"A fascinating near-future exploratic ....ps, sustainability, and power. An extraordinarily accomplished debut novel."

— JEFF VANDERMEER, author of *Borne* and *Annihilation*

"So good, so dark, so funny, so cruelly smart about where we are
and where we're going. This book is a petri dish growing a new
strain of heartbreak. I'm sick with love for it."

— SHELLEY JACKSON, author of *Riddance* and *Half Life*

"With wit and precision, Elvia Wilk pinpoints the moment when
neoliberalism metastasizes into something far more sinister."

— TOM MCCARTHY, author of *Satin Island* and *Remainder*

"J. G. Ballard meets William Gibson meets Jeff VanderMeer. *Oval*
is an up-to-the-minute story about the twilight zones of corporate
design, aesthetics, pharmacy, and bioengineering, where there's
nothing consultants won't break in the quest for 'innovation.'
What could possibly go wrong? Find out in Elvia Wilk's crisp and
stylish debut book."

— MCKENZIE WARK, author of *Molecular Red*
and *A Hacker Manifesto*

"Everything is work—mourning, clubbing, reading your partner's
moods. And everything is a scam—plants that become buildings,
jobs that become consultancies, apps that become jobs. With as-
tonishing emotional accuracy, *Oval* records what it feels like to
hover between two poles."

— SASHA FRERE-JONES

"Wonderfully clever and beguiling. The circle may be absolute, but the oval remains restless and bursts with potential."

—CHLOE ARIDJIS, author of *Sea Monsters* and *Book of Clouds*

"As a social comedy of modern relationships and gentrifying Berlin, Elvia Wilk's debut is exquisitely funny and exquisitely well observed. But it also has something weirder spliced into its DNA: fragments of the future that transform this story into a fabulous biopunk hybrid that's not quite like anything else I've ever read."

—NED BEAUMAN, author of *Madness Is Better Than Defeat* and *The Teleportation Accident*

OVAL

OVAL

ELVIA WILK

SOFT SKULL ✺ NEW YORK

Library of Congress Cataloging-in-Publication Data
Names: Wilk, Elvia, author.
Title: Oval / Elvia Wilk.
Description: New York : Soft Skull, 2019.
Identifiers: LCCN 2018045888 | ISBN 9781593764050 (pbk. : alk. paper)
Subjects: | GSAFD: Science fiction. | Dystopias.
Classification: LCC PS3623.I5452 O93 2019 | DDC 813/.6—dc23
LC record available at https://lccn.loc.gov/2018045888

Cover design & art direction by salu.io
Book design by Jordan Koluch

Published by Soft Skull Press
1140 Broadway, Suite 704
New York, NY 10001
www.softskull.com

Soft Skull titles are distributed to the trade by Publishers Group West
Phone: 866-400-5351

Printed in the United States of America
10 9 8 7 6 5 4 3 2 1

FOR MY FRIENDS

PART ONE

I wish that people who are conventionally supposed to love each other would say to each other, when they fight, "Please—a little less love, and a little more common decency."

—KURT VONNEGUT

1

AFTER DEATH, BUREAUCRACY TAKES THE WHEEL. FUNERAL arrangements, bank account closures, insurance payouts. Unpaid taxes. Unforgiven debts. For some, the cascade of paperwork adds an unbearable layer of responsibility. For others, the onslaught helps to smother the grief. Louis, Anja decided, was clearly the latter.

The bureaucracy was all he could talk about. The only information he sent her way while he was gone came as a series of text messages describing the string of post-death logistics. He was *at the lawyer's office again*. He was *packing boxes*. Then he was *buying more Sprite and crackers for the retirees*. Emoji, emoji. Blaming the time difference, he never found a moment to talk on the phone.

The last time she had heard his voice was when he had called two weeks before from the departure lounge at Brandenburg to tell her the news. His mom, dead. His voice had sounded so unconcerned she had asked if he was joking. Apparently, he had booked a flight back to the U.S., left work, and headed straight for the airport, all before calling his girlfriend. Anja was sure he was in shock. She was the one who broke down crying when he called.

He hadn't told her he was coming back to Berlin until he was already at the airport at the opposite end in Indianapolis. Just a one-line text message listing his arrival time, with hearts planted between the numbers.

Anja was waiting for him when his plane landed in the early afternoon. Arrivals, with its faceted glass ceiling, felt like a cramped greenhouse or the inside of an empty perfume bottle with foul mist trapped inside. Around her, families regrouped, Erasmus students came home from semesters abroad, one-night partiers without any luggage searched for the bus that would drop them off nearest the door of the club.

Anja was startled by how awful Louis looked when he emerged from the crowd. His physical appearance was at odds with the nonchalance of those text messages; he looked miserable. He didn't make any jokes to apologize for his condition, just hugged her weakly, took her hand, and followed her to the taxi stand.

In the back seat of the cab he leaned his head on her shoulder and showed her a fruit-flinging game on an iPad he said he'd inherited. The tablet seemed to be the only new thing he'd come home with.

The driver dropped them off at the base of the mountain with an apology: it was too muddy for him to go any farther. The cable car that should have been waiting to carry them up was still languishing lifelessly in the dirt by the path, where it had been since they moved in. Anja helped Louis haul his carry-on up the sloping path, lifting it over the bigger rocks and puddles. By the time they made it to the house, they were both soaked with sweat, the underarms of Anja's gray Lycra top marked with salt arcs.

"Like the shore of the Dead Sea," she said.

Louis, winded, bent over his knees. "Buns of steel," he said, as he always did when they reached the top. The familiar refrain didn't reassure her. It made her uneasy. An echo across an uncanny valley.

While Anja dug around for her keys, Louis wiped his fingers across the damp wood grain of the front door. "She's sweating, too," he said.

The house had gained a female pronoun early in their inhabitation. Something to do with a made-for-TV movie Louis had seen as a kid, about a smart-house that went haywire.

Anja nodded. "She has been all week." The interior was so humid that condensation had gathered on every surface, and now the untreated wood was engorged. "The window frames are too swollen," she said. "I haven't been able to open the windows to let the moisture out."

He laughed. "Menopause? But she's so young."

Anja unlocked the door and heaved it open with her hip. "No, just vindictive. She's sad that you left."

It was too hot to sleep, and Anja woke up before it was bright outside, rolling over to find Louis sprawled out on his stomach. He was naked, cuddling the tablet in the crook of his arm and jabbing at zombies floating across the screen. She got out of bed, wiped her face with a towel bunched on the dresser, and found a T-shirt, feeling her way down the hall while pulling the shirt over her head. The porous floor was cool and slippery; she steadied herself with a palm on the wall.

In the kitchen, she knelt under the sink and pulled out the main monitoring system. It was supposed to transmit real-time home-climate statistics wirelessly to the unattractive tech watches they'd been given, but the metal casing of the drawer blocked the signal. They'd debated removing the drawer front completely to let the signal through, but Anja, imagining in-house tornadoes, had decided they shouldn't fiddle with it themselves. The contract they'd signed before move-in had been very clear about tampering. Eventually, they'd given up wearing the watches and given up talking about it too.

She peered at the dim readout for a few moments and sighed, slamming the drawer back into place, then padded back down the hall, nearly slipping before reaching the bedroom archway.

She posed in the arch with one hip jutting out, a Carrie Bradshaw move she had once postured as a joke that had by now lost its original template and become a reflex. "The monitor says there's too much waste under the flooring, and the rate of composition is too high. It's hot in here, but the floor feels cold to me. Shouldn't we feel the heat coming up?"

He laughed, still tapping his pet screen. "Too much waste? You've been here without me for two weeks."

"I haven't had any internal plumbing problems. All is running smoothly." She ran her hand over the side of one hip.

"Cheeky." He pressed the round button on the tablet and slid it under the pillow beneath his head, twisting his neck toward her. "So if we can't blame your digestion?"

She nodded. "I'll call Howard in a few hours." She climbed into bed beside him. The top sheet, IKEA blue, was damp with sweat in two oblong patches: hips and shoulders. Avoiding her own imprint, she rolled halfway onto him.

He scrutinized her face. She scrutinized back. He looked like sweet, normal Louis. She frowned.

"Is everything okay with you?" he asked.

"What?" She was supposed to be the one asking that question. She pulled her face a few centimeters back. "Are *you* okay?"

"I'm fine."

"You seemed *not fine* yesterday." She paused to allow it to slip from observation to evaluation. He nodded. That was a good sign. Self-awareness.

"I was just exhausted," he said, shrugging beneath her. That was not a good sign. "Hey," he protested. "Don't give me that look."

"I'm not giving you a look."

"You are, a little."

"It's just hot rays of love."

"Okay, but don't burn me."

She searched his face for traces of yesterday's sadness. Yesterday had been Sunday. The day his mom usually called.

"I can't go back to sleep," he said. "I'm too jet-lagged." He gestured toward the shower. "Should we start the day?"

She sat up beside him, pulling up her knees to avoid the sweat stains. "I never understand what it means when you say that. *We* don't start the day."

"Who starts it?"

"It just starts. The sun, the cosmic rotation."

"My day starts in me." He pointed to his stomach. "Internal rotation, the cosmos inside." He got up and stepped toward the bathroom, grinning.

"Gross," said Anja. She laughed. "Living in this house has made us too comfortable talking about our shit."

At eight a.m. Howard didn't pick up his phone, so she sent him an email, which he responded to immediately. No, he wouldn't be available to talk until eleven, but why didn't she stop by his place instead of going straight to work? He had to talk to her about something work-related anyway. In the meantime, he'd send someone by to check on the house's perspiration situation. He signed his email "cheers," the sarcasm level of which she couldn't decipher.

She and Louis drank smoothies at the kitchen counter. The kitchen, though the most over-the-top room in the house, flaunting its utilities and abilities, was also by far the loveliest. The light filtering in through the strip of windows lining two east-facing walls cast enough brightness for them to forgo artificial lighting in the space for most of the day, and the recycled-plastic-and-something countertops successfully reflected the rays with minimum glare but maximum illumination, as they were designed to do.

"Won't they let you take some more time off?" Anja refilled Louis's smoothie. He had fallen asleep again after his shower and woken up in another time zone, distant and disengaged. Jet lag—soul delay.

"Of course. They keep saying I should take another week, but what else am I supposed to do with my time?"

"I don't know. Sleep? Process? Take a break?"

"I need distraction. And it's really busy there right now. Big project coming up."

"Are you sure?" She reached out and hugged the back of his neck with her hand.

"I'm seriously fine." He took the hand. "All I need is to get back to small talk, logistics, menial tasks."

She smiled. "A typical day in the creative industries."

"A unique privilege. The manual labor of the elite."

She moved the smoothie machine into the sink and turned on the water to rinse it. The water came out of the tap in irregular spurts.

"Have you ever done real manual labor?"

"Sure." He wiped the rim of the glass with his finger and licked it. "I did construction one summer in San Francisco. During grad school."

"Ever feel like going back to it?"

"All the time. I could quit my idealistic job and fix this sustainable mess we live in. Do something practical. Become a stay-at-home environmentalist."

"I'd be the breadwinner? But I don't make enough money."

"You'd have to tap into that trust *fun*."

She banged on the tap in case it was clogged. It wasn't. The water slowed to a trickle. "It's not fun. See how people like you are always bringing it up?"

She glanced at him across the island. He seemed calmed by the familiar banter. She had learned to play this game expertly over time, the game of endlessly countering and counter countering and punning, a uniquely American mechanical spiral of conversation whose pleasure was purely semantic and whose meaning was always secondary to the way it was said.

Louis needed a regular dose of banter, and she had, over the course of their bonding phase while she learned to play, unexpectedly learned to need it too. At the beginning, she had been typically European about it, considering it shallow small talk, but she became convinced over time that it was not only harmless but constituted an important kind of meta-content. Chatting didn't negate an emotional bond; it reinforced it. Her English had become a flawless porcelain veneer in the process.

He stood up and palmed her face, so she could rest her cheek in his hand. "At least you know I don't love you only for your money, since you never spend any of it."

She rolled her eyes. This old joke had run the full course from provocation > slightly offensive but funny > actually offensive from overuse > permissible > endearing relic of relationship past. Was resorting to old inside jokes a good thing?

"Howard asked me to go straight to his place instead of going to work this morning," she said.

"Weird. Do you think I should come with? Is it about house stuff?"

"I'm sure it's fine. He probably just wants to ask me to *pleeeease* stop complaining," she said, affecting a British accent.

Louis left the house buoyantly, leaving Anja still hunched over her half-finished smoothie, inspecting the avocado chunks that had sunk to the bottom, feeling nauseated. She told herself not to obsess over his behavior. And yet he seemed so unthinkably normal that it was surely an abnormality. There was not a trace of grief left in him today. The sallow face of yesterday was gone, instead he looked slightly puffy, pink and fresh. It was indecent, almost offensive. All those nights awake and worrying about him, loyally depressed, wallowing on his behalf. Repeatedly calling her own parents just to check that they were alive. It was obvious she was appropriating something, and it had to stop.

Then she thought, fuck griefmantra.com and supportcycle .net—there was such a thing as a wrong way to deal with emotions. Assuming it could only be posturing, was posturing normality in fact a very bad sign? Should she be prepared for some crazy shit on the horizon? Or could he really be exactly like before, as he seemed on the surface? What was before?

Once, in the Before, at a dinner party, Louis had retold a story he'd read in *The New Yorker*. The article was an exposé on Russian prisons in what was known as the "Black Zone," a lawless section of the penitentiary where there was little supervision from above, and the prisoners were basically left to govern themselves. In the Black Zone, rigid customs had developed that newcomers had to learn if they didn't want to get knifed. Most of the customs had originally been created for practical reasons, but by now they'd become arbitrary rules whose only function was to enforce a sense of social cohesion. For example, there was one major taboo against throwing away crusts of moldy bread. Back in the early years of the Black Zone, when food had been scarce, it was necessary to conserve every morsel. Today, a healthy black market supplied champagne and caviar to the inmates—and yet the taboo against wasting bread remained. Throwing away rotten food marked the newcomer as an outsider, someone who didn't understand the history of want and deprivation from which the rules had evolved. With regards to bread, explained Louis, the culture of the Black Zone was a culture of inclusion via conservation.

This was more or less the situation in Louis and Anja's six-household eco-settlement, or eco-colony, or colonoscopy, an assortment of experimental architecture clustered a thousand meters up the side of the Berg. The no-waste principle, according to which all inhabitants were responsible for monitoring the internal ecosystems and microclimates of their homes, was enforced by an internalized pressure based on imaginary rules rather than any actual supervision from Finster Corp. above. The tiny red lights of the cameras blinking in every room were a sort of mental reminder of Finster's presence—of the abstract idea of monitoring—but Anja was sure nobody was actually watching. The contract was clear: the only spying being done was by a machine-vision algorithm whose job was to spot anomalies and flag worst case scenarios. Tornadoes. Fire.

This lack of explicit instruction had led to some conundrums. When they had first moved in, Anja would hike up the mountain each evening with a backpack full of biodegradables and other trash she had accrued throughout the day, in order to dump them down the disposal and enter her total net waste into the recycling system. It was her waste, wherever she produced it, and she was going to be honest about it. But the surplus of wrappers and crusts and tissues had started to clog the drain unit and overflow the toilet; Anja was wasting way more matter than the house could make go away.

"Couldn't you throw this stuff away somewhere else?" Louis asked her, scooping chunks of foul-smelling paper pulp from the kitchen drain. He pulled out a long, thick strip of blue-and-brown paper. "What is this, a shopping bag from the mall?"

"I just used it to carry my other trash in. Jesus, it's not like I was shopping at the mall."

He stared at her, dangling the wet strip. "You brought home a random bag from a fast-fashion store, which you only used to carry your other trash in, and you put it down our drain."

"Yes, that's what I did. I used the bag. Ergo, it's part of my waste output."

He frowned. "I think the waste thing only applies when you're at home on the mountain."

"No, I don't think it's spatial. It's about what you waste in your whole life, as a human consumer. The whole point is to cancel us out completely." She realized she was clasping her hands earnestly. Without meaning to, she glanced up toward where she knew the camera was, nestled above the cabinets.

"Right, that's what it says on the website. But everyone knows we're just supposed to be making it *seem* like the house works. We're trying to prove that it's possible to live sustainably and not be such a freak about it. Which means not carrying your trash around everywhere."

Anja unclasped her hands and then reclasped them. "But throwing waste away in other places is cheating," she said. "If the house can't handle all my waste, then the designers didn't do a good job, and they should fix it."

"They obviously did not do a good job, Anja. Nothing in this fucking house works. I'm not going to drag all my trash home every day. It's just not realistic—you want me to save the packaging from my lunch? Where does it stop? Am I supposed to wait to shit until I get home?"

"Wait, why are you eating lunch with disposable packaging? I bought you a lunch box!"

Eventually Louis's practicality had won out, as it tended to. He was right: Anja couldn't wait to shit until she got home, and she couldn't keep track of everything she used; trying to do so had led to an ontological breakdown on the microlevel of her daily life. Were eyelashes and skin cells on par with hair ties and coffee cups? Were paper coffee cups on par with a mug that had to be rewashed using graywater from the house, which cost energy to pump? She couldn't bring herself to ask the neighbors how they were handling things, convinced that everyone else automatically understood the rules. To reveal her confusion would be to reveal all, including her doubts.

That had been only a few months ago, but lately, as more elements of the system were getting clogged or bogged down, the two of them had started to perform exactly the opposite of what Anja had originally done: they carried their trash down the mountain and disposed of it clandestinely in orange trash canisters on the street. At first Anja felt ashamed marching down the slope with a backpack loaded with a bundle of trash flattened against her laptop, but Louis reassured her that they were just doing what was expected of them: putting a good, clean face on sustainability. Eventually, bringing trash off the mountain seemed just as responsible as bringing trash onto it once had.

2

ANJA SKIDDED DOWN THE SLOPE, WHICH WAS BECOMING MUDDY from overuse by feet. It still hadn't been paved or even scattered with gravel, since Finster didn't want to admit that the state of the pathway could no longer reasonably be called temporary. Rather than upgrade the provisional solution to make it slightly more functional in the interminable interim, it was ignored, as a signal that something better, something great—the best possible path— *was coming.*

Louis likened this situation to a general societal problem. The refusal to improve a nonsolution with a makeshift solution, he said, was the attitude that left most of the world in muddy shape in need of repair. Making exactly this argument had in fact consumed a lot of his time in his first year at Basquiatt, the NGO where he worked, which he believed was overrun by an ideological insistence on grand solutions that would be forever unattainable instead of small-scale, implementable compromises. "Let's be realistic" was his self-parody catchphrase. "What can we do *right now* to make things better?"

"Why do you think refugee camps are never outfitted with proper infrastructure?" he'd asked Anja just a few days before he'd been yanked back to the U.S. They were hiking up the mountainside in the rain toward their apartment, torsos harshly angled against the incline, sneakers slipping in the mud, dragging grocery bags; it was pathetic.

"Muddy scenes of neglect," he shouted downhill at her, intent for some reason on having this discussion right at that moment. The worse things had gotten in the house, the more he'd taken to ranting. "The mud is meant as a message that the bad situation isn't going to last forever, no matter how long it's already lasted. They want you to think the camp is just temporary, so nobody actually has to take responsibility for it." His voice rose as she lagged farther behind him. "The quality of the now," he yelled over his shoulder, "is sacrificed for the ideal. Know what I'm saying?"

Of course she knew what he was saying. "But you realize you're comparing the Berg to a refugee camp, right?" That had ended the discussion.

Today she was carrying only a few avocado peelings in the pockets of her vinyl windbreaker. The whole apartment was a hot, puffy bruise; she didn't dare force anything down the drain. She waved to a group of electricians in blue coveralls, who were standing, bored, around a post that was supposed to be supporting one of the vine-cables of the cable car. They had raised the car onto a stack of wooden pallets. One of the workers dropped a cigarette butt onto the exposed end of a vine-cable half-buried in mud, and it let off a sorry spark.

Unhitching her bike from a post at the bottom of the slope, she saw that Louis's racer was still locked to a tree. He must have taken the train. She plugged her phone into the charger between her handlebars, checking it for messages. Dam had already sent out his first weather blast of the day: *dry 35° / lavender / wet west gust.*

She checked her phone's weather app for comparison. High

of 24 degrees, calm, clear. The gap between the official version and Dam's version—the real version—shouldn't have still bothered her, but it did. She slotted an earbud in each ear and began the long ride up to Prenzlauer Berg, to Howard's. It would normally take half an hour, the length of one podcast, but she was lumbering on the pedals today, swinging from side to side with each push. She was exhausted, and, true to Dam's forecast, there was a hot wind coming from the west. The sky was purplish with stratified layers of clouds, each like identical, faded copies of one another. Add a layer. Add a layer. Duplicate this layer. Flatten visible.

She listened to the podcast with one part of her brain, thinking with another part about what must have been happening in the lab at that very moment. She was mildly anxious to be missing the morning there. She probably should have asked Howard to meet in the evening after work instead.

The week before, the simulation she and Michel had been hard-coding for weeks had finally authorized cell culturing; today would be the first day in at least two months that they'd be liberated from their screens, finally doing tiny things with their actual hands in an actual polystyrene dish. It was strange to look forward to an action while knowing already without a doubt how it would unfold. They had seen the routine perform itself again and again in high-definition render; the airtight predictability of the chain of events was the only reason they were allowed to make it happen in a dish at all.

She saw the animation in her mind. One cell membrane swelling to accommodate a new blot on its periphery—for one freak moment an egg with two yolks—then, the new blot forcing itself outward to the splitting point, when the edge of the cell would erupt from its boundary to become a whole new edge, scooping remarkably away and burping into its own self-contained shape—from impossible to possible. "Plop," said Michel each time they watched the duplication unfold on-screen. "Plop-plop-plop."

She consoled herself with the fact that today wouldn't really be the most important day. It would be tomorrow, when a surface visible to the naked eye would begin to form from all those slow plops. The plops were designed to perform very slowly—growing into a skein of tangible matter. The surface would be translucent at first, shaping itself over the hours into a perfectly symmetrical double wave, like the contour of the roof of a mouth, but impossibly smooth. And so small, conformed perfectly to its given constraints, the shallow dish only 88 millimeters in diameter, the simulated site map of the simulated shelter, the architecture's designated terrain. By the end of the second day the duplicating cells would have built a delicate little home, rising layer upon parametric layer until it was exactly right, a perfectly circular double-arched roof. Then it would stop. Cartilage in its first official architectural application. A perfect, growable, reproducible, scalable, durable roof, which Finster could send anywhere in the world as a tiny bundle of cells that would sprout on demand. Cells that would be first grown in their lab at RANDI.

She could already see Michel struggling to repress his excitement. She'd mock him, call him Dr. Evil, but they'd both give in to self-congratulation for a few minutes when the thing was finished growing. This week would offer a release valve from the tedious months plugging variables into a giant data sheet and pretending not to give any fucks about their jobs. (On the other hand, they would have to admit to each other with a few uncomfortable glances, the success was a turning point, it made them responsible for what they were doing at RANDI. Until now, the eye rolling and the sarcasm had masked the unease, but soon they'd have to pretend even harder not to care, work even harder not to know where this was all headed. She'd think about that next week, once they had accomplished this small exercise in form, a proof of concept that was surely just a small step in a process that would take years before implementation.)

The stoplight at Jannowitzbrücke gave pause to the pedaling and the imaginary cell growth. A swarm of teenagers in red caps crossed the street, briefly enveloping her. A trio of girls wearing their caps backward—oh, pitiful resistance!—followed closely behind one another. It was easy to spot the popular girl at the front of the pack right away, simply from the geometry of the flock in motion. What was it about the girl, Anja wondered, the homely girl preoccupied with her phone, that made her the focal point, the yolk at the center of attention? What was the factor upon which the self-replicating algorithm turned, that remarkably consistent geometry of popularity? How had Anja still not figured out the answer, the hidden parametric logic to social arrangements, even after all these years, even as an *adult scientist*?

The light turned yellow, and the group hurried by, ushered forth by a red-shirted chaperone. At the same time, according to the podcast she now zoned back into, jellyfish were taking over the oceans as other species died out in the too-warm water and made way for them to proliferate, spreading across the surface in a thick quilt, clogging the gears of power plants and blocking the flow of oxygen to the depths of the sea.

Howard made her wait two minutes, almost long enough to ring him again, before he buzzed her into the front door of his building. She knew he could see her through the little camera above the buzzer and wondered if he had taken the time to inspect her before pressing the button. She hauled her sticky body up to the top floor, pausing on the landing to wipe the area under her eyes with a tissue from her pocket. A lot of her supposedly waterproof mascara had melted below the lashes. Sweating burns calories, her sister would say.

Howard opened the door and gave each hot cheek a kiss. She noticed a mist on the top of his head—the head was sweating, which she'd somehow never incorporated into the realm of possibility. But, of course, a bald head sweats, just like any other head. She remembered not to stare—men didn't like that—but then, this was Howard; he was secure. He'd been bald for so long that he wore his skull without the anxiety of a man who it happens to later in life, and so he didn't associate it with waning virility or whatever else.

He wore most of his distinguishing traits in that way, as incidental and entirely unremarkable. Such as the fact that he was the only Black person in Finster's upper echelons in Germany, which he never, ever spoke about. He was technically in PR at Finster, but Anja had come to understand that the kind of soft power he'd acquired over the years was much more substantial than his official title accounted for. He would never move back to London, that was clear. He was firmly planted here. His German was impeccable, it sliced you like a paper cut.

Howard led Anja down the corridor past the living room, a mid-century forest of teak and mahogany, to the narrow kitchen where they always sat. Very far from the bed.

"Just water, thanks," she said to his offer of a mug.

"Detox?"

"A bit jittery. I don't need caffeine."

"Busy in the lab lately?"

"Yes, actually. Or we're about to be. This week is a big one." She scare-quoted "big one."

Without asking, he tipped a packet of electrolytes into the glass of water he'd filled and passed it to her with a spoon to stir.

"This is good timing, then. I have big news." He scare-quoted "big news" in turn. "You probably know this already, but Finster is restructuring some departments at RANDI." She was silent, then capitulated to admitting she didn't know, shaking her head slightly. "Oh," he said. "Well, now you know. They aren't cutting the whole sector or anything, but they're consolidating a lot of the subsectors. Most of Alloys is merging into General Futures. And Cartilage is merging back into Biodegradables, where it probably should have stayed in the first place."

She got a split-second heart palpitation. "Back to Biodegradables? I used to be in that sector, remember, but then we all decided Cartilage should split off, because we were doing construction, not degradation."

"Right. Your special mission, which you've bemoaned so much. But now your mission is complete. *Voilà*."

She chewed the inside of her cheek and fingered the earbuds in her pocket. Ear buds, she thought. Small lumps of cartilage from which ears will sprout.

"It's not technically finished, though," she said slowly. "We still haven't actually grown the thing in the lab that we were supposed to be making."

"I don't know anything about the science," he said, and laughed, "but think of this as a big high five from the top. Apparently, they think you accomplished what you set out to do."

"So we're going back from whence we came. Compost."

"Nope. That's the thing. I don't know about the other guy who you were working with, but they've set *you* free."

"Free? Am I fired?"

"Why do you always expect the worst?" He paused for drama. "In fact, you're promoted straight to consultant. Laboratory Knowledge Management Consultant, I think they're calling it."

She shook her head. It didn't make any sense. "No, Howard. I'm just a lab tech. I haven't done anything they could consult me on." Consultant was not a title she'd ever associated with her present or future. Louis was the consultant, not her.

He seemed to be following her thoughts. "Oh, and Louis has? You know you don't need to have any consulting experience to become a consultant."

She bit back. "Louis is highly qualified for his job, actually."

Howard raised his hands in mock defense. "I didn't mean he wasn't. I'm just saying that the qualification is not what you think it is. The qualification is just that they decide you can do it."

She chewed her cheek, hard. "What does a knowledge manager do?"

"Whatever you want. You get a pay raise and go around telling people what to do. Threaten them if they don't work fast enough. Do audits, interviews, suggest some restructuring where you think it's needed. You know the drill."

"How long?"

"I don't know how long your first term is. Probably a year."

"But why would they want to fire me from my job and hire me back to do nothing for more money?"

He raised his hands. "That's how companies run. You do the time and you move up the ladder, if you're lucky. Why all the questions?"

She swirled her glass of electrolytes without taking a sip. "Here's a question. Since when did you become my boss? HR should be telling me this."

He shrugged innocently. "I was on the phone with HR this

morning, mentioned you were coming by, and they said I should go ahead and tell you myself. Call over if you don't believe me."

Howard had, of course, been involved marginally in her job at RANDI, her house—everything—for a long time. Finster was involved in all of it, and at some point Howard had become her main interface with Finster's back end. Howard knew stuff, Howard was the cloud, that was the point of Howard. In that regard, his giving her this information was not surprising. Nothing was changing between them, not really. But she couldn't ignore the feeling that this news he was bestowing upon her was more intrusive than some of the other ways he'd elbowed into her life.

"Am I being insensitive about this?" Howard asked. "You seem sort of subdued."

"I'll have to think about it."

"Don't be such a girl." He smiled. "Man up. Take what's yours."

"I love it when men tell me to man up."

"Just trying to boost your confidence. But take your time. Someone will email you a draft of the contract to look over. That's all I know."

"Thanks." She tried to sound grateful. Guilt, gratitude: they were always twins. It was time to steer the conversation elsewhere. When Howard chose to play dumb there was no piercing the shell.

"Do you think they'll let me consult on my own house?" she asked. "The Berg could use a scientist."

Howard laughed. "I doubt it. The Berg is a whole beast of its own. How are things at home? I guess that's what you actually came to talk about."

She realized that, actually, she didn't have a very good reason for having come here, any more than Howard had a good reason for being the one to fire and rehire her. Neither the technical malfunction in her home nor her job officially had anything to do with him. What she had really come here for was Howard himself: his signature blend of affection, approval, and authority. He would, as he always did, oblige her complaints in exchange for feeling depended upon. He liked to be needed; she offered an assortment of needs.

"I was just wondering if you have any sort of . . . overview about what's going on with the mountain," she said. "The temperature and everything is totally erratic. All the doors are swollen shut. People must be complaining."

"Not as much as you guys," he said, smiling. "Have you been talking to the neighbors?"

"A few."

This was a lie. Anja and Louis never talked to the neighbors. At the start, Anja had spent a few afternoons with a middle-aged couple of Danish consultants who had befriended her, but they'd left for vacation months earlier and had never come back. Come to think of it, at least three of the houses were empty most of the time. One of them was used intermittently as a studio for photo shoots of some sort.

"I know you guys don't like the whole community vibe, but you could be a little more outgoing."

Her phone vibrated in her pocket and she checked it under the table. Louis: *flowers on my desk this morning, for mourning. a touching bribe :)*

She wedged the phone between her legs and looked up. "Neither of us signed up to live in a commune."

"True. I'm just saying that it's easier to handle if you all talk to each other. Everyone up there is figuring out how to deal with the same issues. Renewable energy isn't foolproof; you can't depend on it like clockwork. You know that. All the risks are in your contract."

"I know. Sorry for freaking out. It's just that"—a moment on the edge, wavering—"we're kind of stressed right now." With the "we" she'd let Louis into the conversation, and the real reason for her being here rose to the surface. She was handing the need to Howard on a platter.

At least she had a punch line, a shoe to drop: the death of Louis's mom, how awful it sounded, how unarguable.

But Howard was already nodding in anticipation, "I didn't want to intrude," he said, "but I heard about Louis's mother, and I'm so sorry. It's really awful."

This was the worst shock of the morning—an intrusive, many-layered shock. She'd thought the death was hers to tell. Only now that she'd been robbed of it did she realize how tightly she'd been clutching the news to herself. She'd thought many times already of how to deliver the news to Howard, somberly, using "passed away" instead of "dead," blinking back tears. She remembered the dark thrill of saying the words to her own parents and his friends who "deserved to know," the assuredness that she was the one entrusted to disseminate the privileged information.

Knowing before anyone else, knowing first, had been proof of something. The thinness of the proof, now disintegrated, revealed the pettiness of the need.

"How did you hear?" she asked, knowing before she had said it that the question was dumb. Louis had been out of town for two weeks. Nothing like this was ever a secret. Death unfolded private pain into the open.

"I was over at Basquiatt last week doing some consulting," he said. "I'm sorry. I wanted to send my condolences earlier, but like I said, I didn't want to intrude." But of course he wanted to intrude. "How is he?"

"I don't know. He's fine."

"It must be tough."

"I don't know what he wants me to do."

"You just have to be there for him."

"That's what everyone keeps saying. But where am I supposed to be being? Where is there?"

"You know what it means. It means being present and attentive. He probably just wants to get back to normal."

"That seems fucked up on some level, though." She shook her head. "Normalcy seems cruel in this situation."

"Maybe he needs to repress."

"Everyone wants to repress! That doesn't mean it's a good idea."

"You can't expect a person to suffer all the time. He has to compartmentalize if he's going to survive a death."

"Survive a death," she repeated, remembering that Howard's dad was gone, had died a long time ago. They'd never really talked about it. She contemplated flipping the conversation around on him. It wouldn't work.

"There's no predicting what's going to happen or what he's going to need," Howard said in his reassuring voice. "Just be patient. Trauma works in mysterious ways."

"But aren't there also universal things? It's just categorically bad when a parent dies. Even if you're ambivalent about them, or you hate them, it's just overall bad when they die."

"Maybe it's not that bad for everyone."

"If my parents died I would want everyone to act insane, burning shit and ruining everything."

"But it didn't happen to you. It happened to him."

She sucked air in, then opened up all the way. "I know I'm not supposed to map my own feelings onto him, but I don't want to be waiting around, unsuspecting, when he snaps."

"He might never snap. Life is just easier for some people."

"Do you seriously think that? That's privilege speaking."

He circled his face with his finger. Look at me. A minority.

"Oh, come on. You know about privilege." She circled the air more widely, mimicking his gesture, indicating the renovated Altbau kitchen, with its blue ceramic sink and stainless-steel dishwasher.

"All I'm saying is, Louis is in some ways an uncomplicated person." The not-so-subtle digs at Louis were piling up. She ignored them. She had asked for advice; she had to take what came with it. "You tend to get overly involved in the lives of people you care about," he said, "which is very endearing and commendable, but doesn't always serve you. Put on your own oxygen mask first."

"All right. That's enough paternal advice for the day."

"It's just the accent that makes me seem condescending."

"You always say that." They smiled at each other, and then she asked: "And how are your—things? Do you have any of your own issues?" The classic false overture. They both knew their dynamic. It was off-kilter, but it was stable. His knowing her was what she knew about him.

He leaned forward slightly, a barely perceptible shift that wouldn't have been possible to construe as anything meaningful by anyone watching, but which transmitted a message all the more intimate precisely because it was so stunted.

"Since you ask, we are having a bit of a PR crisis at the moment," he said.

"Oh?"

"Just between us."

"Okay."

"Not even for Louis."

"I get it."

"To be perfectly candid," he said, placing all his fingertips on the table, creating little tents with his palms, "some of the problems with the Berg aren't just tech issues." She looked at him blankly, worried for a moment that he knew about their cheating with the trash. No one was watching, she reminded herself. Just the silent, rotating lens of the cameras. "There's been some infighting among the consulting architects, the engineers, even PR. Things are stalled because of the disagreement."

"Disagreement about what?"

"They never officially agreed on how much tech should actually *be* on the mountain. Some of the architects don't think you guys should be so comfy. Some of them don't believe it's really authentic for you to have climate control, for instance."

"But the climate-control system is independent of the central grid. It's a thousand percent carbon neutral. It's not doing any harm to the environment."

"Obviously. I'm on your side. It's always an arbitrary decision, what you call natural and what you call artificial. Those choices are all symbolic, and they each represent a political position."

"But if someone decides that our heating and cooling are unnatural, what's next? Then someone will decide that clean water is fake, and then someone will decide that LEDs are fake, and then someone will say we can't eat anything we don't grow ourselves. Who actually decides these things?"

"That's sort of the other problem. A group of the architects have quit. They're upset that their plans were treated like suggestions and not blueprints."

"And nobody knows about this."

"Thus the PR element. It's a lot of work for me to keep a lid on this. We don't want to freak people out."

"You don't seem worried about freaking me out."

"I think you can handle it."

"I can handle it. But what are we supposed to do? We can't wait forever in that place. You got us into this, you know."

"Oh, be patient. As soon as they make some executive decisions, the solutions are simple. To fix the heating, I think they just have to reconnect some severed wires to the beating heart, or whatever they're calling it, the CPU thing."

"You really don't know anything about the tech."

"Not even a little. I stick to politics. I mean PR."

Her sister was the one who had convinced Anja to stop seeing Howard. "He's projecting an imaginary fantasy onto you," Eva had said. "How old is he, forty-five? He wants someone permanently young. He thinks you're fine with being a piece on the side. He'll never commit."

Anja hadn't been looking for Howard to commit—actually, that was exactly what she hadn't wanted—but the idea of being a "piece on the side" (on the side of what?) in the eyes of anyone else was bad enough to convince her to end it. Somehow unable to cut things off, she managed to trick herself into feeling rejected by him, leading herself down a tunnel of body dysmorphia. She convinced herself that Howard was looking for some ideal of girlish perfection that any lump would disqualify her from. It couldn't be that she was maybe not that interested in him romantically; no, that was not an option; he was a powerful person; the only option was that she was inadequate.

She let herself be consumed by self-doubt, shielding her arms, her calves, her breasts in his presence, becoming volatile and causing increasingly embarrassing scenes. At the low point, she accused him of grabbing the fattiest parts of her body during sex. He'd said, "Obviously, I like them best," and that was the end of that.

Of Louis, Eva approved. "I found his picture online," she said. "He's hot. See, it only took you a month to find someone better. You should think more highly of yourself."

Anja decided not to listen to Eva on these topics anymore. She'd decided that before and always relapsed, but with Louis she finally managed to stop feeding Eva details; Louis was going to stay a sacred space, free from probing. "You must be serious about him," Eva had said. "I never hear a peep. Is he taking advantage of you? I just read an article online about this thing called mansplaining."

She couldn't blame Eva's bad advice when she and Louis hit a breaking point after only a few months of dating. It was the fault of their living situation—which was Anja's fault. They were deadlocked about where to go after the impending loss of the garden house, which they were living in illegally and which was on the verge of demolition. The whole age-old Schrebergarten was going to be flattened for an apartment block as soon as a final piece of paper got stamped somewhere deep inside the Ordungsamt. You could complain about losing history and heritage, but you could complain louder about the lack of affordable housing, and so the development had moved forward with very little protest.

Their garden allotment was just inside the S-Ring, which demarcated the limit of the conveniently livable part of the city. Once upon a time, the thousands of subdivided gardens had been built as urban escapes, chunks of nature scattered across the city where hearty children could be set loose. But when food was suddenly in short supply during the first war, the little gardens were quickly converted into urban farms, amounting to an ur-sustainable-living movement. Later, when the war ended and the embargoes were lifted and the bombed-out city was temporarily left to its own devices, displaced people set up camp in the gardens. Sheds became homes. Temporary visitation became habitation. But before anyone could get too comfortable, the next war emptied the gardens again and the spaces were left to grow wild, reverting to real nature for the first time in maybe a thousand years.

In the next postwar phase, the period of grand division, some gardens were sliced down the middle and became portals for smuggling among the overgrowth. Eventually, Wall came down, or rather Wall was torn down in bits by thousands of hands and machines; city was once again an enormous expanse of empty real estate; gardens were once again parceled and converted into weekend leisure destinations; and the forebears of urbanites like Anja and Louis started to show up. One by one each tiny garden and all its historical baggage became a sliver of private vacation property. The whole thing, meaning the whole city, was going in circles, history looping and tangling itself like hairs clogging a drain.

By the time Anja arrived in the city, when rents everywhere inside the S-Ring were at an all-time high, the central Schrebergarten had all been renovated and taken over, not overdeveloped like most city blocks but rather their miniature charm canonized into tiny overpriced rentals for urban getaway "experiences." Only a few of the far-flung gardens beyond the periphery were still neglected and unregulated. Anja had discovered hers on a long weekend walk due south. Far from any train station, she came upon the fenced-in cluster of twelve little houses separated by scraggly hedges, which all together occupied only two city blocks. Most of them were squatted, but three were empty, and one of those had a decent roof. After coming back a few times and sniffing around, she'd found the woman who seemed to be improvising administration and paid her in cash for six months upfront.

After the six months were up, by which time Louis had moved into the garden with her, they couldn't decide what to do. They agreed that the house was unlivable for much longer, the roof becoming less decent by the day, but finding and paying for a real apartment seemed impossible. Anja was making ridiculously little money at the time, still technically a RANDI intern, and she neither wanted to tap into her trust fund to contribute half the rent for a new apartment nor allow Louis to pay for the majority himself. Louis didn't care if he had to pay (he could easily cover the rent for a new place with his ballooning Basquiatt salary), he just wanted to get out of the wet, crumbling, doomed garden house. And yet Anja was adamant that letting him pay would create an unhealthy dependency. They couldn't agree on how to move forward; they were teetering on the edge of a breakup.

Out of nowhere, the six-page formal invitation letter to join the new socio-environmental living experiment had arrived at their post office box. It was written in complex bureaucratic German, which Louis had tried to plug into Google Translate before Anja got home, which caused him to panic, thinking it was a notice saying they were about to be evicted. Scanning the first page, Anja immediately understood who was responsible.

(Howard was well aware of the garden house's ramshackle condition, having slept there a few times himself in the pre-Louis days. Its shabbiness appealed to him, as it offered tangible proof that he was having sex with a twenty-six-year-old. Being with her on the floor mattress made him feel open-minded.)

The letter was an ostentatious display of magnanimity, whose scale alone—the number of social and professional levers Howard must have had to push and pull to accomplish the feat—practically billboarded his history with Anja, while boasting the extent of his influence. She understood the submessage easily. Howard was a mature adult who did not hold grudges. He had not only bestowed on her a free place to live, loaded with cultural and ethical capital, but a place for *both* of them to live: Anja plus Louis, the guy who had replaced him. Had she expected petty jealousy or vindictiveness?

She'd hesitated to take the offer, but Louis was firm. The eco-village was too good to pass up, no matter how it had come about. Jealousy was not an issue for him, which, overall, she decided she was grateful for.

3

LOUIS HAD NEVER BEEN GOOD ON THE PHONE. HE WAS IMPER-sonal and distracted, always as though he were speaking from a room where he didn't want anyone to overhear him. It was typically mannish and not the worst thing. The only reason it still bothered Anja was because it reminded her obliquely of her parents' inability to telecommunicate. Weeks without checking in, unreachable in a jumble of time zones, and then suddenly a slew of intrusive voice messages: *Are you ok??? Answer us???* And then, just as quickly, going dark again.

After leaving Howard's, she decided to text instead of call Louis, waiting to have the conversation later when he was his full embodied self. But after she texted him with a short update her phone rang straightaway. She was just getting balanced on her bike and had to put the kickstand down again, then remembered to un-plug the headphones when she heard his voice so close in her ears.

"This is the best!" He sounded like he was smiling into the phone. "They finally recognize you!"

She frowned. "It's not like I've just been waiting around to be recognized."

"Don't be so modest."

"I'm not being modest. I just don't feel like I'm in a position yet to—"

"You were going to get here eventually. It just came sooner than expected."

"But I didn't expect. Being a consultant is not what I was ever going for."

"You have to own it! It's your destiny," he said, laughing. "We'll be a family of consultants."

"I wanted to keep doing research."

"You can keep doing research."

"I don't know. This is real consulting. You know what I mean. I'm not an artist like you. I'll have to do efficiency studies and audits and all the rest."

"Every job has red tape. You know I spend half my time in my inbox. But in the rest of your time you'll be able to do what you want. You can look at what needs to be better and just make it better. How many consultants does RANDI have right now? Only twenty or so? This is huge!"

As he went on encouraging, his enthusiasm seemed to have less and less to do with her. She felt embarrassed by it. She derailed the compliments and asked about his return to work. He promised to bring home one of the bouquets he'd been gifted. His inbox was legendarily full, the backlog seemingly impenetrable; he'd set the interns on it like a pack of dogs.

"Prinz says hi, by the way." So Prinz was with him. This wasn't unusual, on the surface; Prinz was always lingering around.

"What are you guys up to?"

"He just bought me this book about psychotropics that he's been telling me about."

Next, a tangent on psychotropic substances that could restructure human memory, altering the structure of the brain to heal the damage caused by negative events. Anja might have thought it was interesting, but she was too busy mentally trying to reconcile Louis with this person who was voluntarily telling her so many things on the phone. "Prinz says the book says sometimes people look twenty years younger after their memories are hardwired. The stories are wild."

"Is he staying there all day or something?"

"He just wanted to check up on me."

"That's nice of him."

"Yep."

She paused. "Working late?"

"I don't know. Depends how much I get done on this project that's finally taking off."

"Cool." The question hung in the pause; she breathed it into the phone, lodging it in the hardware. She wasn't going to ask. She hedged her bet. "I guess we'll talk later, then."

"Prinz and I were thinking we might grab a bite for dinner."

"Of course. Have fun." She was careful not to inflect with bitterness.

"Come! Why don't you come with us?"

"Don't worry about it. You guys should hang out."

She was thinking so hard about each of her responses that she wasn't sure whether she was responding in real time or if there was a perceptible delay. The dynamic between them in this conversation was so out of whack and yet so locked in place. She couldn't figure out how to reroute it. Her very worst insecurities—his lack of dependence on her, his turning to the social sphere for fulfillment instead of to her, his smooth invulnerability—which hadn't reared their heads in ages, were bucking again now. Why were they back? Was she the one driving the dynamic, or he? Or no one?

"I already talked to Dam and Laura about maybe having dinner with them anyway," she lied.

"Oh, okay. Never mind." He managed to sound mildly rejected.

She backtracked, "I wasn't sure of your plans . . ."

"It's fine. We'll see each other later tonight."

No, she decided, if there was someone making the conversation go this way, it was him. He always knew what he was doing.

Anja knew she was whining and she also knew Laura and Dam wouldn't penalize her for it. She had eaten only three shrimp, picking them out from their little corn tortilla cradles with her fingers, but had compensated for the lack of calories with straight vodka.

"Since he got back it seems like all our conversations have a subtext," she said, in Laura's direction. "There's fishy shadows under the water."

"Every relationship has fish," Laura said. "The question is why you're looking below deck."

"Such wisdom. My sister is very wise late at night," Dam put in.

"I know," said Anja. "I'm looking for them on purpose, it's like I want to find them. But I know a big fish is coming. I can feel the fish."

"How long has he even been back for? Twenty-four hours? Stop freaking out," said Laura. "You'll make things worse if you freak out."

"I always make things worse by freaking out."

She had retreated to Laura and Dam's house for dinner without even calling ahead to invite herself. Maybe a remnant of Spanish home life, the two of them ate together most weeknights, after which Dam would do the dishes and then do drugs and leave for a dark place where he hoped to arrive before they took hold. He was already dressed to go out, a black triangle bra visible beneath a loosely woven yellow tank top, knee-high boots propped up against the wall by the door, vinyl trench coat hung over the back of his chair. There were two long dreads trailing from his scalp that hadn't been there the week before.

Laura said, "You know the big relationship fish is always coming. If it's not the breakup fish now, it will be the death fish someday. You can only hope it's a slow, crippled fish."

"At least you got a fish," said Dam. Anja registered that he was hunched over his plate, red-faced and droopy-eyed.

"Are you just drinking in solidarity with me?" she asked.

"Solidarity, baby. I'm also experiencing that fundamental human conflict between reason and emotion within myself." He checked his phone, which he had been doing compulsively as they ate, then closed his eyes and pressed it dramatically to his heart.

"Uh-oh. Who is he?"

"Federico."

"Frederico?"

"*Fed*erico. He's a horrible little old troll. He's a misogynist and I'm pretty sure he's racist. He's the absolute worst."

"Then why are you so desperate for him to call?"

Dam made the shape of a big O with his hands. "He's also the wurst," he said, grinning. "But all he does is work all the time. He works at Finster, actually, managing something."

"Who doesn't work at Finster," Laura said.

"Do you think he could explain to me what's going on over there?" Anja asked.

"Not unless he texts me back. It's been six hours!" Dam shouted, flinging his phone across the room. It ricocheted off the wall molding and ended up near the bookshelf. Dam leaped out of his chair toward it. After checking it for messages one last time, he clutched it in his palm and smashed it against the windowpane. There was a loud crack.

"It's fine," he said, turning the phone over to inspect it. "The protective case works after all." He looked up at the window. "The window's cracked, though."

They made a toast to Federico, who Dam agreed it was time to let go of, and Laura stood, wobbly, to plug her phone into the cuboid speaker hovering near the window.

Even though the speaker was floating three feet above the floor, magnetized as advertised, its Bluetooth connection had never worked, so they had to connect content-filled devices to it with a long black USB cable, which undermined the aesthetic effect. The tether wound upward from the floor to its floating dock, feeding content into the mothership.

"Just another reason the past is prologue," said Laura, fumbling with the cord until a sound stuttered through. "You heard this mix by Koolhaas yet?"

Anja shook her head humbly. It was clear from the way Laura had asked whether she knew the mix, not the producer, that she had missed something, a scrap of cultural matter that was inconsequential on its own but when combined with a whole lot of other things she didn't know could became liability—could make her into a person who didn't know things.

Anja didn't pretend to know things she didn't know. She was

peripherally aware that she had other options besides admitting ignorance, but she rarely exercised them. She gave in automatically when her knowledge on a topic came under question, unwilling to deflect or lie. She hoped this sometimes had the effect of rendering the question irrelevant; more often she knew it made her seem naïve.

"Really? You never heard this?" Laura gave her another chance.

"Really."

"I don't know Koolhaas either," said Dam. He was twirling his dreads with one hand and pouting. Anja noticed a shiny dragon tattoo snaking up the side of his neck. It hadn't been there last week either.

"You're the one who parties every night," said Laura. "You should actually know about music."

Dam opened his mouth and extended his tongue toward Laura, exposing a decimated half-chewed shrimp.

"Yeah, we see your food," said Anja. She got up to look at Laura's phone and check the name of the mix so she could find it again later, but Dam's MacBook cable wrapped around her ankle like a little noose and caught its own tail on the tiny clip meant to act as a hook for easy winding, packing, and traveling: Serra's verb list for the digital age. She skidded across the floor, hands out, knees and ankles twisting, wrist driving downward to catch her fall and on the way dislodging the speaker from its calibrated position in the air. The speaker came down with her, edging the floor with a thud before bobbing back up into place.

"Shit," Dam said, lunging after her. "I'm so sorry, babe."

"Damian! I always tell you not to leave your cord tangled like that," Laura scolded him.

Anja was laughing. A bruise was curling around the knob of

her left wrist. She looked at it with affection. The fall was a comic rupture and she was glad she would have this purpled comma to remind her not to take everything so fucking seriously. One slip was all it took. She should learn to float better, to accommodate the tides.

"You know what? I haven't even told you," she said, getting up and limping toward the sofa. The siblings looked at her, Dam squinting, all of them more drunk than she'd realized. She felt herself expand with gratitude for them, the only two people genetically tied together who she knew in Berlin, the most familial connection she had by dint of their familial connection to each other. They were a mess, but they were hers. Who knew why they'd let her into their fold in the first place, but once she was in, she was in.

"I got fired today," she announced, flopping down on the sofa. "But then I got rehired immediately. I'm a consultant now. Ta da."

"Is that a good thing?" said Dam. He joined her on the sofa. "I don't get it."

"I wasn't sure at first, but maybe it's a good thing."

He kissed her cheek and whispered, "You're badass, you know that?" before sliding down into her lap and closing his eyes.

"What are you supposed to consult on? Like what's your area of 'expertise'?" asked Laura.

"That's not clear. Howard said—"

"Howard?"

Eva was not the only one vehemently opposed to the existence of Howard. Anja had deciphered a quality of protectiveness in Laura's hatred, and tried to appreciate the sentiment behind it, though Laura usually seemed to frame her protection as an accusation.

"Don't ask. It was a very weird morning. Anyway, I called HR from the lab and they said they don't know why it happened either, but it's real." The HR lady had sounded just as annoyed as confused, which made Anja wonder whether anyone really knew the reason for the changes. "My new job sounds like bullshit, though. Here, I'll show you, throw me my phone." Laura tossed Anja her phone and Anja caught it. She opened her inbox, scrolled to the message from HR, and downloaded the attachment.

"Listen to this, it's my contract. 'Consultant will provide unimpeded expertise in relevant field. Consultant will not hold any knowledge back at any time that could be deemed applicable.' Period. Any knowledge that could be deemed applicable. That's an entire clause! Applicable to what? And here, further down. 'Consultant will stay up to date with advancements in the field of: *Biological Science*.' They filled in the name of the field in a different font. This is a formula contract. It was probably generated automatically."

"Are you supposed to be reading it out loud, though?" Laura asked.

"Good question. There's a big confidentiality section down at the end I haven't gotten to."

"It seems really unsecure to send it to you as an email attachment."

"True."

"Is this a scam?"

"I don't know."

"Would they try to scam you out of a job?" Protectiveness again, couched in an accusatory tone, as if Anja should be protecting herself better. "What about that guy you work with, did he get bumped up too?"

"Michel? I don't know." Michel had been texting her since the morning. She hadn't responded yet, unsure what to say. It seemed better to avoid him until she'd thought it through on her own.

"Don't worry, I forwarded the contract to my family lawyer already. She can tell me if there's anything suspicious about the legal stuff."

Laura nodded, mollified that Anja was making sure not to be taken advantage of. Anja was not paranoid about being taken advantage of like Laura was, but she was paranoid about being judged by Laura.

"This reminds me of an episode of *Celebrity Court* I just watched," said Laura. "Want to watch it?"

"Not tonight. I should probably get home in case Louis gets back from hanging out with Prinz."

"I'll send you the link."

"Do you think that's pathetic?"

"What's pathetic about *Celebrity Court*?"

"No, me worrying about Louis. Shouldn't I just call him and see if he's okay instead of worrying about him?"

"I don't get it. If you're worried about him, why wouldn't you call him?"

"I don't want to act weird. He's acting so normal. He's pretending everything is the same, and I think he wants me to pretend everything's the same too. I don't want to fuck up the illusion."

"So then pretend for a while and see how it goes. Don't rush him."

"Am I projecting?"

"Yes, definitely. Let him do his thing. Grief isn't contagious. You don't have any reason to be scared."

Anja considered this for a whole minute. How odd. Fear, that's what it was.

"Whatever else is going on, he loves you," said Laura. "He's a huge pain in the ass, but he obviously loves you."

"Oh." Anja smiled, in spite of herself. "I guess so. Thanks."

She shook Dam by the arm and his eyes rolled partway open, looking up at her from her lap. "Dam. Are you going out tonight or what?"

He frowned. "Hell, no. I'm not going outside. Didn't you notice how foggy it's been today? There's a weird smell in the air. I don't trust it." He found his phone in a pocket of his cargo pants. "I should probably send out a blast now." He started typing without looking at the screen.

"How can you send a weather update without even going outside?"

He rolled his eyes. "Intuition. Rumors. People send me news from around the city all day. I just consolidate. Anyway," he said, smiling, "I don't feel like going out and I don't want anyone partying without me. Might as well scare them with the forecast." He glanced over at Laura, who was tipping her chair back against the wall. She'd undone the top button of her pants and was rubbing her full stomach. "Laurita, look at yourself. You're acting just like Mom after she eats too much. Button your goddamn pants."

heatwave dry / smell of decay / rec. stay inside w paranoid thoughts . . .

No sign of Louis when she heaved the door open at midnight. There were traces of others, though, some muddy footprints on the kitchen floor near the sink. Howard had apparently convinced somebody to trudge up the hill and pretend to fix things. Raw-ended wires were sticking out of the control panel drawer. They had only made a mess: the illusion of progress. She scuttled out of the kitchen, deciding to sleep or pretend to sleep until Louis got home.

She was used to him coming home late from the studio at

Basquiatt. Nobody was forcing him to pull long hours, but if he wasn't passionate enough to stay late, why did he even have the job? She wondered if she would be in the same boat now, a consultant without a real schedule. But she wasn't him. He'd always been this way.

Basquiatt was not a large NGO, and it took on only one artist-consultant at a time—besides however many freelance, short-term creatives were needed on a project—so the one they picked needed to be a real "disruptor." Louis was it.

His job was twofold: to generate press-garnering experiments on the edge of what could be called traditional corporate boundaries, and in the process to enhance the corporate culture and strengthen corporate values from within. He was not supposed to be tinkering with one specific issue in any specific area—say, urbanism in Lagos or sanctions against vaccines in the Philippines—he was not to make this place or that place a better place, but to make Basquiatt a better place and therefore to help Basquiatt make The World a better place. He showed the institution how to think better, how to critique its institutionality. He kept the institution hip and fresh just by being there. His creativity was both the means and the end.

Basquiatt retained its elite status via its closed and rigorous selection process for investors. Stock was not publicly offered: it was offered to targeted investors with track records of ethical practice, who submitted to several rounds of audits before being allowed to buy in. Every few years there was a scandal when a Basquiatt shareholder was exposed as a secret arms dealer or money launderer, but the purging of rotten apples was just part of the necessary routine to maintain the appearance of general purity. Every apple has a worm or two. Best to expose and expel them dramatically.

Anja found the new tablet under Louis's pillow and slid her finger across the screen to unlock it. She swiped through the pages, games upon games, thinking it a healthy sign that Louis had left it behind in favor of other activities, and then remembering that he was out somewhere with Prinz. They had probably met up with some others and gone to a bar. She should have joined them, but she felt weak in the body. Louis's lungs could withstand the secondhand smoke of social life better than hers could. She would get a sinus infection if she sat in a smoke-filled bar for more than a few hours. Berlin, the last place on Earth you could smoke indoors.

Automatically her finger opened the email app on the tablet. Seeing the entirety of Louis's life splay open, she sat up, finger hovering, undecided. She felt around in herself for actual suspicion, for an urge to dig. He'd left the thing at home—unlocked—because he had nothing to hide. And what would be hiding in the machine? The single golden key to his emotional state? The password for feeling completely secure in their relationship?

If there was no secret, there was no reason not to scroll through the messages. They looked at each other's screens all the time. That was what intimacy *meant*.

She limited herself to a casual perusal of subject lines. Plenty of internal Basquiatt emails. He had all the nonsensitive ones forwarded to his general inbox. It was pointless to artificially separate work and life like that.

Re: meeting weds.

PRESS RELEASE urgent :)

Condolences.

There were a few of those, from Basquiatt addresses and others. *Sending hugs. b well.*

There were plenty from Prinz, mostly without subjects,

probably memes. There was one she very nearly opened from an address that looked like a law firm. *Next steps: inheritance tax.* This was something they had discussed very little. All she knew was that the assets were negligible.

An unopened message from that afternoon stopped her cold, finger hovering: 4 p.m. howard@finster-pr.de. The address was commonplace in her inbox, but alien here. It sat among the other unread messages like a row of ripe cherries on a slot machine.

The subject line had its lips sealed. *Feedback.*

Her phone dinged and jolted her heart. Louis, on his way home. She exhaled, closed all apps, and nudged the tablet back under his pillow.

His pillow, impressed and indented by his head. His head on his pillow in their bed. The extra-wide bed you got to have if you were a couple. Anja knew they were just another banal pair nestled in their pocket of intimacy, convinced they were especially unique and worthy, when all around the world there were couples just like them, clutching each other smugly, identical in their uniqueness. Coupling was the most normative thing in the world. It was impossible to know whether you were coupling because it was available or because you really wanted it. Either way, it was a fundamentally unspecial thing to do.

And yet she had always suspected that they really were special, for reasons that had to do with Louis being special. Louis's desire to do good for the world was constantly grappling with his desire for success at any cost—these threatened to merge constantly, but with her he couldn't get away with masking the latter with the former: he couldn't cloak his aspiration with moral goodness. Her job was to gently remind him of this, to disallow him from lying to himself. It was their love that held him to account, and this was important.

What did he do for her? Simple: he removed the pressure on her to perform. She was let off the hook. No performing her wealth, no performing outgoingness, no performing a grand vision for the world. These performances could be outsourced to him. She could spend her time under the bright lights of the basement lab, deep underground with the company of congealing and separating cellular matter, secure that he was performing well on her behalf, up above on land. If this arrangement happened to conform to traditional gender roles, so be it. Sometimes the stereotype was also the truth. (But is he a feminist? Laura had asked once, eyebrow arched. Anja had laughed. What did that even mean?)

She did not worship him, and she did not think he was perfect—he was missing crucial abilities, anybody could see that. Such as time management. Such as the ability to act on his own judgments by, say, openly disagreeing with people he didn't agree with. But no one could be completely whole. Where he was underdeveloped she was overdeveloped, and vice versa, ergo they fit.

Those aspects of their everyday life together—the static on the bathroom radio, the way Louis flicked water off himself after a shower, the condensation on the insides of the windows in the morning from their heat in sleep, Anja picking a bright blue label off an unripe pear, the precise kind of mess Louis made (where everything had its place even though objects looked randomly strewn about), the glass of water she kept by the bed, the green seat cushions of the chairs on the back patio warmed in stripes of sunlight, Louis watering the vine climbing up the back of the house, Louis watching an instructional video about how to fold a fitted sheet—those were holy and they amounted to more than the sum of their parts. As an undergirding of the grandiose possibilities of their lives—his life—in public, what could be more sacred than the ordinariness of their love?

4

MOST MORNINGS SHE WOKE UP WITH A PAIN IN HER NECK. THE symmetrical tension was always there, clenching on either side of the vertebrae where muscle broadens to clasp neck to shoulder. She could feel the supportive tissue protesting against bone. The morning soreness had always been there, before Louis, before Howard, before anyone else had ever been in her bed. She hadn't properly evolved, something was missing in her spine's supply chain upholding her skull. She wasn't accurately constructed. It was a fact.

Usually after waking up she did a special set of stretches on the yoga mat permanently unrolled at the foot of the bed, while Louis was still asleep.

That morning she woke to find him already on the mat himself, doing some kind of bastardized yogic movement. She dangled her head over the bed, tilting it sideways to watch him as he leaned forward and tried to maneuver his elbows into the triangle of his groin.

"When I was little, my sister used to tell me that if I could lick my own elbow I'd turn into a boy," she said to him. He flinched and glanced up, surprised for some reason to see her.

"Did you ever get there?"

"Nope."

"Maybe all that trying is why your neck always hurts."

Sometimes he massaged her neck, which helped in an emotional more than a physical way. She thought of asking, since she was feeling particularly out of sorts, but he was busy on the floor forcing his forearms further into his crotch.

In the bathroom she switched on the radio above the toilet before unscrewing the shower nozzle to give permission for that morning enemy, gravity, to slowly empty the bladder of collected rainwater in a shower-like drizzle. An upbeat German voice spoke from the radio. Reassuring weather words. Mostly sunny all day, calm, sun showers in the afternoon. Wholly untrustworthy and untethered from reality. She couldn't remember when the discrepancy had expanded from acceptable error to flagrant contradiction. In Dam's mind, the inaccuracy of all official weather reports was not an accident, but a surefire conspiracy on a massive scale. Whose conspiracy, he was not so sure. Sometimes the news stations, sometimes the internet service providers, sometimes the city government. Anja found it difficult to muster the paranoia to get behind any of his rotating hypotheses, but she also had a hard time coming up with another, less sinister explanation. Dam wasn't the only one speculating; there were plenty of others staying up late on Reddit swapping theories. There was something pitiful about hanging life's meaning on the borrowed scaffolding of the conspiracy plot, but Dam did give it a certain poetics. She remembered his blast from the night before. *friendly skies, calm waters / immense gratitude / 30°*

She tuned the radio to NPR. This was the second element of the morning ritual after her stretching. Louis said the English-speaking voices reminded him of morning car rides to school, harkening nostalgically back to a swiftly disappearing kind of neolib Americana. The sound of NPR was a message in a bottle from the homeland, written by someone who would only have had to pay attention to the content of the message to know the medium of its transmission was no longer valid. And yet the voices still carried on in genial two-minute news segments, even now, even here in Europe, reassuring generations of expats that the hegemony of the English language would endure and that at least *All Things* would still be *Considered*, whether those things were true or not. There's nothing inherently immoral about nostalgia, Louis had said in defense of his radio.

The water was lukewarm and didn't smell quite right. Anja cut the shower short and enacted element three of the routine: tracing an emoticon with her finger in the shower mist on the mirror. She drew a face with a question mark for a mouth :-? When Louis's shower fogged up the glass again, the face would reappear, and this way he would know her mood of the day, even if she'd already left the house by the time he woke up. She toweled off carefully and left the radio on for Louis, noting that the seeming remoteness of the American voices was compounded by the bad reception in the bathroom.

Thursday. It was only his fourth day home, and already they'd rope-led each other back into mornings as usual. Howard and Laura may have reassured her—Laura more than once—but Anja was still unsure that normalcy was the best policy in the wake of tragedy, vexing herself with the worry that she was repressing Louis by not talking about *it*. It wasn't like he'd said so—but he was undeniably different now, whether he admitted it or not. His body was a different body: a body without any parents. There must have been a physical trace, a scoop missing out of him somewhere, but she couldn't identify where it was.

Scooped out or not, the Louis she knew was aware of how to act in any situation, and this was not the way to act like a grieving man in touch with his feelings, who was supposed to be able to talk about those feelings. More than anyone she had ever met, Louis understood the patterns of behavior that kept consensus social reality running comfortably—he knew the rules so innately that he could mess with them as he saw fit, but he never broke the rules by accident. He knew what he was doing. He must have known that acting sad after the death of a parent was the way to act. He must have known that acting fine was not normal and that, even if he really did feel fine, he should give some indication of awareness that this did not match the expectation; he should act just a little bit sad. He was the one who was supposed to take the lead on these things, and without any real guidance from his side, she had no clue how to act, how to complete the pattern that he was supposed to lay out.

One possibility was that Anja was dead wrong about the social expectation here, and that acting fine was actually the right and normal thing to do. In that case, Louis was simply parroting being a man in denial. And if he was actually setting the pace, she should follow suit. What bothered her about this possibility was that a man parroting denial was indistinguishable from a man in denial. Even if he was faking denial, he was also in it.

The other possibility, which was much more disconcerting, was that Louis had really broken the script, that grief had plunged him so far underwater that he had lost the ability or the desire to adhere to the rules. In a circular way, she thought, this possibility offered the strongest evidence that he was in an unprecedented amount of pain.

She moved into the kitchen to start preparing smoothies,

the final event in the morning series, and as she took out the blender, it occurred to her that her mental articulation of the morning steps was something new. She had never exactly conceived of the mornings as a routine; she was doing so now only because the routine had gained symbolic importance. She had become aware of the norm because she was on the lookout for any minor deviation. So concerned was she with the After resembling the Before, she was seeking a barometer for measurement.

This meant she was surely blowing the deviations out of proportion. That Louis had been awake before her that morning couldn't really be significant. There must have been hundreds of mornings that also didn't conform to the schedule. He must have woken up earlier than she had any number of times. But in that moment, smoothie machine grinding away at chunks of fruit flesh, she could not remember a single one.

She was finishing her smoothie when Louis entered the kitchen. He made a twisty expression with his mouth that was meant to resemble the face in the shower mist. He didn't want the rest of the green material in the blender, he said, he wanted an English muffin. The spirulina will go bad if you don't drink it, she was about to say, but caught herself and opened the toaster. At all costs, she would not let her obsessive thoughts out; she would not pressure him to drink a bad-tasting smoothie. He could never know that she was scrutinizing him. She must not take his coolness as a dare, because she had no empirical proof that he was daring her at all—because she had no empirical proof that he was in pain and hiding it. Pretending to be fine and being fine looked the same from the outside, and the outside was all she had. She must not admit she desired to see him in pain, for that would suggest that she desired for him to be in pain. Either desire was perverse. She had to focus on loving him, very normally.

A flash of pink appeared below her on the path as she turned at one of its many joints. There was no reason, as far as she could guess, for the path to curve around so much according to variations in the terrain, given that every centimeter of the mountain was designed and therefore could have been designed for a straight path from top to bottom. No reason but propping up the silly pretense of naturalness. When the path straightened out again, she saw Matilda, one of the neighbors, who was wearing a hot pink cardigan. Encountering Matilda was a surprise. It had been at least two weeks since she'd crossed paths with anyone ascending or descending the mountain.

"Hey," Matilda called out, huffing slightly as she climbed toward Anja. In one arm she was holding a small, fat dog with yellow fur. Its tongue was poking out of its mouth, which was rimmed with a light froth of drool. "He gets tired on the hike up," Matilda said as she walked closer, patting the dog. "I always have to carry him part of the way."

"I feel the same," said Anja. "I wish someone would carry me."

Matilda stopped half a meter away, hoisting the dog so his nose was near her ear. "How are things? We haven't seen you in ages."

By we, Matilda meant herself and her husband, whose name Anja couldn't remember. They were the Danish couple, in their forties probably, both very handsome. Stately, even.

"Oh, all good here. Minus, you know. A few house things." She gestured upward.

Matilda rolled her eyes and they both laughed. "Well, we signed up for it, didn't we?"

"We did."

They would not talk about the specifics, that was clear. The neighbors were all private about their situations; there was no sense of camaraderie. Maybe she and Louis had just cut themselves out of the group, but she didn't think so. Everyone had moved in at different times and had been briefed separately. "I'm glad everyone is trying to maintain the delusion that this is high-status," Louis had said. "Campfires and barbecues would ruin the game."

"We aren't allowed to have any open-air fires here anyway," Anja had pointed out.

Matilda and her husband lived in the house closest to Anja and Louis, maybe a hundred meters downhill. They couldn't see each other's houses from their own lots, due to the placement of the foliage, and it was easy for Anja to forget that anyone else might be within earshot at a given moment. Isolation by design.

"It's partially our fault we haven't seen you lately," Matilda said. "We've been back and forth to Copenhagen a lot."

"For work?"

"Yes, and family. Our daughter. We still have our place there." She cleared her throat.

Primary residence was supposed to be the Berg, but of course nobody was going to chase them down and insist they stay there all the time. A lot of the others probably still had apartments elsewhere, places they could retreat to when tired of lukewarm showers.

"And you?" Matilda smiled. "Still working in biology?"

Anja nodded and said it was going very well, thanks. She wasn't grateful for the reminder. She thought, with guilt, of

Michel, who had been texting her with some regularity. This was the longest she'd gone in ages without seeing him. She'd taken his reliable Monday-through-Friday presence for granted. It made sense to talk to him about what was happening to them now, to him more than anyone else, actually, but she couldn't bring herself to call him just yet. She wasn't sure why. It also made sense to ask Matilda whether her garbage disposal system had ever worked, which she wouldn't do either.

Matilda asked about Louis, and it took all of Anja's powers of self-presentation to keep a placid face. She didn't know Matilda well. She couldn't just go around telling everyone.

"He's fine," she said. "Busy, like always."

The conversation was boring and they were both glancing behind each other, signaling that it was time to move on.

"You should come over and see us one of these days," said Matilda. "We'd love to make you dinner."

"I'll talk to Louis about what day would be best." They both knew she wouldn't.

Matilda took a step up the path and Anja took a step down the path and they said how nice it was to see each other. When they had reversed altitude, Anja now looking up to make eye contact and Matilda looking down, Matilda said, "Also, if you wouldn't mind not mentioning Cheeto to anyone." She lifted the dog again and let him wet the side of her face with his little snout. "He doesn't normally stay with us. It's just, you know."

"Of course not."

At night she had very little to report. The day had been spent re-reading her contract and watching *The Bachelor* with Laura.

"Laura's been watching too much TV" was her only conclusion. "She needs a job."

"What's wrong with watching TV?" Louis asked. "Does she actually need a job?"

It was around midnight, and it was predictably hot inside. He'd come home late, they'd had sex, he'd showered. She watched while he flicked water off his sides, air-drying. His outline was perfect.

"Yeah, she needs a job. But she's treating TV like her job. She's super deep in all these forums. Like she's studying up for something. She was nonstop with the trivia today, and she was really, overly upset when her choice contestant got kicked off."

"I didn't know *The Bachelor* had contestants. I thought it was a dating show, not a game show."

"Technically they aren't called contestants."

"Do they win money?"

"No, they just win a husband. But then they get all sorts of product sponsorships and talk-show-hosting deals, so indirectly, yes, they win money."

"It's always seemed off to me that Laura watches that shit. Didn't she used to be some kind of anarchist?"

"Yeah, she used to be full-on black bloc."

"Sound like the biggest cliché of disillusionment."

"No, not exactly. She's really anthropological about it. She calls it *critical visual engagement*."

"Or maybe she just loves watching TV. I'd be more on board with it if she didn't try to frame it as something intellectual."

"You should be grateful Laura makes me watch so much TV, otherwise I wouldn't understand any of your cultural references."

"But I never watch TV."

"You don't have to, you grew up in the States. I'm sure you watched TV when you were a kid."

"Never. Pat wouldn't let me."

Interesting. This was a new fact for the pile.

Louis called his mother by her first name, that was a known fact. Anja had learned such facts about Louis incidentally, through osmosis. Unlike most couples, they had never done the background check when they first got together, that protracted period of revealing narratives of self, sharing biographical data and the resulting conclusions about their psychological makeup. From earlier relationships, even from her term with Howard, she had anticipated and even looked forward to this process, and she was disoriented when Louis showed little interest in learning details about her early life and evolution, mistaking it for a lack of interest about her in general.

But it was obvious that their conversations were infinitely more entertaining and enlightening than the predetermined kind from the relationship handbook; they were learning from each other and rewriting those stale narratives about who they were instead of reinforcing them. Generating new content, that was what they were doing. Did it matter what had actually "happened" to Louis before her? The web of references and jokes and ideas evolving in the present was more real than that cause-and-effect type of historical self-interpretation. They had more interesting things to talk about. They laughed all the time.

For two years they had sidled sideways together, allowing the steps of monogamy (exclusivity, going to parties as a unit, introducing their friends to each other, moving in) to arrive without fanfare. These were crab steps into logical territory rather than increments of upward movement, the kind Anja had heard many times referred to by women as some sort of accomplishment. And the steps were rarely discussed as if they were momentous decisions. Louis was capable of making plans, but he never made promises. He didn't need to.

And yet—she did not try to resist the urge to piece together a basic biographical scaffolding for her boyfriend. She carefully gleaned facts that he tossed off incidentally, crusts from other stories. She compiled the facts carefully. It was important that she knew him better than anyone else.

Louis's father had been a mechanical engineer who worked in a blue-and-gray office building across the highway from the diesel engine plant in Columbus, Indiana. Also the Sunday organist at First Christian Church, his father had contracted heart disease at some point when Louis was young (est. 10 y/o), and suffered a pulmonary embolism during choir rehearsal, dead right there on the stool.

Pulmonary embolism was the only description she ever received of the dad, not even a name, just pulmonary embolism, the face a round blot of coagulated fat and blood, arms dangling loosely at his sides, or maybe his lifeless wrists hitting the keys with a clang. All very morbid.

Mom, having been alive until recently, naturally had a name. Pat's story began where the other parent's left off. After three months deployed and eight months of rehabilitation, Pat arrived home from her tour of Iraq only shortly before the pulmonary embolism happened. She was still adjusting to her new legs when she was stranded alone with Louis—becoming a single mom into perpetuity. But she had also become bionic, superhuman: those remarkable mechanical limbs, which Louis had imagined would look like sausage-logs before he saw them, impressed him deeply. Pat took the loss of her legs, much like the loss of her husband, in stride (there was some evidence of hardness or apathy running in the family; Anja took note).

Through his teenage years Louis revered Pat and was desperate to impress her. He shadowed her in all her good-person activities. She worked for the veterans' advocacy group, the city architectural board, the public library, the church cleanup crew. At some point she went from cursory Sunday hits of Episcopalia to mainlining the stuff four days a week.

That was how Louis ended up at Saturday School and Sunday School and After-school Choir and Fellowship Luncheon and Youth Raise Hands Camp and more than one Lock-In. He didn't have to be prodded; church was a sanctioned place to play basketball and meet girls. He never once believed in God, but he did believe in those two things, and he believed in Pat. Pat had no interest in remarrying, from what Louis could tell, and carried on driving Louis to school and to basketball and to the movies in her fully automated, army-financed van, right up until he left for college. (That Louis hated to operate a vehicle himself became clear during that terrible road trip to Hamburg, when he veered off the autobahn.)

As soon as he made it to undergrad in New York, not the city but the state, Louis learned that having an army veteran for a parent did not carry the same moral heft it did in the Midwest. He learned to downplay his middlebrow upbringing, studying frantically to compensate—not his homework, which he could do with his eyes closed, but the highbrow references he had been so cruelly denied by his provincial origins (much as Anja acquired them now from him, second- or thirdhand). He was embarrassed by Pat for the first time in his life when she visited him at school, driving up in the brown van with veteran bumper stickers all over its rear end. She assumed he was embarrassed by her disability—though this was not at all the issue—and a period of distance ensued between them. She burrowed deeper into church.

During the two MFA years in California the shame of Indiana wore off. A lot of the friends he made in his program had emerged from similarly cultureless deserts, climbed the dunes of liberal arts, and surfaced at the top with the satisfaction of having overcome unfair circumstances. That shared climb from mediocrity was precisely what gave them the *right* to be artists—unlike all those jacked-up trust-fund sons and daughters of collectors and curators. Pat was welcomed back into his life as evidence of how far he had come.

In California, he started to produce artwork in earnest. He spent most of the second year on a single project, producing a series of tiny drone helicopters. The drones had wide-lens cameras, with which they could scout wide areas and zero in on telltale signs of poverty: dilapidated roofs, litter, distance from water source, proximity to dangerous waste. These factors were built into its image-recognition system. Based on what the drone found, it was hypothetically possible, Louis said, to determine the zones where development aid would be best spent. For his final thesis exhibition he showed wall-sized and remarkably high-resolution prints of an area the drone had captured from above and highlighted as a danger zone: the university campus. Crumbling buildings, piles of trash, and dangerous proximity to a chemical plant had identified the underfunded campus as a candidate for targeted aid.

His five-year contract with Basquiatt was already halfway over by now. They'd hired him onto the payroll straight out of his MFA, ticket to Berlin the week after graduation. He was the only one from his class to shoot straight to consultant. Many of his classmates would end up on that track, but they'd have to at least develop the pretense of having done something upon which to be consulted first.

(His Berlin period was pretty clear; Anja had lots of data on him from the past three years. Plenty of mutual friends to suck details from. There had been a few women before her, but only a few.)

These were the facts upon which she built her assumptions about what Louis's return to Indiana for the funeral had been like, the story she told herself. Some information he volunteered—for instance, kidney failure. It's a common cause of death for women over sixty, he'd said. She was over sixty? Fifty-nine.

So Pat hadn't let him watch TV. The fact itself was information number one. But the detail also had secondary import: he was voluntarily bringing Pat into conversation now. He hadn't mentioned her name since he'd gotten home.

"You haven't mentioned Pat since you got home," Anja said.

He nodded. "I know, it's weird. I've barely thought about her. And I haven't cried since the funeral." He was fully dry from the shower now and was putting shorts on. She stared.

"You cried at the funeral?"

"Yeah, the way they've ripped up the church is fucking awful."

"The church?"

"First Christian, where my dad used to play."

Cross-check: yes.

"What's happened to it?"

"They tore down the pulpit, which was this beautiful off-center wooden throne, because apparently it's not hip for a preacher to stand still anymore, they're supposed to walk around like Jesus's salesmen. They installed a huge pull-down screen for movies and a stereo system for Christian rock. I guess nobody has the attention span to sit through a sermon that isn't a multimedia experience anymore. What they don't get is that this building is incompatible, it's just not suited to become a megachurch."

"It's the one by Eero Saarinen, right?" Supplementary information, thank you, Google. Columbus, Anja knew, was a hotbed of modern architecture. A shining beacon of culture in the Midwest, its landscape was dotted with big names. Louis had returned to this topic many times before, rewriting its significance each time.

"No, Eliel, his dad. It was the first big architecture ever built in Columbus."

"Aren't there historical preservation laws?"

He sat on the side of the bed and pulled on his socks, which he usually slept wearing. "There's a high-low twang to Columbus that's really hard to explain. Architectural masterpieces are interspersed with strip malls and run-down garages and trailer parks. People don't even notice the public library is an I. M. Pei, teenagers just know there are dark corners to make out in. Then there's this huge ring of industrial buildings all around town, since the engine company paid for the fancy architecture but they never updated their own factories. So most people actually live and work in those shitty buildings, even though the town still looks nice to tourists."

"The engine company paid for the architecture?" Scanning. No hit.

"It was a corporate philanthropy thing. One of the first corporate philanthropy things ever."

She knew where this was going. This was going very far away from Pat, from emotional to intellectual content. And he'd accused Laura of masking her engagement with a pretense of academic interest. It took one to know one.

She went along, following the script. "What did the engine company get out of paying for the architecture?"

"That's the thing about corporate philanthropy, it's not obvious what you get out of it. You do it for a lot of reasons, like public image and employee morale. But also in a bigger sense, it's one way big business convinces people that you don't need the government to support public services. If corporations are benevolent and investing in plant-a-tree day and nice buildings then people won't pressure government to do its job and interfere. Philanthropy is the cornerstone of neoliberalism, as they say."

He walked back into the bathroom and came out again with his toothbrush in hand. "Wait, how long has *The Bachelor* even been running? I thought it came out twenty years ago."

"Longer than that. It's the longest-running reality show ever. Aside from maybe *Big Brother.*"

"Hard to believe," Louis said, back in the bathroom, brushing his teeth.

She called out: "How does an engine company get into modern architecture, though? Seems like a bit of a niche interest."

"There was a mastermind at work," he garbled back. She listened for the spit, the drain.

"A mastermind, you say." He emerged from the bathroom and perched on the side of the bed.

"Yes, a mastermind!" He pulled back to look at her. "J. Irwin Miller, the proto-ethical CEO of the future."

She laughed. "Would you care to tell me the whole story?"

"A bedtime story. Let me think for a second." He mimicked stroking his chin, obviously not needing to think about anything. He was born prepared. "Let's begin in the 1940s." She laughed again.

"It's the middle of World War Two."

"Okay."

"J. Irwin Miller, a native of Columbus, takes over the Cummins Engine Company when his uncle dies."

"Okay. Then what?"

"The company isn't doing so well. But even though he doesn't know anything about running a company, he turns it around really fast. He's naturally a great manager and everyone loves him. He's a humanitarian and a Christian and he's developed this fetish for the working class while he was away in the Navy working alongside the masses. He's all for workers' rights. He actually helps his own workers unionize."

"What's the catch?"

"No catch." Louis smiled, half-serious, as always. "He's a good Christian. So eventually the company has grown so much that the size of the whole town has doubled. None of the schools or public buildings are big enough anymore, and the government is building all these shitty buildings really fast to try to fit people. So our hero, J. Irwin, decides to use company profits to pay for real architects to come design them instead."

"He pays for the whole thing?"

"He pays the extra on top of the government budget that it costs to get a good architect instead of a prefab thing."

"So he builds your church first."

"The church is his own special project. It's kind of a test run to convince the town that modernism is okay. The backwater Midwesterners don't 'get' modernism until he shoves it down their throats via religion. He convinces the congregation to do it by making them feel involved in the design process. He asks them what they actually want in a church."

"Participatory bottom-up spatial praxis!"

"Exactly." Louis laughed. "So ahead of his time."

"How do you know so much about this?"

"I wrote a paper in college."

"What was the paper?

He cleared his throat and mimed pushing glasses up his nose.

"*Well*, I argued that Irwin invented the creative city concept, by building architecture to suck smart young people to the middle of nowhere to work for his engine company. He built up the town's cultural capital and he got to hang out with famous architects. And all the while he created this elaborate tax dodge. He invented corporate philanthropy as an advertising scheme and a way of getting out of taxes. He made public, private, and personal interests align. The perfect trifecta."

"What's Cummins doing today?"

"Nothing really. Diesel's not a thing anymore. And after Irwin died they stopped innovating. No money left to build new architecture or keep my church in shape."

My church. An odd indication of ownership. Ownership arising through lack.

"Maybe they need a new Irwin," she said.

"The world needs a new Irwin."

"Maybe you're the new Irwin."

"Probably not." He looked away, toward the window, the total darkness outside. "You know what I realized when I was home?"

"What?"

"I don't have any reason to go back to Columbus again."

They had come full circle, as she had assumed they would. She could let him spin his hands in the air, drawing loops around concepts, following his own train of thought while she drew new loops silently on her own. Eventually he would return to base camp and she'd be able to decipher why he'd gone where he'd gone. The route was new each time—that was why she went along with it—but the method of leaving in order to return was so predictable, and so inefficient.

For the first time, she felt acutely annoyed that Louis had to leave himself in order to return to himself. If he could articulate the world, he should also be able to directly articulate his own being. Otherwise, what was the point of all that traveling in circles?

5

ON FRIDAY, LOUIS WAS ENTHUSIASTIC ABOUT GOING OUT. PRINZ was at a tiki bar in the west, and they were going to meet him. This seemed normal and fine, and Anja was *fine* with it. On the other hand, she felt soggy and incapable of small talk. All her clothes smelled like they'd been left in the washing machine for too long. She selected a damp knitted yellow top, white linen pants, and platforms with little plastic flowers separating the toes, then spritzed her whole body with a spray bottle of Febreze.

"Resort wear!" Louis called approvingly from the bed, while texting someone. He was wearing his hair in a long fishtail braid and had a leather jacket hanging around his shoulders. He never really put coats on, as in actually threading his arms through the armholes, but swung them over his back with the empty chutes dangling from his neck as if he were a coatrack.

Louis could wear anything. It was incredible. He could wear tasseled loafers, he could wear board shorts, he could wear a pin-striped blazer. This was disconcerting when you first met him—the randomness of the clothes and also that he didn't have the affect of the heavily ironic person you'd expect to be wearing them. He didn't have to. Aesthetic trump card was always the body, and the sheer quality of the skin of the forehead, the long fine nose, the exquisite divot above the top lip, the trapezoid of the torso, those ropey legs—you forgot all about the clothes; they only threw him into relief. Tweed jacket, white sport socks, hair tied back with a piece of rope. It was awful and it was ostentatious, and next to him, carefully curated men looked shrunken and pretentious.

Anja worked hard for a coherent appearance. With each outfit she tried to present a delicate, well-balanced constellation of interconnected nodes. The selection usually went according to a single theme from head to toe. Squeaky Fabrics, Grunge, Business Uncasual, Yellow, Branded, Unbranded, Denim with Silk. She was aware that she had small, sharp facial features protruding from extremely accurate coordinates on the map, and she aimed to replicate that physical precision with her outfits. Louis had told her once that her face in profile was noticeably incongruent with its frontal display, which fascinated him. It was as if she existed in two separate planes.

Her resort wear was appropriate for the weather in the house, but it was the wrong choice for the weather in the world, which had become suddenly chilly, the humidity frozen in midair, sticking to everything in a dust of frost. It became noticeably colder as they descended, as if the mountain were generating its own microclimate. In a sense, this was true; their houses probably gave off extra heat as they tried to regulate their internal temperatures. They were halfway down the mountain when Anja had to run back up to the house for a jacket. "My little fashion victim," Louis said to her affectionately when she met him at the bottom of the mountain. She noticed he had put his arms through the sleeves of his jacket.

In front of the tiki bar, Prinz was planted on a tall stool. Sara and Sascha were perched on either side of him. Anja looked at Louis. She had not expected the Event Planners to be there. He shrugged. Sara and Sascha could be a drag—Louis agreed, though in that case Anja couldn't understand why he loved Prinz so much, when to her, Prinz, Sara, and Sascha were birds of a feather. The thought had crossed her mind that maybe characteristics like gossipy, petty, and manipulative were more permissible when exhibited in men.

The floor inside the tiki bar as well as the sidewalk in front of it were covered in a thin layer of loose sand. Ace of Base was playing from a speaker above their heads, badly equalized and causing the sand to quake slightly. Anja clambered onto a stool and Louis went inside to order a round of mai tais.

Conversation clicked into German in his absence.

"The weather!" said Sara. "Right?"

"Sorry," said Sascha to Anja. "We didn't know it was going to get so cold. Wrong night to tiki."

"No worries," said Anja. "It's so hot in our house that it seems kind of nice outside."

"Are you coming out with us later?" said Sara, right on cue.

"Last time was so much fun. You have to come with us this time," said Sascha, as if someone had pushed a button on her forehead. "Prinz has guest list." Sara and Sascha reliably spoke about events that had happened or were about to happen, with minimal interpretation of those events. The simple fact that events happened and that Sara and/or Sascha knew about them was their reason for having conversations at all. The secondary goal was to create a constant strain of anxiety on your part (and possibly on each other's part) that there could ever be something happening to which you were not privy. Left unchecked, they could carry on forever with preemptive or retroactive scheduling talk, especially if you let on that it made you uncomfortable.

"Sure," said Anja. "Louis was talking about going to the

Baron." Prinz nodded and confirmed they could all get in with his bounty of plus ones.

S and S clapped their hands approvingly. They were wearing different colors of the same mesh top. Seeing Anja glance back and forth, Sara said, "I know, so embarrassing. We both got them at work today and didn't compare outfits before leaving the house." They worked at a clothing store in Mitte together, while pursuing master's in something. Art history. Sociology. Feminism? The top looked better on Sara.

Louis returned with the drinks, and she felt relieved. He'd carry the conversation for her now. She could let the baton circulate without the responsibility of holding it for at least a half hour; he could say funny things on her behalf.

Everyone raised their glasses. The artificial taste of the mai tai brought back a scene from a poolside bar a long time ago. Eva, in a zebra-print swimsuit, stretched out on a lounge chair, her skin evenly tanned and glistening, stomach rising and falling slowly in the sun like the hairless belly of a Chihuahua. Anja wondered what Eva would have to say about this tiki bar. Disgusting, no doubt.

"When I was a teenager," Prinz was saying, "I used to come to this bar all the time." He'd grown up in Berlin and liked to tell stories that illustrated his unique claim on the urban space. "I drank some of my first beers here," he went on, launching into a story. Anja zoned in and out, catching the gist.

One day an older friend told young Prinz that the waiter at the tiki bar sold weed, and that *Fanta* was the code word. Of course Prinz tried the scheme immediately. He cut class to make sure he ran into the right waiter, sat down, and when he was asked for his order he said the word slyly. The waiter looked him up and down and shook his head. We're all out, he said. The refusal infuriated

Prinz so much that he resolved to get amateur revenge. He spent the rest of the day drinking colas at the bar, and then at closing time he went to a restaurant around the corner to continue consuming liquid. He didn't use the toilet for seven hours. In the wee hours of the morning he returned to the scene of his humiliation and pissed all over the sand in front of the bar.

"That's why you never want to come here?" asked Sara, who was staring intently down at the sand at their feet.

"I haven't been avoiding it on purpose. I just always felt weird about it after that."

"It hurt your pride," said Louis. "Teenage humiliation can be very traumatizing. I sympathize with that."

"Hey," said Sara, "what if we order Fantas now? Do you think it still works?"

"Definitely not," said Prinz. "Berlin has changed."

"Amen," said Louis. Everyone shook their heads in reverence.

"Where's the next place, though?" said Sascha.

"I heard Dublin," said Sara. "Or Vilnius?"

"No way," said Louis. He put his arm around Anja and kissed her cheek. "This is the end of the line. Nowhere to go from here."

black sun, definitive night / the shiver (−1°)

They wanted to take a cab, but there were five of them and it was Friday night and a big taxi under surge pricing was going to cost as much as three rounds of drinks, so they gave in and went to wait for the bus, standing huddled against the wind in two clumps: boys and girls.

Sara leaned in and stroked Anja on the arm. "Is everything okay with Louis?" She was oozing with concern. Sara glanced meaningfully over at Louis and Prinz, who were bleating with laughter.

"He's fine," said Anja. "He's really doing okay. Thanks for asking." She wasn't sure if she should be grateful or offended about the breach of scheduling banter.

"He must be sooooo sad," Sara said. "Is there anything we can do?" They both had their hands on her. Their faces were eager, not to help but to acquire information, even information in the form of an emotional reaction. Anja shrank away. She felt herself diminishing in importance, nothing but a conduit. Death as gossip, death as currency.

"Don't worry, he just wants to get back to normal," she said. "You're so sweet. Really, don't worry."

At the Baron they jumped to the front of the line, skipping the hour-long wait but still paying the cover. The bouncer was characteristically hostile, almost comically so. He inspected Prinz's email, displayed on his screen, cross-checking the signatures with the list of people on his glowing tablet before waving them in. Anja focused on the familiar faded barbed-wire tattoo circling the joints of the bouncer's fingers on his left hand. A spider crawled up the wrist of the other.

The Baron had been remodeled a few years back to look like a cave inside, complete with stalactites hanging from the ceiling, and it smelled like sulfur in some corners, maybe not artificially so. Once inside, Louis and Anja leaned against the bar and shared a cigarette with satisfaction. Smoking was banned on the Berg. People filtered by, smiling and stopping to chat occasionally. Louis put his hand on Anja's back, and they whispered together about who they saw and what people were wearing.

"I feel like a sponge," said Anja. "So soggy."

"The body is a porous interface," said Louis, which made her laugh, although she couldn't remember the source of the quote.

It seemed like everyone they talked to had come from an opening Anja didn't know about, an open house at a Finster-owned publisher launching a new ebook series.

Process-based novel, she heard someone say. Net worth up by .07 percent. Third-quarter review.

Anja texted Dam repeatedly, wishing he were here, but he said he was out with the gays tonight, sorry. She was on her own.

Prinz snuck up behind them and whispered in Louis's ear, who put his arm around Anja and pointed to the bathroom.

The drugs were suppositories—not exactly a social experience, but the three of them crowded into a stall together, Louis and Anja reaching around in each other's underwear and giggling.

Prinz rolled his eyes. "Let's get out of here, Snow White's on."

All three stumbled out of the bathroom and pushed to the front of the crowd encircling Snow White, who was squatting on a white plinth. He had on a Viking helmet with three plasticky blond braids tacked to the back of his head, and wore an electric guitar slung lamely over his shoulder like a useless, vestigial limb. He was bellowing a country ballad into a handheld microphone.

Snow White was Louis's friend Andy. He was finishing his contract with O'Reilly this year, and he'd probably start right in somewhere else at the top. Finster was the current rumor. At O'Reilly, Andy's presence had done little more than demonstrate how hopelessly out of touch the company had become. With his carefully designed disregard for rules, he stood out like a sequin from the company's cadre of glassy-eyed Ivy League consultants, kids who'd never learned that fulfilling their terms of contract wasn't going to get them anywhere—you had to subvert or disrupt something. You had to influence.

On the side, as part of his influencer brand, Andy cultivated a late-night performance persona. He offered a much-needed halftime act between DJ sets, a similar function to the squad of spangled gymnasts who leap out between the halves of a football game. He did Disney musicals, cabaret, concrete poetry, whatever the night called for. Probably because of his consistent presence at parties, Andy had reached the top rung of the ladder of local celebrities—he had transitioned, incredibly, to the status of minor celebrity outside Berlin. This was the ultimate goal of anyone who'd accepted a Berlin-based contract. To be successfully *based* in Berlin you had to be famous elsewhere.

The crowd was becoming fuller and people were yelling song requests up toward Andy. "'This Kiss'!" Anja realized Louis was shouting. Was it the name of a country song? But Andy didn't seem to be taking requests. He stuck to his repertoire. She tried to follow the lyrics, but she had trouble focusing on the words. The problem was that her hearing was becoming difficult to separate from her vision. The two senses were interfering with each other. First Andy's face would zoom into focus, and then his voice. She noticed an O'Reilly sticker on his arm. The arm was waving in time to the music, but the movement seemed to be driving, rather than following, the sounds. She felt herself echolocating, like a bat.

Louis mumbled into her ear: "Did you know this bar used to be called Kit n' Caboodle's Mix-Up Joint? Back when this was East Berlin."

She shook her head. That made no sense. Optionable options, variable variables. She asked him words with no voice, his soft eyes close to hers. Weighty propositions stuck on her tongue.

Should we? How to? She was grabbing at him, to make sure he was still there. He fidgeted and stared rapturously up at Andy. Her knees were dead weights. They kept swaying in unison, as if her joints formed the balls of two pendulums. Her butthole was stinging, and she wondered if it was somehow conspicuous, if other people could tell she was thinking about it. She looked at Louis and wondered if that was why he was fidgeting so much, because he was thinking about his own butt.

She looked at him again and he wasn't there anymore, so she wandered back over to the bar, put a forearm down on the sticky glass, and put her forehead down on the sticky arm. She felt a nudge in her ribs but didn't budge, thinking vaguely that she might feel embarrassed tomorrow when remembering this moment of self-comprehension, the moment of realizing how flat out high she was. The thought passed. That's why she'd bought those purple packets of detox tea, for tomorrows like tomorrow. "It's cool," she said to no one, barely lifting her head.

Sara was standing a few paces away. "I have faith!" she shouted to Anja. Sara approached and flopped over on top of her, conforming to her slumped shape like a flow of lava. Anja wondered if Sara had fallen asleep, but then Sara whispered, "He does this on purpose, I know he does."

"Who?"

"He shows up when I'm high, late at night when I'm the most, when I'm, you know, like this."

"Who, Howard?"

Sara lifted her head to look at Anja and gave Anja's head a shove.

"Mahatma, obviously." She straightened and shot a forlorn look toward the far end of the bar. Mahatma was standing there with a red bandana tied around his forehead, talking to some girl.

"Um, groovy," said Anja.

"I know. The sex was just so . . ."

Mahatma glanced in their direction and then turned away to focus on the girl he was talking to.

"He shows up like this and doesn't even come say hi to me, like he doesn't know me at all. But he's always *looking* at me."

Sara had moved to Berlin following a boyfriend, who'd gotten famous within the span of a year and then dropped her for someone else, or many others. Sara had nonetheless held her grip on the dream of domestic coupling, seeking a cliché of straight romance and always pursuing the absolute worst men for the job. If you could look past her clothes, her outlook was fully conservative.

"Fuck him," said Anja. "Find someone else."

"There aren't any," said Sara. "All the good ones are taken." She pinched Anja's sides with both her hands, like pincers. "I guess *you* would know that." She was glaring at Mahatma's back now. He was moving in the direction of the bathroom, following a girl in front of him.

"Who's Harold?" Sara shot out, then seemed to forget to wait for the answer and drifted away toward the receding red handkerchief.

The main dance floor was filling up and people lining up for the bar were brutely nudging her aside. There must be some retreat, a hiding spot, for times like this. Yes, she recalled that there was a void down at the end of the bar. The void was not just a hole in the floor. It had steps leading down to other subterranean depths. A cave below a cave. She peeled herself away from her roost and slunk down the steps, to the low-ceilinged crawl space beneath the dance floor. It was lit by a single, flammable-looking yellow bulb, and there were six or eight people stashed among various cartons and boxes. It was extremely hot.

"Anja!" said someone, and she sought the source, spotting a claw-foot tub in a far corner with Didi's head poking out. "Get in!" Didi was calling.

Where did she know Didi from? Was her name Didi?

Besides Didi there were two other girls in the tub whom Anja definitely didn't know, all tangled together. Anja slid in close beside Didi, the other girls' heads at the opposite end, their dirty spike heels crisscrossed around Anja's shoulders.

"Sardines!" said Didi.

"Snakes!" yelled one of the girls.

"Sausages!" yelled the other.

Anja tried to introduce herself to the heads brushing against her feet, and names were exchanged, uselessly. "They just got to Berlin," said Didi. "Summer internships."

"Where are you guys interning?" called Anja, and one of them said, "PornPals!"

"PornPals has interns?" Anja asked Didi.

"Ya, why not. Social media, marketing."

Didi pulled her shirt up high over her bra.

"Nice boobs," said Anja.

"Thanks. How have you been? I heard about Louis's mom."

"Yeah."

"I'm so sorry. Tell him I'm sorry."

"Thanks, Didi. I like you." She did like Didi.

Down toward her feet: "So do you guys have experience in porn?"

"Not porn, LIFESTYLE," came a voice. The one with her hair in pigtails.

"Like vegan porn?" said Didi to Anja, laughing.

"Porn lifestyle is our thesis research," said pigtails.

"That's really interesting," said Anja.

"I'm doing web statistics, I'm a MATH MAJOR." One of them was now kicking her in the shoulder.

"I GET IT," shouted Anja. "IT'S COOL."

Getting out of the tub was infinitely harder than getting in; the sides of the thing had grown at least a foot taller. Anja used both arms to struggle out, gasping, her foot lodged under someone, like she was trying to pull herself out of a pool but her ankle was tangled in the lane-divider rope.

"You have weird knees," said one of the PornPals.

How could they see her knees? She was wearing wide-leg pants. She looked back and realized her leg was wrenched at an odd angle. It started to hurt.

She limped upstairs and pushed her way through bodies to the bathroom. Leaned into the mirror, eyes focusing on pores and unplucked eyebrows. Couldn't figure out if she looked young or old. Rising anxiety about appearance. Why did they have mirrors in here at all? Clubbing didn't used to be like this, you didn't have to look at your pores in the mirror and you didn't have to talk so much.

You will get old, she said to herself, possibly out loud. This face will not always be your face. You'll have to change your habits at some point. Clubbing, drugs. Then again, Eva hadn't changed any of her habits. She'd never grown up. But she had Botox.

A round of girls huddled into the bathroom. Anja had met at least two of them several times but they'd never spoken more than blanks together, blank phrases meaning nothing, signifying nothing except that they knew each other, like Mad Libs for social acquaintance. Anja shook her head. What was the point? Are you having a good night. What did you do earlier. Where are you going later. Blank blank blank.

"Anja! We're doing face scrubs!" said one of the girls, holding out a white bottle from O'Reilly. A face scrub was not going to be enough to counteract what this place was doing to their pores. But scrub they would. Girls. Women. *Weeeeemen.*

The longer she spent looking for Louis, trudging through sedimentary layers of cigarette butts and across organic slime trails, the more unsure she became about whether this night was going well. She took a break in her search and ordered a beer, absently peeling the label off and feeling conspicuously alone. Some tall guy standing next to her asked what her star sign was, and she made him guess, and he guessed wrong, and they talked about the iconography of the signs, how odd it was that every sign was a living being except for Libra, the inanimate scales. "I'm a Scorpio," he revealed, and she took off.

After an unknown expanse of time had crashed into itself— she remembered dancing—Louis found her near the exit. She thrust her peeled Becks at him.

"No, thanks."

"Where've you been?"

"Outside with Prinz and the girls."

"I was looking for you."

"No, I don't want any more to drink. Just leave it here."

"I couldn't find you for so long."

"I didn't see you either."

"I hate beer."

"Should we get going?"

He took her by her hand, which was wadded up into a ball, and they walked out into the cold morning. Prinz, Sara, and Sascha were squatting outside on the curb, where they'd all four been presumably waiting for ages while Anja wandered around alone inside. A huddle of homeless people was packed in sleeping bags on the sidewalk a few meters away.

Sara was in full Mahatma meltdown; Sascha was in charge of consoling her. Anja hugged everyone and told Sara she'd text her later, which she wouldn't. Louis waved down a cab and called over his shoulder toward the three on the curb: "The light of morning breaks upon our sorrows!" Sascha laughed, too loud. Sara waved sorrowfully, wiping her nose.

The taxi left them at the foot of the mountain. The driver apologized for not being able to drive any farther, his wheels couldn't handle the incline. Anja heard herself shouting at him, saying taxis had made it up before—so aggressive, why?—but Louis said it was fine, they could walk, then paid and tipped. So American, Anja thought as she stepped out of the car. She nearly bumped into a man with his arm deep in a trash can, the same can where she'd deposited some plastic packaging that morning. Louis reached into his pocket and tipped the trash-searcher too.

As they climbed, Louis pointed straight up to the sky, where they could see the moon fading in the daylight, a jet weaving through a cloud of clouds around it. Louis clasped her hand again, squeezed, and she stood for a moment with her head back, mouth gaping. Suddenly her perspective swung around, as if she were looking sideways at the cloud above her, as if on the same level, eye-to-eye. She squinted. Was the cloud denser on the left edge? Was it too heavy on the left side? A three-legged cloud? She should take more time to really look at the clouds from now on, she thought, before recognizing it as a sentimental, drugged thought that would seem stupid in the morning. At least self-awareness was on its way back.

The door to the house opened easily, and it was surprisingly cool, even chilly inside. "I told you they'd work out the temperature situation soon," Louis said, "you don't need to worry so much." Pulling her by the waist, biting her neck.

She woke up at the foot of the bed, partly clothed and parched. Louis looked up at her from the yoga mat, placing the tablet face-down on the floor.

"You alive? Want some tea?"

6

"THE LAWYER SAYS EVERYTHING LOOKS FINE WITH THE CON-tract," said Anja.

"Famous last words. You should get that on your tombstone," said Laura.

"Ha."

"So you're going to take the job?" asked Dam.

"The lawyer said the contract is legit, technically speaking. But what the job entails is still pretty vague."

"Okay, so what does it *entail*, vaguely?" said Laura, fingers drumming on the table.

"I can't tell you, even vaguely. You were right, there's an NDA tacked on at the end. Another standard form, automatically generated, and electronically signed by a bunch of people I've never heard of."

There was a groan. This came from Eric, a twenty-two-year-old blond Dam had found in some crevice of the internet. "How can you even sell your soul to big pharma like that?"

Dam smiled at him and petted him on the head. "Sweetheart, we can't all be as pure of heart as you."

The four of them were sitting in the darkest corner of the

faux-Kneipe around the corner from Laura and Dam's place. Anja could still remember when the faux-Kneipe had been a real Kneipe, run by a sad old couple still running on DDR time. One of their regular clientele, a pensioner often seen howling on the street corner, had passed out in a snowdrift on the Kneipe's front step one night and died, frozen or alcohol-poisoned or both. A week later the bar had closed for good and the place was immediately bought up by some energetic young French guys. Experimental video screenings on Fridays, imported IPA. Fifty years of smoke etched from the walls, which were then immediately re-aged with a gray wash of paint. Anja's back was rubbing up against a spindly, dried-up palm tree starved for rays in the corner.

"Anyone else want a beer?" said Eric, standing abruptly.

"Yes, please," said Anja. "I need it to dull the shame of working for the Man."

"Get four, please, honey," said Dam.

When Eric was at the bar Laura leaned in and whisper-yelled, "You have to get rid of him, Dam. He's the worst one yet."

"Oh, relax. He's harmless."

Dam was trying harder than usual. His lips were glossed with glitter. The dragon tattoo on his neck had been scrubbed off and replaced with some kind of tribal mark, and he'd shaved a thin strap of beard around his chin. His tight shirt said CHOLO in big bubble letters.

"Whatever." Laura redirected to Anja: "Can you at least say how much you're going to be making? Or how long the contract is for?"

"I don't really remember what I'm allowed to tell you. But basically I'm making a shit ton of money for a year, and then they can get rid of me if I don't meet some criteria I don't understand."

Dam clapped. "Good for you, girl. That sounds better than any job I've ever had."

"Honestly," Laura said, "I've never really understood what goes on at RANDI in the first place. Is it really 'big pharma'?"

"No, not at all. We don't make stuff with use value. I mean, Finster does, but not at RANDI."

"I don't get the distinction."

"We do Research About Nature, Indefinitely." Anja smiled helplessly. "What's to get?"

"Why would they tack on 'indefinite' at the end?" asked Dam, stroking his chin strap. "It makes the whole thing weird. Like why would you need to specify that? Why would it be 'definite' in the first place?"

"They needed the 'I' on the end, that's why," Laura snapped. "They can't just call themselves RAND."

"Why not?"

"Really, brother?" said Laura.

"All right, all right," said Anja. "Officially, the 'I' is because there's supposed to be no definite goal to the research. It's research for the sake of discovery, science as the means to its own end, which is the means to a better end for humanity."

"A better *end* for humanity?" Dam cocked his head.

"A better end *goal*. Haven't you ever googled it?"

Laura dutifully pulled out her phone and started padding in the letters.

"So you've never understood the point of what you do there," said Dam.

"There is no point, per se." She glanced over at the next table, where two women had started shouting at each other. They looked like a couple arguing. "We're just exploring new concepts without finite applications. It's like a think tank that isn't influenced by academia or the market."

She couldn't help glancing over at the other table again. The yelling had stopped. One woman was sobbing and the other was gulping a pint of beer.

"But in practice," said Laura, "you probably have some inkling of the commercial applications of your research. Or millllllitary?" She raised her eyebrows.

"You sound just as suspicious as Dam is about the weather," Anja said. "There's no conspiracy. The only reason that I can't tell you about my specific project is that I'm guarded by a wall of NDAs."

One of the women at the other table scooted her chair back with a screech. Anja watched the woman peripherally as she picked up her coat and hurried out.

"Which just makes it seem infinitely more suspicious," said Dam, titillated by the prospect of a new conspiracy.

Laura had found the website and was scanning and scrolling. "Ahem," she said. She put on an authoritative voice. "RANDI is nothing more and nothing less than a place to tackle our world's greatest challenges by resolutely not tackling them. We have hand-picked the best and most cutting edge thinkers across sci entific disciplines in order to finally resolve humanity's most profound questions about nature, not through products and solutions but through speculative speculations on the future. After half a decade of collaboration with external consultants in the field of knowledge management, we at Finster have discovered that the key to advancing scientific research in the laboratory context is not to try to advance science but to try to advance creativity."

Laura paused to catch her breath.

"See, the internet can answer all your questions," said Anja.

"You've been on the cutting edge this whole time, and we didn't even know it!" said Dam.

Laura cleared her throat and continued in a more assertive, TED-talk voice. "But you must be wondering: what do we mean by 'indefinite'?" She glanced up at Anja, who nodded. "To us, indefinite means the kind of research without an end goal besides knowledge itself. Indefinite means a new way of doing research to produce maximum knowledge-based nonresults at an unprecedented pace."

Laura laughed harshly, waved away Anja's protest against her continuing, then returned to her phone. "In all seriousness, we do have some ideas about where to begin, from biome conservation to reduction of fossil fuels to medical advancements, but the direction of the research at RANDI arises organically through collabo . . . oollop . . . peration?" She squinted. "Is that a typo? Collaboroop . . ."

"No," said Anja. "That's the portmanteau some consultants came up with. No one knows how to say it."

"Lord." Laura went on, speeding through to the end. "RANDI busts down stale and dangerous barriers between old and new, between research and praxis, between science as a means to an end and science as a means to its own end that can ultimately help us all reach a better end. At this crucial moment in history, nature is our most precious resource, and we want our relationship with nature to be a long-lasting one—dare we say . . . indefinite."

"I can't even," said Dam, laughing. "The jargon! That's just like how my ex used to talk. The consultant."

"Your paraphrase from before was remarkably accurate," said Laura to Anja.

"I am legitimately shocked that you guys have never looked this up before. I've been working there for years."

"You're blind to the faults of the ones you love," said Dam.

Eric approached the table unsteadily with three beers triangled between his hands. "I only had enough cash for three. They don't take credit cards here, still."

"They're trying to stay authentic," said Laura.

"That's pathetic," said Eric, sloshing beer on his khakis as he scooted the glasses onto the table.

"You're from a younger generation, you wouldn't get it." Laura grabbed one of the beers.

"Aren't you like, twenty-eight?" Eric spat back.

"Generations turn over fast these days. You young kids and all your new technology."

"It's true," said Dam. "They're way ahead of us. Eric was just telling me about this new app that I've never even heard of." He beamed at Eric.

"Well?" said Laura.

"I signed an NDA," said Eric. He glared at Dam but without any real vitriol.

Laura slammed her glass on the table, spilling more beer. "Are we allowed to talk about *anything* tonight?"

"Come on, you can tell them," said Dam.

Eric was obviously going to tell them, he just wanted to be egged on a bit first. He pouted for a requisite moment and then said, "It's just a little microtrading app for intangible capital."

Laura sighed loudly. "Treat us like we're your grandparents."

"How am I supposed to know how much you know?" He sighed, loudly. "You know what trading is, right? Like the stock market?" Seeing the look on Laura's face, Anja laughed. "Fine, so this is a trading system for nonmonetizable things, like your personal network of connections. Basically social capital as opposed to financial capital. Do you follow?"

They were all silent. "Maybe give an example?" said Anja, finally.

"Okay. Say you have a hookup to rent a cheap apartment because of someone you know, a friend in the building. You haven't paid for anything, there's no money involved yet, you just have the connection. So that's your capital. Not the apartment, the connection."

Dam cut in enthusiastically: "So you can trade your social connection for something else you want, right, babe?"

Eric waved Dam off. "I'm getting there. So you have the apartment hookup, but you decide you don't want it after all. Maybe you're leaving the city, I don't know. But there is something else you really want. Something else you can't exactly pay for."

"Like a plus one to get into a club," said Dam. "Right?"

"I'm *getting there.* Plus ones are big. So are letters of recommendation. Or, say you need proof of employment to get a visa, someone has to write you a letter who trusts you to not actually hit them up for employment after you get your visa. So you can buy a letter now, with your social capital."

"Hold on," said Laura. "Who decides how much these things are worth? Is there a point system or something?"

"That's the proprietary part of the app. The *algorithm.*" Eric was visibly pleased to use these words. "It has a special rating system based on social media and news aggregators. Things change in relation to each other all the time. So one day, a plus one might be worth as much as being second in line for an apartment in a shitty neighborhood, then the next day it could be worthless if the club gets lame or if the neighborhood gets cool or any number of things."

Laura raised a finger in the air. "Aren't people speculating on the value then? Some kind of secondary market?"

He frowned. "They're trying to discourage that."

Anja did a quick inventory of her life's intangible worth. Plus ones—check, through Prinz via Louis. Knowledge of events and gossip—check, through Sara/Sascha via Louis. Real estate—check, through Howard. Employment—check, through Louis, Howard. She was secure, until she considered how vastly her connection points would be reduced were Louis and Howard not a part of her chain of connections.

"It seems like, maybe, it would just make relationships into commodities," said Anja, looking at her hands, suspecting she was repeating something she'd heard elsewhere.

"Yet again!" said Eric. "I will say this yet again! There is no money involved!"

"No, she's right," said Laura. "Whether or not there's actual money changing hands, the system is turning relationships into calculations. It might be called 'trading' to sound more like a swap meet or a flea market, but it's really just buying and selling without cash."

"But . . ." Anja opened and closed her mouth.

"Go ahead," said Laura.

"I don't know, maybe this is wrong, but it's also a way to give rich people a way to buy social capital. Like if you don't have any friends in Berlin but you have a lot of money to bribe your way into getting an apartment, now you can trade that thing you paid for to get something that you aren't able to pay for."

Eric was silent for a long moment, gathering his resources, digging around for bits of argumentation he'd picked up at some party or other. "If rich people get a few plus ones, so what?" He shrugged. "The point is that great people can leverage their cultural value to survive." Then he seemed to hit on what he was supposed to say here: "Think about it. What if all you needed to survive was *community*?"

Seeing that Laura was heating up, Dam cut in, "Can you invite us to the app?"

Eric looked haughtily down at all of them. "You can't ask to be invited. You have to be picked. Otherwise where would the trust come from?"

Dam looked back and forth between Eric and Laura, who were becoming less compatible by the second, weighed his options, and made a choice based entirely on his crotch.

"Oh, Laura," he said. "You're just bitter because you've blown all your cash, and you know your cultural capital can't help you now." He watched Anja for her reaction.

Anja reacted dutifully. She was grateful for the shift of gear. The app wasn't worth arguing about. She wished she could get herself to feel as strongly about things as Laura could—Laura argued for argument's sake: there was something admirable in that. "What happened?" she asked. Laura shrugged and drank.

"She's developed a little gambling habit recently," said Dam. "Four thousand euros down the toilet at once."

"It's not gambling," said Laura coolly. "It's like fantasy sports. It's harmless."

Anja remembered how upset Laura had been after watching *The Bachelor* the week before. "Shit. What shows are you betting on?"

"Only *The Bachelor*. It's just an experiment."

"Sure, it's an experiment in figuring out how we're going to pay rent," said Dam, sneaking a look at Eric, who was staring off into the distance.

"I've been doing really well until this week," said Laura. "I never lost before now."

"That's what people who are addicted to gambling say," said Dam.

"So you're part of a reality TV betting ring," Anja said, putting her arm around Laura. "That's not the worst thing in the world." Laura glared at her. "I'm not being sarcastic," Anja said. "I think you've got your finger on the pulse. I was worried you'd been wasting your talent."

"Don't encourage her," said Dam.

Laura composed herself. "Next week is the grand finale, and I have solid intel on the winner of the Final Rose. I just wasn't sure of the order the others would get kicked off. But now I have everything under control."

Eric tapped the table excitedly, apparently paying attention again. "You know what, this could be a really good addition to the app. Insider TV knowledge. I'm going to run this by the founders and see what they say."

Laura face-palmed. The conversation didn't pick up again after that. Eric finished his beer in a heroic swig and took off, alluding to an important tech party he had to get to. Dam watched him leave, stricken at the thought of having to endure a whole other social event with Eric in order to get him into bed. Laura retreated home to "check some stats." Dam volunteered to walk Anja to the foot of the mountain.

As they pushed open the door, leaving the Kneipe, they ran into the man who sold roses in the neighborhood, rearranging his bundle of unripe buds, which he raised in greeting. They recognized each other by now, or at least Anja and Dam recognized him. He probably saw too many faces every night. He was familiar and easy to talk to, always lifting the flowers in a perfunctory gesture but never pressuring anyone to buy. Anja was sure she had bought one, once, but it had been a long time ago. Now the question of purchase seemed beside the point; they met each other as acquaintances, which was nicer than a transaction, wasn't it? Or would he really have preferred Anja and Dam cut the crap and just buy a flower?

They said hello to him and asked after his family. "All good," he said. "The smallest one is teething, so I'm not too sad to be out of the house." He stepped over the threshold into the bar. "But it's so cold tonight."

They agreed, zipping their jackets against an icy wind. The air bit their faces the way it could only bite in Berlin. Anja wrapped her scarf around her face and realized she was clenching all her muscles in an automatic brace against the cold walk ahead. She should have been wearing long underwear—but how could you know what to put on, when the weather was always changing so fast?

"He's right, do you feel this?" Dam said to Anja as they headed south. "I mean really feel it?"

"Are you walking me home as an excuse to try some new weather theory on me?"

"No, but just hear me out for one second. Does this look like rain to you?" The cobblestones were running with an icy slush.

"Well, it's not snow either," said Anja.

"Exactly. It's an ambiguous substance that is not liquid water but not frozen snowflakes. It's undefinable, it doesn't fit into normal app categories, there's no little phone icon for *porridge falling from the sky*. Isn't that convenient?"

"Convenient for who? I mean for whom?"

"You think I know English better than you? Never mind."

"Come on. Tell me the current theory on the block."

He shoved his hands deeper into his jacket pockets and squinted at her. "Have you ever heard of Operation Popeye?"

She laughed, then clamped her mouth shut. Her teeth chattered. "No. Tell me."

"During the Vietnam War, the U.S. government had a secret program called Operation Popeye. Their job was to try to fuck with the weather over Southeast Asia to beat the Vietnamese and win the war. Mainly they tried to make it rain, to extend the monsoon season so it would never stop raining and there would be flooding and landslides that would make fighting impossible."

She rubbed her jaw to calm its chattering. "Is that real?"

"What do you mean?"

"Like did this really happen or is it an internet story?"

"It definitely happened. They released all the classified papers a long time ago."

"How does someone make it rain on purpose?"

"Basically you shoot chemicals like silver iodide into a cloud until it explodes into water droplets. It's called cloud seeding."

They paused so a bus could go by before crossing the street. The streets were almost empty otherwise, no traffic and only a few people hurrying home from bars with their faces angled against the wind. "So you think someone is seeding clouds over Berlin and making it rain," said Anja.

"Not just seeding clouds. That's just the best known kind of environmental warfare, the only kind that's been made public. There are tons of others. Earthquake warfare, wind warfare."

"Or maybe it's just climate change."

The wind picked up, as if for emphasis. A siren blared in the distance.

"Climate change would explain seasons with extreme heat or extreme cold. Or even a few really hot or really cold decades, extra long seasons. There was a little ice age in Europe in the 1600s when it was freezing for like fifty years—even that would make sense. But that's not what's happening now. We don't have consistent seasons at all. It's different every single day."

She nodded. This much was true. The four discrete sections of the year had entirely fractured at some point, first into months and then into weeks and then into days and maybe now into minutes. There was no steady expanse of time when you could expect to be able to wear the same outfit. No continuity. No semblance of a cycle. The last real summer had been a few years ago, although she couldn't remember exactly how many years—maybe, she realized, because there was no such thing as a year anymore. If the clock hands don't go clockwise, you can't tell time.

"I don't have all the answers," said Dam. "I just know this isn't real."

Anja looped her arm through his and pulled him close for warmth, but also to signal camaraderie. "Have you noticed your tendency toward conspiracy gets stronger when you're worried about money?" she asked.

Dam thought a moment, sucking in cold, dry air. "That's plausible."

"How are you going to pay Laura's half of the rent?"

"I don't know. Maybe Laura can suck it up and get an actual job. I'm so sick of her whole thing about the evils of taxable labor. She's just lazy."

Anja didn't point out that Dam's weather blog wasn't the highest-grossing way he could be spending his time. Instead she said, "Want a present?"

Dam was in the inner sanctum, so she was allowed to occasionally offer him money without offending him, though he usually rejected it. In times like these she wished he and Laura would just let her give them cash; it would be so much easier and less slippery than always buying them dinners and paying for cabs. In cash she could get it done in a fell swoop instead of leaking money to them in uncalculated sums late at night. Get rid of the constant unexpressed expectation that she would cover them in indirect ways.

"Danke, but no danke. You can just get dinner next time," he said.

A homeless woman emerged suddenly from her crouching place in a doorway a few meters ahead. She shuffled toward them. Small puffs of steam rose up from the ground around her feet.

"No," said Dam. "I can't handle this right now." He grabbed Anja's elbow and steered her across the street toward the opposite sidewalk.

"I didn't know we were running away from homeless people now," she said when they had landed on the other side.

"What else are we supposed to do? I can't give them anything and I can't deal with the guilt of saying no. It's like the precarious are expected to support the downtrodden in this city. Have you noticed how many bums are around lately?"

"I don't think you're supposed to call them bums."

"What are you supposed to call them? They're everywhere."

"Homeless?"

"But if the only thing separating me from them is a home I don't know. It's not a wide enough gap."

"There's obviously more than that separating you."

"Such as?"

She stopped walking and reached her arms out in a gesture of exasperation. "Seriously. I'm here. I know we have some unspoken taboo against charity, but I don't have anything else I'd rather spend money on than you guys. Plus, if I sign this consulting contract—"

"Abend," a voice cracked. They glanced back and saw that

the homeless woman had followed them. She coughed wretchedly at them. "Bitte," she mumbled. "Etwas warmes zu essen." Anja reached into her purse and produced ten euros. The woman reached out to snatch it, not making eye contact, and hurried back across the street.

"Now we're both exonerated for the evening," said Anja. "Maybe you should take a different route home, though, or she'll catch you again on the way back."

Dam left her by the orange trash can at the base of the Berg. She paused before heading up, texting Louis first, just in case the reception in the house wasn't good that night. She felt her gut drop as she sent the message, knowing he wouldn't be home for a while. He was out eating meat somewhere with Prinz, schnitzel with ketchup, hamburgers, Korean hot pot. He hadn't been home before midnight in a full week. And he'd stopped apologizing for being absent; whatever he was working on or doing must have been justifiable, important enough in his mind, or maybe he had just forgotten, forgotten the private zones of morning and evening. She waited for him to respond to her message, trying not to stare at the screen in her hand, trying not to seem desperate to herself.

She peered up at the mountain. The whole mound seemed to disappear as it rose in the dim haze, the path receding entirely into the bush after only a few meters. This fat stack of dirt had been dumped here before she'd ever met Louis. Their whole relationship had existed in a world where the Berg was already real. Louis's whole Berlin, in fact, had been a post-Berg one. He'd never set foot on Tempelhof airfield; all he knew of this giant swath of the city was a harsh climb upward, all vertical, no horizontal.

Years ago, that had been one of her favorite things to do at this time of night: a slow, horizontal walk around the landing strip in a prescribed oval under the low sky. The city always a receding shore on the other side of the expanse. The smell of grass, unextinguished barbecues, weed, dog shit. Flat, flat ground: a perfectly unplanted plot. Sentimentality crept in like bushes on either side of her line of vision. Louis would never see it. You couldn't undo a mountain.

7

LOUIS MATERIALIZED IN THE WORLD AT A PARTY. A PARTY, THE place where new people materialized. After you met them, you always realized you'd seen them somewhere on the internet already. But you still had to go to parties to get them: new friends, new people to have sex with. Anja had heard of people meeting each other on the subway or standing in line for coffee, but this had never happened to her. It seemed improbable.

The party that invented Louis was an after-party at an investor's house. It was the after-party for the final show of a famous consultant finishing her term at a consumer electronics conglomerate. The consultant was now most definitely on the downhill slide of her career. She'd been "emerging" forever, up into her forties, but instead of making the transition to "mid-career" that should have happened by this time, she'd veered off course. She hadn't been rehired by her company and she hadn't been hired anywhere else.

Both the event and its after-party had a melancholy tinge. The consultant was obviously not allowed to act like she had ended up at a celebration of her own failure, but everyone else was allowed to act like that.

Anja was annoyed while watching the final performance, both because the performance was hard to watch and because Dam hadn't shown up to meet her as he was supposed to (she had only agreed to go after succumbing to his pleading). So she watched alone, standing uncomfortably as a solo agent in a crowded space with a glass of white wine as her only protection from prying eyes.

The consultant's main material in her work was her own body. Her consulting strategy since she was very young had been to urge office productivity by exposing her naked self to the gaze of the office workers whenever productivity waned. It was oddly effective in those early years to have a beautiful, unclothed woman showing up at strange hours in the office, dead-seriously glaring at everyone and beating her chest. She had hit on something counterintuitive: men (of whom the employees mostly consisted) were disturbed (shamed?) rather than titillated by the intrusion, and their desire to avoid the recurring spectacle was enough to keep them fulfilling their ever-rising quotas.

But as her body had aged, she had also aged out of the original premise of her project. Now she was middle-aged, and as a woman, she was no longer the same protagonist. No one looked at her when she came into the office now, there was no intimidation factor, and in the interim the company had been forced to meet a new kind of quota by filling half the lower-level positions with women employees, who reacted in various unpredictable ways, including an anti-exploitation campaign. Anja suspected there was potential somewhere for the consultant to flip the whole approach on its head, but instead she kept performing the same tired provocation, relying on the assumption that she was still the default subject of seeing rather than figuring out how to make herself be seen.

After the consultant's final performance for a bored audience, a repeat of what she'd always been doing and seemed doomed into doing forever—Anja considered the idea that the repetition was in fact a pointed refusal to alter her method rather than an inability to evolve, but then rejected that hypothesis—clumps of selected guests piled into taxis to head to the after-party at the investor's house. Anja found herself chatting with someone in a clump and was quickly absorbed into the group.

Squished against the window in a taxi of people she didn't know, Anja watched the dark city hiss past. They traveled for over a half hour to a suburb she'd never seen before—she couldn't even figure out which direction they were exiting the city. Dam wasn't texting her back and she was growing anxious that he wouldn't show. She wasn't sure she could fend for herself at a party in the suburbs where there was no easy escape. The person next to her chatted on, clearly mistaking Anja for someone else. When they arrived she was first to leap out of the car, unable to keep up the charade for a second longer.

The social choreography of the evening was orchestrated enough that she was relieved of improvisation for the first hour. A flying buffet in the backyard under a huge tent canopy, like a prom party or a small wedding celebration. Tiny burgers of venison meat, tall champagne flutes with red berries floating in the liquid, drugs circulating on silver platters through the crowd, an ice cream vendor parked outside the canopy with a monkey on his shoulder. A llama and a small goat in a pen nearby for petting. It was absurd and people seemed slightly hysterical, completely intimidated but pretending to be casual about the excess. Anja found a cluster of people whose names she knew and joined their group, leaning against a tall, unstable, hourglass-shaped table with a drink in each of her hands. She noticed she was imitating the precise pose of the woman next to her, down to the angle of her elbow. The same way she often copied someone's dance moves without realizing it until they were totally in sync. She consciously tried to alter her position and sloshed wine over her wrist.

Out of nowhere, the shadow fell across her face. The shadow was rare and blessed and she could not control its arrival. It offered social protection. When it fell, harsh looks and judgmental remarks didn't land. It wasn't a mask, just a shadow, which cooled and calmed her. The calmness freed her up to act without anxiety, to take risks. The only proof she had that the shadow state was not only internally felt but also externally manifest was the way men responded to her while she was in it.

She tucked her phone into her bag and stopped checking for a response from Dam. She let herself be led into the house by the group she was standing with, remembering to put her drinks down first. The only risk of the shadow state was the possibility of getting teeth-crunchingly drunk if she took the invincibility for granted.

The house splayed itself out obscenely: marble walls, a spiral staircase with golden banisters, floor-to-ceiling windows. A pastiche of wealth signifiers no less effective than old money would have been. Money was money was money. Anja and the people around her nodded at each of the features nonchalantly—yes, yes, we feel comfortable here, nothing to remark upon.

The investors' children were chasing each other maniacally through the foyer, screaming and knocking into things. The girl banged into a plinth Anja was standing next to, rattling the contents of the vitrine balanced on top of it. Anja reached out to steady it and felt a hand on her arm. It was the kids' mother, who had come bounding over to make sure everything inside the vitrine was undisturbed.

"It's past their fucking bedtime," the mother said to Anja.

"They're not usually allowed downstairs at all." She wrapped her arms around the vitrine and inspected its contents anxiously. Anja peered into the vitrine too.

Sunken onto three shiny purple cushions were three tiny, shriveled, brittle heads. A fine powder had been shaken loose from the one on the left. Anja shook her head, unsure what they were. Objets d'art? Artifacts?

"Just look how he's been rattled," the mother said, jabbing her finger onto the Plexiglas. "Gerald. My favorite! His skin is flaking off!" The woman's hands were shaking, she looked like she was on the verge.

One of the kids flew by again, and she grabbed him expertly by the wrist and dragged him toward the stairs. "Stay there!" she shouted at Anja. "Make sure no one touches the glass!" Smacking her child on the top of the head, she rasped, "Wir haben Respekt vor Schrumpfköpfen," and headed up the spiral staircase.

Others were watching now and backing away. Anja was left alone next to the scene of the crime, unsure if she was really supposed to obey or whether this was a task meant to humiliate her in lieu of humiliating this mess of a family. Before she could make a move to escape, someone joined her at the plinth, someone whose name she had heard but couldn't remember. She'd seen him earlier strutting around the backyard so confidently she could barely stand it.

"Making friends?" he asked. She was uncertain whether he was talking about the investors or the heads in the vitrine.

She tapped the glass with a finger. "Whose are they?"

He raised his eyebrows, evaluating her. "The investors own them. The people whose house we're at."

"No, I mean whose heads did they *used* to be."

He laughed. "You don't know?"

She shrugged. "I'm not in the business."

"Two overdoses and a suicide," he said, rapping his knuckles loudly on the glass. "Nobody wants to be supported by these people anymore. They're obviously bad luck." He took a step back from the case, almost as if he regretted touching it.

"Bad luck?"

"Three deaths in the last ten years. Why take the chance?" He shrugged. "It's either bad luck or something worse."

She'd heard of this somewhere. The heads, she guessed, were consultants who'd died before their terms of contract had ended and whose heads had been all the investors had left to collect. It was hideous, but it wasn't outrageous. It followed the logic of a system where a person's whole life was part of someone else's investment portfolio. She wrinkled her nose at the thought. "So how do they shrink them?"

"They send them to Jay. He's here somewhere. You should ask him. Want to meet him?" Each sentence he dropped was a smooth pellet of social capital.

"Not really. I have my own shrink." He laughed again, but she kept her expression straight. It hadn't been a good joke. "Don't they collect anything else besides these?" She looked around the foyer. Other than the vitrine on the plinth, the space was completely empty.

"Of course. They've still got five or ten living investments. And there's a vault of art objects in the basement, but they never pull them out. Really spooky down there."

She ducked out of the conversation as soon as she could, leaving him and the helpless little heads together in the foyer, and stepped out the side entrance toward the pool. There were four or five other plinths dotting the dining room she walked through, but no more heads. Just little remnants from performances by consultants. Pathetic souvenirs. These were relatively young investors—so on-trend with the immaterial thing. The older ones, the smarter ones who'd weathered more than one boom-bust cycle, they still had beautiful objects around, not just flaking skulls in a jar.

She sat on the edge of the pool, took her shoes off, and put her feet in the water. She waved at three topless women swimming by, but didn't start up a conversation. Her phone buzzed. Dam was held up, he was so sorry, he couldn't make it after all. Of course.

"Not going to swim?" She didn't look up. Him again, following her.

"I'm not the type."

"What type are you?"

"I stay on land."

"Me too," he said. She waited, still not looking up at him, to see if he would sit down. He did. He took off his Tevas, rolled up his seersucker pants, and tested the water. He wasn't looking at her. The women across the pool called out to him and he consented to a casual wave in their direction. Then he looked at her, in order to show that he was not staring at the topless women. This was a clear signal. She glanced back at him.

"Done babysitting the heads?" she asked.

"I never want to see them again. It's like the worst possible version of my future. I don't need to see it displayed in a glass coffin."

He was under thirty, she guessed. Not yet consigned to the crypt. "You've got investors already, though?"

"Yeah. But things would have to get pretty desperate for me to sign my head away at this point."

"Have you been given the option?"

"Of what?"

"Of signing away your head."

"Sure, it's always an option. But it makes you look desperate if you do it too soon."

She swirled her feet in the water, toes puckering from the excess chlorine. "What about that artist who sold her bones to a museum so they could make her into a diamond after she died? She was young when she did it. She got famous."

"True, but that was decades ago. The first time that sort of thing happens it's always a big deal. But the next hundred times—it's imitation, not innovation. You have to innovate faster than the imitators."

"You need the imitators to get famous, though. The imitation proves the innovation."

"I've thought about that a lot," he said, warming. She noticed a slight lisp had emerged in his speech, the corners of the words softening. She thanked the shadow. "The copy reinforces the importance of the original, as they say."

"That sounds like something you've said before."

"Maybe on a panel discussion or two," he said, laughing to let her know this was a joke that was also true.

"I guess you're just reinforcing the power of the first time you said it each time you repeat yourself."

There was enough for them to go on to continue like this, he looking at the side of her face while she looked across the pool, and then she looking at him while he looked across the pool, swapping vectors of vision, occasionally overlapping. She was startled when they were interrupted by a group of people who showed up and crowded around him, one of them kneeing his shoulders to get his attention. "Be right back," he said, and stood up to chat.

On another night she would have retreated, embarrassed to be exposed alone like that for too long, but she waited calmly with her feet in the water, still secreted in the safety of the shadow. It was awfully confident to sit there assuming he'd be back. But she did, and he would. The group moved on, and he took his place beside her again, not any closer, just comfortably angled in her direction. Months later, he would tell her this was the exact moment love hit him on the head like a hammer.

He apologized, gesturing in the general direction of the crowd behind them. "Networking. I have to pay my dues."

This was meant to be a compliment—it meant talking to her was *not* networking, it was the opposite, a choice—but at the same time he was pointing out that she wasn't worth networking with.

"It's fine. I'm not on the job like you. I'm happily useless."

"I doubt you're useless."

"Really. I have nothing to gain or give. This is just a party for me."

"Do you mean—are you a genuine member of the public?" He mimed a gasp.

"I'm a real layperson."

She didn't tell him then that she'd made it through almost a year at art school before calling it quits. It was too long ago to count for anything. All it had given her was a lot of anxiety— taught her she was meant to be a watcher, not watched.

"How did you possibly end up here?"

She turned her palms up and shrugged. "My friend begged me to be his wingman, then didn't show up."

He asked what she did, and was astonished to hear she was a scientist. "You have practical skills," he said. "I'm the useless one."

About this and all things he self-deprecated in a way that she might normally have found tiresome—would have found tiresome an hour before. And yet from his lips, just then, it sounded genuine, less like humble-bragging and more like he was coping rather well with the burden of being a very impressive person. He also readily deprecated the party, as if his being present were a necessary evil. Paying his dues.

He was from middle-of-nowhere America. He talked about the architecture there. Apparently there were a lot of modernist buildings. His name, he explained hesitantly, was a bastardized version of Loos, the Austrian modernist.

"I don't usually tell people about that," he said. "It's pretty embarrassing."

By way of explanation, he said his mom had always had high-culture aspirations but had never made it to Europe. "She keeps saying she's going to visit me, but she never does. I think the idea of Europe has inflated too much in her mind."

After this Anja was surprised that he took up asking her questions. This was not a characteristic she expected from men, much less one like him. She talked freely about her work, telling him about cartilage and its applications: coral reef balls, city sub-structures, whole self-generating satellites launched into space. He listened and occasionally made a remark indicating he had understood. He knew something about everything. And yet his knowledge always came out in the form of another question. He seemed, she could not deny, interested.

They left together without much discussion, and without walking back out through the crowd to say goodbye to anyone, just stepping through the thick row of hedges separating the sanctum from the street. He told her there was an S-Bahn fifteen minutes away and they walked slowly in the right direction, not touching. The shadow veil quavered but didn't lift.

When she woke up it was gone, and her eyes stung in the raw light of day and the raw shape of Louis.

She had woken up in a slightly different dimension: a

dimension with Louis in it, a dimension with a bed with Louis in it. Light bent differently in this dimension, words bent differently. Her eyelids strained to open wide enough to take in the human anomaly beside her, and she saw the air warp around him. A haze, the sheen of an oil spill, a skidded frame. She felt his hand encircling her ankle. The hand was curious, but it was also confident. It asked a question already knowing the answer.

smooth clouds with a chance of secrets / rough winds / 19°

The audience sat on collapsible stool-like things made of folded recyclable cardboard that existed for no reason other than to not be normal chairs. To subvert "the chair." The institution was critical of institutions: this was the message they were supposed to get from the wobbly stools.

The panel discussion was preceded by a performance with two feminist artists in their seventies who were legendary if you were into that sort of thing. One of them was wearing a sailor outfit. During the performance she kept saying "cunt" in a way that was meant to be shocking. She said "slimy cunt, with ooze and pus." She said "patri-capitalism" and "fuck me, daddy." In case you hadn't gotten the message, she said, "We are the only transgressors left."

Anja put her forehead in her hands. "This is making me really sad," she whispered. Louis whispered back, asking whether she had ever actually seen something good at this particular institution. Anja said she had not. She said they must be suckers for coming back again and again. Louis said they'd better head to the bar.

In the basement of the complex, which had once been a church and then a military hospital and then a civilian hospital and was now a warehouse for artworks with nowhere else to go and an event space for artists who'd never adjusted to lending their lives to companies, who instead spent all their energy sucking the last remaining government resources dry, Anja and Louis sat at a small round table upon what had once been some kind of stage, a raised platform for priests and, later, surgeons.

"This whole place is the pits," said Anja.

"Why do we keep coming here?" said Louis. He laughed.

She thought for a moment. "I'm nostalgic for institutional art, and you're trying to find meaningful political engagement."

"Maybe. I think it's more that I'm looking for some evidence of transgression. Or looking to see if transgression is possible anymore."

"It probably isn't. The whole idea is outdated."

"I know! But I can't stop thinking that if I were *really* a creative, good person, I'd find a way."

She laughed. "Everyone has a reason for not transgressing. For me, I'm too shy."

"Maybe your shyness *is* transgressive."

She frowned. "No, it's debilitating."

People thought of shyness as a choice or affectation rather than a real personality trait, which was why people, mainly women, thought it was okay to pretend to be shy. They thought it was cute. Anja knew the truth: timidity was a terrible disease.

"Sometimes you flip in public," he said. "Just like that, you decide not to be shy for a while. Or something comes over you and it goes away." She knew he was thinking of the shadow. She'd never explained it to him.

"I don't decide to be shy or not to be shy. I can't help it." She waved at a server who had emerged from behind the bar and was actively not looking in their direction.

"I used to be shy too, when I was really young," said Louis, also waving at the server. "Pat taught me to be outgoing in high school. She forced me to do sports and go to church camp. I made myself act like an extrovert just to impress her."

Anja got stuck, dropping her train of thought. They had been going along in a comfortable pattern, and now Pat suddenly appeared in the room between them, rising up uninvited like one of those inflatable waving balloon people. Louis hadn't lapsed even once since coming home; he'd insisted with every word and action that he was *not thinking of Pat*. Weeks without a mention or even a gesture toward the lack, toward any sort of grief process, as if he had successfully repressed it and was just going to move on. And now he introduced her as a casual memory, without emotion, without context. As if Pat were not dead. As if mentioning her would not conjure her death, would not require acknowledgment that death was on his mind. Was this a sign he wanted to talk about it, or a sign that he didn't want to talk about it? Was it an invitation or was it bait? Or was it a total red herring?

At a loss for how to react, Anja resolved to carry on the conversation until another sign presented itself. "So, for you," she said slowly, "it was possible to just decide to be an extrovert."

"I guess so." He was unfazed. Good, so moving forward had been the right choice. "I did it on purpose. I thought I had to just to survive. But then here you are, being shy and walking around, doing things and being loved, and I realize I could have stayed the way I was. You're evidence shyness works."

That's nice, she thought. I'm being loved, apparently. "Maybe being outgoing is like learning a language," she said. "You have to learn it while you're still young."

A waitress finally emerged, came over, took their orders for Aperol spritzes, offered them menus.

"I didn't know they had food here," said Anja. "Should we eat?" Louis nodded. She was not even slightly hungry, her stomach wasn't behaving these days, but she nodded back.

He pointed at the menu, and when the waitress came back Anja ordered for both of them in German. Trout for her, goulash for him.

"Groß oder Klein?" the waitress asked Anja, nodding toward Louis as if he were a child.

"Big bowl or small bowl?" she asked Louis.

"Groß," he said to the waitress, his ß a gentle lisp, the O a flat vowel not found in German.

"Brot dazu?" the waitress responded. Louis looked at Anja.

"Bread?" she mouthed at him.

"*Gerrrne*," he said to the waitress.

"What?" the waitress said in English.

"Yes," said Anja, "he wants bread." Louis gave the waitress a winning smile.

Even if Americans learned the technicalities of a foreign language, most of them couldn't handle making the actual mouth movements necessary to be intelligible. They could memorize the words, but they came out in the shape of American sounds. Anja saw this as a cultural inability to recognize phonemes as anything but literal; it was like Newspeak but for pronunciation. Americans believed that letters should act like what they looked like to the American eye, nothing more and nothing less, signifier swallowing signified down its wide open gullet, the vertical relationship between the sign and its referent rendered entirely irrelevant because the lips and tongue just didn't think it mattered whether the vowel sounds were melted properly. Once, in Prague, Anja had seen a sign outside a bakery advertising *Kwassah*. She'd sent a photo to Louis.

Louis was apologetic in a socially necessary way—"So American, I know"—but nobody really expected him to learn German; he had more interesting things to do. He let Anja order for him in restaurants. She liked it, mostly. It was a nice sort of caring labor. She got to be his interface with the German-speaking world. Translating for him was a way of staying indispensable, and keeping him out of German preserved the English-language arena of their private life. The same way she handled the map when they traveled. There was intimacy in dependence. Also, infantilization.

She'd been speaking English since she could speak; not learning it had not been an option. Her papa was technically Austrian, but her mom was truly American, and the "international" of the international schools Anja had hopped between really meant "American" too. The English words arrived effortlessly, most of the time, without the need to home in on the construction—the English world arrived in whole scenes rather than sentences. Before Louis, there'd been hiccups to her colloquialisms, but English was completely common territory for them now, her mouth matching his.

Louis was staring intently at the back of the waitress, who was punching in their orders by the bar. "It's so weird," he said. "Pat used to have that haircut."

Anja froze. She looked at the waitress, waiting for her to turn around. The waitress's blond hair was bobbed. From this angle she bore absolutely no resemblance to Pat. Not that Anja had ever met Pat in person, but according to what she'd seen on screens, the comparison was off.

"I thought Pat had dark hair," she said gingerly.

"It's something about the shape," he said. "I don't know." He sipped his spritz blankly and gave her nothing else.

Was it a provocation or was he oblivious? If he truly recognized

Pat in random waitresses, clearly she was haunting him constantly, but he just went on as if everything were the same. Here was his chance to say *I miss her* or *Here is the spot on my body where the needle of death has entered my bones.* Instead, a cliché: that person looks like the dead person I miss.

For someone so resistant to culturally received plans of action, Louis still did not seem to understand that his silence on the topic of his emotions accorded with clichés about male behavior. It wasn't that he'd ever been overly expressive of his feelings, but he'd always acknowledged them without shame, treating them as subjects for analysis. His fascination with human behavior had included his own, which had always required a certain introspection. Maybe now he was playing the masculine role because, for once, he thought going through the typical motions might help move him along. Maybe he was so submerged in pain that he could imagine no other recourse for action. But it was also possible that grief had turned him into a one-dimensional male person, blind to his own motives, unable to articulate his feelings, waving around blunt instruments of communication like *she looks like my mom.*

Anja tried to formulate a way of saying all this—of asking how he felt, asking whether he was all right, asking if he missed Pat, anything—but she had let the break in conversation extend too long, and Louis closed the gap. Either her chance to say something had passed or she hadn't had a chance at all. He started talking about the feminists again, those aging losers who couldn't update their OS. She nodded without really listening to the content of the words. From the tone of his voice it was clear he was saying things he knew to be clever. He was so insightful, she thought again, and yet so unable to reflect it, to *apply* it, onto himself.

When the food came she knew she'd made the wrong choice. The fish was huge and threatening, eyeballing her with its flat jelly-eye and smelling like what it was: a dead thing.

Louis had already finished half his goulash, eating without pause, shoveling signifier into signified, when he noticed she had only picked at her side salad.

He paused, spoon to mouth. "You don't like the fish?"

"I just don't know how . . . to approach it. It's full of bones."

"Don't panic. I got this." He reached across the table, sleeves skimming goulash, and grinned sweetly at her while expertly slicing the fish laterally and flipping it open. Greasy, translucent skeleton was drawn out of flesh, positioned elegantly on the small extra plate. Animal graciously relieved of its spine. She looked at the fish and looked at Louis and didn't make any moves to interact with either of them. Her eyes wobbled, filled with jelly, her vision slipped, Louis became blurry, momentarily disappeared.

He was alarmed, and took her hand. "That was sudden," he said. "What's wrong?"

"I don't like this fish at all," she said. She wiped her eyes with the back of her sleeve. She heard herself make a conciliatory laugh. Had she known she was going to laugh? Had she known she was going to cry?

With the unoccupied fingers of the hand Louis wasn't holding she plucked a thin, decorative lemon slice from her plate and sucked on it. "Sorry," she said, "I don't know what just happened," and replaced the lemon slice on the plate, its rind half-mooned with a perfect ring of pink lipstick. Usually she didn't wear lipstick because it was an impediment to kissing, but that afternoon she had put it on instinctively. A symbol of self-protection. If that's what it was, it hadn't worked. He was comforting her now, instead of the other way around.

She'd known she was going to cry and hadn't known she'd known it. She was no better than him. They were both utterly blind to themselves.

The restaurant had filled up. All the other tables on the small stage had couples sitting at them now. Anja wondered if anybody had noticed her short outburst of tears. She side-eyed the table next to them, a long glance at the couple sitting there across from each other, who were leaning toward each other and speaking their own private language.

Just cut me some fucking slack, Anja thought, toward the couple at the other table. I'm trying my best here.

Louis had withdrawn his hand and was back to eating his goulash.

8

Management Discussion and Analysis (MD&A):

An MD&A report is a clear narrative explanation, through the eyes of management, of how your company performed during the period covered by the strategic innovation plan, and of your company's condition and future prospects with regard to speed of innovation. MD&A complements and supplements your innovation status report but does not constitute part of your innovation status report.

Your objective when preparing the MD&A should be to improve your sector's overall transparency of innovation by giving a balanced yet honest discussion of the sector's results of innovative operations and innovation condition, including, without limitation, such considerations as liquidity and illiquidity, personnel and ill personnel, openly reporting bad eggs as well as good. Your MD&A should:

- Help current and prospective investors understand what innovation statements show and do
  not show.
- Transmit material information that may not be
  fully reflected in innovation status reports, such
  as contingent liabilities, human resource debt,
  off-balance knowledge investment, or other un-
  fulfilled contractual obligations.
- Discuss important trends and risks that have af-
  fected the innovation statements, and trends and
  risks that are reasonably likely to affect them in the
  future.
- Provide information about the quality and potential variability of your sector's current knowledge
  capital and information flow, to assist investors in
  affirming that past innovation performance is in-
  dicative of future performance.

Anja slid the open folder across the table toward Howard. He was sipping coffee. They were back in the kitchen, squared off on ei-ther side of the teak table

"I went to grad school for biology," she said, "not accounting."

"Who says you're an accountant?" He picked up the packet of information she'd been sent from human resources after signing her new contract and opened it to the page she had been reading from.

"What you're looking at," she said, "is a lightly paraphrased version from a manual on tax auditing committees that was writ-ten in 2002. I found the whole PDF online. Finster replaced words like *finance* with *innovation*, but all that does is make it sound even more like bullshit than it originally did."

Howard giggled. "It really doesn't make any sense, does it," he said, flipping pages.

"No, Howard, it doesn't."

He looked up at her, arched his eyebrows, and closed the folder slowly. He slid it back across the table toward her. The table was sticky and so it skidded a bit on the way.

"Don't shoot the messenger," he said, raising his hands in a gesture of disarmament.

"You're not just the messenger! You're Public Relations. You know everything that goes on at Finster. How can you pretend you're as in the dark as I am?"

"I knew I shouldn't have told you about the job. Should have let you hear it from HR. You've been upset with me ever since. Admit it."

"Of course I'm upset about the job. It's not a real job. It's a bullshit job. Do you know what a bullshit job is?"

"I can guess."

"A bullshit job is a job that should have been made obsolete by technology but that has instead been created to turn the human worker into a bureaucratic functionary. That way the human worker doesn't have time to do any interesting thinking that may involve questioning the order of things. A bullshit job is a distractor designed to waste a person's life with things like"—she flipped open the folder again—"Management Discussion & Analysis."

Howard smoothed out his forehead with his fingers, reminding himself not to engrave the worry lines. "If you want my help, dear, this is the wrong way to get it."

"Oh. I see. You're saying you can help, but that I have to flatter you into doing it."

She knew she was misdirecting her anger—but by gaslighting her now he was justifying it. If he hadn't been guilty of something when she walked into the kitchen, he was now.

"Your problem is that you don't know how to do PR on the microlevel," she said. "You can manage a campaign, but you have no idea how to manage a relationship. You just try to apply the same tactics on the human scale as you do on the company level."

He was taken aback. "Hey. I'm sorry." She looked down, then at the sink, dishless. "I know this has been a hectic few weeks for you. You're going through some stuff that can't be easy."

Against her better judgment she let herself feel subdued. Then she did an inventory of her insides for any evidence that she was planning to cry without her own knowledge. No. All stable. She could let herself be coddled a bit.

"How's stuff with Louis?"

She sighed, eyes still cast toward the sink, then the counter. Then down to her hands. "Not great."

"Is it that bad?"

"He just—he's different, but he can't see it, or doesn't want to admit it."

"Different how?"

She told him about how Pat had appeared in conversation at dinner, and how she'd come up again the next day, and the day after that. "It's all the time now. He says her name and then he changes the subject. He wants to talk about it but he doesn't know how."

"And you don't ask him?"

"I want to ask him, but I don't think he wants to talk about it. *Everything's fine.* I don't want to be the one to ruin it."

Howard thought for a moment. "Maybe he should see someone."

"Like a therapist?" She laughed. "He'd never go for that."

"Why not? There are lots of people trained to deal with grief. You're not."

"You mean I'm not enough."

"Come on. That's not what I'm saying. Just that you can't do everything, and maybe he needs someone else who isn't so—involved."

She considered this. She was certain that it would be a mistake to mention a therapist to Louis. But what a relief it would be to invoke an authority. An authority who would side with her.

"I'm surprised he hasn't gone to see someone already," said Howard. "It's the first thing a lot of people would do."

"Louis doesn't just *do* what everyone else does," she said with an eye roll. Applying sarcasm to Louis felt rich and yucky, like junk food she'd regret having eaten.

Appeased, Howard eventually promised to sniff around at RANDI for her. "I really don't think there's anything I can do about the job situation, but I'll see what I can find out."

"Any news about the Berg coup?" she asked. "Those rogue architects?"

"Not yet. Everyone is lawyering up right now. It's going to take some time."

"Starting to seem like the whole thing was just show business all along."

"Nonsense." He smiled. "It's an honest effort to see if people can live sustainably together."

There wasn't much more to say to each other. He'd diffused

her anger in a matter of minutes, a process in which she was once again complicit. She didn't trust a word he said, but still. But still.

On the way downstairs she finally texted Michel, her long-lost lab partner. It had been days since his last message asking her to meet up, and she still hadn't responded, feeling too embarrassed about how upset she was, suspecting that extending a work relationship outside its terms of contract would be to admit that their work, and therefore their friendship, had ever been something more than a contract job.

sorry I've been MIA. u survive the recession? she typed.

He wrote back immediately. *meet up @plants?*

She biked all the way to the botanical gardens. She couldn't think of a reason why Michel had asked to meet there, deep in Dahlem, besides the fact that it was far away from everything else. She had been to the gardens only once before, with Louis, to walk around in the North American section of the expansive outdoor landscape, which was segregated into simulacra of territories in the northern hemisphere. It was deep autumn then, and acorns and hickory nuts were falling from the trees with hard thumps, scattering the dry mulch and the reddened leaves crunching under their feet. *It smells like fall in Indiana!* Posing against a maple tree with his arms across his chest. *This is just like my senior photo!* He was the picture of wholesomeness.

In the northeastern part of the gardens was the greenhouse, a proud, voluminous glass dome with two chains of long glass pavilions extending from its sides, forming two hugging arms around a central courtyard. The central dome, the Großes Tropenhaus, was large enough to hold tall old trees, their tips forever lightly pruned so as to stay just shy of the building's crown. From the outside, the arching steel frames of the dome and the pavilions shone silver or white depending on the light—from inside, they read as green, reflecting the color of the plants. Anja imagined the dome as a zeppelin, a lost technological artifact inflated by misplaced hopes and colonial fantasy. Most of the species in the greenhouse had been first imported by nineteenth-century European plant-lovers racing each other across Africa, scraping and plucking specimens to carry home and show off in their capital cities. The elegant Art Nouveau of the greenhouse had been chosen specially to boast the material rewards of occupation, of Enlightenment taxonomies reaching like so many steel arches across the biomes of the globe.

Michel was in the cactus room, kneeling on the pathway and gently stroking a small furry plant. When she found him he stood up, kissed her on both cheeks. His familiar smell reminded her of the lab. They toured the cacti together, pointing out species in scientific-sounding language, making up fake Latin names.

"*Expecto cactonus*," Michel said, jabbing at a saguaro with a forefinger. He barely missed spiking himself.

They clambered across a small bridge straddling a carp pond and entered the next room, South Africa, where the air was instantly more humid. A new simulated topography. The insides of the glass ran with droplets of condensation. The air was thick with soil, a sweet wetness.

They agreed to disregard their NDAs as long as they were in the greenhouse.

"Don't worry, the plants will encrypt us," said Michel. "They cleanse the air." He pointed to the next room. "Those ones are carnivorous."

She learned that he'd received the same abrupt severance as her, the same job offer and contract, the same useless packet of information detailing his new duties. He was reluctant to tell her his new salary, nervous it would be higher than hers. It was, but only slightly.

"It's not your fault you're a guy," she said, mentally adding this to the list of Howard-related grievances.

Michel was usually all energy, too much energy, but he seemed calm and steady here. Maybe this was what he was like outside the lab, away from RANDI. When was the last time she'd seen him somewhere else? He never came to performances or product launches or clubs. He seemed categorically immune to the lures of that world and its churning gossip, which she relayed to him sometimes and at which he rolled his eyes, amused at her investment but not at all enticed by it. He was living proof that it was possible to just opt out of the whole thing. Sometimes he mentioned friends of his, people he knew whom she'd never heard of, suggesting that there were more like him who just didn't care to participate in the scene. This was hard to believe, but there it was.

"The thing I don't understand," he said, pausing beside a rotting stump, "is the blatantness of it all. It's so obvious that something went wrong with our sector. Or our experiment. And it's so obvious that they hastily scraped together our contracts as an excuse to get us out of the lab."

"I know, these jobs are so obviously bullshit."

"They are definitely bullshit. Ha!" He snorted. "But hey, at least I'll be allowed to wear open-toed shoes now." He pointed down to his Birkenstocks. The toenail he'd lost last year after dropping a case of hard drives on his foot was slowly growing back into a little yellow stub. After the incident, open-toed shoes had been explicitly banned in all the labs, which was not something anyone had thought necessary before. This was a favorite subject for jokes—who the fuck wears sandals to work in a lab? (Michel: What's the issue? I do my best work when I'm comfortable.)

She leaned down to look at the baby toenail. "So you signed the contract already."

"Yeah."

"Me too."

"I thought of trying to negotiate, but Claudette in HR told me just to take it."

"What else did Claudette say?"

"Well, she said I should be thankful for the salary, treat it like a drawn-out severance package, and start looking for a job asap for when our contract expires in a year. Ha!" The snort again. He kicked the stump lightly with a Birkenstock. "Claudette got offered a consultancy position too, you know. Same time period as ours, but way more cash."

Anja didn't know. She hadn't been in touch with anyone from work. It made sense that Claudette had been promoted, though—she was surely more qualified, having been a lab HR supervisor for years, meaning that she was already basically a bureaucrat. She hadn't touched any equipment in a long time, spending her days in meetings, watching PowerPoints, looking at graphs, arguing about the allocation of funds and writing performance reviews. Claudette had been a kind of academic prodigy at one point, Anja remembered hearing, but any intellectual curiosity had long since been bled dry.

"It makes sense for her," said Anja. "Not for us. I don't have any experience with the kind of stuff in the manual. Do you?"

"No, of course not. They should have just hired us on as

research consultants, not management consultants. We could have essentially kept doing the research we were already doing, but freelance, and they could have paid us less."

"This has nothing to do with budget, though. Like you said, it's obvious, they don't want us to finish our project. The jobs are like—like a bribe to get us out of the lab."

They started moving again and arrived in the main dome. Above them, beyond the glass, a puckered stratocumulus huffed quickly across the sky, its gray shadow incongruous with the heat inside. Enormous palm trees reached up toward the apex of the structure, forever aspiring beyond its confines.

They found a pair of wrought-iron stools to sit on. "What happened to the interns?" Anja asked.

"Fired."

"Have you heard of any changes in other departments?"

"Two other departments are merging, I think."

She fingered a dry fern leaning over her shoulder. A bird whistled from the canopy above. She hadn't known there were animals in here besides the fish. She scratched her forearm instinctively, thinking of mosquitoes. She found her thoughts moving from English to German. She could switch with Michel, if she wanted—he was another mongrel polyglot, having grown up in one of those regions of Switzerland where you had to speak four languages just to go to school—but English had always been their default, because they had to speak it in the lab. Once she'd heard him curse in Swiss-German and the lab's ceiling camera had beeped twice. Michel had glared at it and repeated the curse in English.

"There's only one thing we can do," she said suddenly.

She listened to herself as if at a distance from her voice. It was happening again. Some part of her she was not familiar with, dictating her speech. Where was the speech arising? She searched her reflexes, and felt the same existential vertigo as when trying to imagine the hormones and chemicals governing her brain's circuitry, or when trying to imagine the scale of the universe in deep time. Her thoughts stuttered.

Michel was waiting for an answer. "Why would we do something?" he repeated.

"Think about it for a sec," she said, buying time while she waited for her brain to articulate what it was thinking. They both thought about it for some secs.

"Nope, no clue," he said.

"They cut us off on the exact day of the trial run. That can't be a coincidence." She knew she was right. That day had been the juncture between the Before and the After, the precipice between the simulation and the reality. She saw it now. "So we have to do exactly what they don't want us to do." She was nodding. "We have to finish the experiment."

"Cell culturing? Why? We've already watched it a thousand times."

"No, we haven't. We've watched a simulation of it. We know it's 99.99999 percent probable that it will happen as planned, but not with certainty."

"Those are pretty good odds."

"But we need to find out how it happens in real life. We need to follow through."

Michel smiled. "Listen to you, drawing divisions between the virtual and the actual. Ha! Haven't you read your object-oriented philosophy?"

"Sure, sure, everything's a real object." She waved him off. "But you know, if there was ever really evidence that reality might be different than the simulation, it's the fact that we got fired between the two."

He considered this, tensing and releasing his forehead slightly, just sitting there being Michel, a smart, like-minded individual, a male colleague. She had watched him sit there and consider a proposition like this countless times: she proposed an idea, he worked through the various options by flexing his lobes, and then he came out either in the same place as her or somewhere very different. She'd enjoyed proposing ridiculous things sometimes just to watch him take them seriously.

"Correct," he said in a robotic voice after a long wait. "The specific timing of our firing is highly suspicious." He shook his head. "How*ever*. We didn't just watch that simulation, we *input* that simulation, and we went through it a thousand times. It would have to be magic if it didn't—I mean, the probability is too low, it's too much—there's—it's pointless. I know we did the simulation right."

Magic. Yes, it would have to be magic. Or proof they were shit scientists. There was no other option.

"Fine," she said, and smiled a bit. "You're right."

It was fine to have tried this on him. He was a safe space, free from judgment. She could communicate with little calculation; her internal monologue softened around him. Of course, Michel's softness also repelled her. She needed to stay alert.

Michel stood up and stepped across the path, pointing at a plaque at the base of a gruff little pine tree. "*Lebendes Fossil*," he read out loud. "It says this species is two hundred million years old."

After a short look at the orchids in a pavilion on the other side of the dome, they left through the main entrance. He walked with her toward where she had left her bike, at the western exit, but before they got to the edge of the park, he said, "Hold on. Want to see my favorite part?"

She followed him back across the lawn to a little fenced-in garden. The apothecary plots, he explained as they kneeled between rows, were laid out in the shape of a human body, with the medicinal plants grown in the areas corresponding to the body part they were supposed to heal.

There was something kind of morbid about it, she thought. This corpse planted in the ground, roots tangling in the wet soil. "What body part are we in now?" she asked.

He leaned forward. "Looks like milk thistle." He reached out to feel a jagged leaf. "Probably liver. Or spleen."

"What's this herb hobby of yours? I had no idea you were such an expert."

He pulled the leaf until it snapped off, then stood. "Oh, you know." He smiled in a gently self-mocking way. "Just trying to avoid the medical-industrial complex."

"Are you a witch?"

"I wouldn't tell you if I were."

She stood up too and they walked in silence to the gate of the gardens. Exiting the park dissolved their breach of nondisclosure. They shook hands at the street corner, smiling businesslike, lips sealed.

Eva was in Dubai. Anja learned this from scrolling on her phone. Eva was posed in front of the Palm Jumeira hotel wearing a sarong and thousand-euro sunglasses; Eva was clinking glasses with a bloated, goateed man. Eva was beautiful, really beautiful. She would never have made sense in Berlin, she was too perfect. Hers was the kind of beauty that paired well with money, was buffed and shined by money, was brought to bloom by money.

She would make no sense in the gray gloom of this city, much less in a cave of a place like the Baron, in the filth that came with being a "creative." Anja was pretty, yes, but less straightforwardly so; she was the same height and rough outline as Eva, but compressed. Anja's features were more sharply angled and her limbs more bone than flesh. She moved gracelessly. She looked best in cut and mangled clothes, fabric wrapped around her in unorthodox ways. Anja hypothesized that the reason she and Eva inhabited such different social worlds was traceable to this basic physical differentiation. Their bodies lent them to certain crowds.

Anja considered writing to Eva, but what was the point? What would she ask—What are you doing in Dubai? Are you wearing sunscreen? Don't you know it's offensive to show so much skin in the Emirates? How's the oil crisis? Have you caught sight of the slave laborers who built your hotel? Eva was so, so disengaged from the painful realities of the planet. But maybe Eva was right, maybe it was all a lost cause—might as well enjoy the widening of the ozone hole to get a better tan. Maybe engaging with the ongoing disaster of the planet was pointless, unhealthy. In her own way, Anja avoided engaging with it too, down in the lab with the cells, never asking where all those numbers she generated would end up.

They might have both inherited that slight remove from the world from their parents, whose notion of political engagement was limited to a series of rote procedures: meetings, receptions, speeches for other people just like them. They were busy, which gave them a good excuse for being so remote from their daughters most of the time. Long periods of absence, punctuated by random moments of grand intrusion when they showed up and poked around in Anja's life. You need decent furniture, you need some art on the walls, wouldn't you like to live in the London flat for a few months? Maybe get into science policy? Your sister's so adventurous, don't you feel stuck in Berlin? Anja only knew her side of it, but they probably did the same to Eva: You can't live in hotels for the rest of your life, why not get a real degree like your sister?

Anja was without doubt the responsible one. This meant that she would be the one to handle the inheritance someday. Mom in particular purported to believe it was caring and responsible to regularly bring up the issue of inheritance—who would get what and when—but to Anja it seemed a transparent desire to induce closeness by invoking death. The desire for connection was always couched in practicality, which was the only vocabulary Mom had access to. Anja knew the strategy worked on her. Mom had had difficulty sounding sympathetic when Anja called to tell her about Pat's death; Anja was sure all her mother was thinking about in that moment was her own. But then, so was Anja.

Louis had been there to see her parents arrive and depart from Berlin. Dinner at the steak house, brunch at the hotel. He was a steady wingman throughout and helped her dissect the experiences afterward. Narcissa and Narcissus, he'd called them, after waving goodbye.

But things didn't go in the other direction. Pat never came to visit. His Sunday phone calls to Indiana were unremarkable, composed of diligent small talk, but pleasant and natural-sounding. The only reason she knew the calls were important to him was that he always stuck to the phone appointment, week after week, regardless of hangover. In all that time, Anja had spoken to Pat only once. Louis had been out in the garden and she'd answered his phone without thinking.

"I thought you'd have an accent!" Pat laughed. "But don't you sound perfectly American!"

Pat had been through a war; she had lost her legs. A bomb had blown them off. It was all Anja could think about when she heard her voice.

9

THE GYM WAS CROWDED, SO CROWDED THERE WAS A LINE FORM-
ing at the showers, so many white bodies so close to each other,
so close to touching. There was something as sinister as sisterly
about all those bodies lined up in the tiled room, bodies with
the same attributes in different variations, two of these, two
of these, one of these. The gym was already a sort of selector
for the healthy and the able, and so the variations were minor,
unremarkable until unclothed and paraded all around in one
damp space. Darker nipple, lighter nipple. Puffy nipple, flat nipple. Nipples, all of them.

In the sauna, where Anja went to wait for the shower line to
diminish, she was surrounded by bodies still, but bodies that were
being still, elbows folded in against sweaty sides, breasts flattened
unthreateningly upon reclining rib cages. She knew she was an
alien. There they were, inhabiting their bodies, and here she was,
rocking around inside hers. They knew what their bodies looked
like, and they knew what their attitudes toward their bodies
looked like—sanctioned variations on confidence and insecurity:
this one likes her legs but worries about her lopsided shoulder;
this one hunches because she's too tall; this one defies anyone to

call her thighs too big and so wears very tight pants; this one is warm and round and doesn't self-criticize, but she does work her upper body extra hard on Tuesdays.

Anja didn't know how to classify her body, she only knew that whatever it was, it wasn't her fault. She was naturally thin, and that was supposed to be good. But she had gotten even thinner than usual in the last weeks, which was supposed to be not good. She had noticed some weird bumps on one of her forearms, which was definitely not good. Disease was easy to pinpoint as objectively bad. But the fact that being thin was supposed to be good seemed irrelevant, since in past eras it would have been better to be plump. It was hard to rest on any single aspect for reassurance, knowing it to be simply an accident of being born in a century that aligned its aesthetic ideals with her genes. Could the goodness of a body transcend time? The question was null. Her body was never the same body. It never looked the same. It was swollen in one spot and limp in another. Parts of it seemed older than other parts. The whole thing would be old soon. It got used and it responded to the various uses, sighing to good treatment, prickling to bad. But then, it also sometimes responded well to very bad treatment.

The sauna women knew their bodies' singular worth. They had been children, and they had been teenagers, and so they had experienced the paranoia that comes with physical change. Now they were adults, meaning they were fixed entities—unlike Anja, who was technically grown up but still waiting for a solid shape. They had achieved a sort of continuity that she had not. Many of them had probably given birth. Many of them had probably dieted to extremes. Maybe some of them had hurt themselves badly, or suffered through long illnesses. But now they all looked stable, as if they had achieved equilibrium, stasis.

In the reddish light cast by the hot stove in the sauna, all she could see in the other bodies was her own shape thrown into relief. Do my ankles look like hers, or like hers? She mentally pieced together her own shape from parts of theirs. Then she tried to see the parts of their bodies as beloved shapes for the circling hand or puckering mouth of the people who loved them. She saw them and she envisioned the way their lovers saw them. She saw them and she saw, reflexively, how she might be seen, as a recipient for a hand or a mouth, as Louis must have seen her—as too soft here and too gaunt here and too pallid around the corners here, but nonetheless the ideal arrangement of positive and negative spaces for his positive and negative spaces to fit around. He had never said she was perfect, but it was clear he thought her perfectly formed for him. His complementary match. Things she had never considered laudatory, like the smooth complexion of the skin of her back, the high arches of her feet, he noted and treated with reverence. He had called her arches aristocratic.

The line for the showers dwindled and she left the sauna, found her flip-flops, and chose a stall in the back where she could rinse without being confronted by other bodies. Maybe Germany just isn't a nice place for communal showers, she thought, and shut the water off.

Fumbling around in the inconveniently shaped locker to find her underwear, she realized she was gripping her rented towel too tightly, and that she ought to exercise a more casual relationship to the towel and therefore to her nakedness. She ought to demonstrate that she was not afraid of all that dumb vigorousness around her, ladies with towels draped around their shoulders and trailing between their feet. One woman's tampon string was hanging freely between her legs as she bent, back straight, to root through her bag. Anja drew the thin towel together and tied it in a knot around her chest. Its bottom edge skimmed the bottom edge of her bottom. This was as far as she would go today in claiming herself as a native creature in this place. This place, where they all went together, women and men, to put their bodies into machines, to move in time with music coming from other machines in their ears, to drink water that they had carried all the way here in little plastic bottles that had been manufactured and shipped from other countries inside machines. They were here to scrunch their muscle groups into painful knots and then to retreat to a dark and hot room where they could mingle their sweat, putting their naked bodies as close to one another as possible without quite touching: no, this place was not a natural place.

She'd been shown the machines and locker rooms when she signed up, but nobody had ever given her a tour and said: this is the little cubby where you will place your toiletries while you shower, but you will have to open your eyes filled with soap while you are reaching for them lest you graze knuckles with the woman using the shower next to you; this is the row of lockers that you should never choose, because opening one of these lockers will require kneeling under some other woman's damp crotch; this is the mirror before which you will stand to dry your hair and stare at all the women lined up next to you, who are all standing there with elbows raised, using a wind-making device invented for the sole purpose of removing the water from their hairs—an activity that all of them likely spend ten to twenty minutes on every day, just waving a machine around to blow on the hairs to speed up the evaporation process—women who are all doing the same thing and watching you do it too, but who are somehow less curious about you than you are about them. This is the place you will learn not to stare.

ice ice bb 0°0°0° hats on today

A new ritual took shape. Louis wasn't coming home any earlier, but each night Anja waited for him, and when he showed up she'd strap on her boots and they'd head out the door together right away.

One purpose of the walk up the mountain was to not be in the house, where the question of sex would inevitably arise. The house was too hot, something smelled rank in the bathroom, and neither of them wanted to rub sweaty bodies together in the bedroom, but they didn't want to acknowledge the estrangement. Laura had told Anja that her cousin had "gone through some really weird sexual phases" after his dad died—apparently that was a common aspect of the grief process—but nothing really weird had happened to Louis's libido that couldn't be chalked up to the house and their schedule. He still seemed physically affectionate and capable.

Another purpose of the walk was for Louis to circle around his feelings in long rants, sometimes getting closer, sometimes further away. After her miniature crying jag at the restaurant, she had resolved not to worry about any of his behavior anymore and resigned herself to simply wait. It would all break eventually. She couldn't blame him for how he was acting. He wasn't himself.

Lately Louis had taken to venting about the superficiality of their social world, his job, their lives in general. The consultants, the false friends, the bottom-feeders, the assistants, the interns, the long lines to get into the clubs. Everyone except Anja, though he never exactly said she was exempt.

"The only real difference between the people working in the creative industry and the people working at the airline counter is that the creatives are rude," he said. "Everyone we know assumes they're intellectually and morally superior to normal people, but our friends are just as normal, just as conservative and boring as anyone else. The main difference is that they're rude all the time. And they pan that rudeness off as authenticity."

They were holding gloved hands and taking long strides up through the frozen mud. Anja was silent, letting him carry on. He was more vehement than usual.

"And the ones at Basquiatt are the worst—they really think they have the moral high ground. Most of my interns would be better off working at EasyJet than pretending they care about the world. At least then they'd be honest about their complicity— might as well be fielding lost luggage instead of antiretroviral injection shipments—it's all the same skill set, nothing more glamorous than knowing how to use a computer. And if they just admitted they were in customer service they wouldn't be so goddamn rude!"

"The people working at EasyJet don't exactly have the best manners either—"

"Normal people might be boring, but at least they aren't trying to subvert societal norms by being outright shits to each other. They're not proving their superiority by 'subverting' the rules of conduct."

"Um. Who thinks they're subverting the rules of conduct?"

"Everyone! They think they're being subversive, but they're just fucking *rude*. We need new friends—the whole economy has made our scene corrupt, like a sick tower crumbling from within, like an ethical Ponzi scheme—"

She cut him off. "Did something happen today at work?"

"No, no. It's just the general rudeness of everyone. They need to learn to *empathize*. Nobody thinks about anybody else's feelings. Nobody knows how to treat me anymore. After all this happened"—by "all this" she supposed he was referring to the sudden death of his only parent—"after all this, I finally found out who's a good person, not just an opportunist. People who seemed like idiots to me before turn out to be really nice. They don't care how meaningless politeness is, they're just polite. And it helps."

"You're upset because you want people to be nicer to you, even though you think niceties are meaningless?"

"They might be meaningless in content, but they mean everything in form. It's just the form, the act of saying them."

Louis was judgmental—oh, was he judgmental—but he had a way of bending his judgment to suit his needs. And in general, his judgment had always been much more lighthearted than this, more like a bonding mechanism with the person he was talking to than true shit-talking. It never prevented him from befriending the object of his earlier criticism. Until now she'd understood this as generosity, not hypocrisy.

But at that moment Anja could feel him verging on the kind of vehemence that prevents you from going back on what you said. If he trashed everyone to this extent, it would take a lot of justifying to reverse course.

"Babe," she said, "you've been acting so normal that no one would know you needed any . . . special treatment right now. Usually you hate chitchat. People probably think you'd be embarrassed if they offered you their condolences, or whatever it is that these supposedly polite people are telling you."

"No, I wouldn't hate it. Why can't anyone understand the difference between politeness and banality?"

She stopped walking. They were almost at the peak, and the wind was picking up. "All right. What is the difference, in your opinion, between politeness and banality? Because in my opinion, the only difference is your opinion. It really sounds like you're theorizing around the fact that your feelings are hurt. Someone must have upset you."

There was simply no rubric for processing grief in their social world. Life and death: there was no space for these at the club, the studio, anywhere.

"I'm not talking about any one person," he said.

"Is it me?"

"What?"

"Is it me? Have I not offered my condolences enough?"

"It's not you—"

"Because I would have really liked to offer some condolences. But you wouldn't even give me the address of your house in Indiana so I could send flowers for the funeral . . ."

"I told you, we didn't need any more flowers."

She threw her hands up. "It wasn't about you *needing* them. Politeness isn't about need. It's about form. That's what you just said." Of course, in a way it had been about need—her need to feel like she was doing something. She shook her head. "I think the problem isn't lack of condolences," she said, "it's that no amount of condolences is going to help."

She turned and pushed up the path without waiting for a response, weaving up through the trees, all the way to the small viewing platform topping the bald scalp of the mountain. She sat on the wooden bench overlooking the city, where no tourist had ever sat. The muddy climb was still deemed too unstable for visitors, and the perimeter of the whole mountain was encircled by a net of drones, which tended to intimidate curious explorers who might have tried to sneak up. Anja had caught sight of the drones only a few times, but she was sure they were there, hermetically sealing their total aloneness on the Berg. She and Louis might as well have been living under a giant glass dome.

Louis sat next to her on the bench. They both looked out and down at the view. The TV tower blinked to the left of her field of vision. In front of her, blue-white streetlights lit the western half of the city, while yellow-white lights lit the right half, a remnant from when the city had been divided and the lamps had been electric on one side and gas on the other. Radiating out from the Berg, now, was a dimmer greenish stretch of lights, where the old lamps had begun to be replaced with solar-powered ones. A taste test for the city, a sample of the sustainable color all of Berlin would soon be. With the green lights, the formerly double-sided urban space was transformed into a new ratio with a third variable, a new possibility expanding from its core, the old bisection being eaten away by the green future descending from the mountain. The city extended out as far as Anja could see, ring upon ring of new growth.

"I'm sorry," said Louis quietly. "I'm discombobulated. I've been having bad dreams."

"I know. I hear you making noises in your sleep."

"I'm sorry," he repeated.

She looked away from the expanse and toward him, long focus to short focus—zoom, swing, tilt, shift. She felt suddenly, horrifically guilty for losing her temper. Berating him wasn't part of the plan.

"I'd ask what your bad dreams are about, but I don't know how dreams fit into your current rubric of politeness and banality." That still sounded meaner than she wanted it to, but she couldn't imagine how to dial down the emotional valence of the situation.

He looked back out to the city. "I've been dreaming about my mom," he said. "I have this dream where she's in the house with me." He paused, squinted into the distance as if he were trying to make out a particular landmark. "I dream that I'm sleeping in our bed, and then she wakes me up by touching me on the forehead." He reached a hand up and lightly patted his own head, the gesture itself impossibly childish. Anja put her arm around him. "She wakes me up and when I open my eyes I see that she's all torn up."

"What do you mean?"

"She's all bloody. Her legs have bones sticking out of them." Anja breathed in sharply. "Then I notice that the whole room is bombed out. We're in a giant crater."

"What's a crater?" A word escaped her, for once.

"A huge hole—like we're in a war zone."

"Oh."

"Then I look down and I see that my legs are gone too, and I feel better."

"Why would you feel better?"

"I don't know. Maybe because we match."

"What else happens?"

"I just lie there. Sometimes she stays until I wake up. Sometimes she goes."

"Shit, I'm really sorry."

He patted her arm. "It's okay. It's not that bad."

"I mean, it sounds extremely bad." The whole point of this dream was badness. It was the real reason he didn't want to be in the house at night. The house had become the scene of a crime.

"No, you don't get it. She's there with me in the dream. But then I wake up and she's not in the room anymore." He touched his forehead again, once. "That's the bad part."

Anja pictured the two of them waking up in the morning. Anja, scrolling on her phone, reading the news, waiting for him to wake up. Louis, shifting on his pillow, groggy, rolling back and forth, opening his eyes to see her beside him. She now saw what he saw when he woke up. He didn't see her at all: he saw someone who wasn't Pat.

"I get it" was all she could say.

"Can I ask you something, and you promise not to get mad?"

"Of course," she said, knowing that she had zero choice, no matter what followed. Unexpected pain bloomed in her gut and then tightened as she repressed it. She hadn't eaten anything for dinner.

"Would you hate me if I stayed at the studio for a few nights? There's the pullout couch, and I could use a solid sleep. I think it might be the humidity and the temperature in the house causing me to have the dreams, actually. And I have this big project going on. It would be great to just wake up and get going."

There was no arguing. He was going to leave her alone in the crater.

"Of course. Anything you need."

"You should come by and see me there, though. I want to show you the project." He was always dropping hints about this new thing he was working on without fleshing out any details.

But then, there were so many details that were missing at this point. So many things she should be able to ask him but couldn't. The ghost of Pat. The late nights at the studio. That email from Howard in his inbox. She was afraid he would refuse to explain if she asked—but she was afraid of the explanation.

"Of course I'll come visit," she said.

Going back home after this seemed unbearable, but they did.

They got in bed. Anja was big spoon. Despite all, Louis fell asleep instantly, and Anja lay there around him, imitating his shape, and waited for him to enter dream state. She waited with her eyes wide open in the darkness, staring at the tiny red light of the ceiling camera blinking like a slow, regular heartbeat. She waited for Pat to show up.

10

ADAM HAD AN ACUTE PHOBIA OF BEDBUGS AFTER THAT ONE SUM-
mer he'd lived in New York.

"You can stay here as long as you want," he'd told Anja over
the phone, "but you have to disinfect yourself first."

When she rang the buzzer at 128, his voice said: "Take your
clothes off in the hall."

"Seriously?"

No answer from the metal grate.

On the second-floor landing he was waiting for her with a
black plastic trash bag and a towel. "Hand everything over," he
said.

"What am I going to wear if you take all my stuff?" she said,
holding up her giant tote stuffed with clothes, makeup, laptop.

"Gimme that." He reached out a blue-gloved hand, snatched
her bag, and held it far away from his body. He handed her the
trash bag. He was wearing a blue checked apron and a matching
bandana wrapped around his forehead. "Go on, strip!"

She dutifully pulled off her sweatsuit. "That's right," he said.
"All of it." Each item she placed in the trash bag. "Your skin isn't

as bad as you made it sound, but you look thin as death. Let mama put some meat on those bones." He held out his uncontaminated arm and she took the towel from him, wrapping herself and following him inside. "These go in the incinerator," he said, holding up the bags, "and you, direkt to ze shower!"

She was relieved to be among humans again. Louis had absconded days ago with a duffel of shirts and underwear, enough to last a month if you were a guy, and, faced with the prospect of his interminable absence, she had gotten into bed. Her work contract didn't start for another week and she had plenty of TV shows to catch up on, doled out by Laura like assignments.

Her bedroom was as sticky as always, and at some point during her tenth or twelfth episode, she'd realized parts of her body weren't just sweaty but really fucking itchy. The litter of pink bumps trailing across her forearms and up one side of her neck, which she'd taken for a sun allergy, had gelled into a raised rash, intensely itchy and unattractive.

A hurried Google Image search for bedbug bites and fleabites and scabies ensued, but it was clear that the bumps were not bites; there was no prick at the top, no target-like pattern. It was a rash. A cellular protest that had gained a critical mass of participants and become a crowd. Her body was protesting being left alone. Or maybe it was just reacting to the mold that had taken over the bathroom.

Dam was rooting around in the cabinet full of crusty liquor bottles when she got out of the shower. "You can wear my kimono," he said, pointing to the blue silk laid out on the sofa. "I put your clothes in the washer and disinfected your laptop. It's drying on the balcony."

"Drying?"

"Relax, it's not like I washed it with a sponge." He knocked over a bottle, arm-deep in the cabinet. "What kind of day is today? Martini? Pernod?"

"Let's make gin and tonics."

"There's no tonic."

"Let's make gin."

"Good point." He found two large bottles with a finger or two of liquid left in them and emptied them into champagne flutes. "So shut up and tell me what's going on. Is your house being fumigated? I could practically smell your bug spray through the phone when you called."

"I told you, it's not bedbugs. I don't know what it is."

"How do you know?"

"The internet."

"Right. The internet." He swirled the champagne flutes. "What about Louis?"

"He's totally fine."

"He's at home alone?"

"No, he left a few days ago. He's at the studio."

"So it's just you. With the skin thing." He scanned her skeptically while popping heart-shaped ice from a red rubber tray into two cups.

"Don't you dare tell me this is psychosomatic." She turned her head to show off the blotchiest part of her neck. "Does this look imaginary to you?"

"Psychosomatic illness is the realest of the real, honey. Nothing fake about it." He handed her a glass and they toasted. Dam was no stranger to undiagnosed disease. Neither the source of his famous allergies nor a cure had ever been identified. Always a new acupuncturist, a new bottle of homeopathic droplets. "What's going on at la Casa de Malos Sueños, then? Anyone from Finster show up and try to fix things?"

"I got a ton of emails from Howard yesterday, but I just can't be bothered."

"Good. He's a jealous son of a bitch. Keep him out of things."

"Actually, he's trying to help, but I don't know how much he can do. There's some kind of problem with the architects."

"That place has been bad news from the start."

She changed the subject to Eric. She was not in the mood to open the floodgates. Dam was happy to talk about Eric anyway, or rather to complain about him. Eric, he told her, was *so* shameless in instrumentalizing people to get what he wanted, so transparent in his self-serving motives, that everyone just fell at his feet. There was an honesty to his way of operating that sliced through all the usual pretenses of networking, and strangely, people loved it. They loved the transparency. Dam was in awe. He'd followed Eric to a party the night before, where Eric had gotten soullessly drunk, and even in his blind belligerence seduced three consultants into some kind of creative collaboration on an ad campaign. The next morning he was already emailing them.

"What does Eric actually do for a living?" Anja asked. She sipped her gin, imagining it as antiseptic.

"Nothing. He just climbs. He calls himself a promoter, but I don't know what that means."

"I guess he has that app, though. The one he was telling us about. He probably gets everything through there."

Dam told her a lengthy story about a multiple trade Eric had recently made involving a license to travel with a dog, which was apparently very hard to acquire without a "vet connection"; a building permit; a publishing deal; and a consulting gig. What

Eric got out of it, after all that, was nothing more than an invitation to an exclusive dinner. *The* dinner, Dam insisted.

It was impossible to think about the app and not scan your life for unmet needs and potential offers. The app couldn't fix a relationship, but maybe it could help with all those other tangibles that held up a relationship. A decent, unsustainable apartment. A dog.

She looked down at her body and saw that she had been scratching her elbow so hard while listening to the tale of Eric that the skin had split. She interrupted Dam. "Do you think that app could get me a fancy doctor's appointment?"

"Of course," he said. "If Eric can get a letter from a vet, a human doctor can't be that hard."

"Ask him for me."

"No way he'll help you. He likes to lord this sort of stuff over me. If there's no direct benefit for him, he's not going to do me any favors. I'm telling you, he's absolutely shameless."

It was no use suggesting to Dam that pursuing Eric was a bad choice. She'd watched Dam do this time and again, and there was no rerouting him from his course of pursuing men whom he despised in order to be abused by them and therefore confirm his assumptions about the world. He was like Sara and Sascha in that way: so sentimental and so in need of care, and yet so incapable of seeking love from a person who could provide it. Unlike Sara and Sascha, though, he was perfectly aware of his own hypocrisy. By seeking compassion in the wrong places, he tried to dull his needs by proving to himself that they were impossible to meet. The satisfaction of rejection was the only kind he seemed to know how to feel.

"You don't need to tell me," Dam said, preemptively defensive. "I know there are a few red flags with Eric."

It occurred to Anja that her relationship might also look unhealthy to people on the outside who didn't understand it. No, she thought, nobody should judge a relationship except for the people in it. Only the participants could understand what existed between them. And after it was formed, the relationship became a fully autonomous, uncontrollable being. People liked to think they were having a relationship with each other, but really they were having a relationship with the relationship itself.

calm cloudless sailor moon / ?°

She jerked awake around noon with a nasty headache and a furious itch on her thigh. Laura was back from her two-day trip to Barcelona and was in the kitchen making coffee.

"You slept late," Laura said, back turned.

"I know. Lots of gin yesterday. Wait—is that my phone ringing?" Anja flailed, tossing magazines off the table. "Do you hear it?"

"Phantom," Laura said flatly. She was right, the phone was dead; the imaginary sound was an echo of desperation. Anja had dreamed about Louis all night. She went to find her charger and when she came back Laura said: "Did Dam tell you?"

"Tell me what?" She plugged her phone into the floor socket and jabbed at the power button.

Laura sighed. "Lazy shit. He's so afraid of conflict that he winds up causing conflict. Every damn time." Anja waited. "He just doesn't want to upset you," Laura said, glancing over her shoulder.

"I'm not that fragile."

"That's what I told him." Laura doled out spoonfuls of sugar, which she used in huge quantities. Sugar, salt, fried things. The more she watched TV, the worse her diet got.

"Well?"

"Fine. I'll do the dirty work." She licked the sugar spoon before putting it back in the dish. "The big news is that our little piece of Neubau here is about to get an upgrade. We'll be priced out next month."

Anja realized she'd been expecting some awful rumor about Louis, which was absurd. She snapped to attention.

"Seriously?"

"Seriously."

Anja diligently went through the requisite questioning. She assembled the story from Laura's short, recalcitrant yesses and nos.

What had changed? The building had been sold. Who had bought the building? Finster, of course, which now owned every building on the street. What was the justification? It fell far short of the recommended standards for environmental sustainability and it needed, said Finster, new organic insulation, efficient lighting, solar panels, water filtration. A long list of efficiency improvements that would cost a few million euros to implement, and naturally as a result the rents would triple. Everyone knew the improvements were a scam—for one, these old buildings were pretty well insulated already.

"How is no one protesting?" Anja demanded.

"It's useless. People are bored of this story by now. Even I'm tired of it. It's happening everywhere. You can't argue with sustainability."

Laura used to take part in every protest she could. She used to shame Anja for her lack of participation, until one day Anja accompanied her to a Refugees Welcome rally and they'd watched in horror while two of the guys they'd been marching alongside attacked a man carrying a Palestinian flag. "Anti-Semite!" they'd screamed as they kicked him to the ground. Anja had started crying and Laura had stopped pestering her to join after that. Laura's participation had also waned until it was largely theoretical.

"Show me the letter," Anja said, meaning the letter from Finster. There was always a letter.

Laura leaned over the desk in the corner and dug around. Anja averted her eyes from the pitiful digging. Her friends' disorganization pained her. It was pathetic. Every time they got a scary letter in German they buried it instead of dealing with it, so the scary letters multiplied, referring to one another, building an impenetrable web, piling up in a crumpled mass on the desk.

If you'd just paid this fine when you got the first letter, Anja would say, anguished, you wouldn't have had this problem! If you had just brought the first letter to me! If you had just called the number on the letter and asked them to explain! Laura would swear, defiant, that they'd never gotten the original letter, and yet after a half hour peeling coffee-stained paperwork from the stash on the desk Anja would find it, dated eight months back and labeled MAHNUNG. This is a final notice! You're being sued! Why can't you get a fucking file folder!

It wasn't so much their dependence on her for dealing with these things that upset her, it was the very shape of the paperwork on the desk, the random mess of it all. You have to accept that you live in Germany, she'd say, I don't care if it doesn't make any sense to you! It comes with the territory!

The letter that Laura produced this time, without too much digging, was a short one. It explained the newish provision of the city code whereby environmental upgrades overrode rent caps, so apparently there was no recourse to appeal. There was a phone number in the letterhead.

"I'll give them a call," Anja said.

"Don't worry about it."

"It's worth a shot."

"Really, it's not."

She took a photo of the letter, resolving to call later. "Do you have a plan?"

Laura poured the coffee grounds into the sink. Anja wondered if it would stop up the drain, reminded briefly of her own kitchen sink and its stubborn disposal.

"That's the thing Dam doesn't want to tell you," said Laura.

Anja looked at her blankly, and then remembered where Laura had just been. "No! Laura, you *hate* Spain!"

"I don't hate the price of living there."

"You hate it!"

Laura stared blankly out the window for a moment. "Berlin has changed since we moved here," she said finally. "None of the reasons we came apply anymore. It was freedom—now it's a trap."

"You honestly think things are going to be better anywhere else?"

"Don't get me wrong. I'm sad about it. We just don't really have any options left. We'd have to move to Spandau if we wanted to find a new place in this city."

Anja was incredulous. It was unimaginable, Berlin without Laura and Dam. The whole city would drop out from under her.

It was Dam whom she had met first and whom she called her best friend, but over the past five years she'd spent more time with Laura. Laura, without whom she had become unable to make decisions, to sort out her thoughts. Laura, the brilliant and the bitchy. Laura, the least likely candidate for a best female friend. Against all odds she'd managed to win Laura's friendship—even though she was apolitical, even though she was rich, even though she was shy. She'd won Laura and now she would lose her.

Anja narrowed her eyes. "Be honest. Is this about the *Bachelor* thing?"

"What? No. Let it go. I won that money back already. I told you I had the Final Rose in the bag. But even if I keep winning, it's not sustainable for us. We can't stay forever."

Anja stood up and leaned against her chair. "I can't believe you're so chill about this."

"Everyone is chill about all this." Laura shrugged. "The entire last decade in Berlin has been everyone sitting around and asking each other, how can you be so chill about all this? and then going on being chill. Everyone is chill because everyone else is chill, and it never ends."

"But that's the point of Berlin. It's the only chill place left."

"Yeah, but it's over. How can you not see that? These were our Weimar years, and we spent them doing nothing."

"We do things."

"No. We get fucked up, we spend our time in dark rooms, we don't make anything. Protests are basically street parties. When we see the news we watch it through a filter, because none of it's real to us—we cry about it sometimes, but it doesn't really touch us, it's not real, we feel safe. We drink it off and then the badness of our hangovers gives us a good excuse not to do anything the next day. And the whole time things are getting more and more expensive, and people are leaving, and each time we think, how sad, another person has left, but actually it's an exodus now. There's no reason to stay any longer, now that it looks just like the rest of the world. Have you even read about what's been happening on the outside?"

Anja felt herself flush; she wasn't up on the news at all. She had been entirely absorbed by herself.

Laura wiped her upper lip, which was lined with a light brown fuzz. "We've been so ahead, and so behind. But it's ending. Can't avoid it any longer."

Anja pictured those green lights spreading out from the base of the Berg. The fluctuating weather, snowflakes, sunburns. The tinge of sickness, dysfunction. The humidity in her bedroom, the waste disposal unit spitting out bits of plastic.

"The city isn't postwar, post-Wall anymore—it's pre–something else," said Laura. "You're right that there's no place left. But this place isn't left either."

Anja ran her hands through her hair, tugging on it. "If every place is ruined, why not just sit it out here? Spain will be even worse."

"Better to be somewhere where the apocalypse has already happened than sit through another one." Laura sipped her coffee. "Dystopia takes some time to set in."

Anja responded by holding up her forearms. Laura understood. She leaned in and inspected Anja's rash, feeling it with her fingertips. She said she'd go pick up something from the health-food place. Then she asked about the house, about Louis. But Anja felt even less like opening up than she had with Dam. She had woken up planning to replay every event and conversation for Laura to analyze, to flip over and see from another angle, but she restrained herself. She didn't want a rational opinion. She wanted to think and say irrational things that she would regret.

11

LOUIS SAT ON THE EDGE OF THE BATHTUB. HE DIPPED HIS PINKY in the filmy green water and took a lick.

She opened her eyes: there was no Louis. She was alone in the bathtub in Dam and Laura's beige-tiled bathroom. She closed her eyes again and blotted out his absence, concentrating on the little eukaryotes of algae fastening and unfastening from her skin.

Instead of medicine, Laura had brought home a packet of green powder and a jug of filthy water from the canal. "I read about it online," she said. "The powder causes the algae from the canal water to multiply and take off a layer of skin. It's good for eczema and rashes and things."

Why would you think canal water is safe to bathe in? would have been the proper response. Or, how much skin does it take off, exactly? But Anja just said thanks and retreated to the bathroom. She ran half a tub of scalding water and then dumped the jug and the powder in before thinking to read the instructions on the back of the packet.

Half a packet sufficient for one bath, it said. Combine with six tablespoons of fresh pond water. Test pH level using enclosed blotter paper before making contact with skin.

Anja uncorked the half-empty bottle of Bordeaux Laura had given her along with the bath ingredients and took a swig. Then she sank her foot into the frothing water. It was way too hot, but it felt fine otherwise. She wondered what Michel would say about this particular medicinal plant. Maybe she'd ask him. Algae hadn't been in that section of the garden, the section in the shape of a body. It was more like the shape of a gingerbread man. Or a swollen corpse. She hadn't liked the concept of the thing as much as Michel had seemed to.

She was chest-deep in the mush for twenty minutes before the creases of her elbows and knees started to sting—the places where the thin skin was the thinnest and was being sloughed off by the algae quickest. She lifted a foot out of the water to check whether the rash was improving, but it was hard to say because the whole foot was so red from the heat. She breathed deeply, focusing on the stinging to keep Louis out of her mind, and with each breath she saw her nipples poking up through the green surface, causing tiny ripples. She checked her foot again. That pair of freckles near its bony apex—was something different about them? The freckles, she was sure, were closer together than they had been before.

"Why would your freckles be moving?" Louis smiled from his perch on the edge of the tub.

"I don't know, maybe I'm evolving."

"Maybe you're devolving and becoming a swamp creature."

She heard his friendly laugh again, a laugh that could cover anything up, even the most cutting comment—you wouldn't even realize it had cut you until you replayed the conversation in your head again late at night. How many times had she heard him mask the things he said with that laugh?

She pulled the foot with the freckles closer and grabbed hold of it, mushing the skin with her thumb to see if it felt at all mutable, putty-like, but it just felt like a hot, raw foot. She touched the freckles lightly. No, at closer range they were certainly normal, no movement.

But of course. She was confusing her freckles with Louis's freckles, the two on his arm that formed the handle of the Big Dipper. That was his body, not hers. She'd appropriated them. Funny, this had only ever happened before with Eva: the mistaking of one body for another. Of course it made sense with Eva—their bodies were made of essentially the same stuff in different tinctures. They were both women who came from the same woman. The uncanny sight of Eva's legs, so similar to her own, had jolted Anja out of her own body more than once.

There was that time she and Eva had gotten terrible poison ivy at day camp during their year in Connecticut. Their mother had picked them up, swung them back to the rental home, and forced them both into an oatmeal bath. They were too old to be bathing together, and Anja remembered the unwelcome feeling of their legs bumping in the oatmeal mush, her sister's leg's already smooth shaven, Anja's still softly frosted in kid hair. It was a repulsive feeling, leg against leg in oatmeal water.

A quarter bottle of Bordeaux in, she decided the stinging had gotten intense enough. She pulled the drain plug and, blood pounding in her temples, stumbled naked, red-faced, and covered in green scum into Laura's room, where this time she was sure she could hear her phone ringing. Three missed calls: Papa, Howard, Louis. She took her phone back to the bathroom, lay down on the bath mat, and started dialing from the top.

Papa's phone rang endlessly. She dialed again. Algae was crusting into a variegated topography on her stomach; she decided not to wash it off, to let it settle. A green stain was spreading around her onto the beige bath mat.

His voice arrived unexpectedly. "Darling! We're just about to board." (French.)

"Oh, where?" (German.)

"Schiphol."

"To where?" (German.)

"Frankfurt."

"Until?" (German.)

"Sunday. Then back to Vienna, finally." (French.)

Vienna was the landing pad. Technically it had been Anja's permanent home during the growing-up process, but she'd spent very little time there altogether, just stints between different postings: always a new school in the fall, a new camp in the summer. The familiar questioning refrain of one international school kid to another: Celebrity, Diplomat, Oil? Double Dip, that was Anja's stock answer. Both parents.

Anja had taken Louis to the Vienna apartment the winter before. The house was empty—Anja had chosen those dates because it would be. Shining parquet boasted across all seven rooms; southeast-facing windows let in sunlight in glorious strips across the vast floors; crown molding iced the ten-foot ceilings; Talavera tiles floored the bathroom and Delft tiles framed the kitchen. Louis fawned over the orange tree, so ambitiously branching toward the bay window in the sitting room.

In fact, Louis was enthusiastic about all of it. How honest this old Viennese grandeur, compared to Berlin's new money! How figurative the buildings! How casually the assets displayed themselves! She was surprised that the city appealed to him so much, but of course, she reminded herself, it was all new to him. Waking up beside him in the four-poster bed, she tried to imagine the house he'd grown up in, that little brown square of a roof she'd located after searching on Google Maps. Wall-to-wall pile carpets?

Recliners? A TV in the kitchen? (Fast-forward and scratch that: no TV.) She had been born into a world of private schools—he had ended up beside her in this vast antique bed entirely on merit, on the merit of being so brilliant he was lovable. He'd achieved his achievements. She'd never be able to say that of herself.

Venturing beyond the apartment, though, Louis had to admit that the architecture could be over-the-top. Column after column after balustrade. Grimaces leering from every corner. Gargoyles on gargoyles. Leaning against the scalloped railing of the raised entrance to the Albertina Museum, he expressed a kind of historical vertigo while trying to make geometrical sense of the view: three eras of intensely ornamented façades converging at odd angles to one another, like railway tracks merging unsuccessfully.

Below them, Anja explained, the vectors of history also tunneled all the way into the earth. The Albertina had recently opened a whole new viewing hall in a sub-subbasement, beneath which were even more sub-sub-subbasements, climate-controlled halls of storage. Wedged between untouchable historic buildings on either side and unwilling to stop acquiring objects, the Albertina had opted to dig down. The museum a spaceship, a crypt. Anja's family owned a whole chunk of real estate down there—she didn't mention that.

"Come visit," Papa was saying into the phone. "We'll be in Vienna almost the whole month."

"I'm busy, actually. I have a new job. And anyway I shouldn't travel, I'm sick or something. I'm all patchy." She checked her foot again, the one with the freckles. Under the green film the red rash was still firmly printed.

"What kind of patchy?"

"A rash."

"What kind of rash?"

"I don't know. A red one."

"Your commune has lice?"

"I know. You told me so."

"I did tell you so, but we all have to make our own mistakes. When I was your age I lived in a farming cooperative in Copenhagen, growing my own beets and radishes."

"I know, you've told me that, too."

"That was when I developed my psoriasis, from all the stress of living together and the lack of hygiene. What does your rash look like?"

"Papa, it's not psoriasis."

"Psoriasis can easily spread and inflame the joints if you don't catch it in time."

"It's not psoriasis."

"Why don't you take a picture with your camera phone and send me a multimedia message? I'll tell you if it looks like psoriasis."

"What difference would it make? There's no cure for psoriasis."

"Maybe not today, but soon! By the time you're my age they'll have a cure for all these things. Cancer, obviously—heart disease, a thing of the past. You and Eva will live forever."

"Everyone wants to think their kids will live forever."

"But think of what's happened in just the last fifty years, the science is enormous! Compared to the sixties—have I ever told you about my waking tonsillectomy?"

"Yes."

"See, there's reason to hope. The future—but hold on—" She heard mumbling, her mother's voice in the background. "Sorry, love," he said, "we've really got to board now."

"All right, well."

"You sound down, darling. Do you need anything?"

"I'm fine, just—" The speaker scratched as Mom grabbed the phone. "No," Anja said, "I don't need to talk to—"

"Anja," Mom yelled into the mouthpiece, fumbling with the device and breathing hard. Airports had started giving her migraines; she was particularly unpleasant when she was inside them, which was frequently. She seemed to think she could counteract the process of aging by accelerating air travel to the point that it was nonstop. Turn endless movement into a state of constancy and voilà, you'd be stable. A rat in formaldehyde, endless suspension.

"Is it our American friend? Has he deserted?"

"Not exactly," Anja said. "Remember about his mom, though. I told you."

"Jesus, I'd forgotten. What a tragedy—but hold on, your— we've really got to run—"

"Okay. We'll talk later."

"Why! What's he done?"

"Who?"

"Your . . . boyfriend."

Anja was tempted to press her into saying his name, but she resisted. "*Louis*," she reminded. "*Louis* hasn't *done* anything. He's grieving, Mom."

"You can't let him walk all over you, Anja. Take some control. You don't need him."

Time passed differently for Mom. She lived inside her own schedule, forgetting the existence of anyone not standing directly in front of her. But when you did cross her field of vision she latched on hard, flipping from absent to overbearing in a second. There was no third mode. Eva had long since learned to avoid speaking to her mother on the phone. Both she and Anja had generally learned to use her father as the go-between, but Anja still gave in, in moments of weakness, reaching out to make sure her mother was still alive.

"Where did you get this idea that everyone is trying to take advantage of me?"

Anja knew the answer. It was because her mother had been born in America, and so had been born ready to sue anyone, legally or emotionally, at any moment.

"You're too good for him—he's from the Midwest, for god's sake. There are more fish. You're still young. I have to go now, we're already on the tunnel to the plane, what's it called, the tunnel thing?"

"A jet bridge."

"No, that's not it. Anyway, your father will get you a plane ticket to come to Vienna for a few days. You'll feel better once you get home. You can see Doctor What's his name."

Papa's voice entered the phone for a moment, but she couldn't tell what he was saying. The line cut out.

Howard answered immediately. "Finally."

She sat up and leaned against the bathtub, pulling the bath mat up over her legs, which were shivering. "It's only been like three days since we talked," she said. "What's up?"

"Where are you?"

"I'm at—wait, why?"

"Everyone else is at the Best Western."

She laughed. "Who's everyone?"

"Everyone from the Berg, the whole community. This morning we relocated all of you, except *you two*."

"Come on, half of the houses have been empty for weeks."

He turned on his official voice. "Everyone who was still living on the Berg is now here. At the hotel."

"So you finally realized it's unlivable up there."

"They can't fix the system with everyone on site. This is just a temporary vacation for you while they solve the last little issues."

"That means they decided on the way to go? How natural our lifestyles should be?"

"All buttoned up."

"And?"

"You'll be getting all the luxuries you deserve."

"Heat and running water."

"For starters."

"And what are you telling the press about having emptied us from the biome we are supposed to be a part of?"

"Nothing. That's why you should probably be over at the hotel."

"Yikes, Howard. This must be a nasty PR situation." She checked the wine level in the bottle beside her. "A little out of your depth, maybe?"

"Watch it." He sounded less in control than usual, not absorbing the jabs. "Wash your mouth out with soap and get over here. I mean it."

She stood to look in the mirror and inspect the burgundy skid mark on her tongue. "Hold on, you're right." She rubbed her tongue with a white bar of soap next to the sink, which tasted like lavender, then sipped water from the tap, gargled, and coughed into the basin.

"It's the Best Western in Mitte," he said. "Do you need the address?"

"Chill for a second. I have to go home and pick up some stuff before I can do anything. I didn't bring enough clothes."

"We've got things cordoned off, so no, you can't go back. If you had just picked up your phone—"

"I have another job now, remember? I'm a very busy con-sul-tant."

"You're at work?"

"No. I'm working on myself."

She heard another phone ring in the background on his end. Howard put his hand over the microphone and said something muffled in German. She realized they had been speaking English together on this call, which sometimes made their interactions more antagonistic. He abruptly returned to the speaker. "Remember the NDA you guys signed," he said loudly. "It covers this exact potential scenario. You really can't be talking about it with anyone."

"Really, this exact scenario? This very exact particular one?"

"It covers all potential scenarios, one of which has become an actual scenario. That's how legal contracts work. They account for multiple universes, and this is the universe we happen to find ourselves in."

He sounded manic. Artificially induced. Mom had, conversely, sounded sedated. Maybe it was time Anja met everyone else on their level: heavily medicated.

"It's not possible to write an NDA that covers every possible reality," she said.

She could imagine Howard's blood pressure rising, his veins opening, the click in his brain that told him to switch the focus back to her. "What's going on with you?"

"I have a rash. It flares up in the afternoon."

She reached across the floor to dig around in the hamper of treatments she'd assembled from Laura and Dam's cabinets. Vitamin B_{12} sublingual capsules, colloidal silver nasal spray, valerian root extract, quick-dissolving mineral salts, homeopathic nothing-tablets, teal ceramic neti pot with an Om symbol engraved on the side. She found the calamine lotion and squirted out a thin pink worm on her thigh, then rubbed the elbow of the arm holding the phone into the goo.

"I'm sorry to hear that. I could find you a doctor to meet you at the hotel?"

"Is the Best Western seriously the best you could do in this situation?"

"It's four stars."

"I have to rinse off this algae, it's really stinging again. I'll get back to you."

"Where's Louis? Is he with you?"

"I'll get back to you."

After rinsing and inspecting her blotchy patches, which had flattened into faint pink outlines but not stopped itching, she put Dam's kimono back on and got into his bed. She stared at her phone in preparation and dialed Louis.

He was bright and loud when he answered. The room he was in sounded noisy. He asked about her rash in a concerned tone.

"I'll be fine. Probably just some kind of allergy."

"I feel so much better after getting out of the house. I'm sure you will too."

"Good for you." She knew she sounded sour. She wanted to sound sour. He was supposed to ask her to come stay with him.

He was supposed to ask if she wanted to get a hotel room, a new apartment, to move forward or go back in time.

"What?" he said defensively. "Are you annoyed I'm staying here?"

"No. But we could stay somewhere together."

"The pullout sofa here isn't big enough for two people."

"I know, you've said that."

"Hey, come see for yourself. Come by here and look at the sofa, you can decide if you want to sleep on it with me."

"We could go stay at the Best Western with everyone else."

"Best Western?"

"Howard says everyone from the Berg was relocated. They want us to go there right away."

He laughed. "The Best Western was the best they could do?"

"That's what I said."

"Sounds like a terrible idea. Have you ever been inside a Best Western? Your rash would probably get worse."

"Hasn't Howard called you like a hundred times today?"

"I'm not taking calls besides yours right now. We're in full brainstorming mode over here. Innovation is going *down*, babe."

She laughed, but then wondered if she hadn't been supposed to laugh. Maybe he was serious? Innovation? Going down?

"Just come see me," he said. "I miss you."

It was a neon fishhook in the dark, which she bit down upon slowly, feeling it pierce the roof of her mouth.

"We'll see us tomorrow," she said, deliberately inserting the common German error into her English, something he'd once thought was funny.

The calamine lotion wasn't working to dull the itch and her elbow was urgently prickling, inflamed and demanding scratching.

After she ended the call, she recklessly hacked away at the skin with her bitten fingernails, wondering yet again whether *she* was the cause of this new and odd state of affairs between them, or whether *he* was the cause, or whether the relationship was an organism independent of either of their intentions that would always morph in ways useless to try to control.

12

LOUIS WAS PHOTOGRAPHING THE VIEW FROM THE WINDOWS OF his studio with his tablet when Anja came in. He smiled over his shoulder. It was *slobbering wet / bright rays / strawberry* outside, and the light was filtering in through the southwest windows of the building, of which he had an entire floor sandwiched between West Africa below and Digital Development above. An eighteenth-century sanitation factory had been knocked down a few years ago and rebuilt anew exactly the same, down to the fixtures, but with one entire south-facing façade replaced by a sheet of triple-enforced glass. This was Basquiatt HQ.

Louis's desk rolled itself around the room to follow the sunlight, performing asanas, but everyone in the room except Louis was down at the darker end of the space, cast in shadow. There were five or so of them huddled around a large monitor on a regular stationary table. Anja waved, but they didn't seem to notice, too engrossed in whatever they were looking at. She moved up behind Louis and laid her cheek flat on his back, wrapping her arms around his chest between scratchy wool sweater and soft cotton shirt, smelling the familiar detergent they had at home, which was supposed to be unscented.

"Gimme a wet one," he said, turning to wrap around her.

They sat together on the white leather IKEA two-seater in the sunniest corner. Anja tried to position herself in a confident recline, imagining she was one of those gym women whose bodies knew what to do without conscious instruction. Louis said how excited he was to see her, she reciprocated, they made physical contact easily, it was all natural. Just like that, they were together again. Who had decided it would be this way? No one: it just was.

One of the people from the clump at the other end of the room had broken off and was creeping along the wall toward the sofa, looking privately thrilled.

"Hey, Belinda," called Louis. He and Belinda were grinning at each other, Belinda more giddily so. She giggled as she inched closer. Anja started to reach out a hand to introduce herself, but Belinda leaped upon Anja and wrapped her arms around Anja's head. She gave Anja a kiss on the side of her face.

"A real wet one," said Anja, wiping her cheek.

Belinda fell across the sofa, stretching herself over their laps. She swung one arm upward until it was a few centimeters in front of Louis's face. The hand held a USB stick shaped like a pink breast-cancer-awareness ribbon. "What's this?" asked Louis.

"The final vector files. Signed sealed and delivered!" She was American, maybe Canadian.

"Thank you!" Louis plucked the USB stick from her hand and Belinda beamed up at him from his lap. "Belinda's a graphic designer," he said to Anja. "She's consulting on this project I want to show you."

Belinda sat up and shifted so she was curled around Anja, resting her head against Anja's shoulder with the kind of unabashed intimacy that Anja associated with bathtubs in the basements of clubs. Belinda slithered a hand onto Anja's thigh, and Anja reflexively slapped it away. Belinda didn't seem bothered. She rolled her face back in Louis's direction and said, "We decided to give you the mock-ups for free. No need to reimburse us. After all, how often do we get to serve a higher purpose?" She closed her eyes serenely and signed off: "With very best wishes."

"Of course we'll pay you, Belinda." Louis laughed. "We couldn't cancel your contract even if we tried."

Belinda waggled a finger in the air. "That's the problem with everything," she slurred. "They don't let you give anything away for free." She jolted awake and then appeared to drift off again.

Anja shook her head. "I want the opposite of whatever she's taking," she said.

Louis frowned. "Really? That's your first reaction?"

"What are these mock-ups for?"

"Well, *her*, basically," he said, looking at Belinda. "Here"—he waved the USB stick—"I'll show you." He jiggled his knee and Belinda gently rolled off their laps, giggling, then sunk over to the far side of the office again.

They stood together at his desk while Louis maneuvered the unwieldy cancer ribbon into the USB socket of his computer. The stick's plastic appendage blocked the other ports, so he had to unplug his power cable to get it in. "Not sure why we're still using USBs here," he muttered. "This place is so behind."

He downloaded a file called "Relinquish_Super_Ego" onto his desktop, unzipped it, and opened a 3D rendering. He rotated the rendering so she could see all sides of the object. It was an oblong, light purple capsule, with a groove etched on one side, following its contour. Two concentric ovals.

She squinted. "It's a pill?"

"Designer drug, literally." He pointed at the group at the far end of the room, ostensibly a whole squadron of designers. "It doesn't look too perfect, though, right? They tried to undesign it after they designed it. We don't want it to look corporate." Then he jumped. "Oh god, I forgot. Don't hate me. Can you sign a waiver?"

"An NDA?"

"I just—" He pointed at the nearest ceiling camera.

"Whatever. These don't seem to mean much anymore."

Louis handed her his tablet and she signed the screen sloppily with a finger. He kissed her cheek. "Now I can show you." He pulled up another folder from the drive labeled "ChariteX" and opened a slew of files.

There were TIFFs of molecular structures, peptide bonds, brain scans, the eyeballs of mice and apes under the influence. PDFs of biology papers. A science collage. He clicked through photos, animations, renderings. "This is the mood board," he said, "just to give you an idea."

She took in the mood uneasily. "Maybe give me the elevator pitch."

"Right." They paused to look over at Belinda, who was saying something not quite intelligible from her position on the floor nearby, on her knees with arms stretched out before her in an approximation of a child's pose. Louis looked like he wanted to call out to her, but shook his head and turned back to Anja.

"Let me set the scene," said Louis, licking his lips and entering the present tense, as he usually did for story time. "It's the 1980s. We're in Rio de Janeiro." Seeing Anja's arched eyebrows, he laughed—that laugh was the real elevator pitch, she thought. That laugh could soften you into agreeing to anything.

"Like I said, we're in Rio, okay? So there's this guy who runs a french fry stand on Copacabana Beach. He sells the fries for a few bucks and makes a living, just like everyone else. He's normal. Okay. But then something happens. One day something falls on his head, I don't know, a volleyball or something, and he suddenly changes. He keeps making fries, but he starts giving them away for free to anyone who asks. He won't take money. He just wants to give all his food away. And he's actually pretty poor, but he just can't help himself. It just makes him so happy to see people's faces when he gives them free fries from his stand. Then he realizes he can give other things away too, and soon he starts giving away all his possessions and his money. His family and friends try to stop him, but he can't stop. It's like he's *high off his own generosity*. Something has happened to the reward centers of his brain and generosity gives him insane pleasure. People take advantage of him and he runs up a huge debt. Nobody knows what to do with him—until some researchers from LA hear about it, fly down immediately, and get him into an MRI machine. When they look at his brain, they see that one spot is damaged, this little tiny risk-and-reward region. It's like his reward centers have been rewired and now the reward he used to feel from earning money, from getting stuff, he only feels by giving things away."

Anja took a deep breath. "I think I get where this is going." She looked at the giant purple capsule on the screen. "The pill turns you into the french fry man."

"Yes. Or, sort of."

"Through brain damage."

The laugh again. "Obviously we're not advocating any permanent changes in brain chemistry yet. The compound is designed to pass through your system in maximum eight hours."

"So for eight hours, you feel artificially high when you give things away for free?"

"No, there's no artificiality to it. It just *removes a barrier*. That's the important thing about the french fry story. Generosity is already in the brain, just waiting to be unlocked. It takes the *tiniest change* to make giving feel better than taking."

"But taking feels good because we're self-preserving animals. We evolved this way for a reason."

"Yeah, and look where that got us." He waved a hand around himself in a circle, indicating the entire failing planet. "Survival of the richest. Endless selfish consumption, climate change. This is the end of the line if we keep going like we are. Obviously we're going to have to evolve in a new direction if we're going to survive for another generation. We're going to have to undergo an actual physical change. Capitalism—it's in the *brain*." He pointed to an area near the front of his skull where she supposed the capitalism was sequestered. "But it can be changed."

"So you take it and it turns off your . . . capitalism?" She laughed in spite of herself.

The earnestness in his face read like an autocorrect mistake that accidentally formed a double entendre.

"Eventually, I hope." He nodded. "But for the period of influence you just feel really amazing when you do something generous, especially something financially generous. Over time you might start to associate those things: being nice and feeling good. Brain training. Like one of those mindfulness apps, but actually effective. The implications of that small rewiring . . . over time you could start to realize there's another way of living and exchanging."

She thought of young Eric at the bar, idiotically arguing that the cultural-capital app would create a new friend-based economy beyond hard capital. *Another way of living and exchanging.*

"Who's supposed to be taking this pill?" she asked. "Who's going to voluntarily turn off the capitalist part of their brain?"

"Everyone. We do it all the time." His eyes were shining. "Think about it. Everyone we know takes drugs every weekend in order to do some version of exactly that. We take drugs to change the reward centers of our brains. Touching people, being around people, exchanging experiences, that's why you do drugs. Aren't you always complaining about how much money you spend when you're high?"

She shifted from foot to foot. She had indeed often complained about it, rolling in bed hungover, recounting lost cash. "So it's like MDMA or something."

"Nope. Nope, nope. It's highly selective. This thing is focused very specifically on the economic centers of the brain. The spendy bits. We found the main money spot, it's in the hippocampus or something, this little groove of risk and reward, gain and loss, a pressure point of financial risk in the something cortex. If you activate—or I guess deactivate—that spot, then people become temporarily generous, especially with their money. Boom."

Anja was silent, ordering her thoughts. What good would it do to loosen up people's wallets at a club? What was the point?

Glancing around the room, she remembered what building

they were in. Who Louis worked for. The file name. "Oh, god. Are you trying to get clubbers to donate to charity?"

He was prepared for this, excited. "No! It's about *people,* not causes. It's concrete, not abstract."

"Come again?"

"That's the most important part. The generosity doesn't work on an abstract level. It's person-to-person."

"I don't get it. What's the point of getting generous at the Baron?"

"Think about it," he said again. She *was* thinking about it. "You leave the club at six a.m. Who do you see? Who's also out on the street at that hour?"

"Joggers?"

"Homeless people. People who really need your generosity."

She was on the verge of understanding, but there was still too much in the way. "Getting high will make you want to give spare change away . . ."

"And eventually you'll make a connection between person-to-person charity and goodness. Eventually. When you start to associate generosity with pleasure, you'll choose, on your own, to care about the world. Start local, act global."

"And the target group is our friends." She shook her head.

"Think about them, the people we know. The art world, whatever it is. Think about how hermetic we are, how apolitical. We spend all our time at parties, trying to get on the guest list, being completely selfish. Making money and spending it on ourselves. Imagine what would happen if we turned outward and started giving a shit about the rest of the world."

"But most people we know don't make much money."

"Most of them have a lot more than they admit." She looked down, reddened. He reached out and squeezed her shoulder.

"It's fine, it's what we've been taught to do. Not to show off. Not to talk about it. But there's actually a lot of money tied up in the culture class, I've got a lot of data on that. We just have to change the culture. The issue is, we all think we're doing enough good just by being creative or whatever. We think if we exist for ourselves—we've talked about this before, remember, babe? Everyone thinks they're transgressive, but actually they're just fucking selfish."

She remembered their last walk up the mountain, his tirade on behalf of politeness.

"It still seems like you should be starting at the top," she said. "Like where the structural problems are, corporations and stuff. Not with us, the people we know."

"No, it has to start with us. *Bottom up.* Artists used to show the world what ethics looked like. Now everyone's a consultant. The ones on the bottom are as corrupt as the guys at the top. We've all sold ourselves. If the only way to get some compassion and political responsibility back is chemical, so be it. We have to lead by example. We're the last hope."

She looked to Belinda, rolling around on the floor, and then out the window, at the roofs and windows wet with rain and shining with sunlight. "But the giving won't be real," she said quietly. "It's about feeling good, not about doing the right thing."

"That's how humans work. You have to incentivize them. Moral commitment is always selfish, on some level."

She chewed a whip of hair, realized she was doing it, and pulled it out of her mouth. "I don't think so. Giving money away because it feels good is not the same thing as actual kindness."

"I know, babe. But on the receiving end, does it make any difference?"

Belinda's voice wafted over. She had taken off her shoes and was dancing by herself near the window, singing at full volume. *This is the perfect time . . . a worthy climb . . .* Some song from the radio that Anja had heard in a cab. *Good is here and bad is done . . . we're running running running straight into the sun . . .*

Anja snapped back to attention. "How is Basquiatt letting you do any of this?"

"So far, they think it's all a PR project. Speculative design." He laughed, genuinely amused. "They're so used to consultants making up abstract provocations that don't go anywhere, they never considered I would actually try to do something real."

"At some point you'll have to tell them."

"Obviously. The real artwork, though, in my opinion, is going to be my selling the idea to them. I've got someone coming in this week to help me do that." He ruffled his own hair. "I need consultation on how to sell my consultation—this is the world we live in."

"What happens if they don't take it?"

"I'm almost positive they'll bite. Basquiatt has been wanting to get the creative class to care about humanitarian shit for years, but the people allocating the cash couldn't manage to switch their focus away from Africa."

"Isn't Africa their whole reason for existing?" She had, in fact, learned to look down on the concept of philanthropy—learned of its colonial legacy, learned how it functioned as a form of money laundering—from Louis.

"Of course. But they're misguided. So let's take their resources and set up our own peer-to-peer version of charity instead. We need to start helping the people directly around us. Maybe charity is corrupt, maybe political activism is dead, but that doesn't mean we have zero responsibility. It's time to invent something better."

"With money from Basquiatt . . ."

"Unless someone else comes along to pay for it." He smiled quizzically at her, and she couldn't tell if he was seriously implying something. She ignored it.

"This whole time I've been here," he said, "I've thought of humanity as some abstract concept, while the homeless guy sitting out front of this building is starving to death. Have you seen the numbers? Homelessness in Berlin has tripled this decade. There's no reason for me to have this job if I go on being decorative, playing the role of the artist for the investors to fetishize and make them feel like they're doing something abstractly good by investing in me. I finally realized I have to follow through on this project if I ever want to actualize something—actual. Actually good."

The membrane between actual and virtual. The Before and the After.

She stepped back and examined him. "When did you decide to go through with this?"

"I don't know. Sometime in the last weeks."

Her mouth screwed up into a tight pucker and her eyes narrowed, skewing the coordinates of her face. Pity filling the gaps.

"No, no." He shook his head and sighed. "Come on. It's not about *her*."

Anja unscrewed her mouth. Silence persisted. She was pathologizing him again. Howard had gotten into her head with the therapy stuff.

"Why does trying to do good always have to be *about*

something?" he insisted. "If you think everything is about some-thing, you'll never do anything."

Anja lifted her hand to reach out to him, unsure of what to do other than make physical contact. He asked her: "It's worth trying, don't you think?"

She avoided the voices in her head, which were saying things like Absolutely Fucking Not, Who Do You Think You Are, etc., and looked at the person standing in front of her, who was the same beloved person he had always been, who was asking for her approval although he didn't need it, who was including her and trusting her. This was surely a kind gesture, meant to make her feel better as much as to help him. "Of course," she said. "Any-thing you come up with is worth trying." He hugged her with one arm. She closed her eyes for a moment, then opened them and straightened her back. "So," she asked, "how does it start? Are you going to give it to doctors?"

"We'll deal it in clubs. Or actually, we'll feed it to dealers who won't say where they got it."

There was no reason to poke at the weak spots in this plan. "Who gets the cash?"

"We do, minus a cut for the dealers. Think about how much *equity* Basquiatt is going to make off this. It's a double-header: we get the selfish class hooked on supporting the needy, and we make Basquiatt the main supplier of their moral high."

"And you're experimenting already?" She turned toward Be-linda, who was tangled in an undefinable pose on the sofa.

He followed her gaze toward Belinda. "She volunteered. I guess I shouldn't have let her take so much."

Anja nodded. She would have to process this all later, slowly. "What are you calling this thing?"

"That's what I thought you could help with."

"Me?"

"Come on, you're so good at this stuff. You could really be a consultant." She didn't remind him that this conditional had also become an actual. "We don't have a name for on-the-ground yet. We had a title just for internal use . . ."

"ChariteX. I saw."

"Yeah. Maybe we could use some kind of abbreviation—"

"Ex? That might already be taken."

"Good point."

"Let's look at the designs again."

They leaned over the monitor together, Louis with his hand on the back of Anja's neck, and he scrolled through a long PowerPoint of design inspirations. There were no chemistry references in this folder. The nitty-gritty, he told her, was being taken care of at a lab in Düsseldorf. "No time to get a PhD, this shit is time-sensitive."

"Maybe you should go for form instead of content," she said. "Like the Pill. Except that's already taken too."

"I get it. Seeming transparent, but without being too transparent."

He continued scrolling. Sunsets and sunrises that had inspired the pastel color scheme, the light lavender, a gentle and encouraging shade. Symbols that had inspired the groove in the pill's surface—ancient engravings in stone, concentric circles. Fairy rings, toadstools, crop circles.

"Circles," she said. "The shape is what's important. Something more Judd . . ."

"The pill isn't a circle, though."

"A circle is an oval, but an oval isn't a circle?"

"Right, like spaghetti is a pasta."

"Then go for the genus, not the species."

"Oval?"

She thought about it. "Oval."

Louis put a soccer-referee hand in the air. "Oval," he repeated a third time.

"It's good."

"It's beautiful." He nodded. "It's perfect."

He stood up straight, awash in the discovery. She stood, too. Her cheek was itching, the rash revving up again. She scratched at it. The pride she instinctually felt in pleasing him was hollow. Cleverness was cheap. "You're welcome," she said. "Magic pill has a name."

"You think I'm crazy," he said. He looked, indeed, slightly crazy. "I know, it probably sounds like my ego's out of control." He batted her hand away from her face, like he did when she bit her nails. "But as soon as I take a few—Ovals, my ego will calm down. Self-satisfaction out the window. Problem solved."

Her hand returned to her cheek, scratching vigorously now. "As soon as you take a few? How many have you tried so far?"

"None yet. I wanted to wait until the prototype was finished. I want to sample it for the first time in an on-the-ground situation."

"When?"

"Soon. In a couple weeks. With you."

"Just me?"

"At a party. But we'll be the only ones taking it. Maybe when people see us it'll feed the hype in advance. Beef up the demand side."

Anja's eyes were stinging. The rash, real or imagined, expanding hot across her face. "I don't know."

"Why not? You can be my guinea pig." He reached out to run his fingers across her bumpy cheek and frowned. "A guinea pig with a bit of a cage rash. Maybe not the most accurate control group. Let's see if we can't get you some ointment."

PART TWO

. . . biologists give cellular death an ethical inflec-
tion. Cells are said to have a proper and improper
death—in a good death, a tidy death, the cell
self-destructs; in an untidy death it swells, leaks,
explodes . . .

—ELIZABETH A. POVINELLI

13

THE GYM HAD NEVER FELT MORE LIKE WHAT IT WAS: A BODY FAC-
tory. Ellipticals and stair-steppers and stationary bikes were
shoved together in a non-Cartesian array on a small section of
newly laln imltatlon-hardwood floor. The greater portion of the
space was still under construction, with its concrete subfloor exposed. Given the shortage of wall outlets, most of the machines
were scattered across the middle of the space without power, cords
trailing around them in futile loops. People circled the machines
in search of a working one, dodging one another's pumping arms
and legs in the dogged pursuit of fitness.

Anja found a rowing machine that was plugged in, but its
miniature screen displayed only PRESS CTRL+ALT+DELETE.
The front end of the gym's OS had cracked open, revealing faulty
code.

The exposure of the gym floor as an arbitrary construction
was jarring. Until then she'd thought of its layout as a natural
landscape. Previously the gym had allowed a renunciation of
her relationship to dimensional space—a way to move without
moving anywhere—but now, randomly configured, the machines asserted themselves as dimensional objects with tangents

and coordinates, setting up new and strange relations between one another and the bodies touching them. They were no longer machines for forgetting. They were forklifts for moving soft goods.

Below the gym there was a hardware store, a massive four-level warehouse. Everything from fine-grained sandpaper to Swarovski-encrusted toilet brushes. Gilded picture frames and fluorescent lights, sawhorses and stacks of linoleum. Anja wondered if the new flooring being laid across the gym floor had been brought up from the store, loaded piece by piece into the service elevator, and installed under cover of night. How pointed, to keep the gym open throughout its renovation. *We don't take a day off from our self-improvement—how could you?*

Instead of waiting for a free machine, she gave up on body renovations for the day, sat down in the mini-café, and ordered a kale smoothie. She spotted two electricians in blue coveralls squatting nearby, fiddling with an outlet. They looked like they were doing a good job. They looked like they were working hard.

The workers hired by Finster had been categorically unavailable since the start, and nobody she tried to hire on her own would agree to hike up the mountain. The materiality of the Berg seemed incompatible with just about any service or bureaucracy. There had been the insurance companies, the various delivery services who refused to deliver, the Bürgeramt, which didn't know how to register the address, and of course the bank, which still refused to go paperless. In order to activate her credit card, she had to first receive a series of special codes, hidden inside an envelope behind a magnetized strip. The envelope could only be delivered to her home address, therefore it couldn't be delivered, therefore no credit card.

Customer service stories were so universal and so useless to repeat: the second you started telling one, people's eyes would glaze over. Everyone knew the gist, and nobody really cared about the details. To give in to the urge to tell a customer service story was like an admission of defeat. This is really so important to you? You don't have any more interesting content to impart? Have you really become an adult, a parent of your own life, whose entanglements with infrastructure are now central enough to share?

It was best to limit the telling of customer service stories to your partner, if you had one. That was part of the agreed-upon division of labor between Anja and Louis: she dealt with the bureaucracy, so he had to listen to her complain about it. "I'm going on Human Strike," she'd announce, waving her phone while dialing yet another hotline number. "You can't make me do all the reproductive labor just because you don't speak German." But they both knew how it went when he tried to handle it.

Overall, the labor evened out. Louis did the laundry. Louis did the dishes. Louis initiated sex. And Louis provided an audience for stories about logistics.

She was, she knew, the kind of person who took care of things, and there was an inertia to that identity. Louis everyone praised her "natural" skill at dealing with the regime of bureau-power surrounding them. There was a modicum of pride in this. She sometimes felt an animal satisfaction running her hands over the binders of hole-punched and sorted paperwork in the house.

But the expectation of competence was also oppressive. Truthfully, she didn't have any more or less "skill" at dealing with the overwhelming amount of problems, she was just more diligent. A safe realm to exercise the control she didn't have over most areas of life. Naturalizing it made sure that she was the one who had to do it. The more everyone depended on her, the less possible it was to denaturalize the activity.

Thinking about customer service usually made her agitated, but she remained cool sitting there at the gym café with her green smoothie and a view of the exercise floor, watching the horde of exercisers slotted into their machines. And she continued to stay cool, even after going to fetch her things from the locker room and realizing her key card had stopped working and then waiting twenty minutes for a bulked-up gym person to come open her locker with a master key. She stayed cool, even after the gym person tried to blame her for somehow breaking the lock mechanism. Cool, even after the elevator to the ground floor was full of weight lifters who eyed her a little too lustily when she squeezed in between them. Cool, even after it took two full cycles of the traffic light to get across the intersection and enter the train station. Even after her train was delayed by twelve minutes. Even as she considered how Louis, the person she had loved the most violently in her life, was shedding his skin and becoming an unknown creature. She stayed very cool. She played Candy Crush for eight minutes. The train came.

The car was full of white people, except for one elderly black man. The seats on either side of him were empty, maybe because they were those hinged seats that you have to push down in order to get them horizontal; no one liked those. A finger scratched in Anja's brain: sit next to him. In solidarity—against what? Was she appropriating something again?

Another finger scratched in her brain. The voice of a woman who had just entered the car. She was clutching a transparent file folder in which was wedged an outdated issue of a monthly magazine the homeless were given to sell by prostrating themselves before a subway audience. Holding the monthly was how they proved that they were homeless, just a signifier, a badge. Nobody bought it. A monologue was streaming out of the woman's mouth as if it had broken off mid-sentence in the previous train car and was simply picking up where it had left off, like a half-finished video that starts playing immediately, unbeckoned, when you open your laptop. . . . *kein Dach kein Job . . . was zu Essen ein Bißchen Geld Kleingeld zwanzig Cent dreizig Cent ein Cent vielleicht . . . nichts zu essen nichts entschuldigen Sie bitte die kurze Störung . . .*

The Störung—the interruption—*was* an interruption, an interruption of the private thoughts of each person in the car, whose expressions had become pitying or grim or defiant in response to said interruption. Except the two adolescent girls loudly gossiping behind their hands, unshaken by empathy or culpability or anger or disgust because the only thing stronger than those feelings is the social pressure of high school . . . *können Sie ein Bißchen Kleingeld vielleicht* . . . The woman scooted down the car, her litany echoing from a subterranean, ancient place, like a shaman channeling a dead spirit, so glazed over was her expression and so unanimated her gestures. There was more cadence to a voice you'd hear on the other end of the insurance company hotline, more human specificity even in the repeated *Was kann ich für Sie tun?* of the customer service representative.

The Störung was an interruption not because it was commanding or harassing, but because it was so benign yet so unignorable. It fell into the uncanny valley of empathic response. As Louis might say, there was no "specificity" to the struggle, no "human story" compelling you to act. How would Louis react if he were in the subway with her? Had he solved the problem of how to puncture the banal wretchedness of these encounters? Wasn't his solution, Oval, ultimately just an amplified version of tossing change into a cup? It didn't really change the binary nature of the encounter, didn't provide a new option outside the fixed choices: to give or not to give. Oval just compelled you to give more. It didn't resolve the paradox wherein ignoring another's suffering was impossible (that would be inhuman) but fully letting in the awfulness of it was also impossible (because then how could you go on living your ridiculous privileged life?) and so you either plunked some change in the bucket or you averted your eyes just like everyone else as the source of the Störung approached.

. . . Danke, danke für Ihre Aufmerksamkeit . . . The lack of originality in the woman's performance extended to the halting movements, the downturned chin, the flinching expression. Universal physical effects of marginalization, pain, poverty? Or learned behaviors? How had the woman discovered this litany she was now producing? Had she subconsciously internalized the words years before, as a comfortable, seated subway passenger, listening to someone else sing them and memorizing them, until a calamity suddenly befell her and she ended up on the other side of the valley, only to find that she could recite the whole speech with innate ease? (The finger scratched in Anja's brain: she'd never have to recite these words; she was immunized by wealth. She thought of her parents.)

Because no amount of spare change would matter, and because she was not Louis and could not think of anything more creative to do, Anja decided not to donate today to the society of predictable, memorizable ills. The woman was slowing in front of her anyway, stopping now very close to her; her labored breathing came into focus, her filthy jeans, her sour smell; Anja felt panicked, stared down at her lap . . . *Danke vielen Dank schönen Tag* . . . Anja was being thanked, for some reason, though she had shrunken fully into herself, gutted by the thought of Louis watching her, and yet driven to be even more belligerently un-generous by the same thought. The woman moved on and Anja looked up to see the man next to her arching his body up to slip his wallet back into the pocket of his slacks. He had produced an offering. The muscles of everyone sitting around them seemed to relax; they had been absolved of responsibility for the time being. He'd taken care of it.

Anja looked down and saw that a very small dog was trailing the woman. She smiled at the dog in a way she had not smiled—would never smile—at its owner. If the dog had begged her for something, how easily she would have given it. The dog was white with a light brown spot on its flank and a dark brown spot on the top of its head. The dog and its owner were now stationed in front of the doors at the other end of the car, waiting for them to open, after which the dog would obediently rise and follow its owner out onto the platform and ostensibly repeat this humiliating process again and again into perpetuity. Only maybe it was not humiliat-ing at all, maybe that was an unfair assumption. The dog, for one, was not humiliated. It was as happy with the homeless woman as it would have been running circles in the backyard of the house of the Danish couple on the Berg. The dog loved the owner, was now clinging to the flaccid denim rag that had become of her jeans Keeping in step with her gray Skechers.

Woman and dog exited the train, and at the other end of the car, another pair entered: a homeless man and a pit bull wearing a spiked collar. Anja looked to her left, at the man next to her. Would he give again? Would she? What would Louis do? The eter-nal question: What would Louis do?

Once, while stroking his hair, Anja had said to Louis: "I'm petting you like a dog." He had told her: "No, people pet dogs like they should pet people." Beloved Louis, the funnel through which all the anguish of life leaked. He revealed and then healed through the revelation. He was the only problem and he was the only solution. He was the plague and the pox and the salve and the salvation.

14

POTSDAMER PLATZ WAS BURIED IN SAND DUNES. HEAT LAMPS dangled all the way down from the ceiling on spindly chains, emanating a red glow. The flamboyant spike pointing straight down from the center of the domed arcade seemed more menacing than usual, hardly restrained by the BabyBjörn of steel cables holding it fast to the ceiling. Children were playing and digging around in the sandy mess beneath the spike. The sand was a tossed salad of scattered ticket stubs and jumbo plastic cups and dog shit.

Anja could remember every season having been staged beneath the canopy over time, as if the decorators were reminding people what time of year it was supposed to be. There had been fake snow at one point, with a miniature white Berg for kids to roll down; once, real dried leaves had been imported from somewhere. She'd read that an upscale department store near this same spot had posed similar spectacles in the 1920s, marking all the seasonal holidays with extravagant store-window displays. Online, there were plenty of photos of what the Platz had looked like in Grand Old Europe, before it was completely blasted and then eventually bifurcated and then reconstructed in some ambivalent combination of past references and future imaginaries—the same story repeated everywhere across the city: disintegration, division, reunification, squatting, then sale to Finster and clad in glass, with plaques explaining how the new design referenced the original architecture or paid tribute to the lives lost in one of the disasters on the spot. Every once in a while something would instead be reconstructed exactly as the old photos depicted it—like the Prussian palace the government was erecting in the city center—in order to retain the touch of empire that they believed tourists wanted to experience. But most places ended up something like this commercial arcade at Potsdamer Platz, which had reached its historical terminus in the form of a cluster of chain restaurants and movie theaters huddled under a canopy of lights and wires held taught by a central vertical spike.

Louis loved Potsdamer Platz. Anja half expected to see his blond head poking up from the crowd of tables outside the chain restaurants, his throat reddish from the cold, teasingly vulnerable. The vulnerability planned, but also real.

She forced herself not to look for him. He wouldn't be there, he was working, whatever that meant. He'd been texting her from the studio, enthusiastically planning their "trial run" at a point "very soon." He seemed to think they were on the same track. Or he was trying to skip straight to dessert without eating his vegetables.

Anja bought tickets and 3D glasses for Dam and Laura and the three of them descended into the pit where the twelve theaters lay, deep underground beneath the spike. She and Dam waited in line for popcorn while Laura went to find seats.

"Are you mad I didn't tell you about our apartment?" Dam said, wiping his endlessly running nose on the back of his sleeve. "Don't be mad."

"I'm not mad," Anja said. His sleeve was caked with dried snot. "You should take an allergy pill."

"I knew you were going to be mad. That's why I didn't want to tell you." He sniffed and picked at the edge of his nostril.

"I'm not mad."

"It's not like I want this to be happening. I'm in denial. You know I can't deal with real-life stuff like this."

It was so like him to label himself as someone who could or couldn't or did or didn't do certain things. I'm not a jealous person, he would say, as if that negated his obvious jealousy. I don't drink coffee in the afternoon, he'd say, in order to explain why the coffee he was drinking at three p.m. was a bad idea. He deviated constantly from his list of self-defined traits and behaviors, but no amount of deviation prompted him to change the list. I'm not that type of person, therefore my actions can't be interpreted as such, ergo I'm not that type of person. A tautology of personality. Anja ran this through her head, standing beside him in line. In her teens, before she'd had real friends, she'd imagined that real friendship meant you didn't have an interior monologue running constantly about your friends—but maybe the interior monologue just got more accurate.

They'd reached the front of the line and were expected to in dicate what they wanted to buy for twenty euros. Dam put his arm around her. "Libation of choice?" He pandered to her, speaking her thesaurus words.

"Whatever you want to buy me."

He asked for two big beers and a giant popcorn, which he pushed in her direction. "You need to eat. You've got nothing left to hold on to."

She shrugged. Her stomach acids curdled at the sight of food. She knew she had become even more spindly; she was fine with it. It showed solidarity with the grief Louis was supposed to be experiencing (though she couldn't help noticing he had in fact put on a few kilos) and indicted him for the way he was acting. *I feel his pain* plus *just look at what he's doing to me.*

It occurred to her that Laura might have been wrong. Maybe grief was contagious.

They found Laura in the very middle of the second row of the theater. "You want to give us a stroke?" said Dam. Laura nodded and slipped on her 3D glasses and put her feet up on the seat in front of her.

"Hey D," said Anja once they were deep in the red velvet seats, "can you write some messages for me?"

"There's no signal in here."

"They'll send automatically when we leave."

"Will you forgive me if I do this for you?"

"Yes." She handed him her phone. She hated typing on tiny screens. Her fingers weren't good at it—some innate incompatibility with the object. "Find Howard first." If only she could outsource all communication like this.

"Where . . . Okay, here he is. Howard says: *WHERE ARE YOU.* All caps. A little aggressive, no?"

"Definitely. Write back in all caps. Say: *AT THE MOVIES.* Caps."

"Passive-aggressive. I like it." He typed quickly. "Sent." He raised his voice over the surround sound, which had just picked up, and glanced at the screen. "The trailers are starting."

"Find Louis. He sent me something earlier."

"Here's Louis: *Are we on for Friday? My oval heart beats for you.* Heart emoji."

"Something noncommittal."

"Dolphin?"

"Good."

He pressed send with a flourish. "What else?" He raised his 3D glasses from his nose to get a glimpse of what was happening on-screen.

"Who else wrote me?"

He lowered the glasses to the tip of his nose again. "One from Sara, one from Michel, and one from your dad." He opened the top one. "Sara wants to know: *Wie gehts dir und lou? Lang nichts mehr von euch gehört, alles okay?*" Dam frowned. "Why is this person even messaging you? Are you actually friends with her?"

"Not really. She gets a dolphin too."

"Okay." He glanced at the movie screen, then back down. "Michel wants to know if you'll meet him Monday morning before heading—quote—*into the belly of the beast*—unquote."

"Sure. Yeah, just give a thumbs-up or something."

"Lots of emojis today."

"What did my dad say?"

"Something about the *docteur.*"

"Just say I'll call him later."

"In French?"

"Doesn't matter."

"Okay." He tapped away faster than she ever could have. "That all?"

"For now. Thank you."

"Kiss your secretary on the cheek."

She did, then leaned back into the red faux-velvet seat. Instead of following Dam's gaze toward the logical point of attention at the front of the theater, she stared at his profile, then turned to look at Laura's. The two of them were so alike from this side angle, bookending her. She was safe here between their matching faces—or she had been. Where now? They would always have each other as defaults; she wouldn't have anyone by default without Louis.

She cast about in her mind for a node. The only person she could think of was her sister, which would have been logical except that Eva was such a horrible bitch. Money had ruined her—seeing this was what had polarized Anja into hating and hiding it. While Eva wasted herself, Anja's guilt complex grew until she'd reached total paralysis during the years finishing her master's and then living in the garden house. In that time she'd indulged in the shame of privilege, obsessed herself with growing her own food, recycling, borrowing, trading. Living sustainably for her in those days was a flimsy cover-up. In retrospect it was an embarrassing overcompensation, but the basic premise still held: inherited wealth was inherently unfair, and if she wasn't capable of doing something *good* with it, then she'd better clam up and never spend it, lest she become like Eva. Eva, who was permanently unattached to anything or anyone. Eva, who was possibly unlovable. According to the internet, Eva was in Australia now, learning to surf.

Laura seized the opportunity of the bus ride home to rant about the movie. She wanted to know why anyone would agree to star in an all-white Hollywood movie as a token hot-dumb female character.

"You just wish you looked like her," said Dam, referring to the actress in question.

"No, I don't. I actually don't. It would be such a burden." They were standing on the rubber accordion-like part of the bus that allowed it to bend around corners. All three lurched when the bus made a turn.

"You look great," said Anja. She'd been with Laura to the sauna and to the FKK side of the lake. Laura had a nice shape naked, but her whole sense of style was based around trying to desexualize herself, maybe hiding her body the same way that Anja hid her bank account. Her frizzed-out hair was chopped bluntly into the shape of a triangle around her head. Sometimes she bleached it, then dyed it back; this was as far as she went toward altering her given appearance. It dawned on Anja that Laura hadn't dated anyone, man or woman, in at least a year.

Laura rolled her eyes. "My brother's prettier than me." Dam batted his eyelashes and said something to her in Spanish that Anja didn't catch. Laura turned sharply to Anja. "Don't *you* feel burdened?"

"Me?"

"Come on. You know you're *hot*."

"Stop it."

"No," said Dam, "you can't argue with that. Plus you get extra points for anorexia right now. And you have money. Total package."

"You don't feel objectified, just by being you?" said Laura.

"Of course I do, all women do."

"Isn't it worse for you?"

Anja steadied herself as the bus took another turn. "How would I know? I'm me."

"Don't worry," said Dam kindly. "We love having a hot friend."

"Admit you like it," said Laura.

"Being thin, white, and straight? Yeah, it's great."

"Good. As long as you admit it. Then you're allowed to have problems."

"Tell us your problems," said Dam.

"Yeah, tell us. We have no idea what's going on with you lately."

Anja sighed. The mild attack had been leading up to a display of concern. "I can't tell you anything," she said. "I've signed too many NDAs."

"What was Louis texting you about?" asked Dam. "Something on Friday?"

"He just wants to go out together. Some party."

"So you guys are fine?"

Anja shrugged. She wasn't going to give them the whole story. It wasn't the right time to bring up Oval. Laura would only make fun of it. Dam would want to try it. But mostly she just didn't want to hear herself say the words out loud. *He wants to drug people into kindness. He thinks he's making the ultimate artwork.* It just wouldn't sound so good coming from her mouth. Plus there was still a chance it would blow over. Maybe she'd never have to mention it, until it was just an inside joke receding on the horizon.

dry sahara / scheherazade skies / 35°

She wasn't sleeping well on the sofa. The living room had no curtains and it was always bright and noisy, windows facing the street below. She was up three hours before she had to leave the house on Monday morning, jittery. From the way her jaw felt, she must have been grinding her teeth in her sleep. And she had been sweating; she could smell herself. Stretched out with the blanket bunched near her feet, she recalled being visited in her dream by Hans, her first boyfriend. She hadn't thought of Hans in ages. Hans's memory didn't demand much attention. When she knew him he'd been so eager and unassuming, with that soft-hard becoming-body of late-teenage. They'd been together for two years, long distance for most of the time as she got carted around by her parents, until he left Vienna to do economics at Oxford and they'd eventually lost touch. She saw him online every few months when the algorithm of her feed decided to show him, noted that he was coupled up now with someone equally bland. Beach vacations, a four-bedroom in Notting Hill. Baby? She couldn't remember.

His dream presence had been an affectionate one, not exactly sexual, just physically reassuring. Arms around arms: you're safe. She felt a minor thrill from dreaming about someone who was not Louis, but then her face got hot as she imagined Louis dreaming about someone else too, how he looked at other women sometimes, how he might describe her to Prinz . . . This could go on and on, so she launched herself off the sofa and across the room to the cabinet where Dam's rotating circus of bottles was kept, letting her hand roam around and find something to disinfect her thoughts. She'd be sober enough again by the time she had to leave the house at nine a.m.

Michel was waiting for her outside RANDI in the shade under the lone tree on the block. They were both tense, which made them embarrassed. Michel also seemed to have retreated inside his own brain, thinking hard, working through something.

Anja held out the folder of nonsense information they'd both received.

"Forgot mine," he said.

"Great. Now I look too enthusiastic."

Instead of taking the elevator down to the subterranean levels of labs as usual, they headed up to the fourth floor. An intern showed them down the hall. On the way Anja noticed a tall, thin plinth in a corner of the reception room with a tiny head mounted inside the glass case on top. She hadn't seen one of those in a long time.

The intern led them into a conference room, which had two treadmill desks pushed against one wall and a giant screen mounted on the other.

"Don't worry, you don't have to work out during your

presentation," the intern said, gesturing to the treadmills with a smile. "I'll grab you some chairs."

She left the room and Anja raised her eyebrows high at Michel. "Our presentation?" she mouthed. The intern returned with two brown metal folding chairs banging together in her arms and handed one to each of them.

Anja touched the woman lightly on the arm when she turned to leave. "What did you mean about the treadmills?"

The intern laughed. "Oh, you really don't have to use them. No one does. They've been sitting there forever."

"But you said we didn't have to use them during our presentation. We thought we were supposed to be getting a presentation, not giving one."

The intern frowned, pulled out her phone from a back pocket, then flipped it around to show Anja the meeting label: *new consultants x2 innovation pres.* "I just assumed you were the one doing the *pres*," she said. "Must be my mistake." She looked them over without attempting to hide the appraisal. "You guys are new?"

"Not really, we've been at RANDI for like—a few years?"

"Oh?"

Michel nodded and Anja pointed down to the basement. "Biodegradables. Then Cartilage."

"Ah." She nodded slowly. "Gotcha. You're the ones." As she left she said over her shoulder, "Welcome upstairs."

They set up their folding chairs in the empty center of the room, facing each other awkwardly at a 45-degree angle, as if around an invisible table. Before sitting down, Michel took off his brown suede jacket. Underneath was a gray turtleneck, probably cashmere. Slim-fitting, dark-wash jeans. Clean black Adidas. He dressed like men in other cities—real cities—men who commuted to work in cars, men who were on the market for marriage and reproduction. He dressed like an adult. Timeless, or something. She pictured herself sitting beside him. They didn't match at all.

"Seems like they should put some other furniture in here if they don't use the treadmills anymore," said Michel, leaning forward in the empty space and resting his elbows on his knees.

They were left alone for fifteen minutes, long enough to make Anja nervous. She was considering getting up to look for the intern again when two white guys finally sauntered in. Both of them were wearing different washes of low-slung jeans with white Calvin waistbands rising up beneath, blazers, branded T-shirts, and some kind of advanced high-tops. One had a string of prayer beads circling his wrist. The other had a tattoo of a lion peeping up from his shirt collar.

She shuddered: Mitte. Germans who clumsily aspired to look like Americans. Germans who picked and replicated with absurd precision the cultural markers they wanted to appropriate, without understanding that some of those signifiers were politically charged and therefore unsuitable for random adoption and recombination. And Eva always asked why Anja tried so hard to act American. Because this was what you got when you fell short of the mark.

(On the other hand, she reminded herself, Americans invariably did the same thing when they got to Berlin. In a matter of weeks they decorated themselves indiscriminately with whatever cultural ornaments appealed to them—blue construction-worker coveralls, Soviet-era furs, East German leftovers from paisley polyester to fake Levi's. Even Louis listened to Turkish rap.)

Michel was grinning at Prayer Beads and Lion Tattoo, clearly thinking something similar. They were carrying brown folding chairs under their arms, which they set up ceremoniously, angling them to complete the square at the center of the room, before introducing themselves.

"Daniel, pleasure," the one with the tattoo said, smiling in a practiced way. He leaned in to shake her hand and she was struck by the perfection of the little brown mustache sculpted above his chapsticked lips, which were parted to reveal a row of gleaming teeth as staged and unified under a common cause as the characters in a Nativity scene. Anja preferred Louis's slightly curved and pointed incisors, but she could appreciate a religious set like his. What she couldn't appreciate was that four teeth in Daniel's bottom row were gold.

They were face-to-face, it seemed, with Finster's middle management.

"So!" announced Daniel, after introducing his colleague—she didn't catch the other's name, momentarily mesmerized by Daniel's mouth region—"Srilled to haffe you on poard." He slapped his thighs to transmit enthusiasm, and Michel barked out a laugh, which he tried to cover up by slapping his thighs in return.

"We are also thrilled," said Michel, straining against his own smile. Anja glared at him and felt her armpits prickle with sweat. She adjusted herself in the chair, which creaked softly.

"Deutsch?" she asked. There was no way Michel was going to survive more than five minutes with Daniel and his Bavarian accent.

Daniel mechanically shook his head, pointing at the ceiling. "Monitoring is *auf Englisch*." Anja nodded. No reason to think it would be any different up here than in the labs. Language policing was probably more intense the higher up you were.

Michel smiled more widely. "No problem."

"Gut! So. Down to pissness. We are looking forfard to what

you can contripute. Innoffasion levels are down across the poard this quarter and we are in need of fresh perspectiffs."

"Yes, thank you for this opportunity," said Anja. She had resolved not to argue until she had the chance to sniff around the lab and see what she could find out about her own firing. There was no option, really—Howard hadn't delivered on his partial promise of finding her another lab position—and she wasn't going to go jobless. She knew she could have spent the last week searching for new jobs in other labs, but she'd spent it wallowing, drinking, and watching reality shows. And now she was here, a consultant being consulted. It was apparent that she and Michel were expected to say something, to justify their presence in a cursory way, even though they had never asked for these unjustifiable positions.

"Will you need a screen?" Daniel nodded to the end of the room, which was sheeted with an enormous LCD screen.

"Actually," said Anja, smiling, "what Michel was going to say is that we haven't prepared anything formal for today. That's because we don't—we don't believe in a formulaic approach with quantitative measurement when it comes to things like . . . innovation. We aren't into special effects, or what you may call quantitative devices. We don't believe it's appropriate to apply numbers to human dynamics . . ."

"Or really to help in any quantitative way at all," said Michel.

Anja cleared her throat. "He means we're into *quality*, not quantity. Interpersonal interactions are at the core of our—of our innovation management philosophy. So our way of working is, we need to get a . . . lay of the land first, to understand how people work, and what they need . . ." She cast about for some Basquiatt formula phrases she'd heard Louis regurgitate at the dinner table. "We do problem solving according to projected future problems instead of existing problems. We have to find and foresee the problems before they exist." Michel snorted. "That's what innovation is, anticipation of future . . . things. Futurities, futurations that haven't happened yet."

She watched Daniel's expression carefully. Louis had a theory about the importance of first impressions that she wasn't sure she believed, but that she did feel superstitious about. He said first impressions could never be rewritten or pasted over, no matter how many years went by. You'd always be that first projection, an indelible mark on the other person's subconscious. To trust or not to trust.

Daniel squinted at her. "Exactly," he said after a long moment. "Innoffation is a *time machine*."

Anja opened her mouth to conjure more managementese, but before she could get a word out Daniel raised a finger in the air and stared directly at her. "In sat case, what ancient zone will you pe inspecting first?"

She responded without looking at Michel. "Downstairs. Progress starts from the bottom up."

O, the heavens cry! *SHOWERS WITH A CHANCE OF BATH*

She smelled him before she saw him, but didn't trust the first sense until it was corroborated by the second. She swiveled to affirm his presence. Howard didn't belong in the lab. He never came belowground. And yet there he was, sight agreed, in the doorway, his face etched in fluorescent light.

"I thought you'd been let loose from the lab," he said. He wasn't smiling. "Yet here you are."

She'd been scrolling on her phone, trying to find a picture of

Daniel with the gold teeth. Michel was at the desk next to her, purportedly doing research. Both of their faces were red from laughing—for the last few days they'd been cracking up like kids in the back of class. All they had to do was look at each other and repeat a bit from the meeting—innovation, time machine—and it was over.

Anja straightened her face. "Howard, have you met Michel?" Howard nodded. Michel nodded back.

"Oh yes," said Howard. "I sit in on the annual performance reviews." There was a dead beat.

"Well, welcome to where the magic happens," said Michel, stupidly.

Howard made his face agreeable. "What sort of magic are you doing, then?"

"We're just sussing out the situation in the lower levels," Anja said. "We're sussing out the human resource performance, the workflow amenities, you know. Whatever our contracts say we're doing."

"Progress starts with our bottoms up," said Michel, glancing at Anja to see if she'd crack a laugh.

"I see," said Howard. "And where are all the other human resources you purport to study?"

"Around. Or at lunch?" said Michel. "It's hard to keep track of everything, being so new at this side of the job. It would help if we had some interns."

"You'd probably have to fill out a request form for that. Explaining what you're doing and what you need them for. What's your end goal this month, Michel?" Howard's eyes were fixed on Anja, who was checking her phone.

Michel raised his tablet, displaying an image search result for UGGs. "Isometric analysis of lower-limb effects on productivity. That's my project this month."

Anja looked up. "He means he's trying to justify open-toed shoes in the lab."

Michel nodded solemnly. "So far the data's on my side."

"Sounds like a wonderful use of your time," said Howard. "I hate to interrupt." He inclined his head slightly and gestured at Anja to follow him.

In the hall he handed her a brown bag. "I thought you might want some lunch," he said. She looked inside. Sushi. "It was meant to be a peace offering. But maybe it just makes me seem parental."

"No—it's nice. Thanks."

"You need to eat." He moved his eyes around her midsection. Was there anyone who didn't feel fit to comment on her weight loss? Was this what it would be like to be pregnant, people constantly asking about your body, reaching out to touch your stomach, gauging your degree of expansion? "Along the lines of parenting, though, you definitely don't need to be working with *that* kid." He jerked his head in Michel's direction. "Let's see you get your own team, yeah?"

She shook her head. "No, thanks. I'm fine where I am."

"He seems pretty immature."

"He's fine. But you know the guys who work up there, in the middle? Daniel and the other guy?"

He laughed. "Maybe you finally appreciate my being the go-between, huh? Now you see what it looks like in there."

"You're right. You're the lesser evil." He shrugged, assenting. "Are you here to hassle me more about the Best Western?"

"No, not today. As long as you're fine and safe and have somewhere to sleep. You're busy, Louis is busy, you're both fine. I overreacted."

An admission that he'd contacted Louis. Now was the moment to ask him point-blank about the email she'd seen on

Louis's tablet. *Feedback*. Now was the time. She opened her mouth and closed it again, like a fish at the edge of the tank. But any question about it would be an admission that she didn't know everything already. Having Howard think she knew what he and Louis were talking about was more important to her than actually knowing it.

"By the way," he said before leaving, "tell your friend the footwear study's already been done. O'Reilly, like five years ago. Conclusively against open-toe. Look it up."

15

HEAD HELD HIGH, CHIN TILTED BACK, CREAMY CHIFFON GOWN parted at the knee, lovely lower leg exposed and foot delicately resting upon on a wedge of hay, Snow White gestured toward the ninety-nine glass cylinders pendulating on chains from the ceiling of the brutalist church. Inside each transparent cylinder burned a small blue flame. Anja thought of Potsdamer Platz.

Snow White opened his mouth. "These handmade, 3D-printed un-icons represent the spirits of the ninety-nine O'Reilly ambassadors living around the world."

His voice echoed in the darkened cavern of fossilized architecture. Not so long ago, the church had housed a traditional commercial gallery that hosted rotating exhibitions of sellable objects. One month they'd be made of cloth and paint, the next rocks or video monitors or flashing lights. Sometimes all the objects were made by one person and other times there was a jumble of contributions from different artists, united by a theme. The reason the particular selection of objects had been chosen was always explained in a press release printed on an A4 sheet at the front desk, like a menu at the entrance to a buffet. Next to the press release, there would be another sheet with CVs of the artist or artists whose work was on display, so visitors could guess how old and famous they were and how much the items on offer were likely worth.

Things got sold, but it was understood that the buyers were buying into the artist's whole brand via the object. The object stood in for something: a share of the artist's sum total life's worth. The object was a token for speculation on that life's worth. Over time, the objects had begun to seem more and more incidental to that speculation. Sponsors realized that using artists as object-makers was a waste of resources. The artists' true value was their proximity to the vanguard, that is, the future, that is, the next niche for market expansion. A corporate lobby may have been full of art objects, but management realized it needed *artists* inside the building to keep a finger on the pulse.

Most of the artists Anja had met had made their real money working for companies—even way back before most of the commercial galleries had transitioned into venues for product launches and release parties and initial coin offerings. It wasn't that objects didn't still show up at these events; sometimes they would decorate the launch, or even constitute the launch. But those objects were not for sale. They were a priori the property of the company or the investors who had invested in the artist. The investor providing the artist's tenure was logically the owner of anything made during the time period. Having a tenure was infinitely more stable for most artists than object-by-object sale had ever been.

If there was a formal device signaling continuity between the old and the new systems (which weren't really so different, Anja thought), it was the press release. The press release was ever-present; you still needed an explanation for what was going on. Anja had one explaining the meaning of Snow White's current actions folded in her purse.

Snow White's voice was being amplified through a tiny flesh-colored microphone Anja could see taped to his face. The flesh tone of the microphone was several shades lighter than Snow White's skin, which, according to the press statement, was meant as a critique of the racialized standards of the beauty industry at large. Snow White's self-proclaimed role as O'Reilly consultant—ambassador, as they called it—was to overturn those standards by bringing *diversity* into the mix.

"Set free from the brittle shells of their physical bodies," he went on, chanting, "their spirits are able to finally transcend the vanity inherent in the cosmetic industry that they are struggling to change from within."

Anja lifted up on her toes and craned her neck around, searching the crowd of faces in the audience for Michel, who was supposed to be meeting her there. She'd pressured him to come, convincing him it would be a perfect opportunity for footwear research—all the O'Reilly higher-ups would be congregated there, undoubtedly wearing shoes of some kind. She had felt a desperate need to go to Andy's performance, probably to prove to herself and the world that she could go anywhere she wanted without Louis leading the way—but she was definitely not capable of going alone.

A low hum started to build up in the room. Andy's voice rising, incantatory.

"The butane powering the flames corresponds to the portion of the world's fossil fuels that each of us will consume over the course of our time on this dying planet! The flames will die at the end of the night, but O'Reilly's commitment to sustainable practices will live on . . ." The sound of a gong struck somewhere in the room. Andy took a deep breath. "In my last hours as a part of this forward-thinking family, who has over the last four years embraced my incisive critique of its practices—leading to the recent expansion of its sustainable market worldwide, particularly in Southeast Asia—I have chosen to honor not the products but the true soul of the company, the human souls who have the power to change the course of history through consumer revolution . . ."

She spotted Prinz across the room. Prinz was mouthing the words along with Andy. Her stomach flipped, eyes darting around the room—but of course Louis wasn't with him. He was in the lab. He'd told her that. He had been messaging her daily with little updates, still trying to plan their trial run. She'd been feigning enthusiasm while putting him off. She assured herself that she'd somehow feel his presence if he showed up in the room. She scratched at her cheek with a fingernail.

The gong struck again and a raging fire appeared on a huge screen behind Andy. Red words written in Comic Sans began to scroll slowly down over the flames. Snow White whispered the words in time, turning over his shoulder only once to check whether he was on-tempo.

> the water of my
> race
> walks with O'Reilly soft touch absorbent
> infallible
> pro-aging
> bamboo follicles
> who will inherit
> the earth

misty plum

[Gong noise]

when your hair is on,

you're on

fire

After a final series of gongs the flames died down and snow
started to fall on the screen. A trio of products appeared in the
foreground on-screen: bottle, pump, tube. The product image was
about three meters tall, completely dwarfing Andy. The products
had matching pale yellow lids and images of Andy's face on the la-
bels: at this scale, quadruple the size of his actual face. The writing
on the products was in Korean.

Andy raised his hand in an elegant arc, and he announced the
name of the line: *Snow Yellow.*

Applause. A bubbling from the crowd, a surge, a press forward. An aging O'Reilly executive moved in from the sidelines
to shake Andy's hand and say some words. The noise in the room
diminished to a pinging of whispers while he spoke. No one was
listening to the formalities.

"Ha!" Loudly, in Anja's ear. "Ha!"

She turned. "There you are."

"I've been here the whole time, unfortunately," said Michel.
He was speaking above normal volume, audible to those surrounding. "What the fuck is this? I can't tell if the whole thing is
a huge joke."

She took him by the elbow, using his arm like a rudder, and
navigated them to a corner of the room.

"Of course it's a joke," she said, once they were sheltered
against the chilly stone wall of the onetime sanctuary. The black

stone was slick, moist. "You think 'Snow Yellow' would be an accident?"

"No one's laughing."

"It's not meant—" She sighed. "It's funny to us, but not meant to be funny to O'Reilly. The joke's on them."

"You honestly think they don't get the joke?"

"Of course they do, but they pretend not to, which is an even bigger joke. And Andy's pretending he doesn't know they're pretending. And that just makes it an even bigger joke. And on and on forever in an endless loop."

"You think everyone knows this is ridiculous, but no one calls anyone's bluff?"

"This way both sides get to feel superior." She shrugged. "That's how consulting works. Each side thinks the other one is the chump."

He paused, as if attempting to apply this template to their own current situation, then nodded, finding a positive match. "But this particular joke is also racist," he said. "Isn't it?"

"Hush," she said, scanning the faces around them. The congratulatory speech was wrapping up at the front of the room. As soon as the spectacle was over, the audience would group into huddles to snicker and critique in ways they thought were incisive but were actually superfluous ("the cylinders looked really good, but the screen was over the top"; "kind of self-indulgent, right?").

This was gossip, not critique. Prinz, for instance, whose gleaming face she could see through the bobbing heads around her, fed on such gossip like a larva absorbing feed—gorging on it as fuel for reinforcement of his own subject position, metabolically churning dissent into self-righteousness. How many times had she listened to Louis and Prinz debating some performance like this one, Louis articulating critique after critique (he got away with criticism, because he could make it *sound* like gossip, rather than the other way around) and Prinz gleefully blanketing it all in statements like "you have to *problematize* situations *further* to resolve them," or "you have to go *through*, not around the problem," or "you have to *offend* to liberate." In group situations, though, Louis would effortlessly switch sides—he'd defend Prinz by taking the weak arguments Prinz had been gesturing toward and articulate them in compelling ways.

That was Louis's peculiar genius, the genius of being on both sides at once. If he were here, he'd whisper one thing in her ear, a criticism not so far from what Michel was saying, but at dinner afterward he'd defend, defend. He took neither side seriously enough to truly advocate for it; the fact that he could make arguments for both sound equally compelling was the ultimate critique. The critique was that there were no political stakes in this type of argument at all.

She shook Louis from her thoughts, physically shaking her head like a Christmas tree losing its dead needles. "Of course it's racist," she said quietly to Michel. "But it's meant as a *critique* of racism, ergo it's not really racist. Or so the thinking goes."

"So if this is all a provocative joke, they aren't actually going to sell these offensive products."

"No, of course they'll sell the products. Not here, though. This is the concept launch. The products will probably go to stores six months from now, in Korea, I'm guessing. Andy's job is just to invent the concept."

Michel groaned. "I can't believe you got me to come to this."

Everyone said that all the time, but Michel was the only person she knew who didn't abuse himself by constantly attending anyway. He was fine not being part of the living, squirming mass; he didn't need to reaffirm himself through proximity to the status quo.

"Why don't you infiltrate the crowd and survey the footwear," she suggested, feeling his negativity radiating from their conversation out into the room.

"I don't know if I can even get close to the O'Reilly people. It's packed in here."

The crowd had begun applauding once more. An enormous amoeba with a thousand wiggling nuclei. Anja had often wondered who the real nucleus of the social scene was, the truly central person who anchored the existence of the blob and kept it internally churning, gave it the life-energy it needed to continue partying and gossiping and having sex with itself and doing drugs into infinity.

Who was the person without whom this crowd simply could not function? Where was its center of gravity, and then where was its outer limit, the membrane?

The center was elusive, almost impossible to identify, but Anja had always been sure it was there. There was an internal logic to the social order, its mechanisms so predictable that there had to be a single actor policing its behavior.

Or maybe, she thought now, observing the shuffle, this was actually a self-regulating organism with distributed, not centralized, intelligence, its logic irreducible to any of its constituent parts. A tensile, redundant mesh network of glances, text messages, sweat droplets, GIFs, jokes, nonjokes, payments, diseases, repulsions, attractions; from afar, everyone looked to be moving in concert, although as individuals they maintained the belief that their behavior was autonomous. Free will.

This night would organically follow the same pattern as every other night:

Performance finishes. Friends of performer push to the front of the crowd to make themselves known. Friends take their places beside performer and turn around, ready to receive congratulations on behalf of performer—adjacency to fame is falsely presumed equivalent to fame. Performer selects friends who will be invited to the Dinner after the event. When the first Dinner guest (Guest Zero) has been appointed, the others will rearrange themselves in proximity to Guest Zero, although Guest Zero may or may not have the ability to actually confer the invitation further—like fame, invitations are falsely presumed contagious.

As invitations are slowly bestowed down the pageant line, the mass continues to jumble itself until a silent call is sent through to the invitees, like an electric zap only they can feel: *The cars for the Dinner are leaving! Say your goodbyes!*

The invitees politely and/or condescendingly disengage from their sorry companions, casually mentioning "a dinner," which everyone knows to be the Dinner, making promises to meet up later, kissing, kissing, then slipping off. The event is left without its lifeblood; the people who own the venue may even be gone; only the interns are left tending to the evaporating crowd. Without a Dinner the aspirational possibilities are temporarily curbed—until the wasted, makeup-smeared regrouping later at the bar or the club, when the hosts and guests of the Dinner will once again mingle with the uninvited. And so, for the time being, the people left over separate into their home groups, their friend alliances, in order to plan their own feeding—because food is going to be necessary at some point if the second, late-night round of opportunism is going to be possible—and certain friend modules will try to sync up with others, extending alliances for the evening ("us three and you four"), which necessitates excluding others ("there isn't room in the car, so sorry"), creating makeshift hierarchies where the major, substructural one has vanished. The amoeba always keeps its shape.

"Where is everyone going?" said Michel. The sifting process had begun.

"To the front of the room. To congratulate Andy. To the Dinner, eventually."

"Who's Andy?"

"Snow White—Yellow."

"You know this guy?"

The typical pride of proximity didn't strike. The link wasn't hers in the first place, really—it was Louis who was friends with Andy—and in Michel's presence—Michel, who was vaccinated against the anxieties of social life—claiming proximity now seemed sort of pathetic.

She pointed to someone she thought worked in press at O'Reilly. "Now's your chance. Eyes on the ground. But don't leave without me."

He vaulted himself into the fray, and she was left alone, unattached and exposed. It wasn't more than thirty seconds until Sara appeared and sucked onto her side. Sascha wasn't with her like usual, but then Sara functioned fine on her own, being the dominant gene as opposed to the recessive. Who knew how the two of them together maintained a delusion that they were social equals? (Or did functional relationships really require a pretense of equality?)

They kissed cheeks, and Sara squeezed Anja's shoulders warmly in what was meant to be interpreted as a gesture of intimacy, looking into her eyes and transmitting empathy. Sara knew about what was going on with Anja, the squeeze said. Sara knew the agony of male rejection and so she knew every ounce of Anja's sadness better than Anja even knew it herself. There was solidarity in the gesture—but there was also condescension. Your pain, my pain, banal pain.

Still, the faux intimacy felt real in the moment, and in spite of herself, Anja warmed to the touch.

"Things are going way better with Mahatma." Sara looked meaningfully across the room to convey that Mahatma was present, at this very moment, suggesting that in fact they had *arrived together as a couple*. "I think we're dating."

Anja wondered how many other people Sara would tell this "secret" to tonight, effortlessly drawing them closer to her. It occurred to her that faux closeness worked because it made you realize how starved you were for actual closeness.

"It's nothing official yet," said Sara. "We're just hanging out again." She looked again across the room. Eye contact was a scarce commodity in this place. Anja glanced back to follow Sara's gaze, spotting Mahatma, standing beside Sascha, who was present after all. Sascha and Mahatma were leaning into each other, giggling, exchanging a single beer and cigarette back and forth. Flirting in the most ostentatious way.

Anja tried to pity Sara, whose entire world was made of unstable alliances. Then she recalled all the minor slights Sara had directed at her over the years. Sara would forever be passing the stings she received from her so-called friends on to the next person down. Through repeated subjugation the victim becomes the victimizer.

"Everything changed after last week at the Baron," Sara said, apparently unperturbed by the sight of best friend and target boyfriend engaged in flirtations.

"Oh?"

"Lou didn't tell you?" Sara feigned surprise.

Anja's face got warm, her body chemistry reacting to the

thought—Louis, doing things she didn't know about—Louis, not telling her things—Louis, *Lou*. She rearranged her face into a dumb smile. She wished the protective shadow of social confidence would appear over her face, but it wasn't coming. She was far too raw, too exposed.

"That's so weird," Sara said, shaking her head. "I guess I asked him not to tell people about me and Mahatma yet, but I assumed he'd tell *you*." She waited for a reaction from Anja, who didn't provide it. "Are things going okay between you?" she prompted, clearly knowing the answer. That's what the shoulder squeeze had been about, hadn't it? Then why was she pretending she didn't already know?

"Um," said Anja, unsure how to give the illusion of candidness without transmitting any real information. "No, I mean, he's living at the studio right now, so."

Sara was all sympathy. "I know he's been struggling, it's so obvious. But I just so hope you guys can work it out. You're the perfect couple. If there's ever anything I can do."

"Thanks," Anja whispered.

"He needs us all to support him right now. You can't blame him for whatever he's going through. And some things are more important than *us*, you know?"

Ah, the blame. Anja locked her lips into the thin line of a nonsmile.

"He told us you came up with the name for Oval though," Sara said. "That's cool."

Anja fidgeted. Heat spread from her face to her body. She squeezed her arms to her side, worried about pit stains. She swallowed this information carefully. He'd already let it leak. This was so far beyond the pale—so reckless. And without her there. "You guys tried it," she said.

"Definitely. But for some reason Lou still won't try it himself."

After she'd put him off for more than a week—dolphins, monkeys, thumbs-up signs—he was still waiting. That counted for something. That justified this period of bizarre estrangement. She swallowed. "How was it?"

"Totally amazing. A total game changer." She pressed her palms forward in the air, fingers spread wide, as if waiting for a double high five.

"Is that when Mahatma—?"

Sara nodded and lowered her hands.

Of course, thought Anja. So many relationships functioned like transactions already. Oval would simply make those transactions more generous. It would feel a lot like love—at least for a few hours.

"It's like we finally get each other," Sara said. "I mean, he's still a guy," she added, looking over Anja's shoulder again. "They always check in and out when they feel like it. They trap you in this role of waiting for them . . ." Anja nodded uneasily. "But when they come back, you can't keep them out, because you've already wasted so much time waiting."

Anja glanced around them, wondering if anyone was close enough to be listening. Groups were clumping together and others were starting to leave, which meant she had better sight lines across the room. She scanned for Prinz—anyone else she knew and might latch on to. She was surprised to find Michel suddenly at her side again.

"Hey," he said. "No dice with the shoes. They're all wearing Moon Boots."

"This is Michel," Anja said to Sara. Michel and Sara exchanged cheek kisses.

"We were just talking about the performance," said Sara,

instantly switching gears, as if nothing had passed between her and Anja. "What did *you* think?" she asked Michel, smiling.

"You mean that racist shit we just saw?"

Sara raised her eyebrows, signaling that this was out-of-bounds. Only sanctioned critiques, please. "Racist? How so?"

"Snow Yellow?"

"I'm pretty sure it's a comment on racism, it's not *doing* racism."

"What's the difference?"

"Um, it's sort of an interrogation into . . . I don't know, notions of authenticity in the Western world. Like gestural marks that are meant to—maybe—provide like, a feedback loop into network ecologies of beauties, and like, other ways of interaction conceived as data flows?"

Michel looked at her incredulously and laughed. "Who has done this terrible thing to your speech?"

"Excuse me?"

"It's like you've memorized the press release and are trying to make it sound like it's spontaneously coming out of your mouth."

"Um."

"Or are you just recombining random phrases from thousands of press releases you've read?"

Sara narrowed her eyes at Anja instead of Michel. Anja had brought this uncouth animal into her range.

Michel persisted. "Seriously, where do you get this stuff?"

Normally Anja would have shifted visibly away from Michel, signaling a distance, but instead she found herself laughing. Michel joined in and the giggling fit that had possessed them at the lab lately took hold again. She shrugged helplessly at Sara.

"I'll leave you guys to it," said Sara. "I have to get to this dinner now anyway."

Sara made the type of abrupt exit that Laura was always complaining about: a demonstration of dominance in the conversation by simply choosing arbitrarily when to end it. "The minute you try to start an actual conversation they literally run away from you," Laura would say. "The whole goal of going out for these people is to rack up goodbyes."

"I can't take you anywhere," Anja said to Michel once they were standing outside, still laughing. "You just pee on the carpet."

"I don't want to be taken anywhere. These people are gremlins. I can't believe you hang out with them."

She cast her eyes downward and stopped laughing. "They're more Louis's friends than mine."

"I see." He walked to the edge of the curb to wave down a taxi. The street was crowded with cars and people, which made it difficult to hail one. "Where is this Louis, anyway?"

Michel had never met Louis. He'd never met anyone, really. This was the closest they'd come to doing something together unrelated to work.

"I don't know where he is." She wasn't sure how to explain any of it, and she wasn't going to try. "Things are kind of amphibious lately."

She had never confided in Michel about her relationship, but it dawned on her that he wasn't exactly unobservant. He had seen her obsessively checking her phone for messages, had heard her complain about her current sleeping arrangement on the sofa of her friends' house, had eaten the leftovers of the muffins that she only picked at sorrowfully. She could assume he'd pieced things together. If nothing else, he must have noticed how much time she was spending with him, and how little with Louis.

He opened the door and shooed her into the cab before him. "Let's drop you off first," he said. She gave the driver Laura and Dam's address.

"So you're half in the water, half out," he said, once they had seat-belted themselves.

"Something like that."

"If the water is full of things like whatever we just watched, with the people we just watched it with, for the record, I think you can do better."

She folded her hands tightly together in her lap. "Why are you in such a bad mood?"

"I asked one O'Reilly guy what the deal was with his Moon Boots, and he told me they're the only footwear to have been proven to enhance not only productivity but authenticity in the workplace. Fucking *Moon Boots*."

"Authenticity?"

"Authenticity! Moon Boots!" He tapped the side of his head against the window in anger. "I don't give a shit about any of this! I'm doing pretend field research at a racist product launch. I miss my lab coat and my antisocial routine."

"Me too. I miss empiricism."

"I miss cartilage." He leaned forward to see what street they were turning down, and when he sat back he said, "Fine. I'm convinced."

"Of Moon Boots?"

"No. Of what you said."

"What did I say?"

"Let's do the experiment."

It took her a moment to register what he was talking about. She'd scrubbed the idea from her mind. "Seriously?"

"Yeah, fuck it. To split the difference is to side with the oppressor."

"What does that mean?"

"It means I don't want to be a consultant anyway. I don't care if we get fired."

16

"IF YOU REALLY WANTED TO BE POPULAR, ALL YOU'D HAVE TO do is devote all your time to hanging out."

Laura reminded Anja of this whenever Anja was feeling insecure about her social shortcomings. "If you went to every party," she'd say, "you'd be invited to every party. All they want is proof of your dedication."

Anja knew this was true, but she still couldn't help but blame her ongoing feelings of social alienation on her inadequacy. She knew what *not* to do at an opening, at a club—she could recognize it when she saw it, e.g., Michel—but she didn't know what to actually do. There was a roof on the acceptable conversation topics that felt so low it wasn't worth standing up. She was perpetually nervous in crowds. Her inner monologue didn't slow down. She got exhausted, even ill, after more than one long night out in a row. Those long stretches required a particular kind of endurance she just didn't have.

"You can't just go to parties," she'd protest to Laura, "you have to know what to do when you get there."

"Going out is not a skill. Literally anyone can stand around and take drugs."

"I get sick if I do too many drugs."

"Why do them at all, then?"

"Nobody can dance for ten hours sober."

"Then go home after two hours."

"Then you're the person who always goes home early."

Sometimes Laura would shrug her off by muttering "first world problems," and Anja would back off. But more often, Laura indulged her. Anja understood the conversations could become pitiful, even harassing, but she also knew that they were polarizing each other to work something out that bothered them both. The question at the base of it was: Why do we willingly submit ourselves to social defeat at the hands of those we don't respect? Why do we play a game with such idiotic rules?

This was mainly posed as a question for Anja to answer, but over time she came to realize that it was also relevant, in a different way, to Laura. Why else would Laura engage in these circular arguments at all?

Laura also cared what people thought. She cared so much that she hated everybody. Hating everybody worked for her—it covered up the fear. She performed the hatred online, where several thousand followers could enjoy her rants. This way of relating to the world suited her. "You're so *of the moment*," Dam would say, reading her feed over her shoulder and sarcastically reciting her posts out loud.

As for going out into the world of physical bodies, Laura did it mostly within a safe sphere of gay men. She'd infiltrated and eventually pirated Dam's nightlife to make it her own. As a bonus, gay guys constituted the demographic most likely to follow reality TV, and so she had an endless mine of content to discuss with them— this relieved the anxiety of inventing topics, of finding common ground, that so plagued Anja.

"Just repeat gossip," Laura said. "Nobody invents content at parties, they just repeat it."

And yet they were both in need of content. (Louis, it seemed, was able to find content everywhere. Here was the main jealousy Anja felt in their relationship: that Louis could find content in a social world that she found barren. It energized him; he needed it.)

"It's a waste of time," said Laura of partying. "You have better things to do."

I do? Anja thought. Am I "above" partying? Am I fulfilled by my work? Do I hold a vestige of the belief in the goodness of *work*?

People who spent all their time out there—people like Prinz— could no longer even draw a distinction between productive and unproductive time. The act of partying had become an act of production: they were producing relations—relations as objects. And objects as opportunities. Content was subordinate.

To liberate herself from the pull of opportunity, she'd worn her career as a jacket of legitimacy: the Real Job jacket. *A scientist, really? Wow, sounds intense.* She had a real place to be on Monday morning. It was all she could use to justify a life not governed by late-night invitations; it was all she could use to prove to herself— to Louis—that she wasn't a social animal because she had more important things to do, not because she was incapable. And now? The excuse of the Real Job was gone. She was exposed.

When Anja got home from Snow White's performance, exhausted, Laura was waiting for her at the kitchen table, scrolling her feeds, poised to listen to Anja's recap.

Anja sat on the floor at Laura's feet. She leaned against her legs.

"Bad night out?" said Laura, squeezing the sides of Anja's head with her shinbones.

"Not great."

"Whose fault?"

"Women's. And men's."

Laura laughed, and then Anja sighed and opened the valve she had been keeping shut. She'd barely lasted a week without spilling. There was no point in keeping quiet. Oval was apparently in the world. Laura would find out soon enough.

But instead of starting with Oval, she found herself starting with Sara. She could only seem to explain things through the lens of Sara's meddling—it was the only thing that made sense. It didn't make any sense for Louis to be estranging himself on behalf of a newfound rainbow of idealism—the estrangement had to be blamed on someone, and Sara had offered herself.

Anja didn't seriously think anything was actually going on between Louis and Sara. This was highly unlikely. Sara had only tried to incite jealousy on the social level, not the sexual. Nonetheless, Anja found herself describing the conversation as if some genuine infidelity had happened.

"Thank god," Laura said when she'd finished. "You're articulate again."

"What?"

"You've been clammed up for weeks. We haven't gotten a true word out of you."

"What's a 'true' word?"

"We count on you to speak the truth. You always point north. Lately not so much."

Laura was speaking in the plural, which meant that she had talked about this with Dam. "You mean I'm usually more needy," said Anja.

"That's a very sober, truthful way to think about it. See, you can't help but be honest."

If truth was her territory, which she had not supposed

until that moment, then Laura was right that she had been skirting it.

"I don't want to tell you the truth, because I don't want you to get sick of me," Anja confessed. "I'm always complaining."

"Everything in the world is terrible. You're not going to blow our minds by saying that. And we're not going to kick you out of the house for being depressed."

"I'm not depressed!"

"I'm not blaming you for it. Depression is structural at this point."

"You think everything's structural."

"Everything *is* structural. Even or especially this Sara situation. The two of you are just following the script."

"What script?"

"The script. You know. I've seen it on like every season of *The Bachelor*."

"Go on."

Laura clapped her hands together loudly. "Fine. So." She clapped again. "Straight couple goes through relationship difficulties that become publicly obvious. Close female friend of couple plays both sides, absorbing the complaints of both and sympathizing. While she's doing face masks, watching movies, and bringing tissues to the girlfriend, she's partying and acting like the cool girl with her friend's estranged boyfriend. Basically massaging the suffering of the girlfriend while flattering the boyfriend into thinking he doesn't need his relationship. She isn't overtly trying to hook up with the boyfriend, but she's definitely treating him like he's single. So the girlfriend stays miserable, while the guy gets to have fun. Unknown to himself, convinced he's simply having a good time to escape from the difficult entanglements of romantic love, the guy lets himself get pulled away from his girl-friend, who now seems lame and melodramatic."

"That's so, so bleak," said Anja.

"I know. Men deal with heartbreak by destroying women. Women deal with heartbreak by destroying each other. Don't fall for it."

Anja shook her head, jostling against Laura's legs.

"It's true," said Laura. "We think we're all struggling here in private, unrelated to the identical struggles of people all across the western hemisphere with internet access. Sara thinks she's living in a unique reality—but she's actually just reliving season three of *The Bachelor*."

"Season three?"

"People just don't get how predictable they are."

Anja spun around to face Laura, and leaned back on her hands, staring up at her. "So according to your structural analysis, where do I fit in?"

"I'd say your version of the story is a bit more complicated," Laura said, without missing a beat, "because you have this death thing in the center of it. So Sara's involvement is also positioned as some kind of caretaking thing. Obviously, by acting maternal to Louis and then weaponizing the knowledge she's gained from it, she's trying to make you jealous. The jealousy is meant to drive a wedge between you and Louis. The more jealous you act, the more you'll drive Louis away, and the cycle perpetuates itself."

"So she might not actually be that close with him, but she's baiting me into thinking she is?"

"Oldest trick in the book. Sow seeds of distrust and watch them flourish."

Anja frowned. She could hear a doorbell ring on another floor of Laura and Dam's building. "But knowing the script does not mean I can change it. It just makes me even more depressed because everything is so predictable and I am but a pawn."

"True. Structural analysis isn't sorcery."

Anja sighed, coming back to earth. She was supposed to be speaking the truth. "The truth is," she said, "Sara isn't really the problem. She's kind of a red herring."

"What—there's more girls?"

"No. It's not more girls. It's way worse." Laura looked perplexed. "He's also cheating on me with, like—I don't know how to say it. Idealism."

Laura was silent for a few moments. "I'm interested. Keep talking."

Anja went back to the beginning. All the way back to the french fry seller on Copacabana. She described the pill, Belinda, the naming ceremony. She tried to explain how Louis's humility had been stripped by this new mania. How he thought his ego would be canceled out by his own invention. How abstraction had become actuality, how irony had given way to earnestness. It wasn't the lack of irony that bothered her, she tried to explain, it was the sentimentality that went with it.

Laura was, thankfully, aghast when she finished. And impressed. "This script is off the rails," she said, wild eyed. "Fuck the script! This is way more exciting than some domestic drama!"

Anja took this as a blow. How petty it had been to dwell on anything else, even for a minute. She'd let herself be occupied with interpersonal squabbles with inconsequential people. She had to learn to separate these things, to put herself and her feelings in perspective compared to things like death, social upheaval, the environment.

"It's like he wants to privatize ethics," Laura said, nearly shouting, rising out of her chair. She pushed the chair back with her foot and started to pace around the table. "He's fully given up on solving structural problems. He just wants to fix each person, one by one." She laughed a bit crazily.

Anja nodded. "Or maybe it's more like he's gone from structural to infrastructural. Like dumping fluoride into the water supply."

"How is that ever going to get past an ethics board?"

"I have no idea. He doesn't seem to care."

Laura shook her head as she circled back to her seat. She lifted a foot and rested it on the chair rather than sitting. "I can't get over how megalomaniac this is."

"I know."

"And how neoliberal! It's just an acceleration of what's already in place. You relocate responsibility for handling human problems from governments to corporations, then you let corporations pass it off to individuals by shaming them."

"Basquiatt's an NGO, not a company."

Laura picked up a couch cushion and squeezed it to her chest. "Didn't you hear? Finster bought Basquiatt last week."

"What?"

"You really have to start reading the news, mamita. Nonprofit is now officially a subsidiary of profit, just like it always was. Shame successfully passed down the food chain. But it ends up on us, the little consumers, the broke kids. They pass the shame all the way down to us. Now they give us medicine to make us cough up our last remaining cash."

"I guess it has to start somewhere?" Anja wished Laura could have been there when Louis was telling her everything. Laura could have argued back in a way Anja never could.

"Don't you see?" demanded Laura. "This drug doesn't change anything—it gives us a way to absolve our shame without actually rethinking reality. It's a quick fix. It's going to make people feel like they're doing good, distracting them from the real issues—"

"I guess he thinks that eventually it will lead to other sorts of generosity . . . beyond cash . . ."

"Sorry, but no. He's just helping everything go faster in the direction things are already going," Laura said.

Anja zoned out for a moment, ordering events in her mind. She thought of something cute she'd once said to Louis about subway cars looking like caterpillars. She could still remember in high resolution the way he'd smiled at her, both as if she were childish and as if her childishness was prized; she could remember that look more clearly than almost anything else. "There was a blip," she said, glancing at Laura.

"A blip."

"A blip between then and now. There's two Louises now, the old one and the new one."

The old Louis was morally superior, not because he was righteous, but because he objectively knew best. He knew the way things really were. He knew the way he really was and the way she really was. He could always explain why he was right, and she would always eventually learn that he was right. He had been right so many times that she hadn't had to question whether his version of reality was the right one. Until now.

"I hate to break it to you," said Laura, shaking her head, "but I think the two Louises are the same one."

Anja frowned. "No, he's different. The old one is still there somewhere. Maybe he does need to take Oval, try it for himself, to get back to the old one . . ."

Laura stood up again. "You mean he hasn't taken it yet?" Her accent emerged more strongly when she was excited like this. Anja had become so used to the way Laura and Dam spoke that she hardly noticed its particular rhythm except at times like this.

"Not yet," she said, shrugging. "He says he's waiting for me to do it with him. I've been putting him off."

"Are you serious? You *have* to try it."

Anja shook her head.

"You have to! How else will you know anything? You have to try it, and you have to report back from the other side."

"I can't."

"Of course you can. You have to. Text him right now."

17

FRIDAY TO MONDAY WAS AN OVAL-SHAPED BINGE. THEIR PUPILS were Ovals, their kidneys elongated themselves into Ovals, all the loose change in their pockets melted into Ovals and spent itself, serotonin molecules morphed into large and bubbly Ovals, Oval sperm jetted from Oval testicles through vaginal canal toward ovarian Ovals. Anja dubbed Louis "The Giver" and together they spent a thousand euros, at least, in forty-eight hours. Most surprising of all, Anja thought, was that her knowledge of the artificial nature of her instincts to spend, to give, and to love during those hours in no way dampened the urges to do those things. Far from detracting from their validity, her knowledge that her feelings were chemically induced by Oval even lent a certain righteousness to her acting upon them, a feeling of fully justified liberation.

No meat was eaten; no taxis were taken. No cigarettes were smoked. ("Think of the environment," they whispered to each other, without sarcasm. Each soft, Oval syllable was sexually charged; the responsibility was titillating.) Alcohol was downed only sparingly, but round after round of drinks was bought for friends. *What are you taking? Where can I get some? What's it called?* Louis would wink at them in a way that only he could get away with (who winks?) and Anja would shrug and giggle. They barely slept—who were they to waste this precious time in which they could do so much?

Most of this helping took place abstractly, during long, dribbling conversations in which they made plans to start a not-for-profit library in a disused building in Friedenau where they would host reading groups, and a community garden out back where they could run an agriculture workshop, and they could start a dog shelter there, and an artist residency, and hold an open call for MFA students to apply . . .

There were also some concrete actions, which were difficult to recall by the time they came down, but according to Anja's credit card statement there were six faux-fur coats bought at KaDeWe that Louis said he was pretty sure she had given to a probably homeless man on the subway platform with a lot of facial piercings and a collie with a rhinestone collar.

On Saturday night at the Baron, watery gin and tonic in hand, Anja made a grand decision: she would buy Laura and Dam's apartment building. She would save her friends from Finster's property developers by taking Finster to court, starting a media campaign about the injustice the corporation was perpetrating on the urban landscape and its needy economic refugees, and scandalize whoever was in charge into preserving the building. Her friends wouldn't have to leave their home, or the city. She'd start her career as a public advocate. How hard could it be? She had all this money sitting around, tied up in various investments—most of them green and clean and ethical, but still—and now she was grown up enough to have identified the Right Cause. She had finally discovered her calling, gyrating slowly to deconstructed classical music at four a.m. in the courtyard behind the club with

Louis, hand in his back pocket, murmuring into his ear the word *revelation*.

And the two of them were nothing if not generous to each other. It was as if no distance had caverned in the space between them in the past weeks, as if they were back at the beginning, two years ago, standing by the swimming pool and nodding their heads in a microcosmic moment of unironic mutual understanding, but this time shudderingly without irony at all. Time collapsed and Anja forgave him, forgetting that to forgive was to admit that he had done something for which one could offer forgiveness, untangling her guts and thanking him profusely for working so hard for this experience, this round shape, this symmetry. She smiled serenely on the second night when he asked to spend an hour alone outside with the moon. His sentimentality was left undisturbed and unhounded. There was no reason to hunt for abnormalities.

But on Sunday night it was time to come down, in the interest of science. Louis insisted that they were morally obliged to experience the comedown in a hermetic environment and to carefully detail the effects, so they stumbled into his studio around ten p.m.—interns and graphic designers long gone—and settled onto the sofa cushions with Starbuckses and a few liters of tap water in bottles they had dug out from trash cans on the street.

It had only been an hour before Anja glimpsed the guilt tunnel.

The guilt was exquisite and manifold. The walls of her asylum were crumbling. She felt stranded alone with her education and her bank account, without the defenses of serotonin or melatonin or oxytocin or dopamine or endorphin in her system to pad her privilege and present her with the Right Cause. Louis remained contemplative, philosophical, nonchalant, while Anja fell into deep despair.

First came the creeping memories of chattering with (at) strangers on public transportation, of tossing a large bill to a wrinkled man with a cane who may or may not have been asking for money, of stroking the faces and arms of friends and nonfriends. Then there were the scattered guilt showers of simply having spent more than forty-eight hours straight on drugs—wasting time, wasting life, wasting brain cells. Then there was the bottomless guilt pit of realizing how easily she had been duped by water from an impure source, an artificial fountain, her own feelings exposed for the rudimentary chemistry they were.

Louis was on the sofa, eyes closed and breathing calmly. "I wonder if, philosophically speaking, it could be considered amoral to let people experience Oval without explaining what it is." He didn't sound disturbed at all by this, just fascinated. "We wouldn't want it to seem like some kind of trick. It should be voluntary."

"They'll figure it out anyway on their own, won't they?"

"Probably. Do you think you would have figured it out?"

"I have no idea."

"On the other hand, maybe it's smarter to let people try it first without preconceptions. So they get the vibe and realize how fun it is, instead of going in with foregone conclusions. Concrete expectations are the worst thing you can have before a new experience."

When they'd first started seeing each other Louis had talked about expectations often. Expectations were the death of a relationship. Holding to expectations didn't allow the other person to change, to evolve. Expectations could only lead to disappointment. Expectations ruined the magic, precluded the possibility of improvisation.

"Ring the alarm," Laura had said when Anja told her about this expectation phobia. It was Laura's opinion that men brought up expectations to lay the groundwork for cheating. It was of the same ilk as "I value my freedom." They'd lump the expectation of monogamy into all those other "assumed" expectations of what coupling looks like—then eventually they'd stray and point out that exclusivity, too, had been an unfounded expectation. "He'll say you never *agreed* you were in a monogamous relationship," said Laura. "He'll say you had unfair and unfounded expectations."

Louis's response to this, when Anja brought it back to him and explained it as if it had been her own line of thought, was that expectations, for him, were things that didn't fall under the rubric of their relationship "contract." Our contract includes exclusivity, he'd said. Monogamy is not us conforming to imagined ideals, it's something we've agreed on because it works for us. Monogamy is a case where our private relationship situation happens to conform to societal structures—we *chose* it. I can't believe you thought *that* was still up for grabs. We're living together, for god's sake.

(To Anja, the question of expectations had always been more of a metaphysical one. Expectations, she thought, were part and parcel of experience. You looked forward to something, you imagined how it would be, and then it happened or it didn't—the prelude to the thing was at least the half of it, and after it happened, the memory took over the thing entirely. The thing itself barely existed.)

Pushing these thoughts aside, she told Louis, "If I hadn't known what I had taken, I wouldn't feel so fucking awful about it now."

"I know what you mean. I feel responsible too. It's one thing to buy drinks for people you know, but totally different to be engaging with unknowns on the street."

Anja felt relief. He understood. They'd given what they wanted to give, not what anybody had asked for. They'd forced their charity, for the sake of their own pleasure, on people they'd assumed wanted it.

"The only way we're going to reroute this whole white-savior aspect is to share the whole experience, both sides of it. People have to be primed to accept things," he said. "Giving is easy, it's taking that's hard."

"I don't think taking is that hard, if it's something you need," Anja said slowly.

"That's why we have to remove all those barriers to communication." He made it sound like he was agreeing again, when he was really either misunderstanding or contradicting her. "The receiver needs to be made unsuspicious of the giver. Say you gave someone an Oval first, and *then* a jacket?"

Anja removed Louis's head from her lap and slid down onto the floor, leaning back against the sofa, and massaged the tendons holding her knees to her shinbones, which were inexplicably sore.

"I just don't get what you think is gonna happen when it's all over, babe. You can't stay on Oval all the time, it has too much other-drug feeling to it. Monday morning rolls around and some of us are gonna have to go back to work." She pictured the old man in the tuxedo pants who was always on the subway early on weekday mornings, playing a six-note tune on his harmonica. His broad shoulders and the remnants of delicate bone structure under the deeply creased skin of his face. Dignity.

"Obviously, that's all part of it." He sounded impatient now. "The point is to break the barrier to make everyone see that other kinds of social contracts are possible. Dissolve the misguided fallout of political correctness. Even if it's just on the weekends at first, over time you can change how you behave. If you condition an emotional response, eventually it should happen, even without the supplement."

"Pharmacological utopia," she spat out, in spite of herself, feeling that she was about to veer off course. She had to keep things intellectual, not personal. She couldn't help it.

Louis was quiet. Breathing. He shifted on the white leather, maybe partially sitting up. "It's a start. Do you have a better idea for how to change things?"

"Oh—shit." She leaned over to grab her bag and rummaged around for her phone, which was on 4 percent battery. "Did I make any phone calls this weekend?" Scrolling through her messages, she found a group chat with Dam and Laura that didn't look so good at a glance. Outgoing calls: five, all to an unknown number. She took a breath and redialed.

"Hello, and thank you for calling GSG Real Estate, a Finster holding," said a voice. "I'm Beate, your gender-neutral automated assistant, and I'm pleased to assist you. Please select one of the following options." Anja clicked the phone off and stood up.

"I should go. I'm exhausted." She took a long look at Louis, his soft hair matted over his forehead, his eyes closed, green veins showing on his eyelids. Those incredibly delicate eyelids, covering the eyes through which the world exposed itself to him—not the world as it was, but the world as it could be.

She imagined placing her thumbs right on top of the bulbs of his eyes, pressing slightly to feel them give. Reshaping them. She could do it, if she wanted to. Eyes were like peeled grapes, she'd been horrified to hear as a kid. They didn't pop, they mushed. She realized her face was hot, her hands shaking, as he lay there inert, unresponsive.

"You know, you haven't been the same," she said. Her voice was wavering, her throat constricting to repress it, but it came out.

"The same?" his eyes stayed closed.

"Yeah, you haven't been the same."

"Since when?" The eyes popped open.

"You're going to make me say it?" He looked up at her impassively. "Fine. You haven't been the same since Pat died."

It was exhilarating—it was insane! This was the fatal move, she saw it in his face, the eyes that squinted up at her. She felt it in her stomach muscles as they cramped and pulled her fully into the alternate reality, which she now recognized as her reality. *Since Pat died.* With the words, she had closed the window so that she could never sneak back into their house. She knew suddenly that she had been planning to say this all along—it had only been a matter of how long she could hold it in. She'd succumbed to the whole experience of Oval with him just to push herself to this point, the breaking point.

"Everything is different," she said, the force of the pent-up words propelling themselves out with spittle. Ugly words on oily froth from her uncontrollable mouth. "You're a different person, and you won't admit it."

He gazed up at her still, contempt drawn across his face. "Of course I'm different," he said, as if she had just said the stupidest thing imaginable. "My fucking mom died. What did you expect?"

Her voice was squished almost beyond recognition, lips wet but tongue dried out. She was in fact coming down from drugs, she remembered distantly. There was a chemical thing going on in her brain and body that was making her thoughts not 100 percent pure. Whatever a pure thought was. "I can't handle this anymore," she said, pinched, struggling. "You're making me feel insane."

He gave her a look of concern. "You know, I'm observing your comedown reactions, and I think we're definitely going to have to make some tweaks in the chemistry."

18

WORDS WERE PHYSICAL REFLEXES; HER BODY HAD DONE THEM to her. They had punched her in the gut and spat themselves on Louis's face. Then, as soon as she'd left his studio, the words had gone missing entirely.

Finster was never going to sell Laura and Dam's apartment building to her; this was painfully obvious in the light of day. She could throw as much money at it as she wanted, but there was no way. It was laughable.

All the same, she felt she had to follow through, at least to ask the question. At least find out how much it would cost. She owed it to herself. To Laura and Dam. To the memory of herself on O.

Howard would know. She asked to drop by his place, without thinking too much about what she would say to him when she got there. She would let her words continue to do the talking. It was better to take a back seat. Thinking she had been in control in the first place had been the problem.

Back in his narrow kitchen, she devoted ten minutes to re-assuring Howard she hadn't breached the NDA. He pestered her about it in a half-assed way. Form for form's sake. He had no evidence that she'd broken the contract (though of course she had), but the burden of proof was on him. That was the absurd thing about NDAs, and the reason they proliferated so wildly: they were flimsy unless someone really had it out for you. Most of the time, all it took to not breach an NDA was to insist that no, you had not disclosed. There: you didn't do it.

Satisfied or bored, he gave up and inspected her, stirring his tea. "You were wearing that shirt the last time I saw you."

"I don't exactly have access to my clothes right now."

"Everyone who showed up at the Best Western was given a budget for incidentals. You could outfit yourself if you just moved in with the tribe."

"You don't think I look good in this?" She smoothed her hands over her stomach, which was verging on concave. Taut and certain of itself. The allure of the restricted body.

"Of course you do. Near-death suits you."

The antagonism was thicker than it had ever been between them, and closer to sexual. She was repulsed by herself, almost to the point of being drawn to him, and he could feel it. It was hard to imagine closing the space between them, but what was stopping it from happening now? The desecration of a memory? And what memory—all she could pull from her memory about sex on O with Louis over the weekend were a few cropped images—hand on thigh, mouth opened in a round shape—hardly enough to feel nostalgic about, hardly enough to compare favorably with the potential of unsatisfactory sex with anyone else.

She knew sleeping with Howard would only exacerbate the lack. The lack was so big that she couldn't see it anymore, she could only feel it rising up around her.

The lack contained in it thousands of other images, which swarmed her as she sat across from Howard. Phantoms: she and Louis viewed from above, paired this way and that, seeking an impossible symmetry. The legs that were both hers and his; the mole on her stomach that was an impression of the mole on his stomach. Her body an indentation, his an exception to the rule. Believing in him had been believing in the existence of nonbanality. There was no reason to aspire any longer.

She looked up at Howard. The images of the two of them that she could conjure were pockmarked with shame.

Howard tried another approach. "How's Louis's project going?" Her ears pricked up. "I heard you came up with the official street name."

She stiffened and withdrew her hands from the table's edge. "Who *hasn't* heard by now? I thought it was still supposed to be under wraps."

He shrugged. "I've been consulting at Basquiatt, you know. A few marketing strategies Louis wanted to run by me."

"You helped?"

"He was delusional if he thought he'd push this through without professional help. Consultants like him will always need consultants like me."

"What's in it for you?"

"Just the good of mankind." If he'd been writing an email, he'd have tacked a smiley on right there. "And a favor for you, actually. I figured you'd appreciate the gesture, but maybe I misjudged the situation. Again."

She realized she hadn't discussed any of the practical side of things with Louis over the weekend. All she knew was what he'd told her while they sat by the canal and waited for it to take hold. She'd asked him how Basquiatt had received the plan, and he'd grinned, saying no other project of his had met with approval so quickly. No mention that it had been thanks to Howard.

She had the feeling again that things were moving around

her that she couldn't see, detritus from the flow only occasionally materializing and coming into focus. She could only try to guess where the shards had come from by the velocity and angle of their approach.

Howard sent another shard her way. "I just heard that you were in on the beta test too. I haven't tried my sample yet—any tips?"

It was happening. Oval was entering orbit, touching down.

"Sure," she said. "Don't take it."

He laughed. "You hooked already?"

"Not exactly. I think the beta still needs a few 'tweaks,' as Louis put it. He didn't like my comedown reaction so much. Neither did I."

"Oh?"

"It's fucking fake, Howard. None of it's real. None of it lasts."

"It doesn't have to be real to make a difference." He cocked his head to the side, watching her carefully.

"No—it doesn't solve any problems. It only makes you blind to the structures behind them. It's just an empty ego-high—it's white-savior complex in pill form."

He forced another laugh, registering that she wasn't in the mood to ease the tension. There was nothing accommodating to her speech; she was saying what she meant. Not playfully combative—she was, maybe, ready for real combat.

"Sounds like you're upset with Louis more than anything else," he said.

"Can you not reduce my political disagreement to a lovers' quarrel?"

"I'm just saying, cut him some slack. It's a work in progress."

"Cut him some slack? Since when are you on his side?"

She knew as she said this that she was invalidating herself.

That's how it was: boys got to believe their private lives were extricable from their politics—*I read feminist theory so it's irrelevant that my girlfriend's career is subordinate to my own; it has nothing to do with our genders*—and yet they never believed your politics were anything but feeling-based. She would never be allowed to have ideas about the world that were not traceable back to a feminine insecurity. *You only wrote a bad review of my book because I wouldn't sleep with you. You voted for him because you think he's hot.*

In a world where her structural critiques were cast as personal insecurities, no one would ever believe that she was politically opposed to O; they'd only believe that she was having problems with her boyfriend.

Howard leaned forward. "Since when are *you* guys on different sides?"

She shook her head. "He's the one who made sides," she said.

She left without asking him the question she had come to ask.

white fog on cats paws / highs of 40°

Her muscles were underfed, unwilling to push the pedals of her bike, so she left the thing hitched to a lamppost outside Howard's. Little chance it would be there tomorrow.

She hadn't taken the subway in a while, and once she was on the train she realized she'd forgotten to buy a ticket, which usually would have made her paranoid, but she found herself pocketing the worry easily. Any quotidian discomfort paled in comparison to prolonged heartbreak. Like stubbing your toe while already doubled over in pain from cramps

She connected her headphones to her ears and scrolled,

searching for a podcast she hadn't heard. She should really be listening to the news, but what was the point? She would never know as much as Laura. No use pretending to be interested. Her finger alighted on an episode from RANDI's science series. "Newly Observed Behaviors in Genetically Modified Insects." It was news, of a sort.

A pleasant voice described the colorless wings of a particular kind of beetle bred to be resistant to diseases that affect edible crops. The modification of its immune system had also resulted in some unexpected phenotypic changes, such as losing the bright pattern on its wings, which had previously been an attractor for mates. In the absence of the ostentatious wing color it had previously possessed, the beetle species had invented a new mating ritual based on chirping.

She let her vision unfocus and her thoughts drift. Was she pathologizing Louis in the same way Howard, and countless males, pathologized her? She had mentally reduced Louis's desire to change the world to a desperate reaction to grief. But maybe his desire was pure. Maybe it wasn't a cause-and-effect reaction. Maybe its coinciding with the hinge of the death event was superfluous. Who was she to act as arbiter when it came to motive anyway? Was there such a thing as a purely positive motive? And did it matter why a person did something? Motive was not necessarily traceable in worldly effects. It couldn't be—it just wasn't possible for a person to exert that much control. Reactions, collisions. Hadn't every major technological innovation in history been appropriated for uses beyond the inventor's intention?

She knew the story. Intellectuals hunch deep down in academia somewhere, throwing molecules against one another until they finally release energy—these molecular reactions are later weaponized to kill millions. A military task force invents a portable blood-infusion device for use on the battlefield—it becomes a lifesaver in civilian hospitals around the world. Beetles are modified so as not to be vectors for disease—and look, now they have a new wing color. Now they mate differently.

Oval, she told herself, was just another emergent technology like all the rest, and one invented by an artist in an NGO—not the most damning of possible contexts. Whether the artist was aware of why he was doing it, this was superfluous. The pill was simply a kernel; the change would proceed, autonomous, from the source.

It was lunch hour and the train car had quickly become over-crowded, standing room only. Her back was pressed up against someone's front. The person was a heavy breather and she could feel his chest moving as the air rattled in and out. The train lurched and he jostled too close to her, making a full plane of contact against her body, and she felt her bag move against her side, a sure feeling that someone was fumbling in it, but when she reached down to check it no hand was there.

A man whose nose was full of heavy metal rings—three, four piercings in one nostril—squeezed himself in through the doors at the next stop. A pair of Turkish men in tracksuits mut-tered something in his direction. Anja scrolled numbly on her phone, holding it tilted up and close to her body, and focused on the voice in her headphones. The man had started shouting; she averted her eyes. But the words felt somehow directed. She glanced up. It occurred to her that he was shouting at her—the girl absorbed in her phone—and he was very close, only sepa-rated by the width of one person, an elderly woman cowering against the pole in the center of the car. Anja couldn't move; her back was still wedged against the breather, and to her left and right others pressed against her.

Yes, the words were directional. The man was accusing

her, just her, in words that were garbled but intelligible. *Every-one is obsessed with their phones*, that was the gist. But then he was saying something about a fur coat. She willed herself to glance at him. Yes, he was wearing what looked like an expensive coat made of rabbit fur. "Erinnerst du dich nicht?" he insisted. *You must remember me.* Something had passed between them over the weekend, but she couldn't remember what it was anymore. Were they now acquaintances? What more did he want from her?

The male beetle has learned to vibrate its wings fast enough to produce a high-pitched sound only the other sex can hear. The man was daring her to respond to him and panic burst in her chest. She felt the eyes of everyone in the car flicker in her direction.

On O, she would have smiled at the ranter, tossed her phone aside, started chatting, given him whatever she had. She tried to conjure the feeling of common humanity, and the feeling of joy she supposed she had experienced over the weekend—but the illusion could not hold when confronted, sober on the subway, with this everyday horror. If she'd really talked to this raving man over the weekend, exchanged more than material goods with him. The urge to spend money induced by O would have to extend to other urges: to spend time, to spend care. Maybe the urges were linked in a way she didn't want to admit.

The man's voice was now hoarse from yelling; he was smacking his own forehead. Here she had a choice, to prove that taking O wasn't necessary in order to act like a compassionate human. She could try, but the prospect froze her. Engaging a lunatic as a token of respect would in no way diminish his pain. She felt his pain—everyone in the subway car was in some kind of pain—but there wasn't anything to *do* about it. She was shy,

shy, shy. And she was afraid of doing the wrong thing, much less the right one.

Anja gave in and checked her feed. She had been avoiding the icon on her phone for days, thumb hovering above it like it was a hot pimple that needed popping. When she finally pressed on it she quickly found what she was looking for. She searched for Sara's profile and there it was: third post from the top. In the fenced-in, grass-trampled backyard of the Baron, sun rising. Louis leaning on Prinz to support Sara's weight on his shoulders. Sara's thighs around Prinz's neck. Sara's hand in the air, ecstatic. Sascha's face on his other side, level with Louis's, the molecules of their cheeks making contact. The four of them in perfect formation. United by O. No filter.

Laura came charging into the living room in her underwear. "I just saw something so fucking weird."

Anja dropped her phone on the floor next to her, snapping out of stalker mode. "Down there?" she asked, gesturing toward Laura's crotch.

Laura rolled her eyes. "Outside. I was smoking a cigarette out the window ."

"I thought you quit smoking."

"I did. As I was saying. I was looking out the window and I saw this lady jogging by, listening to her headphones. She was wearing one of those armband phone-holder things."

"The thing that looks like a blood-pressure cuff?"

"Yeah. Maybe it does that, too. So the lady was jogging by and she passed this homeless guy, who was passed out on a pile of cardboard boxes. When she saw him, she stopped all of a sudden and reversed herself back to him—she didn't turn around, she just jogged *backward*—and then she sort of poked him awake with her *foot*, and then he started rolling around confused, and she ripped out her headphone jack, took her phone out of the armband, and bent down and gave the phone to him."

Anja had a sinking feeling. "That's all?"

"No—then she leaned down and kissed his face. He seemed like he was trying to talk to her, but then she just stood up and started jogging again. She was still holding her headphones, which was kind of weird. I guess she thought he didn't need those . . ."

"What did the girl look like?"

"I don't know. Blond."

"Did she look like she'd been out partying?"

"No, she looked like a jogger. What do you—oh my god, you don't think . . ." Anja stared at her blankly. "Jesus."

Laura sank onto the sofa and Anja pulled her legs up to make room, scrunching up the blankets around her. She had been awake for what felt like hours already.

"Where's Dam?" asked Anja. "He hasn't sent any weather blasts in a few days. Actually, I haven't seen him in ages."

Laura sighed. "He's in Barcelona. Looking at places."

"Shit." Anja rubbed her eyes, which felt like they were stuck open. Secondhand grief was pickling her into a smooth, shiny vegetable. At least her rash was less fervent today. "I can't believe you're serious about this move."

"Looks like it. Not sure how to go backward on this one. You know," Laura gestured toward her bedroom, "the jogging backward is what really gets me about that whole interaction. Like she had a switch go off in her brain and then—ee-yoo-ee-yoo . . ." She made the noise of truck reversing, moving her forearms up and down as if directing it where to park. "She just, like, reversed herself when she saw him."

"While I was tripping over the weekend I had the stupidest idea," said Anja. She hadn't been planning to say anything, but it seemed so silly now, what was the harm? "I was convinced I had the solution."

"To what?"

"To you guys leaving."

Laura wrapped her arms around her long, tan legs. She hadn't shaved any part of her body in a long time and the black hairs were healthy, thriving. Actually, Laura as a whole looked healthy, alive and well. Anja felt the warmth of her friend's body through the blanket and gazed at her with love. Love, and comparison. She wondered if she would ever simply admire another woman's body, or whether she'd always be compelled to compare herself, centimeter by centimeter.

"I had this idea," Anja said, laughing hoarsely, "that I would try to buy your building off Finster. I even called their real estate subsidiary while I was high, apparently. Thank god I didn't get through to anyone."

"Damn," said Laura after a pause. "But would you—I mean, is there any way that's possible?"

"Of course not. It makes no sense. Finster wants to monopolize this whole block. Why would they sell off the final piece to some random person?"

"I guess. Could you afford it, though? How much does a whole building cost?"

"No idea. Howard laughed in my face when I asked," Anja lied. It didn't matter that she hadn't asked him, she told herself. It was impossible.

Laura leaned her head back against the wall and then lifted it, knocked it back again, lifted it, knocked it back. Gently banging the back of her head against the paper-thin interior wall, plastered with Raufasertapete, the disgusting wood-chip wallpaper that had been plastered over so many interiors at some point before the end of the Wall, supposedly for insulation. The same era when they'd chopped up all the Altbau buildings, like this one, converting them from grand homes into single-family apartments—creating long, narrow hallways, tunnel-like kitchens, and closet-like bathrooms. The room they were in now might have once been a third of a large drawing room, with a maid's quarters on the floor above. Now it was a strangely shaped extra-large kitchen-living area. After living in Berlin long enough, everyone got accustomed, even attached, to the hacked configurations. It was liberating when things weren't the way they were designed to be; it made you feel you could do whatever you wanted with them. For a time. Now it seemed claustrophobic.

"It's a lost cause," said Anja, picturing the glassy loft that would become of this space.

"How rich are you, really?" asked Laura suddenly. "Could you afford a building?"

Anja crossed her arms. "I don't know." She didn't know how much buildings cost, but she did know she had as much in her investment account as Eva, and Eva had skated by without working a day in thirty-five years. "Probably," she admitted. Her heart was beating uncomfortably fast. This was the first time she and Laura had ever had an explicit conversation about money. The risk of sounding like a poor little rich girl had always been too high.

Laura cocked her head and asked, "What would it take for you to spend some of it? Don't you ever want to buy something big?"

Anja didn't know what to say. Once or twice she and Louis

had fantasized about using the money to build their own little village somewhere, a thousand times better than the Berg, where all their friends could come live. A real commune, a real community. They could take over one of those crumbling brick sanatoria on the Polish border, or hire an architect and start from scratch on a mountain in Switzerland. But they both knew she'd never take the leap. The first time she'd ever found herself truly tempted—compelled, unafraid—to go all in was when she'd been spiraling on O.

"I could never decide what the most important cause would be."

Laura shrugged. "Causes are Louis's thing. Look how that's turning out."

"But I can't justify spending it on myself either."

Laura examined her fingernails, then looked at Anja. She put an arm around one of Anja's knees, which was bent up toward her chest. "You'll figure it out," she said. "When the time is right."

Anja nodded, grateful but unsure whether this was true. She knew she'd moved to Berlin partially so she'd never have to stare down this question, but here it was. The city would soon be too expensive for her to squirrel away her savings forever. Maybe it was time for her to jump ship too. Unlike Eva, who'd replicated their parents' schedule of constant displacement, Anja had dedicated herself to pinning down a steady, stable homestead to counteract all those years of being ripped out at the root. Most international school kids ended up flighty like their parents, but not her. Maybe Berlin had been the wrong choice, but she'd chosen it. It was hers.

19

OLD/NEW LOUIS DIDN'T ANSWER HER MESSAGE. SHE HAD MADE a pact with herself not to send him anything and then promptly broken it. The message she ended up sending, she hoped, sounded casual. It said that she was sorry and hoped they could talk soon.

The real messages, the ones she knew she shouldn't send, she composed in her sleep. She woke up unsure if she'd sent them. She often dreamed that he had written back. But nothing came from him. Twenty-four hours, thirty-six hours, forty-two . . . He hasn't seen it, she told herself—it doesn't have the double check marks saying he's opened it. But his phone had alerts, just like hers, where the preview of the message showed up whether you opened it or not. But maybe his phone was off. But maybe his phone was on . . .

Her phone offered no other clues. Sara's feed had gone dark, and Louis hadn't popped up on anyone else's. He didn't have his own profile: either a brave or elitist choice, depending on how you looked at it. She refreshed Sara's profile once again.

You were supposed to go for a walk when you felt stagnated. She wrapped Dam's kimono around herself and left the house, thinking she would head toward the canal and get an ice cream.

That was how Sundays used to be, in the early Berlin days, when time stretched before her like a boundless airfield. Ice cream, drugs, new people, improvisation—and then all those things anew, with Louis. Last Sunday at this time she'd been with Louis in the corner of his studio, neurons misfiring. How could she have done what she'd done?

Her phone dinged from her pocket and her stomach flipped, but it was just Dam, back from Barcelona. *FFRYING 1 EGG ON ME FORHED RN BRRLIN IS N INFERNO SCAPE WILE U CAN.* A mass text, not even geared toward her. She searched for a podcast on her phone that would override her thoughts.

Dam was right: the sun was harsh. Her armpits moistened and she felt sweat bead up into a mustache of droplets on her upper lip. She pictured the skin cells on the ridges of her cheeks quickly turning precancerous, like an animation from a sunscreen commercial. Sunblock—another thing you were supposed to do. The dirt path by the canal was almost deserted, only a few couples sweating on the strip of grass between the path and the water. The smell of weed drifted from an unknown source. A line of filthy swans trailed through the water near the steep edge of the canal, beady eyes trained on the surface in search of sandwich morsels. One dived down and came up with an empty bag of paprika chips.

The voice in her ears explained how the ozone hole had briefly appeared to be shrinking—but after a second check the meteorologists had apologized: nope, still thinning up there. She glanced up toward the sky. Spreading, spreading, like a cervix dilating.

Someone sidled alarmingly close to her on the path. She pocketed her phone, which she had somehow unconsciously pulled out to check yet again, and veered slightly away from him, monitoring him in her peripheral vision. It was threatening to be approached when both of you were ambulatory, active and directional, two vectors in motion. One party had to be stationary for a nonthreatening transaction: either you're sitting on a bench or at a table and someone comes up to you, or you pass someone kneeling on the street and drop some change into their cup. Not both of you moving in toward each other with the possibility of confrontation.

He was clutching something in his fist. She stepped down onto the grass to avoid him. He revolved on his heel to follow her along the path. She was now approaching another pair of people sitting on the ledge of the canal bank, hunched over what looked like little cartons of takeout sushi. One was stirring wasabi into soy sauce, the other arranging ginger atop a California roll. The man who'd been following her was hiking down the short slope toward them now, chopsticks held high in anticipation. She shook her head at her own assumptions, paranoia.

The city was changing its clothes, or at least wearing a new scarf. Good to be walking along, seeing it happen. The canal was the right place to test the city's social temperature: ground zero for public life.

The summer she met Dam and Laura had been full of canal days. They played bocce for entire weekends at the canalside court between teams of old men who never seemed to finish a game, so busy were they haggling over points. The three of them walked up and down the long stretch by the water, always finding a new perch to dangle their legs over or someone they knew to stand around and chat with. Groups of friends gathered around them and dissipated, but the three of them stuck it out, forming a solid core. Laura always had a bag with a blanket, water, cigarettes. Afternoons, Dam went to pick up pizza, smearing it with chili oil before bringing it back with a slice already missing. Laura liked tuna on her pizza, which was awful, but Anja gave in, willing to let her tastes soften to make these people hers.

Interning four days a week then, Anja was the only person who seemed to have a place to be during the week. The feeling of letdown at the end of a long weekend was new and surprising to her: she wanted these beer-soaked, sun-slurred days to last without end. She wanted to smoke on the grass and let her hair bleach, let the conversation spill over from afternoon to night, then bleach her brain at a club until the next morning and do it all again. She wanted it more than she wanted to be in the lab, for the first time since she'd stepped into one. That had been the last true summer of persistent heat before the weather went haywire and scattered the year into discrete days instead of seasons.

"Hey!" Someone called to her from the other side of the water. She squinted. It was a couple she knew from around, friends of Prinz, maybe. The two guys had been together so long that they looked like each other—or maybe they had always looked like each other, and that was the reason they got together in the first place. The one on the left waved and called her name. She skidded down the slope toward the bank.

"What's up?" she called. They were surrounded by cartons of beer.

"We're emptying some bottles!"

"Why?"

"Gonna give them away!" He appeared to gesture toward the sushi eaters. His partner handed him a bottle, which he cracked open with a lighter and tipped slowly into the murky water. The canal was probably 60 percent beer anyway, she thought. Behind them, the black cat that they brought everywhere was straining at its tether, tied to a tree.

"You're emptying them . . . to give them to those guys?" She jerked her thumb to the right.

"We were collecting empties for a few hours, but it got a little intense. It's nasty in the trash bins."

"Then we realized we could just buy a few six-packs and give the bottles away."

The first one was struggling to pry the top off another bottle with his lighter. Anja wasn't sure what to say. "They wouldn't rather have the cash?" she tried.

"Charity is demeaning," said one, lifting the cat and stroking it between the ears.

"Teach a man to fish!" shouted the one opening bottles.

The other nodded. "You have to nurture the ecosystem of the city so it stays alive."

Remora fish clean sharks. Oxpecker birds eat the flies off cows. He was, it seemed, referring to bottle collecting as part of a kind of urban symbiotic system. She started backing up the bank toward the path.

"You could just give them the full bottles," she said, less loudly.

"We're not about to *give* them a case of beer," the one with the cat said, laughing.

Back on the path, she bumped into a tall girl teetering on clunky platforms, chatting into her phone with one hand and clutching the end of a leash with the other. The leash was attached to the collar of a Weimaraner who was finishing taking a huge, unself-conscious shit in the dust. He stood up, pawed a bit in the dirt to signal his satisfaction, and the two of them walked on, leaving the pile of crap in the middle of the path.

Anja watched them amble on, wondering why you'd want to have a dog in the city. She'd always vetoed the idea, but Louis loved dogs so much, all of them. He had a kind of radar that brought anything under knee height immediately into his awareness. He would grab her arm on the subway and she'd know to look down. Dogs: the great leveler. The lowest common denominator of human compassion. The perversity of pampering your dog while the planet is dying. Sloths are nearly extinct, and here we are breeding bulldogs whose rib cages are too small for their lungs. A slave race of our own making. Louis would say all this, bending down happily to pet a collie.

Nothing looked out of the ordinary at the base of the Berg. It wasn't cordoned off, but the paths leading up the western side where Anja and Michel stood were deserted. None of the usual bottle collectors or birdwatchers or furtive couples sneaking around the trees at the bottom.

They circled around to the southeastern trail, the lesser-used one that led up to the back of the clearing where her house stood, and climbed a few meters into the brush, which had grown surprisingly quickly to meet itself in the middle of the path.

A giant stepped out from nowhere in front of them.

"Nope," he said. He was huge, with arms swollen in a way that didn't look as if he were always at the gym but rather that his body fat was distributed in a way that happened to conform to the shape of muscles. He was wearing a pinstriped shirt that could have been a Karstadt uniform. The shirt bunched at his armpits, straining to contain his chest.

"Private property," he grunted. "Residents only."

"I'm a resident," said Anja, feeling Michel shift nervously beside her.

The giant shook his head, gearing up for the certain pleasure he would experience in contradicting her. "All residents are accounted for." He crossed his arms and stared off behind them.

"And yet here we stand," said Michel.

"All residents are accounted for. I have the list."

"Looks like reality and bureaucracy may not be in alignment on this day of all days," said Michel, digging his toe into the mud. "Maybe Mercury in retrograde."

Anja reached into her bag to find her phone with the requisite residence permit codes on it, and the man's hand instantly went to his hip.

"Whoa," said Michel, stepping forward. "We're harmless."

"I'm just trying to show you my residence permit," said Anja. "I have it on my phone."

"No residents are currently in residence here."

"I just need to pick something up." Anja smiled sweetly up at him. "Maybe you know Howard?" she tried.

She watched carefully for his reaction, to gauge whether he was high enough on the ladder to understand how and when to succumb to this type of coercion—or whether he was immune to name-dropping because he believed power worked in straightforward ways according to protocol. In other words, how German was he? Whatever Laura said, she thought, Germany will never entirely collapse into the next century. Cultural capital, even real capital, will always yield to the rules here.

The giant remained impassive, and she sighed, running through possible tactics. Name-dropping: no. Flirting, no. Indignation, entitlement, rage . . .

He moved his hand away from his waist, and she glanced at it. The hand had faded barbed wire entwined around the fingers. She checked his other hand. A spider extended its legs down the wrist.

She couldn't believe it had taken her so long. "You know me, actually," she said. "Wednesdays and Saturdays are your nights at the Baron." He glared at her. "You always let me in. I'm usually with Prinz and Louis."

The way he scrutinized her was entirely familiar. There was the necessary delay of a few painful seconds, before he would reach out his hand to shove the swinging door open and a warm, wet, smoke-filled puff of air would hit her in the face as she pushed through into the club. The precipice of rejection. The power was petty, but it was entirely his.

Without Louis she knew there was no guarantee she'd get into the Baron, much less the Berg. Alone and not a recognizable regular, she would be easy to dismiss. The social anxiety of possible rejection should have been surging inside of her, but she decided to bluff.

"I was at the Baron last night, actually," she lied. "A little hungover today." The bouncer grunted. She rolled her eyes impatiently.

He looked slowly from right to left, arms still crossed solidly in front of his chest, and took a few steps to the side. She watched him, waiting for the fateful nod. When it came, she tapped Michel and started up the path. As they passed, she nodded back at the bouncer, careful not to seem overly grateful. You wouldn't get in the door next time if you acted relieved when you got in the first time, that's what Sara had once told her. Or would you? The whole thing was a crapshoot. People were constantly trying to come up with repeatable strategies for getting into the club, but the whole process wouldn't work unless it retained some element of randomness. There could be no truly systematic process: every dictator knew that.

"The fuck?" said Michel when he assumed they were out of earshot. "Is that really the bouncer from the Baron?"

"I can't believe I didn't realize sooner."

They veered slightly west in order to stay shielded by foliage until they came up behind the cluster of houses. The trees hadn't had a chance to lose their leaves, but the air was intensely cold, and the ground was brittle, nearly frozen in places. STAY CHILL*YALL had been the message of the morning. The confused peat moss that was grafted on the stones—which were grafted on the soil grafted on the mountain grafted on the airport grafted on the city—had shriveled up into brown pubic-hair masses in the cold, and much of the shrubbery looked like it had passed on to the next life. Too many temperature changes to keep up with.

"Why is it so much cooler up here?" Michel asked when they reached the top. He was panting slightly. It did seem even colder. They stepped silently across the back patio of her house, circling the pair of bamboo recliners where she and Louis had spent so many Sunday mornings. The green seat cushions had a white frosting of some kind on them—mold or dust. Louis always forgot to take the cushions inside.

The door was unlocked, but it was jammed shut; after engorging with humidity the wood had dried out without deflating. Michel hunched over and levered it with the side of his body until it wedged open with a dry creak.

They were met with a smell of decay, but not an entirely unpleasant one. There was, strangely, a note of fresh grass on top of the compost bouquet—slightly sweet. Michel sneezed. "It smells like pot in here." He looked around the living room, taking it in. He was stunned.

She scratched her stomach, maybe a Pavlovian response to the rash she now associated with the place, and scanned the creeping green-brown fuzz dotting the floors. It was much warmer inside. The windows were gently sweating. A remarkable amount of dirt and leaves had collected in the corners. Were those—yes, weeds were growing up through the floor by the sofa.

"Was it like this when you left?" He knelt and patted the concrete composite floor. Its top layer was disintegrating into graham cracker crumbs. "Living here must have been kind of like camping."

"No—it wasn't working so well, but it wasn't like *this*."

"But it wasn't great."

"Not after the first few months."

"Why'd you ever move here?"

"When we first saw it, the house was—" She stopped and shrugged.

The way it looked the first day they saw it had thrilled her. It had been staged with model furniture, a few pieces of which they had decided to buy, and the rooms felt clean and airy. Everything smelled so new—the polar opposite of the garden house. Louis's excitement about the place was impossible not to adopt. They had almost no belongings, and so he ordered them a new mattress, plates and wineglasses, a woven carpet, a bath mat. Those things you don't invest in until you're "serious" about someplace, someone. They hauled boxes up the hill together, laughing at the inconvenience. Moving in had been fun, hilarious at times. Think about it, Louis said, in a city where everyone's counting their square meters and hiding from their neighbors, we have a giant house in the middle of the forest to ourselves.

The Berg had proven their specialness, which they'd suspected all along. Learning the ins and outs of the house had been like a game at first. The first month or two, when the waste system was still sort of cooperating and she was earnestly cooperating too, there had been minor frustrations, but no real worry. *The cable car will be installed any day now. We'll get our own post code soon.*

The wireless will get hooked up this week. Everything had seemed possible.

"Mama mia!" came from the other room. She found Michel standing in the office, in front of the Bureaucracy Bookshelf, which was loaded with three-ring binders labeled and sorted by year.

"This is no joke," he said. "You've got a lot of binders. What's in all of these?"

She ran a finger over the binders on one shelf and it came away covered in dust. "Blue is for taxes. White is for insurance. Gray is for Louis's visa paperwork . . ."

"What's red?" he pointed to the bottom shelf.

"Red's all the Berg stuff. Our contract, manuals, insurance . . . all the NDAs."

"So I shouldn't even know of their existence."

She smiled. "Correct."

"I've never seen someone so organized."

"Runs in the family." She paused. "Actually, no, that's a lie. It's just me."

"I have this little handheld scanner you could use . . ."

"Real Germans don't digitize."

"I thought you were Austrian." He approached the bookshelf, slid out a red binder.

"Same thing when it comes to hard copies." She regarded her collection, so curated it might have been empty decor in an office supply store. "They're the closest I'll ever get to having a pet. Even when I lived in the garden house, I kept them all stacked in the bedroom."

"A garden house, huh." He was struggling to separate the pages threaded onto the rings of the binder he had pulled off the shelf and was holding open. "I hate to break this to you, but I think your hard copies have been made obsolete." He tried to pull the pages apart with two hands, but the clump held fast to itself, a dimpled, brittle plate of paperwork.

She broke into a laugh. "A month ago I would have been heartbroken about that." The records seemed arbitrary now, just fossils. She was detached from whatever they had signified.

"You must have backups somewhere."

"These are the backups. The Berg contract, for one, has a clause saying we aren't allowed to keep any digital copies of our contracts for security reasons."

"You have no way of checking what your actual contract says if the hard copies get lost?"

"Guess not."

He closed the binder and sat on the floor, then crossed his legs in front of him and took off his suede jacket, the one he wore every day. She'd grown to like it. He laid the jacket across the binder and looked up at her. He seemed comfortable, like he wanted to stay sitting there.

"Should we get started?" she said.

She led him to the kitchen. "Let's put the stuff down in here," she said, testing a light switch. No click; no light. The mechanism was only decorative now. Cute, even.

"It's pretty bright in here," she said, gesturing to the windows, "but we're going to need something brighter. I'll go find some flashlights."

There were plenty in the utility closet. Big and small— they'd stocked up at a certain point when it became clear that the experimental aspect of their lifestyle was outweighing the sustainable one.

In the kitchen they rigged up the largest flashlight by taping it to an overturned Tupperware container so that it was pointing directly at the work area. The items were spread out across the kitchen island: a stack of petri dishes each coated with a thin layer of agar, a little toolbox holding various pincers and scoops, a small box of transparent slides to squeeze samples between, a few metal clamps, and the crown jewel, the activator, the soft machine: sixty-four cells of self-replicating engineered cartilage, in the tiniest of the petris, packed in ice inside a tiny cooler.

She stood back and surveyed the small collection. Laid out, it didn't look like much, just a fraction of what you'd think you needed to do a real, cutting-edge science experiment. It looked more like the setup for a high school science fair.

Michel brought out and unfolded the shelter, a microwave-sized Plexi box, which had an airlock gadget on one end for them to poke things through. A simulated lab: a microhermetic environment. He handed an empty dish whose interior was coated with agar and the dish with the precious sample, both still lidded, to Anja, who pinched them with tongs and slid them, one at a time, through the airlock onto the floor of the Plexi chamber.

They were quiet during this process. It was a solemn affair. Both an illicit and a holy operation.

"Good thing I have full charge," Michel said, powering on his laptop once they were set up. "Maybe I intuitively guessed you wouldn't have electricity up here."

"What's the game plan?"

"Basically we have to let the sample defrost halfway inside the box and then move it to the agar. You know the rest—I'll run the simulation at the same time so we can watch to make sure it's happening on schedule. Remember, it's probably going to go at hyperspeed, because it's so warm in here." He checked the room temperature again by holding his phone up, did a quick calculation, and set a timer: twelve minutes to half-defrost. He pressed start.

"Hard to believe how warm it is in here," he said, staring at the timer. Weather talk.

"Must be all the composting going on. It's like we're in a giant kombucha jar."

He looked up at the box and then back at the timer. "So—were you really at the Baron last night?"

"No."

"Where's your . . . Louis these days?"

"I don't know."

"Okay," he said.

"I'm still half in the water, half out."

"We were all amphibians once. It's just a stage in evolution."

They were quiet, a full, wet silence. It was cut when the timer beeped.

Michel stood up straight, ran his finger over the mouse pad on his laptop to wake it up, and she stationed herself by the box. "Ready?" he said.

She sent a pair of long pincers through the airlock and clasped a little lip at the edge of the empty dish, then wiggled it until the lid eased off. She did the same with the dish holding the sample, then quickly pulled out the pincers and sent in another instrument. A gimlet scoop, a long tube that flattened out at one tip, like one of those plastic smoothie straws flattened to a sort of spoon at the end that always cuts your tongue. She scooped the area of the dish that was circled with sharpie where the cells were planted, still half-asleep, waiting to wake up and meet one another. She dug under the cells and scraped the whole chunk out.

Then she shoveled the small clump onto the waiting dish, tapping it down into the thick agar layer, and quickly pulled out the gimlet scoop. She nodded okay to Michel, who tapped a key on his laptop to start the simulation.

She'd been surprised when he agreed without protest to do the experiment on the Berg. The idea had simply occurred to her at some point and inflated in her mind to blot out all other possibilities. He had always been curious about the place, he said. As good a place as any. She didn't point out how unhygienic it was.

Friday, Michel had announced that everything was ready. He had acquired the necessary wetware and hardware. After consulting with some orthopedic experts in Paris who were working on growing outerwear from living tissue, he'd filed an internal request for cartilage cells and equipment for *novel progress in the growth of unique, self-sustaining footwear out of tensile, responsive tissue analog, essential to the productivity of the ambulatory laboratory human resource.* He filed the request under his own name, misspelled by one letter. It was approved by the next morning.

Smuggling it all out of the lab, Anja was sure, should have posed a problem, but Michel was confident they could just walk out. "I mentioned at the bottom of the request that we'll need to do field trials. Don't worry about it. Our smokescreen is intact. We just need to act confident."

"What smokescreen?"

"For me, the shoe thing. For you, being disgruntled."

They sat at the kitchen island together, looking back and forth between the computer simulation, which was proceeding slowly, as it should, and the cells in the box, which still appeared entirely inert to the naked eye. Anja hardly had to watch the simulation to see what it was doing. Before constructing itself, the roof had to build its own support system. Two little columns rising from the dish, inscribing themselves on the empty space, making emptiness into somethingness. They'd fill themselves in as they grew into solid posts, thin and slightly brittle—to be snapped off later when whoever was living under the roof built something else to support it. Theoretically, anyway.

"Good thing I put everything on a flash drive ages ago, right?"

"What?"

"How did you think I got these data sets for the simulation?"

"Preemptive? Before we even got fired?"

"You never know when you'll need a backup." He smiled.

"Impressive."

With his eyes fixed on the screen, he reached into his pocket and pulled out a small vial. "During my stealing rampage I also nicked some burdock root."

"What's that?"

"Witchcraft."

"Oh?"

"No—science." He smiled. "It's a natural antihistamine they've been messing with in Health Trials." He traced his own jawbone and glanced at hers. "I noticed your rash was coming back."

She took the little bottle and opened it, sniffing, slightly embarrassed. "Thanks." She tipped a drop of the liquid onto her finger and wiped it down her cheek. It didn't smell or feel like anything. "My friend says this rash is psychosomatic, though."

"Doesn't make it any less real."

"I guess."

"The power of the subconscious."

"But if my subconscious is doing this to me, it really seems like my conscious should be able to override it."

"Bodies don't have a manual override."

"I know. I have this feeling lately like my body and the world are locked into a pattern I don't understand."

"Sounds like the eternal human condition."

"I used to think free will was a thing."

He gestured to the box in between them. "You've got genotype and phenotype. Environment matters."

"What about self-actualization? Or plastic surgery?"

"Some people might say the urge to change yourself is just another aspect of your innate personality, as conditioned by your shitty cultural environment."

She laughed. He glanced at her and back at the screen, fidgeting. "We should really be seeing something in there already." The set of columns should have been complete, their tips fanning into little trestles to uphold the roof.

"Already?"

"Yeah, it should go like twenty times as fast."

"Maybe it's dead. I wouldn't be surprised if the sample didn't survive the trip."

"I know. This is a hack job."

But they continued to stare intently, and twenty-one minutes after Michel's calculated schedule, Anja tapped the glass. "There she is."

Two baby mushrooms of translucent pinkish material had appeared, blooming from nothing, beyond all reason, in the center of the dish, right where she'd planted them.

"Ha!" Michel threw his arms up. "Ha, ha!"

She realized what it was about his laugh that had been bothering her. His laugh was onomatopoeic, in that each utterance really sounded like he was saying "Ha." Michel was always Michel, a literal, fixed version of himself. Louis, of course, was never quite Louis. The shape that didn't match its outline—the skidded frame.

They watched the performance in rapture.

First the sinewy columns, then the trestles close behind. A stretching and a winnowing. Then the real triumph: the bridging, when the two sides of the roof extended themselves across the expanse between the columns in two arches, meeting in the center like old friends. As the double-wave shape solidified it also crept out in all directions until it was a perfect round blot from above. From straight on, it looked like a wedding arbor.

Anja wiped her nose print from the glass and then put her nose right back against the surface. Time passed in exquisite growth. She was ecstatic, forgetting herself in the movement.

In just over an hour the real roof had been born, matching its blueprint in the simulation: the screen and the petri dish displaying the same complete image. Reality had converged with calculation: world had met abstraction. Anja felt drawn into a moment of literal peace, as in the peace of literalness. This was what it felt like to be exactly yourself.

Then she remembered where they were, what they were doing, why they were doing it. She looked back and forth between the sketch and the structure and let out a ragged sigh.

Michel leaned back, clearly as dejected as she felt. "I know. Shit. I didn't realize until now how much I wanted it to do something else."

"I really thought . . . I don't know what I thought. But I did think."

He leaned in to squint into the box again, frowning hard. "So I guess there's no conspiracy." He forced a Ha. "We're just consultants."

"Just doing our bullshit jobs."

They looked at each other. She was unbearably embarrassed. He leaned across the table.

In the brief moment before his mouth reached hers, curving toward her like one side of the roof pushing itself through the air to meet its other half, Anja consciously experienced three emotions: fear, despair, resignation. When the mouth landed at its destination, it met an immobile counterpart. She could neither conjure the reflex to jerk away nor to kiss back.

The kiss ended as abruptly as it had begun and Michel leaned back and looked away. He made a dejected huffing sound. He shook his head and then he huffed again.

"I don't get it," he said. This was true. He obviously didn't get it, any of it.

"I wasn't expecting that."

"Come on."

"I wasn't."

"You're saying I was imagining it?"

She shook her head. Had she known? Had *she* been imagining things? Had she imagined that she could relax in the presence of a Y chromosome socialized as straight male? Had she imagined that their obvious incompatibility would cut off the possibility of Michel constructing his own fantasy of what they were?

He looked as embarrassed as she felt. "Why did you bring me here, then?"

"To do the experiment." She shook her head. "I thought we were friends."

He stood up and started fussing with the things on the table, stacking some petris and shifting them around. There was something pitiful in his movements. It occurred to her that he was pouting.

"We *were* friends," he said.

The comment stung, but it also seemed pathetic. She noticed a minuscule brown stain on the lip of the collar of his turtleneck. "I'm sorry, but I'm just not capable right now. I'm still half underwater."

He picked up his jacket and shook it out, unnecessarily. "Hey," she said, reaching out a hand. "Really, I'm sorry. But I'd only be doing it out of loneliness."

He put the jacket on one arm, then the other. He shrugged to straighten it across his shoulders. "Ouch," he said.

"I know. That's what I'm saying. I don't want to treat you like a Band-Aid."

His gestures of moving and stacking things had been for show. In the end he didn't bother to gather the instruments on the table, just shoved his laptop into his backpack.

Before leaving, he said, without making eye contact, "You have no idea what's good for you."

20

ANJA HAD ONCE READ THAT DOLPHINS COULD SURFACE TO breathe and birds could keep flying while half-asleep. Evolution had gifted some species with the ability to shut down one hemisphere of the brain at a time. Some animals, like ducks, kept one eye open on the awake side of the head to watch for predators or monitor offspring. Hemispheric sleep was efficient, managerial: tasks could be delegated to one side while the other side rested.

Humans never learned this skill. The hemispheres were too codependent to cleave; the optic nerves didn't like to work alone. Human half-sleep was entirely unsatisfying, with neither half of the brain enjoying a real rest—instead, the whole brain was left just sitting there, simmering below the surface of consciousness, unable to sink.

Home again on the Berg, Anja involuntarily became the first land mammal to develop the skill. The eye nearest her phone was always open, even when closed, and she held entire conversations with people who weren't there, using her still-active language-processing centers.

No one called. After Michel left, the house was silent. She

quickly got used to the smell and the humidity, but the silence pressed in on her as she lay on the floor of the living room, not caring about whatever fungi or creatures crawled across her. There was deep regret, there was a new sense of loss, but she'd had no choice—she couldn't do it. He'd gone and ruined the sense of safety between them, broken the seal. The experiment was over.

Half-asleep, she drew her knees to her chest and waited, hoping to enter full hibernation. If only she could stop her system altogether, no more metabolizing or processing—like a bear halting its digestion before a long winter sleep.

Her thoughts turned to Howard. He was always there, waiting. She could call. He'd be mad that she'd come up here, but she could frame herself as desperate or helpless and he'd arrive like he always did. She considered it and then she tucked it away. She slid her phone under the sofa and let one half of her brain rest while the other kept on whirring.

Right eye pulling left brain awake before dawn, she felt around instinctively for the phone again, panicked when she couldn't find it right away. Panicked again when she realized how low her battery was and where she was—cut off, no one but Michel knowing her location. Her first thought, of course, was to leave the mountain, but she jerked against this possibility. The house was filling with golden streaks of light; she could wait a few hours.

In the kitchen above the sink she noticed a vine creeping through the wall. The wall was crumbling where the vine poked through, but not giving way. She went outside and around the house to see where it was coming from: a whole nest of thick vines was suctioned, octopus-like, onto the corner of the building. From their bright green offshoots she found a cluster of plump round fruits, like small yellow plums. She plucked one and turned it over in her palm. Its skin gave slightly with a squeeze and bounced back like a collagen implant. Without thinking, she bit into it. Sour, but not bad.

On the back terrace, growth was also accelerating. Sprouts were shoving themselves up between the tessellated stones, which had buckled in one corner, and a swarm of gnats concentrated itself over the wet muck that had collected in a crevice in the split surface. Surveying the edge of the clearing, she found an odd mix of growth and decay, like the mountain was eating itself and spitting new things out.

All her life she'd found satisfaction in the cycles of consumption, the pleasure of bringing full containers home and taking empty things out. All those normal entrances and exits: lightbulbs, wine bottles, toilet paper. Bring them in, unpack them, put them where they need to go. When they're done, remove their shells, take them away, put them in the right goodbye containers. But the Berg house had swallowed it all, a hungry, angry child that ate everything and then vomited most of it up.

Bracing herself for heavy nostalgia, she went inside and up to the bedroom. The bed was unmade, of course; clothes dotted the floor, a towel was slung over the door to the bathroom. After inspecting the toilet she decided it was safe to pee. While peeing she inspected her forearms. She'd slathered them with the whole bottle of burdock root after Michel took off. The irritation was faded to the faint imprint of a continent on a sun-spotted map.

She lay down on the bed and spread her limbs, feeling the memory foam give way in a familiar pattern. It would be so easy to take a nap. Her hand hit upon something under the pillow: Louis's tablet. She sat upright, hardly believing he'd left it here for so long, after seeming so attached to it when he got home. Hadn't he been using it at the studio? She looked carefully around the room again. She couldn't remember how it had looked the day she left. But his side of the closet was mostly empty. Had he come home to get more of his stuff without telling her?

Hesitantly, she pressed the tablet's button and was surprised to find it still holding a charge. She held it close to her face, checking for a data connection, which was low but functional.

A little red button hovered atop the inbox icon. It said 36. She felt the weight of the machine, so heavy, a thick slab of flesh. There was no doubt that Louis had outsourced his grief to the machine. She remembered the way it had felt when one day, while they were riding the subway together, he had pressed the tablet against the side of her shoulder to steady it as he composed a message. She could feel each of his taps through the screen, so clearly articulated. She didn't notice when he had removed the tablet and was really tapping her shoulder, trying to tell her they'd reached their stop.

She felt sorry, for a moment, that he didn't have it now. His appendage, which contained his loss. The thing was a part of him, all he had left of Pat, maybe.

Oh well. She tapped open the inbox. The thirty-six unread messages stared her in the face like glittering pebbles. Her pupils dilated, her pulse bounced. She was high on the breach.

Impulsively, she scanned for Sara's name, apparently still in search of the other woman to pin everything on. She knew that, just as it had done to Louis, pain was twisting her toward the cliché: the mainstreaming of emotion. Wasn't there any fucking original way to experience heartbreak?

Be methodical, she told herself. Start from the top. Read the recently opened ones first.

The first batch she scanned was mostly logistical chatter. Louis was a brilliant email writer—she had watched over his shoulder as he constructed messages sometimes, and had asked him to draft hers when she had to handle something particularly delicate. The art of the email was an English skill, or maybe just a human skill, that she'd never fully mastered. It was at its heart the skill of knowing how to ask for things without sounding like you really needed them. Louis knew how to be firm without forcing, to be funny without being unprofessional. In his elegant sentences he was clear and calm; he never pointed fingers, but he never shouldered the blame. He inflected the right amount of humor and familiarity to remind the reader that, while he was responsible, he was a creative, not a cog.

She was surprised at his curtness in several of the exchanges she glossed over. He reprimanded a colleague for "hierarchical" behavior in a meeting. He insisted the receptionist triple-check a delivery was coming on time because of its "vital importance." The events themselves were unremarkable, except that they were things Anja didn't know about, because she was not speaking with Louis on a daily basis anymore. Mundane ticks on the daily meter that she should have heard about over breakfast smoothies, but which were now really none of her business. And yet these normal happenings still had the aura of Louis around them: they weren't normal nothing-mails, because they were his.

On cue, Sara's name popped up in a message from two days before. Anja shuddered and pulled the comforter up around her on the bed.

> hay lou
>
> still on for tonight @barowned? I got the *special delivery* you sent and am gonna find a way to stash it before we go in. is anyone else coming with?
>
> also just wanted to say I'm so sorry abt anja, I know you tried ur best but sometimes things just

aren't meant to be . . . we are gonna take ur mind off

it w dancing ja?? if you need anything at all just lmk

I'm always here to talk etc

sending xoxoxsss!!

She looked down at the tablet with disgust. At least it was clear there had been no hooking up. She could tell by the pandering tone of the message.

Knowing that he wasn't sleeping with Sara should have made her feel better, but it didn't. There was no other concrete reason for Louis's inner disjuncture, no one for her to blame except mortality—except Louis. She realized that the name of the disjuncture—Idealism? Grief? Self-righteousness?—was becoming harder and harder for her to describe. And its occurrence was becoming harder and harder to locate in time. Just like Laura had said, maybe it wasn't there at all. Maybe Louis had been continuous all along. Maybe the disjuncture had happened in her.

The rest was obvious. Sara was in the loop, number one O sidekick, since Anja, the would-be distributor, was now out of the picture.

Louis had responded.

can't wait for ur grand entrance :) I'm gonna get there early around 11, just to czech out the scene, so msg me when you get there and I'll seek u out. snowhite's going on at 4 btw.

x L x

Was it worse or better that he hadn't mentioned Anja at all in his response? Respecting their privacy or just more denial?

She scanned further down the list in the inbox. She clicked

through a few emails from Prinz without subject lines. Links and jokes, links and jokes. She found one that Louis had apparently sent to himself.

> Loos: "The homeless need meaning in their existence and they need beauty. The only way to give this back to them is to reinvent an authentic, craft-based art."

This almost made her laugh. The return of the forsaken namesake. She clicked the next button.

Glaring up at her like a blue evil eye was HOWARD.

> Hi Louis,
>
> Hope all is well with you, congrats on the launch this week!
>
> As promised _here's_ a secure link to the rough cut (expires tmw) of the first episode. Let me know what you think, we're on a bit of a crunch schedule-wise but happy to pass on any feedback as we finish the final edit.
>
> Again: can't thanku enough for the last-minute part you've played in all this. It's really going to make a difference.
>
> Cheers,
>
> H.

She placed a hand on her sternum to repress a wave of nausea.

She clicked through the link and ended up on a long scrolling page. It had a perpetually repeating forest pattern as wallpaper. The repeating image was slightly pixelated: a complex Photoshop effect made to look like it was pushing against visual technology limitations now long since irrelevant.

Times New Roman italic scrolling across the top and bottom of the page announced: *FERN GULLY, Episode 1.*

A video embed was nestled in the forest.

Video playback was automatic. She turned the volume up on the tablet.

A time code flashed across the screen: 9:00 A.M.

Bedroom, aerial view. Dresser, bed with pin-striped sheets, stack of books in the corner. Yoga mat unfurled at the foot of the bed.

She sat up. Her eyes shot around the room. Dresser, bed, books. Yes, these were the same elements, the exact same elements, but in slightly different states. The yoga mat in the room she was in was flopped over itself in the corner. Fewer books were in the stack. The sheets she lay on were flowered, not striped—a different IKEA pattern. An orchid on the windowsill that was still alive in the room on the screen was very dead in the real.

Two images, screen-shallow and room-deep, like a blueprint next to a photograph. Which was which? Her perspective swung around to match the screen view—there: the camera near the ceiling. A small white ovoid shell with the tiniest of apertures. She stared into its glareless lens.

There was a stool by the window, which she dragged to the wall below the seeing eye. She reached up to rip out its cords, but, of course, it was already off. No power, no blinking light. She yanked the cords out of its backside anyway.

The tablet was still playing the video, making noises from its spot on the bed.

She looked down at the screen and saw her head. The back of her head, then the front of her head, the part of her head with her face. She'd never seen herself from that angle before—her face from above, with features foreshortened. A towel was wrapped around her body, which was also foreshortened. She saw herself lift one leg up on the bed and then turn to look over her shoulder into the bathroom. When video Anja turned, so did real Anja, expecting for a second to see someone there. But no one was behind the real bathroom door.

Video Anja had company. She was joined by video Louis, in his underwear. He kissed her and said something; the sound of his voice was muffled. Tiny subtitles popped up at the bottom of the frame to clarify. The bubbles said: *I can't tell your mood of the day since there's no hot water to steam up the shower.* Video Anja laughed and said, loudly enough that subtitles were unnecessary: *What mood do you think I'm in after a cold shower?*

She tapped the video to pause, and stood, triangulating the objects in the room. A page in the back of a magazine: What's the difference between these two cartoons?

The book pile in the video room was double the height it was in the real room, and she recognized the book on the top of the taller pile from its yellow cover, a giant behemoth of a science fiction book Louis had been reading. Reading because of something at work. Something about parachutes. The parachute project. Not so long after they'd moved in. The video image was nearly a year past its expiration date. Since then, their relationship had congealed around an event, then dissolved—and now she was back at the house, in its shell.

When all those terrorist beheading videos had come out, she hadn't been able to bring herself to watch them, but she didn't want to be the only one who hadn't seen them. Caught between horror and curiosity, she'd called Laura, who was inured to televised suffering, and asked her to narrate them while she watched.

"Pleading victim," Laura had said without affect. "Knife is not very long. Seems kind of like a steak knife. Hard to believe it will do the job. But—oh—oh, yeah, damn, it's doing the job. Wait, you can't see the knife because of all the blood. The head is coming away . . ."

Faced with watching the demise of her relationship on candid camera, Anja dialed Laura's number from the tablet.

"Louis?" Laura answered warily.

"No, it's me," Anja said.

"What? Where are you? Are you with him?"

"No, I'm alone. I'm totally fine."

"Are you—"

"Just listen, can you please watch something for me? Don't ask more right now. I'll send you a link."

While she waited for Laura to find her computer and open the page, Anja glimpsed Louis's inbox again. Twenty-eight unread messages, down from thirty-six. He must have been looking through it at this very moment. She closed the window reflexively, as if he could see her in there looking.

"Okay," said Laura. "Ready." Anja waited. She heard the shadow of her own voice, from the video on Laura's laptop, through Louis's tablet.

"What the hell?" Laura said after a little too long. "Is this your house?"

"Yeah. You can fast-forward if you want. I already watched the first four minutes."

"No, I want to watch from the beginning."

Anja opened the inbox again, despite herself. Twenty-one unread messages. She scrolled down through the subject lines of the recently read.

"Okay . . . here you are in the kitchen," said Laura after the bedroom scene had ended. "You're complaining. About Michel. You're saying how annoying he's been lately . . . Louis says . . . Michel's a nice guy . . . but kind of a square." Anja gritted her teeth and massaged her forehead with her temples, imagining Michel watching the video. "Okay," said Laura, "you're getting your food ready . . . you're making a smoothie. Okay. This part is pretty boring."

"Keep going."

"You're asking Louis about his stuffed nose . . . You just asked if he remembered to pick up his nasal spray from the pharmacy . . . no, it looks like he forgot his nasal spray. But he's not going to get it today, he doesn't have time. He's late. Oh, the drama!" Laura snorted. "He has to go to work now . . . you're giving him the trash to take with him . . . hold on . . . okay, you're arguing about whether it's okay to take the trash down instead of putting it in the disposal . . . he's going to take the trash anyway. He is leaving with the trash now. Okay, end of scene. Long pause . . . waiting . . ." She was silent during the apparent pause in action. "Okay. New scene. Now it says it's seven p.m., and we are . . . back in the kitchen. How exciting. You're trying to put something down the disposal . . . you're yelling at it. Whoa, strong language! Okay . . . you're taking stuff out of the fridge . . ."

After the twenty-minute episode finished, Laura agreed with Anja: the only identifiable throughline was Anja and Louis's incompetence when it came to the house. A particularly shameful scene had them sharing a cigarette out the window, laughing about the smoking ban.

"They must have sifted through months of recordings to find the worst parts," said Anja, rubbing her forehead. The scenes had been stitched together from several different days, spaced weeks apart.

"It does kind of seem like you guys aren't doing a great. . . um, job of it."

Anja tried to match her memory with the recording. Maybe they had been at fault for not following the rules. Maybe they could have tried harder. Maybe some of the blame *was* on them. But hadn't Howard admitted it was all a bunch of mismanagement?

She shook her head and sighed into the phone. The truth of the Before wouldn't really matter to anyone else. The only thing that would matter from now on was the representation, the way it was all depicted in this carefully edited home video.

"Where did you get this link?" asked Laura.

"I found it." Laura passed her judgment through the phone. "Okay, I found it in Louis's email. I have his tablet."

"Nice. So I guess he knows about this already."

"Looks like I'm the only one who didn't know."

"You didn't know there were cameras all over your house?"

"Of course . . . just in case of malfunction . . ."

She'd read every sentence of their contract. It had been clear that the video was for posterity—a dead end, a cul-de-sac, feeding itself straight into the bowels of some unhackable server. Maybe this had been true, for a time. But, like all bytes, it was retrievable. She should have known. The membrane between private and public was so slight. She should have known. She hung up.

Spare room, living room, office. All cameras were definitely off, but she severed the cords anyway with nail clippers. The kitchen was harder—she had to climb up on the counter and reach around into the back of the cabinet to find the wires.

While she was up there she surveyed the room and wondered if she was imagining it or whether, since the day before, it had become even more overgrown. The vines reaching through the wall extended far across it now, almost grazing the basin of the sink.

Some particularly hearty weeds were pushing themselves up from the disposal, reaching up to meet the tips of the vines.

The forgotten experiment lay on the island. She and Michel hadn't even bothered to document the little miracle mushroom they'd grown together. Might as well take a picture while it existed.

She hopped down and approached the box where the thing was nestled, raising the tablet to the glass, spreading her fingers to zoom in for the photo.

She stopped. Spread her fingers wider and closer on the screen. Zoom out, zoom in. Look again. Something different. The mushroom. Larger, taller—no, it wasn't like a mushroom at all anymore, not rounded where it should have been, angular instead. Light was glinting off its roof, which had become a flat surface. A hallucination, an overgrown memory.

She put the tablet down and stepped closer to the box. The pink thing in the dish, which had been the roof resting on two columns, had expanded to be much broader and flattened out into two planes, slightly smaller than the circumference of her hand with fingers spread. Where it had been creased in the center, reaching up in an arch on either side of a valley, it was now peaked, as if the crease had exactly inverted itself to become a ridge. Yes, it had peaked in a long line down the middle of the roof and flattened on either side: no longer the roof of a mouth. It was now like the roof of a house.

When she crouched and peered into the box sideways, she could see that a second horizontal plane had webbed itself beneath the roof, about midway between roof and ground, dividing the empty interior into two sections on top of each other: two stories. And this plane was supported by two more newly sprouted columns, so there was now a post on each side of the two-level structure. The whole thing had risen a few centimeters above the agar, now resting on a dense-looking foundation of its own making. It was all still a translucent pink, the color more noticeable in areas of greater density. The makings of a cartilage house. Anja frowned. *But you were only supposed to be a roof.*

She stood again and closed her eyes. There was something familiar about this new shape, the gently angled slopes of the flattened roof, the fact that the columns were placed on the sides of the planes rather than at the corners—it was counterintuitive, not how you would imagine building a Lego house yourself. She leaned back on the kitchen counter, which felt grimy on her forearms, and considered the meaning of "counterintuitive." Intuition was supposed to be a natural, instinctual feeling or desire, but there was really no such thing as instinct. Even what seemed like the deepest inclination was conditioned to some extent by the outside world. Genotype does not determine phenotype. For the physical expression of traits, one has to look to the environment, to circumstance. Nurture determines how nature behaves.

So if there were no such thing as pure intuition, what was counterintuition? The deliberate realization that nothing you took for granted as real had been true in the first place? Howard had told her once he thought she had good intuition, which she had taken as a compliment, but maybe she should have been cultivating counterintuition all along.

She looked back at the roof in the box, which was now much more like a house in a box. She pictured Howard in the kitchen, showing her and Louis around their new house, opening cabinets and turning on the faucet, halfway between proud parent and real estate agent. "This is one of four main vertical beams," he'd said, slapping the wall above the sink. "It's hollow so it can double as a rainwater collector."

Four shafts on the four sides of the house for water collection and ventilation. Of course, she'd seen plenty of diagrams of how it worked. She recoiled from the tiny house in the box, wondering if this were some accident of biomimicry—if it could mimic the house she was in. But really, there was no way this was improvisational; if it were copying its environment, it would be copying skin, not bones, and so far it was all pink interior. It wasn't improvising. It knew what it was doing.

In the back of her mind she must have believed a deviation from the simulation of some kind might happen—why else had she suggested reconstructing the experiment with Michel at all? But the reality of it was too much. If she acknowledged that the little house was mutating without warning, she would feel the whole history of the house—and her life in the house—mutate retroactively. This constituted a betrayal of some sort. Not a surface betrayal, but deep down on the cellular level. A mutation that was a feature, not a bug.

Notice the thought. Acknowledge its presence. Let it pass. Something she'd read on a grief forum. How ridiculous: thoughts never passed on their own. She'd have to do the heavy lifting. So she forced the panic, centimeter by centimeter, from the frontal lobe, off the cliff and down into the depths. There were reasonable actions to take if she could suppress the impulse to freak out.

Michel was right: the paperwork in the binders had massed into solid chunks after weeks of moisture and heat. She found the right red binder with the Berg contract and tried chipping off the first page with a fingernail. The paper flaked in her hand. She needed something to lever each page open with. A search through the pantry and the bathroom cabinet yielded dental floss.

Floss didn't make it easy, but possible. She guessed that the last quarter of the block of paperwork was where the section in question could be found, and she painstakingly seesawed the waxy thread between leaves, nudging them apart one by one, hunched over the binder on the floor by the bookshelf. It was a tedious job. When she had found and separated the right sheets, which were albeit stained, warped, and torn, she needed another twenty minutes to scan them for the clause in question. She knew she'd read this before at some point, alone in the garden house, highlighting passages that had seemed important or confused her.

She had not highlighted the passage about video recording, deeming it irrelevant or too unlikely a scenario to really consider. She cursed Anja of the Before.

Forcefully adjusting her reading mode to that of parsing legal jargon, she read each sentence out loud, slowly, to make the meaning stick.

§ 26 Documentation of Living Arrangement

(1) The undersigned inhabitant(s) consent to unbroken visual and audio recording at any and all times in all _6_ rooms of object, excluding toilet room, for purposes of quality control and safety monitoring. The Recorded Content [RC] is continuously machine monitored according to latest vision algorithm (ICU.7.1 as of date of signing) to check for major anomaly, i.e., flood. Upon special request and agreement of all parties, particular sections of RC may be reviewed by Berg Asset Establishment [BAE] stakeholders and Finster Corp. Relevant Interested Management [RIM] for quality assurance and/or post-facto evidence to determine fault in case of major anomaly, etc. RIM for given situation is to be determined on a case-by-case basis by BAE according to stipulations listed in § 22

(7). RC is considered confidential (for strictly internal use, internal being defined as BAE and RIM) pending special circumstances, being:

(a) As deemed beneficial for the other residents of Berg community or similar communities in development ("similar" as defined by § 42 (4))

(b) As deemed educational for the general public

She wiped at the page, which was stained at this section, and brought it close to her face to make out the words.

> Distribution of RC beyond internal communication requires written permission of signatory. In the case of multiple inhabitation of object (multiple signatories), any form of release of RC beyond BAE stakeholders and RIM depends on permission of one (1) signatory inhabitant.

She dropped the binder and went to the kitchen. She felt around in a bowl she had filled with plums and found a nice big one to drive her teeth into. She glanced at the house in the box, which in the interim had grown stairs, a bathroom, and some kind of fringe around the roof, which she guessed would become gutters and eaves. She sucked on the plum pit. The house was growing without stopping. The house didn't need food; it didn't need a consultant. It didn't need anyone.

21

NOTHING ELSE FROM HOWARD IN LOUIS'S INBOX BESIDES A FEW bland scheduling emails. No trail. Meaning the episode, whatever it was, must have been rolled out behind closed doors, face-to-face. Howard's face to Louis's face. Louis was the one (1) signatory inhabitant needed to release the footage for the *education of the general public.*

It was raining for the first time in weeks, and the mountain was drenched in a lukewarm torrent. The ceiling dripped in the kitchen, the bedroom. Anja ignored the plinking sounds of water hitting furniture and took a pail from the utility closet and a big bowl from the kitchen cabinet and left them outside on the patio to collect water. The raindrops were thick and even. She closed her eyes and wiped her face, bunched her hair, rubbed her fingers around her skull; she was reminded by the weight of her head that her entire reality was created inside it and was subject to change. She took off her shirt, wrung it out. Feeling her forearms against her stomach, she was startled by the smoothness of the skin where for so long it had been irritated.

When she was mostly dry she pulled a stool up to the kitchen island to check on the house, wishing she had the computer simulation to look at and compare to the physical developments. But it wouldn't have mattered. The simulation was designed to time out after the expected physical completion, clipping off the future from its fulfillment. She stared down at what had emerged from the petri dish, having transcended its dish terrain and grown into what was undeniably a house with the shape of the house she was in. She could locate her exact position on the 3D model. Second floor, kitchen. She narrowed her eyes at the spot where she was sitting, willing a replica of herself to grow there. Instead she found a barely perceptible movement in another area, a little stirring in the bathroom. Plumbing.

The real house, on the other hand, was no longer plumbed. The water that came out of the tap upstairs was mucus-like; the tap in the kitchen produced nothing. Certain daily tasks required running water. Obviously, she reminded herself, she could leave. But why? What was waiting for her down below?

She assessed the situation. There was nothing to eat besides some dry granola in the pantry—she didn't dare open the fridge to see what it held—plus the plums and a few cucumbers. She'd found the cucumbers peering in through the foggy living room window at her: oblong finger-size green curls bumping up against the glass. Only five were big enough to eat, but they were crisp and sweet. When plucking them outside in the leftover drizzle, she noticed new anthills dotting the patio. A metallic slug slimed toward one anthill, leaving a wet trail across the wrecked stones. She waved to the slug and checked her water buckets, which were full enough.

There was a backup battery charger in the utility closet that she could use for a few more hours. She plugged her phone in and let it reach 20 percent charge before disconnecting, not wanting to exhaust the charger just yet. When she powered the phone on, she was acutely aware of the low-battery bar on the screen.

She scrolled through her missed calls and messages. Skipped over tons from Dam and Laura, who could probably wait. One from Howard, who could definitely wait.

And Louis. Louis had finally called in the singular moment of white noise when she was unreachable.

In the living room the rain was washing in under the door-frame, pooling in places and sinking into the crumbling floor in others. She thought of sopping it up, but the plants sprouting inside wouldn't mind the moisture, and neither did she, really. She sank her bare feet into a puddle and wiggled her toes in the warm rainwater. She readjusted her stance, gulped in air, and called back. After five leaden rings, he answered.

The curtains opened: How are you, good. How are you, good. Couldn't Americans think of any other way to open an encounter? How are you how are you good good good how are you good good into eternity. You'd have to pack so much nuance into the *good* to make it mean anything that it wasn't worth the effort to draw it out at all—better to get it over with as fast as possible. Hwryugd. Gd.

"What have you been up to?" she asked.

He cleared his throat. "A few product trials. Expanding on our beta test last weekend."

"I see. Approaching the alpha."

"Yep. Hope so."

"Anything else?"

"What do you mean."

"I mean, have you been up to anything else?"

"Anything like what?"

"Oh, anything at all."

"Like what?"

She closed her eyes. She was going to have to wrench it from him. "I heard you've been spending some time with Howard."

He cleared his throat again but didn't speak. She imagined where he might have been standing, near the sun-following desk, or maybe the wall-window, looking out at the parking lot where the receptionist retreated to smoke cigarettes. Maybe he was watching people go in and out of the yoga studio next door, rolled mats in hand.

"I also heard that you signed off on a web series about our life, without telling me," she said.

"Oh. Who told you?"

"That's not really the point, is it."

"Well. I didn't have a choice." He sounded like a teenager begging off a chore. He wasn't even interested enough to make excuses.

She stepped from one puddle to another. "Please clarify."

"It was the only way."

This was like pulling teeth. "Go on."

"It turned out getting Basquiatt to sign off on O wasn't as easy as I thought it would be," he said. "In the end I had to make a trade."

With the phone still pressed to her ear, she walked back into the kitchen, circling the glass vitrine, the little house staring up at her like a tiny head. Her stomach rumbled. She picked up a cucumber from the pile she'd made of them on the table, studied it, and took a bite. A trade. One for one. She remembered: someone had told her that Finster now owned Basquiatt, just like Finster owned everything. Meaning Howard owned everything. All roads led to Oz.

"Howard pushed O through for you, in exchange for your signature," she said at last.

Someone's voice came through in the background on his end. Louis paused to listen, muffled the phone, and asked whoever it was to wait just a minute. "Sometimes you have to make sacrifices," he said into the phone.

She thought of Pat. Pat, who always invaded. Pat, who had sacrificed her own body for a misplaced notion of duty, of obligation to a greater cause.

"Sacrifices. Like me?"

"It wasn't about you."

"Right." She recalled the idea she'd had near the start of their relationship: Louis was able to make plans but not promises. In retrospect, she could see what she had not been able to admit to herself back then. She should have really insisted on some kind of promise.

"Hey, I'm sorry." The apology was flat, like the cap had been left off the bottle overnight. "But if you were paying attention to anything at all, you'd see it was worth it. This is all so much bigger than us."

"Shouldn't I get a say in that?"

"You can't always control everything. Sometimes history runs its course."

"Your history. Your story. Not mine."

"This is just as tough on me as you. It's embarrassing for both of us to be on that website."

"What's the point of embarrassing *us*, then?"

"You should talk to Howard about that."

She took a long breath in and out, chewing the cucumber. *Acknowledge the thought. Dismiss the thought.* "What the fuck is wrong with you?" she said. "Why the fuck didn't you just ask me first?"

He didn't raise his voice in return, just stated, as if the

relationship between cause and effect were clear: "*That's* why. See how you can't even have a normal conversation? You're always suspicious. You assume I'm doing everything in bad faith."

"What did I—?"

"Maybe you shouldn't have brought Pat into things."

Anja was blown aback. *She* shouldn't have brought Pat into "things"? She, Anja, was the one to bring Pat in?

She remembered how she'd inspected him for signs of change in this very kitchen, morning after morning. How she'd repeatedly asked him if he was okay. How she'd been so worried about him that he ended up comforting *her*. How he'd started avoiding her just so he wouldn't have to worry about her worrying about him. How angry she'd gotten with him on their last hike up the mountain as he struggled to deal with his emotions. How incredibly angry she had been with him. How unfair she had been.

In spite of herself, she said it: "I'm sorry too."

"It's fine."

"You still should have told me what you were doing."

"Yeah, and you should have been more supportive." She wiped her streaming nose. "I wouldn't have had to get Howard involved at all if you'd wanted to invest in O yourself."

She sniffed in snot loudly. "What? You wanted me to invest?"

"You could have, if you wanted to. That's what everyone is saying now. Even Howard thought it was weird you didn't offer."

He was invoking the authority of the dysfunctional social scene, of the masses, of the culture at large, even of Howard, to override the private contract of their relationship. Public consensus reigned, the proclamation was in, and she was the traitor. She remembered again their last climb up the mountain together. His hating everyone, his superiority. Yet he was ready to invoke their wisdom now, when it suited him.

She felt her language giving way, the right words not readily accessible. Whatever she said, she knew she'd realize later it was the wrong thing. She hung up.

When the rain stopped in the early evening she put on a T-shirt, shorts, and rain boots and went for a walk. Her route up the mountain was random; she ignored the path and zigzagged recklessly through the wet mud. A thorn tore at her leg and she bent down to inspect its source: a bramble patch thick with berries. One of the berries had oozed onto the skin of her calf, leaving a purplish smear.

Not concentrating on the ground, she stepped carelessly into a hole of eroded muck, stumbling and landing ungracefully on her butt. The mud on the slope continued to shift until it collided with a rocky outcrop a meter or so below her and prompted the rocks loose. Mud and a smatter of stones slid down the hill below her feet in a miniature landslide. She scrambled up away from the action and, picking her steps more carefully, continued to climb.

Reaching a break in the greenery, she peered out at what she could see of the city below. She was surprised to pick up the sound of a steady beat. The sort of music you'd hear at the Baron, a stammering, high-pitched bleating atop heart-seizing bass, which she felt in her chest as much as heard with her ears. The bass was what reached her so high up.

She found a tall, mossy stump and pulled herself onto it with her hands, using all her forearm strength. When standing on the stump, which was a bit slippery, she could see what looked like a huge open-air festival on Hermannplatz. One of those endless festivals, an excuse for day-drinking and overdosing before dark. There was what looked like a rigged stage and, surrounding it, a ton of tiny sparks of light visible in the quickly falling dusk—probably phone screens raised to capture the DJ making the sounds. Judging by how far the little lights spread from the center of the action, the crowd must have been enormous. She couldn't remember having seen a gathering so big on Hermannplatz since a protest Laura had taken her to years ago.

Things were happening on land that she wasn't part of, that she knew nothing about. But they were just new iterations of the same. You were always missing something and you were never missing anything. The mass of social life would be swirling predictably, justifying its own presence with petty dramas. Careers were rising and falling, friends and lovers coming together and splitting up. Everyone was clinging to their individual life experiences, so invested in their existence on ground level that they never saw it from above.

Sara was down there somewhere, still locked in her endless struggle with Mahatma, questing so hard for god knows what. Michel was down there somewhere, brooding and working hard to forget her. He'd eventually find some grown-up woman who wore slacks and turtlenecks and owned a car and who wanted to reproduce with him. Laura and Dam were down there—possibly worried about her, she thought with a pang—but they had their own things to deal with too. And they'd be leaving soon anyway. Better not to bother them, burden them, any more than she already had.

Howard was down there, waiting for her to call him back so he could give her some miserable explanation. She resolved not to call him. She didn't need his explanations. Anyway, it couldn't be more than a day or two until the inevitable press release surfaced.

She noticed a burst of orange appear in the sea of people surrounding the stage. She frowned and squinted into the distance.

It looked like a little spurt of flame with a puff of smoke rising above it. The flame briefly illuminated the crowd, which forced itself back away from the fire in a circle, and she could see just how thick the Platz was with bodies—so many people back-to-front. There was a communal shouting loud enough to rise momentarily above the music as the crowd shifted. She stared down, intently, feet slipping on the stump. It was hard to tell what was going on, but in less than five minutes the fire disappeared. The music lowered in volume, perhaps in response to the emergency. A few minutes later there were sirens.

On her way back to the house, the oddness of the scene struck her. A crowd so packed. It was like a twilight vigil. And a fire—since when did anyone light fires during an open-air concert?

Before going to sleep she double-checked all devices to make sure they were off, conserving every morsel of battery power. She checked the camera in the living room one more time too, knowing full well she'd cut the wires but needing reassurance.

Surprisingly, sleep came easily as soon as she reclined on the sofa, as if her bodily rhythm was tuning itself to the cycle of day and night unadulterated by electricity. Her dreams were furious.

In the morning she had only to refresh her feed to find it. The press release came not in the form of an announcement from Finster, but as a sponsored critique on the front page of *The Guardian*.

Leaked Footage Exposes Cracks in the Foundation of
Pioneer Sustainable Community

An unauthored website titled <u>*Fern Gully*</u> has leaked
fly-on-the-wall video footage from inside a house in

Berlin's new eco-community for sustainable living on the city's "Berg" mountain constructed by the Finster Corporation. The footage suggests that the community inhabitants themselves may have been partially responsible for the settlement's endemic problems, which have only recently come to light.

While the degree of success of the multi-million-euro, carbon-neutral living experiment has been largely shielded from the public until now, a press release issued in response to the video <u>this morning</u> from Finster reveals that all inhabitants have in fact been recently relocated due to difficulties with the extensive demands of rigorous sustainability.

"This grand experiment," states the press release, "is a testament to Finster's investment in sustainable futures. Though the initial hopes for human/nature coexistence were higher, we are proud to have gained this essential knowledge about human limitations through our approach to Indefinite Research. Progress sometimes requires taking small steps backward."

The source of the leak is as yet unclear. The video consists of 20 minutes of compiled footage of the lives of two inhabitants, a young couple whose names are being withheld. The video is telling in its banality. From earnest arguments about how much effort they should expend on things like recycling properly, to blatant mockery of rules such as not smoking (which has <u>been proven</u> to damage the tissue of architecture meant to self-regenerate), the video is a portrait of innate human resistance to micro-governance.

Unfortunately, it seems that is precisely the type of self-regulation that would be required for life on the Berg.

The Berg, an urban development proposal by Finster to "re-nature" Berlin, won the bid for the open tender seven years ago for the controversial development of Tempelhof Airfield, which was previously the largest undeveloped public space in any European metropolis. While all other bids included various mixes of private real estate and retail outlets, Finster made a compelling case for instead increasing the city's green space with a "vertical nature park" that would over time become populated by those willing to live a completely zero-waste lifestyle. After years of vehement resistance to any kind of private development on the airfield, city residents finally agreed on a path forward and voted for Finster's plan.

From the press release recently issued, Finster seems to be considering a temporary halt to the Berg project as well as other flagship eco-communities, two of which are currently under development in Copenhagen and Milan.

The press statement's last lines read: "The greatest lesson from this adventure may well be that, unlike our ancestors, we are no longer capable of living closely with nature. As stewards of our children's future, we cannot simply leave the planet to people anymore. Individuals cannot be left to shoulder the burden of the Anthropocene."

Finster is known as a notorious "greenwasher" of

urban areas such as Berlin—that is, renovating buildings to meet sustainability standards and evicting tenants in the process. Finster and others have persistently argued that this is a necessary step in order to halt or slow climate change, despite the toll it takes on residents.

The letdown of the Berg forces us to ask whether alternate methods for large-scale upgrading of city sustainability are really possible—or whether the square meterage of Tempelhof might be better used for a typical carbon-saving (if not carbon-neutral) commercial housing development.

Given that Finster won the bid for developing Tempelhof based on this scheme, it would not be surprising if the city granted permission in the near future for the mountain to be rethought and, instead, used to make space for commercial real estate in a city with such a strong demand in the housing market.

Responsibility for the Berg's breakdown ultimately falls on many shoulders. On a larger scale, it could be that the urban planning commission did not exercise sufficient oversight during the planning and construction process. On a smaller scale, one gets the sense that Finster's vetting process for participants in this much-anticipated eco-experiment may not have been airtight. But while the two participants whose lives have been exposed in this leak may be especially (even comically) incapable of following basic rules, one also feels sympathy for the conundrums they face, and imagining oneself in their shoes, wonders if one would fare much better.

She turned off the tablet. The stupid object had never been anything but bad news.

Sunlight was blinding in the living room and the house was too warm for her to consider trying to go back to sleep. Outside, who knew what time it was; the sky was doing that purple haze thing again and any moisture from the day before had entirely evaporated. The air was desert-like and the sounds of the city below were muted. Silence. It was orange down by the horizon, but in a uniform way, not like the glow of the sunrise. The sun was impossible to locate in the haze; light was coming from all around and nowhere.

She wished for a fan as she checked the mini house slowly cooking in the kitchen. No movement now; it was certainly in its final stage. The ducts, the disposal system, all of it: pipes had even threaded themselves down into the foundation, leading to a holding tank in the ground that, she knew, was supposed to ferment waste and feed energy back up through a charged mesh of wires, which were too tiny to see on the replica. The whole circuitry of the house had emerged last, making itself visible in translucent incarnation. Veins and organs under the skin. It had grown past embryonic and fetal to become a creepy little house baby now, fully viable on its own.

A hot wind snaked through the kitchen, and she turned around to find the source. The windowpanes were sagging low enough to have separated at the seams from the ceiling, bringing their frames down with them. She could hear a gentle creaking, and wondered absently whether the ceiling was preparing to collapse.

She took a magnifying lens to the living room to take a closer look at some of the vines that had pushed up from under the sofa during the night. The foliage was getting so thick in the room that if she lay with her head against the wall, looking up, the leafy vines almost looked like a field extending into the distance. Or the forest backdrop of the *Fern Gully* site.

She saw through the magnifying glass that the leaf membranes were perfectly regular. Green surfaces edged in purple. The mass of them rustled together on the wall, the orchestrated, infinitely soft sounds giving her pleasant chills.

Outside, she found that the plum vine was naked; she needed to eat. The closest neighbor was only thirty meters down the hill. Nobody else was in any of the houses now—she was sure of it. Why had she stayed moored to her own house like a recluse for so many days? She pulled herself up, put on a shirt and rain boots, not bothering with pants, and took a bucket in case she found anything worth collecting.

She was shocked to find the other house even more overgrown than her own. Not a single window was left unbroken by the aggressive vines overtaking its façade. The decay seemed accelerated, years beyond normal decomposition. She approached the house, where the Danish couple had lived with their secret dog, and stepped tentatively through the doorway. The door was nearly rotted off its hinges, dangling at an unpleasant angle like a broken limb.

The remains of a proud display of designer taste eroded before her. Two plump Soriana lounge chairs pouted at each other over a glass table with complex steel undergirding. The glass bowl of a chandelier had fallen to the floor, somehow without shattering, the long gold chain from which it had hung coiled on top of it. A towering bookshelf boasted expensive knowledge, now moldering; a teak cabinet packed with vinyl records was in the throes of collapse; a hand-knotted carpet sprouted fungus.

No luck with the light switches. But the pantry was full of canned vegetables, tinned sardines, smoked oysters, pâté, flour, sugar. A rancid smell emanated from the fridge, rimmed by orange mold at its edge. There was a secret supply of bottled water under the sink. She smiled. She and Louis hadn't been the only ones cheating. She cracked open a sealed jar of sugar cookies and ate three, placing a whole one in her mouth and letting it saturate with saliva before chewing.

The stairs didn't look so sturdy, so she took the steps slowly, one by one. At the top stair she stopped and gasped. A large, wrist-wide snakeskin was draped over the step. She considered retrieving something sharp from the kitchen, but quickly dismissed the thought. She was going to stab a snake? She thought back to freshman biology. Snakes were most active in darkness, not daylight; she'd be fine.

In the bedroom, which must have once been ruthlessly tidy but was now scattered in dust and fallen ceiling debris, she found herself hit by the melancholy of the simulacrum. While the layout of each Berg house was slightly different in order to give a semblance of uniqueness, the bedrooms were all essentially the same shape and size. She turned around the room, running her finger over surfaces. She admired the placement of the bed, the wall sconces, the carpet, wondering why she and Louis had never tried other arrangements.

The tap in the bathroom wasn't working and the shower was overtaken by an assortment of fungi. The floor of the hallway was riddled with what looked like roots. The utility closet yielded the best booty: a backup solar-powered generator. She tipped it onto its wheels and hauled it down the stairs and over the uneven floor. She piled a bucket full of pilfered food and carried it, along with the generator, up the hill toward her house. She imagined she would set up the generator on her back patio to let it suck in the rays.

Nearing the house with the generator and bucket in tow, she stopped short. She knelt quietly in the tall grass and laid all the objects down beside her, then crawled, low to the ground, toward the trees.

Working hard to control her breathing, she peered out from behind the skinny birch where she squatted. Howard was circling the near side of the building.

The shock was not only in seeing Howard, but in seeing any human at all. She'd grown accustomed to the silence. The sound of someone else brushing through the grass was jarring and invasive. He had punctured her privacy. He absolutely did not belong here.

He called her name. She narrowed her eyes and shielded herself as much as possible behind the tree.

As far as she knew, Howard hadn't been to the house since the week she and Louis came to visit it before moving in. Any awkward tension between him and Louis had lifted that day—or so it had seemed—along with the official handoff of the house and, she supposed, of her.

He stalked back and forth through the grass. He was holding some sort of package. He scanned the tree line, then pivoted at the patio and strode directly toward her hiding spot. She was sure he would see her; she cursed herself for not wearing pants. He would find her pantless, cowering behind a tree.

But when he was a few meters away he turned and continued to troll the clearing rather than heading in her direction. He was either blind or not really looking—not really expecting to see her. The house behind him was so overgrown, maybe he doubted she was really there. Maybe this was a long shot. Or maybe—she realized with a heart stammer—maybe he'd traced her location. She'd been checking Louis's email from the tablet—he could have found out. No, she decided. The simpler scenario was more likely. The bouncer must have told him.

Frustrated, he steered himself into the house. She heard him curse as he banged on something crossing the threshold. She changed her position slightly, moving a few trees down, in the hope of seeing him as he came out without presenting herself at a head-on angle. Now he would surely notice evidence of her in-habitation. The plum pits lined up on the counter. The buckets of rainwater. And—she realized with rage—the remains of the tiny house in the box. He had no right to see the experiment.

She was tempted to run in after him, confront him, yell, ar-gue, swat his hands away from touching anything in there, but her body resisted. She blamed the hesitation on her half-nakedness, and yet she knew she wouldn't have run to him even wearing a snowsuit.

He came out of the house and sat on the green cushion of the bamboo recliner on the patio in a Thinker's pose. She enjoyed the moment of voyeurism: Howard without any audience. His bald head gleamed in the sunlight, which illuminated the wrinkles creasing his forehead. She remembered a conversation they'd had once about Botox: he said he was against it. But he'd said he was against a lot of things.

After he gave up and left, she waited for a long time among the trees to make sure he was really gone before creeping out. The house felt slightly tainted now; it would take her some time to inhabit her aloneness again.

In the kitchen, on top of the Plexi box, she found a handwrit-ten note beside a brown paper bag. The note said, *Everything hap-pens for a reason. Don't worry, it will blow over.* In the bag was a deluxe sushi combo. She forced the plastic box of sushi, through the thick weeds, down the mouth of the kitchen garbage disposal.

She inspected the experiment's box to make sure he hadn't touched anything. It didn't appear that he had. The house in the box was visibly crumbling, though. It was perishing in hypertime, before her eyes. She pulled up the stool again to watch.

It was happening fast. Witnessing the decay was like watching a time-lapse tape. The kitchen wall sagged, the doorway collapsed. Some kind of powder colonized the corners of the structure and what looked like a fine fur of pink mold arose from the rim of the Petri dish. Maybe, she thought, some of the rot from the air in the real house had found its way inside the Plexiglas. Maybe the box was being invaded by its surroundings. The box should have been airtight, but it was always possible for sturdy germs and spores to force themselves inside. Contamination loves a vacuum.

And yet, looking closer, as she always did, it didn't really look like the decay was the random result of foreign influence. The fur wasn't mold—it was just more of the same pink biomass in a shape resembling mold. And it was molding in the exact same places the real house was molding. The wonky angle of the stair-case in the box was the same as the real one. The way the window frames were separating from the walls, leaving gaps like open lips, was the same in both houses. Just as the completed house in the box had matched the shape of the real house at its zenith, now its pattern of degradation mirrored the real house in its current dilapidating state. The reason this had been so hard to recognize was that, while in the human-size house the colors were varied realistically—brown mushrooms, white and orange mold—the tiny house was monochrome.

This suggested that the realistic colors in the real house were an *additive*. There had been food coloring added to the simulation.

Circling the kitchen island, she noticed from one angle that the whole tiny house was sinking into its foundation. She ran outside, past the patio, to take in the elevation of the plot. Sure enough, the actual house—she reminded herself that this was the actual one—was also sinking. It must have been ten or fifteen centimeters below ground level already. Sagging and sinking, as if the day's hot air were pressing down on it, rupturing its seams. The downward movement was imperceptible from inside the house, but from outside it was clear as day.

She sat on the same recliner where Howard had sat, feeling the rough lichen on the cushion scratch against her bare legs.

On her left leg, a yellow-bodied beetle crawled up her thigh. She pinched it between two fingers, and instead of trying to wriggle away it seemed to power down and enter sleep mode, its thorax curling under and its legs moving slowly in perfect sync with one another. She pinched it between two fingers, drew it close to her face, and for a second thought she could see it stuttering like a windup toy.

There was no chance that this horned creature was native to Berlin soil. There was no chance that this creature was native to nature. Its wings slowly clicked and purred with the same lightly perceptible tone as the electronics drawer in their long-suffering kitchen. She recognized the fractal base pattern of the symmetrical, malleable-looking brown antlers fused to its tiny head, the elegant-but-too-smooth cartilage bending at the joints of its forelegs. The joints between the segments were a magnified version, like a blown-up diagram, of the cellular structure of the engineered cartilage she'd spent so much of her life watching grow on a screen. The only differences were the scale and the color. The prototype was forever a pale pink. Maybe the purpose of its monochrome was exactly to make the full-spectrum reality hard to recognize.

It was the same modified, bastardized cartilage that was supposed to have stopped after becoming a roof, but had kept going to become a whole little house, before reversing course and following its own independent trajectory of disintegration. The tiny house: a miniature version of a giant house that had been malfunctioning, on purpose, the whole time she'd lived in it. Their lives on the mountain, she realized, had been just one episode in a long story of planned obsolescence. And then she understood that the symbiotic system of the Berg was not a failure. It was built to fail.

22

AFTER A FEW MORE TRIPS WITH THE LAUNDRY HAMPER DOWN TO the Danish house, she sorted what she'd found. She'd stumbled into a trove of leafy spinach-like greens behind their house, which tasted edible. Maybe it really was spinach—she thought she remembered a neighbor doing some gardening down there. She boiled the leaves with canned vegetables in a tureen on top of Louis's barbecue, a big black dish like a UFO on spindly silver legs. She ate directly from the pot and listened to the sounds around her, anticipating another visitor slithering through the forest, a Howard or a snake as thick as her arm and as long as her leg, but the twilight hour was silent.

Before darkness fell, she spent some time with the plants. She chose the specimen that was growing the fastest, the plum vine, and studied its leaves and stems with the magnifying glass. The joints were exquisite, the shape of each structure perfectly symmetrical. But this method was laughable if she wanted to learn anything. She needed to look closer. She found a pencil and sketched out a plan for a rudimentary microscope.

In the morning she assembled the parts: a lens from Louis's old analog camera, a lens from a video camera she'd found in the neighbors' study, aluminum piping jutting out of the external wall where the drainage system used to be. She painstakingly sawed the pipe to the right size with a serrated knife. She bit off pieces of duct tape and dental floss to wind around it.

She worked until her body clock ticked lunchtime, then ate the remains of the stew. For dessert, berries from the bramble patch where she'd hooked her leg earlier. They were perfectly ripe. She spent the afternoon adjusting the rigged microscope until she could focus an image through it. It was finicky, but it worked.

The day passed easily as she absorbed herself with the temperamental contraption and sketched what she saw through it. Drawing the outlines of the plant's microcomponents brought her back to the best days of grad school. She felt the same relief that had overtaken her when she first entered a lab after struggling through two semesters of art school's relentless critiques. The only reason she'd thought art was a good idea in the first place was because she'd been good at looking. She dropped out, tail between her legs, having learned nothing of use besides the fact that vision had nothing to do with being an artist. Switching to science had been a rare piece of helpful advice from Eva.

She spent mornings gathering food, afternoons absorbed in seeing and sketching, evenings hiking up to the observation stump. She dragged a desk from the neighbors' house all the way to the patio, where she placed it so it could get the best light. The generator, which was fully charged, stayed there beside her unused, like an unwanted machine at the gym. It gave her a feeling of security to have it, but she couldn't think of a reason to use it besides torturing herself in Louis's inbox. And there were better things to do, like crush berries into jam.

Venturing again to the Danish couple's former garden plot, she found several recognizable species. Other plants, invasive weeds and succulents with deep roots that riddled the soil, appeared to be endemic to the mountain: too perfect in structure to have occurred through the random mutation of natural evolution. And they were too deliberate in their behavior. They had a purpose. Their purpose was to digest the mountain. Watching the behavior of an individual plant, she could trace the trajectory of programmed growth and decay. Roots advanced at warp speed a few centimeters under the ground's surface, bursting through and disrupting the others as they spread. The weeds grew to knee height and then quickly withered into compost that gave off an ammoniac scent strong enough to make her pinch her nose. The compost ate away at whatever was below it, decomposing other greenery and leaving the earth below yellow and fallow.

First, she figured, the plants would break down most of the other life on the mountain and make the soil infertile. They would do the same to the houses, invading the constructions and speeding their rate of collapse. The second stage was mold; the rot prepared the ideal condition for fungal spores to take hold, which would sprout and eat through what was left. Then, in an orgy of apoptosis, the plants and fungi would delete themselves along with what they had eaten. Dust to dust. The houses at the bottom of the settlement were in more advanced stages of the process. One had become a barely recognizable, lumpy miniature mountain taken over by a forest of brown mushrooms and white fuzz.

The neighbors' garden was barely recognizable as such, plants mingling and strangling one another in some places. She took to weeding and digging trenches between the plots to create a semblance of order through segregation. The engineered plants were growing so fast that it took only a few days to see the fruits—or vegetables—of her labor. One plentiful evening harvest left her with far too much to eat before it spoiled; she tried brining some of the cucumbers in jars, and they puckered quickly into sour pickles.

While she was screwing a lid onto a pickle jar one evening, it hit her: she hadn't thought of Louis once that day. An entire day without the dread of her own thoughts or the guilt or the replaying of scenes. The relief was outweighed by the sorrow of forgetting. When you're sleepy, you don't want to feel less tired—you want to go to bed. When you lose a person, you don't want to forget the person, you want the person back. But she had to admit: forgetting was easiest. Life was just easier for people who could forget.

The peculiarities of the forest became so familiar on her regular hikes that she could easily note its daily changes. Erosion led to mud pits and small landslides with increasing frequency. She always returned to the slippery stump. It gave her a good enough view. She didn't want to climb all the way to the top of the mountain, for the same reason she hadn't gone back into the bedroom since the first day. She was afraid of the memories it would conjure and the loss it would exacerbate. She slept on the sofa or on the recliner outside.

From the stump she watched as the gatherings on Hermannplatz and elsewhere around the city continued, even seemed to pick up. Endless, undying parties, day and night. FOMO incarnate. But she searched herself for an urge to join in, and found none. Her remove from that world felt, at times, absolute. She was becoming a self-contained organism, unwilling or unable to be subsumed by the mass.

Light did not wake her, but smoke. A gray, acrid tint to the air. The house, she thought—it's finally ready to collapse. But rushing around the rooms, she saw nothing had changed. From the outside, it looked to have sunk to its fullest extent for the time being, roof continuing to sag into the curve of a smile, but frame still holding without any major crashes. A disaster without any disaster. The house inside the box in the kitchen, on the other hand, was disintegrated into nothing more than a flat scrim.

Her abdomen clenched, uterus worrying over the egg that was fixing to release. She groaned, having forgotten about her body's autonomous movements. Trying to clock her last period, she wondered how much time had passed since she'd come up the mountain with Michel.

She considered the possibility that the smoke had been part of her dream, but she could still smell it on the breeze. She filled a glass bottle with water collected from her scattered receptacles and headed outside, up the slope. The time of day wasn't obvious. It could have been early morning or late afternoon. The sun was shrouded in thick cloud cover and the ominous light was further scattered by the trees between her and the sky, illuminating the forest around her in patches.

She had never seen the dirt this dry, dry to the point of crumbling underfoot and scattering in chunks down the hill after each step. The tall bamboo-like stalks near where the path used to be appeared to have died suddenly. Their bases were brown but their tips were still faintly green: power supply cut off before they could completely decay. The collapse she had seen lower down the slope was advancing quickly. Attuning her nostrils to changes in the air, she decided that the scent of smoke was thinning as she rose higher.

She climbed atop the viewing stump and raised one hand to form a visor for her eyes, rubbing her lower stomach with the other. A tilted cone of smoke rose from the west of the map. A south wind was blowing the smoke momentarily away from the mountain, which explained the receding smell. If you didn't trace the smoke back to its source, where it was thickest, the receding haze could almost be a normal cloud sunken from its post. But the gray puffs were moving too fast in directional wisps to be anything but traces of fire. She strained to see where smoke was clotted thickest above the burn, but too much city surface was obscured by the dark churning to make out where it was originating.

The thickness of the smoke down below, compared with its clarity where she was standing, exaggerated the height of the mountain, drawing her ever higher above the splayed city, slamming her with vertigo. Her estrangement from the city was compounded by the silence on the mountaintop. She strained to hear sirens, shouting, anything from below, but only became more aware of the sighing of the trees and her own breath.

Her thoughts turned automatically to her parents. If this were a real disaster, they'd have seen something, and it would have reminded them that she existed. Mom must have been calling her frantically.

Her legs led her back down. She arched against the angle of the slope, leaning back to counter her weight. Reaching the shrinking clearing, she was struck by the spectacular mess of her house; it was thriving, growing, and dying all at once, cannibalizing itself in programmed splendor. She was filled with respect for whoever had designed the species converting this smattering of civilization into a ruin.

She was standing there ogling her house when they came crashing up through the thicket. The silence was split. Twigs snapped and dust rose through the rustle of bushes.

Dam came through first, panting.

"Is she up there?" called Laura from behind him.

"I see her!" said Dam.

"I'm here," said Anja.

They'd pried her whereabouts from Michel, who Laura emphasized had been bitter and unhelpful. Anja was disoriented when they asked how she'd survived for almost an entire month. A month? She'd spoken to Louis only a few days ago. Or had it been a week? Two weeks? The days had crushed together, contracting around the workings of the house and the house inside it.

"You look good," said Laura, reaching out to feel Anja's long, ungroomed hair. Anja looked down at herself and saw a tan, strong pair of legs. Laura and Dam were pallid and strung out in comparison.

Prompted to play host, she remembered the liquor cabinet above the sink. She must have been sober for the longest stretch in her adult life—maybe that was why time was working so unpredictably. She took down a few bottles, wondering where the urge to drink had gone, and uncorked a red someone had given Louis for his birthday.

"Honey, how're you still alive?" said Dam when she came back, sliding an entire cucumber from her stash into his mouth before crunching down on it. "You've been eating animal food." His speech was thick with Spanish, knocked loose by worry. He looked stricken.

Laura was on edge too. They sat together on the living room floor, passing the bottle, and Anja tried to figure out where to begin. As she searched for links to chain the events into an intelligible narrative, she realized Dam and Laura were the ones itching to explain.

"You saw the smoke?" asked Dam. His eyes were ringed with dark circles. She nodded and sniffed. She could smell it in the house again.

He glanced at Laura. It occurred to Anja that their presence might be as much a flight from whatever was happening below as a friendly visit.

Things had changed in her absence, they tried to explain in a rush together. Across the city, a palpable transition, coming from everywhere and nowhere. An uptick in partying, all day and all night. Clubbers sleeping on the subway tracks; homeless people making their way into clubs. Rampant displays of generosity, followed by comedowns full of hostility. Of course they knew the reason. But the effect seemed so *outsized*.

An open-air party had been raging down the block from Dam and Laura's for two straight weeks. Anja realized it must have been one of the parties she'd been observing from her perch. Pounding music, barbecues, beer—everyone welcome, the dividing lines between groups blurred. It had the flavor of a protest, but with no common cause. Everyone was there for a reason, some reason, but once they got there, no one was sober enough to try to figure out what it was. The gatherings amounted to charity carnivals where no funds were being raised. Funds were, rather, being extinguished. People threw change across counters in abandonment. It was blind expenditure ramped up to eleven, the pleasure drive cloaked in righteousness, every excess validated. Those who could afford to give nothing but couldn't resist the urge quickly dug themselves into holes of debt. What should have felt like liberating social disintegration instead felt like another kind of regime. Nothing was solved, only accelerated. Like beating an intricate knot with a hammer instead of untangling it. Dam put his forehead in his hands, trying to describe what he'd seen.

At first, generosity had overridden animosity; who complains about such togetherness, much less free stuff? But over time, as gestures became more outrageous—Laura assured Anja that tipping beer into the canal or giving smartphones away paled in comparison—arguments erupted, not only between those who considered themselves to be the givers and those who had been identified as the takers, but among the givers themselves. Jealousy. Competition. Disagreements about the best ways to do things. Tactics to become the best giver. Tactics to undermine one another's charity. Tactics to preserve the class of takers so that the class of givers could continue to give.

The weird thing was that mutual exchange, as in trading objects of equal value, did not trigger the response that O had promised. Giving and receiving at the same time canceled each other out. The person who gave more felt better.

If unlocking generosity via chemical reward was O's primary function, and if the reward could be repeatedly incited by this one-way act, maybe even in a cumulative process, it followed that the reward, the feeling, the high, would become the basis for addiction—not the act itself. The user would do anything to feel like generosity had been achieved.

Of course circular pay-it-forward systems quickly emerged. I give to you, and you give to the next person, who gives to the next. Nobody in the chain required the gift; the receipt was a favor. The point of charitable donation was not to fulfil a need on the side of the recipient but to fulfil a need on the part of the giver. If Louis had succeeded, he had succeeded in replicating the stucture of worldwide aid on a microscale.

Then, they told her, there had been the wave of break-ins everywhere. Dam described everything from petty pickpocketing to full-on looting. Apparently one had to steal to continue the process if one had run out of things to give. *Counterintution*, Anja thought again.

"You can imagine," said Laura. "You've tried O."

Anja shook her head hard. "It wasn't like that."

"You only tried it once," said Dam. "Imagine taking it every day for weeks."

To Anja's surprise, Laura and even Dam said they had resisted trying it the whole time. Dam claimed to not even have been tempted, after seeing what happened to Eric. He didn't go into any details about that.

"All this generosity has really brought out the dark side in humanity," he said softly.

"I can't believe how fast it happened," said Laura.

The fire had started, of all places, in their building, ripping down the street in the early morning. They'd grabbed their laptops and passports and run straight to the mountain.

Tears streaked Dam's eye makeup. He sniffed. "We were going to have to leave anyway." He wiped his nose with his wrist, a familiar gesture. He was making the same guilty yet defiant face he always made when he knew he had behaved badly. He looked older than he used to, Anja thought.

Laura shot him a look. "It's not like we're going to get any insurance money out of this."

"It was an accident," he said. "Don't be mad."

By dark the smoke had stopped gusting and had become a general haze outside the house. They stayed inside, eating pâté and crackers from the neighbors' stash.

Dam and Laura had been scrolling through their phones until service suddenly cut out. Even text messages were bouncing back now. Dam had sent his last blast out just in time. ***EVAQ8 EVAQ8 NOT A DRILLL****

"The cucumbers gave me a tummy ache," he complained, refreshing his screen, unwilling to believe he was cut off. His top lip was wine-stained in a perfect semicircle. "What should we do?" he asked.

"The news told everyone to evacuate west," said Laura. "Maybe we should head down there."

"The news I read said to go east," said Dam.

None of the news had been particularly helpful. A lot of it had been blatantly inaccurate, according to Laura and Dam's account. One source said the blaze began during an altercation in a kebab shop. Another said that it had been deliberately set off by protestors—protesting what? Another said fireworks. While listening to the two of them call out tidbits from their feeds as they scrolled, Anja had been struck by how the distinction between news and rumor had become so thin it was practically nonexistent. Starting with the weather, everything had now been reduced to gossip. Maybe Dam's weather service really was, as he insisted, the future of news.

Anja patted Dam on the back. "There's still too much smoke for us to go anywhere now. Let's wait here until it clears."

"She's right," said Laura. "We don't know if the fire's still spreading."

He threw his hands in the air. "How do we know the fire won't come up here? We'd be trapped if it did."

Anja shook her head. "It doesn't seem like it's going to."

"What if it does?"

"We'll wait at the top for someone to come find us. It's the most visible spot in the city."

"I wish this mountain was still an airport," he said. "We could just take off."

The airport took over their thoughts for a long, round moment. A stroll at twilight on the tarmac. A cigarette, a beer. Too dark to see all the way across the expanse. A lone skater struggling against the wind. A cold note to the air, the arrival of a new season, one section of months shifting clearly to another. And between each season the feeling of stretching, of adolescence.

Without the full progression of the seasons, the city hadn't been able to grow. Its natural cycle had stuttered and shorted out.

"It feels like the apocalypse," said Anja.

"It *is* the apocalypse," Dam said.

"It was always the apocalypse," Laura said. "You guys just didn't notice until now."

Smoke still clung to the air in the house, but she'd slept with her face pressed into the grassy sofa, and momentarily it was all she noticed: the strong, now-familiar smell of simultaneous growth and decay. Her own sweat-soaked body was a part of it.

Dam and Laura were asleep in the bedroom. After checking on them and then, out of habit, the little house in the box in the kitchen—an indecipherable mass of crusty material—she pulled on her boots and picked up Laura's sweater from the floor to tie around her shoulders.

Her eyes watered intensely from the lingering smoke. She walked slowly, blinking and trying not to rub them. The wind had picked up and dust rose around her in tiny tornadoes. Her abdomen contracted with a spasm of pain. A red line sped down her leg, curving around her knee and stopping as it soaked into the rim of her sock.

The dream from the night before burst in on her suddenly. A red light shining in through the windows of the house. Louis standing in front of her, head tilted to the side. She knew it was him, but she couldn't make out the features of his face. He was speaking, but she couldn't make out the words either. The room was unbearably hot and full of fog, or smoke. Sweat dripped in her eyes and blurred her vision. His image would not resolve. She wanted desperately to reach out to him, but she was frozen. He had to come forward of his own accord. She waited and waited. Tried and failed to speak. Finally he came closer. His hands reached out to grasp the great messy ball of her face. But her face had no outlines—he couldn't find the edge. She could tell he was there, looming in front of her, but they were both too out of focus. His face approached hers until it should have been touching hers, but he went through her, like a cloud—like they were two clouds. Then, in the haze, she felt a mouth open on her lips, and teeth came through. The sharp bite was what woke her.

The force of the letdown hit her as she climbed. There would be no final confrontation, no closure. Closure was a myth. There was nothing to close. The object of affection was no longer itself. An orange that did not smell like oranges. A plum that did not taste like a plum.

The bench was right where they'd left it at the top of the slope. Phantom Louis was there, arms spread wide over the backrest, waiting for her to enter his negative space and be hugged into his side. She shook her head. The night of their last hike up here had been the beginning of the end.

It was tempting to pause for a moment and replay the order of things again, to imagine moments she could have intervened and stopped the landslide, but the regrets were too plentiful to sort through. *Egrets*, as Eva used to call them. Long-legged birds with milk-white wings. "No egrets, Anja. Live your damn life."

The bench waited for her, flaunting its immutability.

Everything else was in flux, but this dumb, silent bench was the same. She walked past it to the edge of the mountain, which was more of a cliff than it had ever been. The soil all along this side of the Berg had shifted and fallen, destabilized by the fire or the wind or the dryness, and roots jutted out from the dirt below her like hands reaching into midair. Below that, emptiness.

A massive billow undulated to the north. In its wake, ash. The canal had not stopped the fire in its tracks; neither had the Spree. All those buildings, updated to meet environmental standards, stuffed to bursting with flammable organic insulation. Block after block flattened. Buildings gutted, reduced to skeletons, or toppled into each other. The wide artery of Karl-Marx-Allee was surprisingly clean and visible far to the north, beneath the shifting smoke and drifting white specks. She carved the path of the former wall with her stinging eyes, following its shape as far as she could. She knew the contours of the streets and blocks so well, but in the absence of landmarks it was hard to piece the coordinates together on this charred spread. One landmark oriented her sight: the TV tower had somehow survived, defiantly retaining the city brand through its total destruction. The magnificent Dome, the Gate, Museum Island—all gone, and the fucking TV tower was what stuck.

She wiped snot from the indentation below her nose, where it had mingled with tears. Her eyes were streaming as much from the smoke as the shock. She wrapped her arms around herself, grasping her own shoulders, and told herself that most people must have gotten out in time.

She looked for Dam and Laura's house, knowing their blue building wouldn't be there. It had indeed been at the epicenter: that was clear from the extent of the wreckage there. She searched for Howard's place next, up north. Nothing. All that teak furniture exploding in the blaze. She followed the tram tracks to where she imagined RANDI had been. Nothing. She winced. But the lab would surely be frozen tight, air-locked belowground.

She looked for Basquiatt HQ last. A monstrous pile of rubble, with jagged shards of glass jutting from the rocks and glinting in flashes of sunlight.

"You got rid of me because I finally saw who you were," she said toward the place where the glorious revised architecture had been.

"You were so afraid that I would change that you changed instead," the hill of ash, metal, and glass said back.

Despite its expansion outward, the fire hadn't closed in on the mountain. It had stopped at the base of the Berg. Maybe this was what happened when you reduced a city's green space to a single hill, leaving the rest dry and brittle. As she tracked the dead city with her eyes looking for greenery, she realized that there hadn't been any large public parks left to burn. Finster had justified confining all the city's nature to the mountain, creating a giant fold in the landscape to expand the surface area of greenery, filling the percentage quota of the planning commission, while justifying leaving the rest of the city for development.

But trees did burn. The mountain should have snatched the flames. Maybe this engineered nature simply wasn't flammable. It was meant for another, more deliberate kind of transformation.

She imagined the view at night from where she was standing. Where green had radiated out from the base of the mountain, there would be total darkness. Where there had been white lights on one side and yellow on the other, there would be total darkness. Darkness—and space entirely empty of all those attachments.

They were fine, of course. Louis, Michel, Howard. They had to be. Those invincible men. They would always be fine. They were fine in the Before, and they were fine in the After. In the Post-After, there was no reason to expect they wouldn't be just as fine.

She looked down at Finster's dead city of lost investments and smiled. In the Before and in the After, the city had offered nothing she could make hers. Nothing to buy that Louis couldn't buy better. Nothing she wanted to own, nothing they'd let her own.

Until now. There had never been such a good time to buy.

Acknowledgments

I have too many people to thank. Thanks to Theresia Enzensberger and Vincenzo Latronico, my first readers and my favorite writers. To Jenna Sutela, Martti Kalliala, Tamen Perez, Alex Turgeon, Beny Wagner, Anna Saulwick, Jessica Bridger, Sophie Lovell, and so many others, for being my Berlin and for several of the stories and ideas that ended up in this book. To William Kherbek, Josie Thaddeus-Johns, Jonathan Lyon, and Vijay Khurana, for years of generous feedback. To my parents, for endless encouragement. Most of all, to Clemens Jahn, who invented love.

I am immensely grateful to Cynthia Cannell for her insight and support, as well as my brilliant editor, Allie Wuest, along with Yuka Igarashi and everyone at Catapult/Soft Skull. Many thanks to the Banff Centre, Rupert, the Helsinki International Artist Programme, and the Rabbit Island Residency, for providing the space and time for the book to be born and reborn.

Finally, I am indebted to Mila Architects for their imaginary mountain, the Berg.

© Nina Subin

ELVIA WILK is a writer and editor living in New York and Berlin. She writes about art, architecture, and technology for several publications, including *frieze, Artforum, e-flux, Metropolis, Mousse, Flash Art, Art in America*, and *Zeit Online*.